The Reincarnationist

"M.J. Rose delivers a tale that goes beyond chills and thrills. It's a delight of intrigue with a clever twist. Not a disappointing page."
—**Steve Berry**, *The Templar Legacy*

"THE REINCARNATIONIST is a riveting thriller – smart, original, and so well written. Rose hooks you on the first pages of the book, where current-day murders pull the reader into ancient secrets and shocking revelations, and keeps you turning till the stunning denouement."
—**Linda Fairstein**, *Bad Blood*

"A breakneck chase across the centuries. Fascinating and fabulous."
—**David Morrell**, *Creepers*

"Both unnerving and mesmerising, THE REINCARNATIONIST by M.J. Rose will excite anyone who's ever had the slightest curiosity about past lives. The story is packed with unforgettable characters, breath-taking drama, and fascinating research, cementing M.J. Rose's reputation as a master storyteller."
—**Gayle Lynds**, *The Last Assassin*

"A triumph! A breathtaking, smart and inventive novel that dazzles while it thrills. THE REINCARNATIONIST is one of the year's best reads."
—**David J. Montgomery**,
Chicago Sun-Times & Philadelphia Inquirer

Also available by ***M.J. Rose***

THE HALO EFFECT
THE DELILAH COMPLEX
THE VENUS FIX

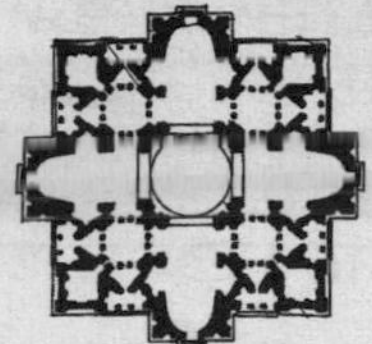

The Reincarnationist

M. J. ROSE

MIRA

MIRA Books, Eton House, 18-24 Paradise Road,
Richmond, Surrey, TW9 1SR

ISBN: 978 0 7783 0197 4

58-0208

Printed in Great Britain
by Clays Ltd, St Ives plc

This book is dedicated to my remarkable editor,
Margaret O'Neil Marbury, who convinced me
I could climb this mountain.

&

To Lisa Tucker and Douglas Clegg, wonderful writers
and friends, who threw me a lifeline every
step of the way.

"I simply believe that some part of the human self or soul is not subject to the laws of space or time."

Carl Jung

Chapter 1

They will come back, come back again,
As long as the red earth rolls.
He never wasted a leaf or a tree.
Do you think he would squander souls?

—Rudyard Kipling

Rome, Italy—sixteen months ago

Josh Ryder looked through the camera's viewfinder, focusing on the security guard arguing with a young mother whose hair was dyed so red it looked like she was on fire. The search of the woman's baby carriage was quickly becoming anything but routine, and Josh moved in closer for his next shot.

He'd just been keeping himself busy while awaiting the arrival of a delegation of peacekeepers from several superpowers who would be meeting with the pope that morning, but like several other members of the press and tourists who'd been ignoring the altercation or losing patience with it, he was becoming concerned. Although searches went on every hour, every day, around the world, the potential for danger hung over everyone's lives, lingering like the smell of fire.

In the distance the sonorous sound of a bell ringing called the religious to prayer, its echo out of sync with the woman's shrill voice as she continued to protest. Then, with a huge shove, she pushed the carriage against the guard's legs, and just as Josh brought the image into that clarity he called "perfect vision," the kind of image that the newspaper would want, the kind of conflict they loved captured on film, he heard the blast.

Then a flash of bluish white light.

The next moment, the world exploded.

In the protective shadows of the altar, Julius and his brother whispered, reviewing their plans for the last part of the rescue and recovery. Each of them kept a hand on his dagger, prepared in case one of the emperor's soldiers sprang out of the darkness. In Rome, in the Year of their Lord 391, temples were no longer sanctuaries for pagan priests. Converting to Christianity was not a choice, but an official mandate. Resisting was a crime punishable by death. Blood spilled in the name of the Church was not a sin, it was the price of victory.

The two brothers strategized—Drago would stay in the temple for an hour longer and then rendezvous with Julius at the tomb by the city gates. As a diversion, that morning's elaborate funeral had been a success, but they were still worried. Everything depended on this last part of their strategy going smoothly.

Julius drew his cape closed, touched his brother's shoulder, bidding him goodbye and good luck, and skulked out of the basilica, keeping to the building's edge in case anyone was watching. He heard approaching horses and the clatter of wheels. Flattening himself against the stone wall, Julius held his breath and didn't move. The chariot passed without stopping.

He'd finally reached the edge of the porch when, behind him, like a sudden avalanche of rocks, he heard an angry shout split open the silence: "Show me where the treasury is!"

This was the disaster Julius and his brother had feared and discussed, but Drago had been clear—even if the temple was attacked, Julius was to continue on. Not turn back. Not try to help him. The treasure Julius needed to save was more important than any one life or any five lives or any fifty lives.

But then a razor-sharp cry of pain rang out, and ignoring the plan, he ran back through the shadows, into the temple and up to the altar.

His brother was not where he'd left him.

"Drago?"

No answer.

"Drago?"

Where was he?

Julius worked his way down one of the dark side aisles of the temple and up the next. When he found Drago, it wasn't by sound or by sight—but by tripping over his brother's supine body.

He pulled him closer to the flickering torches. Drago's skin was already deathly pale, and his torn robe revealed a six-inch horizontal slash on his stomach crossing a vertical gash that cut him all the way down to his groin.

Julius gagged. He'd seen eviscerated carcasses of both man

and beast before and had barely given them a passing glance. Sacrifices, felled soldiers or punished criminals were one thing. But this was Drago. This blood was his blood.

"You weren't...supposed to come back," Drago said, dragging every syllable out as if it was stuck in his throat. "I sent him...to look in the loculi...for the treasures. I thought... Stabbed me, anyway. But there's time...for us to get out... now...now!" Drago struggled to raise himself up to a sitting position, spilling his insides as he moved.

Julius pushed him down.

"Now...we need...to go now." Drago's voice was weakening.

Trying to staunch the blood flow, Julius put pressure on the laceration, willing the intestines and nerves and veins and skin to rejoin and fuse back together, but all he accomplished was staining his hands in the hot, sticky mess.

"Where are the virgins?" The voice erupted like Vesuvius without warning and echoed through the interior nave. Raucous laughter followed.

How many soldiers were there?

"Let's find the booty we came here for," another voice chimed in.

"Not yet, first I want one of the virgins. Where are the virgin whores?"

"The treasury first, you lecherous bastard."

More laughter.

So it wasn't one man; a regiment had stormed the temple. Shouting, demanding, blood-lust coating their words. Let them pillage this place, let them waste their energy, they'd come too late: there were no pagans to convert, no treasure left to find and no women left to rape, they'd all already been killed or sent into hiding.

"We have to go..." Drago whispered as once again he fought to rise.

He'd stayed behind to make sure everyone else got out safely. Why him, why Drago?

"You can't move, you've been hurt—" Julius broke off, not knowing how to tell his brother that half of his internal organs were no longer inside his body.

"Then leave me. You need to get to her... Save her and the treasures.... No one...no one but you..."

It wasn't about the sacred objects anymore. It was about two people who both needed him desperately: the woman he loved and his brother, and the fates were demanding Julius sacrifice one of them for the other.

I can't let her die and I can't leave you to die.

No matter which one he chose, how would he live with the decision?

"Look what I found," one of the soldiers shouted.

Screams of vengeance reverberated through the majestic hall. A shriek rang out above all the other noise. A woman's cry.

Julius crawled out, hid behind a column and peered into the nave. He couldn't see the woman's upper body, but her pale legs were thrashing under the brute as the soldier pumped away so roughly that blood pooled under her. Who was the poor woman? Had she wandered in thinking she'd find a safe haven in the old temple, only to find she'd descended into hell? Could Julius help her? Take the men by surprise? No, there were too many of them. At least eight he could see. By now the rape had attracted more attention, drawing other men who forgot about their search to crowd around and cheer on their compatriot.

And what would happen to Drago if he left his side?

Then the question didn't matter because beneath his hands, Julius felt his brother's heart stop.

He felt his heart stop.

Julius beat Drago's chest, pumping and trying, trying but failing to stimulate the beating. Bending down, he breathed into his brother's mouth, forcing his own air down his throat, waiting for any sign of life.

Finally, his lips still on his brother's lips, his arm around his brother's neck, he wept, knowing he was wasting precious seconds but unable to stop. Now he didn't have to choose between them—he could go to the woman who was waiting for him at the city gates.

He must go to her.

Trying not to attract attention, he abandoned Drago's body, backed up, found the wall and started crawling. There was a break in the columns up ahead; if he could get to it undetected, he might make it out.

And then he heard a soldier shout for him to halt.

If he couldn't save her, Julius would at least die trying, so, ignoring the order, he kept moving.

Outside, the air was thick with the black smoke that burned his lungs and stung his eyes. What were they incinerating now? No time to find out. Barely able to see what lay ahead of him, he kept running down the eerily quiet street. After the cacophony of the scene he'd just left, it was alarming to be able to hear his own footsteps. If someone was on the lookout the sound would give him away, but he needed to risk it.

Picturing her in the crypt, crouched in the weak light, counting the minutes, he worried that she would be anxious that he was late and torment herself that something had gone dangerously wrong. Her bravery had always been as steadfast as the stars; it was difficult even now to imagine her afraid. But this was a far different situation than anything she'd ever faced, and it was all his fault, all his shame. They'd risked too much for each other. He should have been stronger, should have resisted.

And now, because of him, everything they treasured, especially their lives, was at stake.

Tripping over the uneven, cracked surfaces, he stumbled. The muscles in his thighs and calves screamed, and every breath irritated his lungs so harshly he wanted to cry out. Tasting dirt and grit mixed with his salty sweat as it dripped down his face and wet his lips, he would have given anything for water—cold, sweet water from the spring, not this alkaline piss. His feet pounded the stones and more pain shot up through his legs, but still he ran.

Suddenly, raucous shouting and thundering footfalls filled the air. The ground reverberated, and from the intensity he knew the marauders were coming closer. He looked right, left. If he could find a sheltered alcove, he could flatten himself against the wall and pray they'd run past and miss him. As if that would help. He knew all about praying. He'd relied on it, believed in it. But the prayers he'd offered up might as well have been spit in the gutter for the good they'd done.

"The sodomite is getting away!"

"Scum of the earth."

"Scared little pig."

"Did you defecate yourself yet, little pig?"

They laughed, trying to outdo each other with slurs and accusations. Their chortles echoed in the hollow night, lingered on the hot wind, and then, mixed in with their jeers, another voice broke through.

"Josh?"

No, don't listen. Keep going. Everything depends on getting to her in time.

A heavy fog was rolling in. He stumbled, then righted himself. He took the corner.

On both sides of him were identical colonnades with dozens of doors and recessed archways. He knew this place! He could hide here in plain sight and they would run by and—

"Josh?"

The voice sounded as if it was coming to him from a great blue-green distance, but he refused to stop for it.

She was waiting for him...to save her...to save their secrets...and treasures....

"Josh?"

The voice was pulling him up, up through the murky, briny heaviness.

"Josh?"

Reluctantly, he opened his eyes and took in the room, the equipment and his own battered body. Beyond the heart rate, blood oxygen and blood pressure monitor flashing its LED numbers, the IV drip and the EKG machine, he saw a woman's worried face watching him. But it was the wrong face.

This wasn't the woman he'd been running to save.

"Josh? Oh, thank God, Josh. We thought..."

He couldn't be here now. He needed to go back.

The taste of sweat was still on his lips; his lungs still burned. He could hear them coming for him under the steady beat of the machines, but all he could think about was that somewhere she was alone, in the encroaching darkness, and yes, she was afraid, and yes, she was going to suffocate to death if he didn't reach her. He closed his eyes against the onslaught of anguish. If he didn't reach her, he would fail her. And something else, too. The treasures? No. Something more important, something just beyond his consciousness, what was it—

"Josh?"

Grief ripped through him like a knife slitting open his chest, exposing his heart to the raw, harsh reality of having lost her. This wasn't possible. This wasn't real. He'd been remembering the chase and the escape and the rescue as if they had happened to him. But they hadn't. Of course they hadn't.

He wasn't Julius.

He was Josh Ryder. He was alive in the twenty-first century.

This scene belonged sixteen hundred years in the past.

Then why did he feel as if he'd lost everything that had ever mattered to him?

Chapter 2

Rome, Italy—the present
Tuesday, 6:45 a.m.

Sixteen feet underground, the carbine lantern flickered, illuminating the ancient tomb's south wall. Josh Ryder was astounded by what he saw. The flowers in the fresco were as fresh as if they'd been painted days before. Saffron, crimson, vermilion, orange, indigo, canary, violet and salmon blossoms all gathered in a bouquet, stunning against the Pompeii-red background. Beneath him, the floor shimmered with an elaborate mosaic maze done in silver, azure, green, turquoise and cobalt: a pool of watery tiles. Behind him, Professor Rudolfo continued explaining the importance of this late fourth-century tomb in his heavily accented English. At least seventy-five, he was still spry and energetic, with lively, coal-black eyes that sparkled with excitement as he talked about the excavation.

He'd been surprised to have a visitor at such an early hour, but when he heard Josh's name, Rudolfo told the guard on duty that yes, it was fine, he was expecting Mr. Ryder later that morning with the other man from the Phoenix Foundation.

Josh had woken before dawn. He rarely slept well since his accident last year, but last night's insomnia was more likely due to the time change—having just arrived in Rome that day from New York—or the excitement of being back in the city where so many of his memory lurches took place. Too restless to stay in the hotel, he grabbed his camera and went for a walk, not at all sure where he was going. But something happened while he was out.

Despite the darkness and his ignorance of the city's layout, he proceeded as if the route had been mapped out for him. He knew the path, even if he had no idea of his final destination. Deserted avenues lined with expensive stores gave way to narrow streets and ancient buildings. The shadows became more sinister. But he kept going.

If he'd passed anyone else, he hadn't noticed them. And even though it had seemed like a thirty-minute walk, it turned out to have taken more than two hours. Two hours spent in a semi-trance. He'd watched the night change from blue-gray to pale gray to a lemony-pink as the sun came up. He'd seen lush green hills develop the way the images in a photograph did in a chemical bath. From nothing to a shadow to a sense of a shape to a real form, but he didn't know if he'd stopped to take any shots of the scenery. The whole episode was both disconcerting and astonishing when it turned out that, seemingly by chance, he'd stumbled onto the very site he and Malachai Samuels had been invited to view later that morning.

Or not by chance at all.

The professor didn't ask why he was so early or question how he'd found the dig. "If it were me, I wouldn't have been able to sleep, either. Come down, come down."

Content to let the professor assume enthusiasm had brought him there at six-thirty in the morning, Josh breathed deeply and took a first tentative step down the ladder, refusing to allow his mind to dwell on the claustrophobia he'd suffered his whole life and which had intensified since the accident.

Strains of music from *Madame Butterfly* that had first caught Josh's attention and then drawn him up this particular hill were louder now, and he concentrated on the heartbreaking aria as he descended into the dimly lit chamber.

The space was larger than he'd anticipated, and he exhaled, relieved. He'd be able to tolerate being there.

The professor shook his hand, introduced himself, then turned down the volume on the dusty black plastic CD player and began the tour.

"The crypt is—I will do this for you in feet, not meters—eight feet wide by seven feet long. Professor Chase—Gabriella—and I believe it was built in the very last years of the fourth century. Until we have the carbon dating back we can't be positive. But from some of the artifacts here, we think it was 391 A.D., the same year the cult of the Vestal Virgins ended. Such decoration is atypical for this type of burial chamber, so we believe it must have been intended for someone else and then used for the Vestal when her inconstancy was discovered."

Josh lifted his camera to his eye, but before he took a shot he asked if the professor minded. Nothing short of a bomb had ever stopped him from taking a photo when he was working for the Associate Press. Then six months ago he'd taken a leave of absence to work as a videographer and photographer of children who came to the Phoenix Foundation for help with their past-life regression memories. Since then, he'd gotten used to asking for permission before shooting. In return, he had access to the world's largest and most private library on the subject of reincarnation as well as the chance to work with the foundation's principals.

"It's fine, yes, but would you clear it with either Gabriella or me before you show the pictures or release them to anyone? Everything here is still a secret we are trying to keep until we have additional information about exactly what we have discovered. We don't want to create false excitement if we're wrong about our find. Better to be safe, no?"

Josh nodded as he focused and clicked the shutter. "What did you mean by the Vestal's inconstancy?"

"Maybe that is the wrong word, I'm sorry. I meant the breaking of her vows. That's better, no?"

"What vows? Were the Vestals nuns?"

"Pagan nuns, yes. Upon entering the order they took a vow of chastity, and the punishment for breaking that vow was to be buried alive."

Josh felt an oppressive wave of sadness. As if on autopilot, he depressed the shutter. "For falling in love?"

"You are a romantic. You will enjoy Rome." He smiled. "Yes, for falling in love or for giving in to lust."

"But why?"

"You need to understand that the religion of ancient Rome was based on a strict moral code that stressed truthfulness, honor and personal responsibility while demanding steadfastness and devotion to duty. They believed that every creature had a soul, but they were also very superstitious, worshipping gods and spirits who had influence over every aspect of their lives. If all the rituals and sacrifices were performed properly, the Romans believed the gods would be happy and help them. If they weren't, they believed the gods would punish them. Contrary to public misinformation, the ancient religion was quite humane in general. Pagan priests could marry, and have children and…"

The faint scents of jasmine and sandalwood that usually accompanied his memory lurches teased Josh, and he fought to stay attuned to the lecture. He felt as if he'd always known about these painted walls and the maze beneath his feet but had forgotten them until this moment. The sensations that usually accompanied the waking nightmares he'd been experiencing since the accident were rocking him: the slow drift down, the undulating, the prickles of excitement running up his arms and his legs, the submergence into that atmosphere where the very air was thicker and heavier.

He ran in the rain. His soaked robe was heavy on his shoulders. Under his feet the ground was muddy. He could hear shouting. He stumbled. Struggled to get up.

Focus, Josh intoned in some other section of his brain where he remained in the present. *Focus.* He looked through the lens at the professor, who was still talking, using his hands to punctuate his words, causing the light beam to crisscross the tomb wildly, illuminating one corner and then another. As Josh followed with his camera, he felt the grip on his body relax and he let out a sigh of relief before he could stop himself.

"Are you all right?"

Josh heard Rudolfo as if he was on the other side of a glass door.

No. Of course he was not all right.

Sixteen months before, he'd been on assignment here in Rome, which turned out to be the wrong place at the wrong time. One minute he'd been photographing a dispute between a woman with a baby carriage and a guard, and the next a bomb was detonated. The suicide bomber, two bystanders and Adreas Carlucci—the security guard—were killed. Seventeen people were wounded. No motive had been discovered. No terrorist group had claimed the incident.

The doctors later told Josh they hadn't expected him to live, and when he finally came to in the hospital forty-eight hours later, scattered bits of what seemed like memories started to float to the surface of his consciousness. But they were of people he'd never met, in places he'd never been, in centuries he'd never lived.

None of the doctors could explain what was happening to him. Neither could any of the psychiatrists or psychologists he saw once he was released. Yes, there was some depression, which was expected after an almost-fatal accident such as the one he'd suffered. And of course, post-traumatic stress syndrome could produce flashbacks, but not of the type he was suffering: images that burned into his brain so he had no choice but to revisit them over and over, torturing himself as he probed them for meaning, for reason. Nothing like dreams that fade with time until they're all but forgotten, these were endlessly locked sequences that never changed, never developed, never revealed any of the layers that hid beneath their horrific surface.

These were blue-black-scarlet chimeras that came during the day when he was awake. They obsessed him to the point of becoming the final stress in an already-broken marriage and set him apart from an entire phalanx of friends who didn't recognize the haunted man he'd become. All he cared about was finding an explanation for the episodes he'd experienced since the accident. Six full blown, dozens of others he managed to fight back and prevent.

As if they were made of fire, the hallucinations burned and singed and scorched his ability to be who he'd always been, to function, to sustain some semblance of normalcy. Too often, when he caught sight of himself in a mirror, he blanched. His smile didn't work right anymore. The lines in his face had deepened seemingly overnight. The worst of it was in his eyes, as if someone else was in there with him waiting, waiting, to get out. He was haunted by the thoughts he couldn't stop from coming, like a great rising flood.

He lived in fear of his own mind, which projected the fragmented kaleidoscopic images: of a young, troubled man in nineteenth-century New York City, of another in ancient Rome caught up in a violent struggle and of a woman who'd given up everything for their frightening passion. She shimmered in moonlight, glistening with opalescent drops of water, crying out to him, her arms open, offering him the same sanctuary he offered her. The cruelest joke was the intensity of his physical reaction to the visions. The lust. The rock-hard lust that turned his body into a single painful craving to smell her scent, to touch her skin, to see her eyes soaking him up, to feel her taking him into her, looking down at her face softened in pleasure, insanely, obscenely hiding nothing, knowing there was nothing he was holding back, either. They couldn't hold back. That would be unworthy of their crime.

No, these were not posttraumatic stress flashbacks or psychotic episodes. These shook him to his core and interfered with his life. Tormented him, overpowered him, making it impossible for him to return to the world he'd known before the bombing, before the hospital, before his wife ultimately gave up on him.

There was a possibility, the last therapist said, that there was something neurological causing the hallucinations. So Josh visited a top neurologist, hoping—as bizarre as it was to hope such a thing—that the doctor would find some residual brain trauma as a result of the accident, which would explain the waking nightmares that plagued him. He was disconsolate when tests showed none.

Josh was out of choices—nothing was left but to explore the impossible and the irrational. The quest exhausted him, but he couldn't give up; he needed to understand even if it meant accepting something that he couldn't imagine or believe: either he was mad, or he'd developed the ability to revisit lives he'd lived before this one. The only way he would know was to find out if reincarnation was real, if it was truly possible.

That was what brought him to the Phoenix Foundation's Drs. Beryl Talmage and Malachai Samuels, who, for the past twenty-five years, had recorded more than three thousand past-life regressions experienced by children under the age of twelve.

Josh took another photograph of the south corner of the tomb. The smooth, cold metal case felt good in his hands, and the sound of the shutter was reassuring. Recently he'd given up digital equipment and had been using his father's old Leica. It was a connection to real memories, to sanity, to support, to logic. The way a camera worked was simple. Light exposed the image onto the emulsion. Developing the film was basic chemistry. Known elements interacted with paper treated with yet other known elements. A facsimile of an actual object became a new object—but a real one—a photograph. A mystery unless you understood the science. Knowledge. That was all he wanted. To know more—to know everything—about the two men he had been channeling since the accident. Damn, he hated that word and its association with New Age psychics and shamans. Josh's black-and-white view of the world, his need to capture on film the harsh reality of the terror-filled times, did not jibe with someone who channeled anything.

"Are you all right?" the professor asked again. "You look haunted."

Josh knew that, had seen it when he looked in the mirror; glimpsed the ghosts hiding in the shadows of his expression.

"I'm amazed, that's all. The past is so close here. It's incredible." It was easy enough to say because it was the truth, but there was more he hadn't said that was amazing. As Josh Ryder, he'd never before stood in that crypt sixteen feet under the earth. So then how did he know that behind him, in a dark corner of the tomb the professor hadn't yet shown him or shone the light on, there were jugs, lamps and a funerary bed painted with real gold?

He tried to peer into the darkness.

"Ah, you are like all Americans." The professor smiled.

"What do you mean?"

"Impertinent…no…impatient." The professor smiled yet again. "So what it is it you are looking for?"

"There's more back there, isn't there?"

"Yes."

"A funerary bed?" Josh asked, testing the memory. Or the guess. After all, they were in a tomb.

Rudolfo shined the light into the farthest corner, and Josh found himself staring at a wooden divan decorated with carved peacocks adorned with gold leaf and studded with pieces of malachite and lapis lazuli.

Something was wrong: he'd expected there to be a woman's body lying on it. A woman's body dressed in a white robe. He was both desperate to see her and dreading it at the same time.

"Where is she?" Josh was embarrassed by the plaintive despair in his voice and relieved when the professor anticipated his question and answered it.

"Over there, she's hard to see in this light, no?" In a long slow move, the professor swept the lantern across the room until it illuminated the alcove in the far corner of the west wall.

She was crouched on the floor.

Slowly, as if he were in a funeral procession, walking down a hundred-foot aisle and not a seven-foot span, Josh made his way to her, knelt beside her and stared at what was left of her, gripped by a grief so intense he could barely breathe. How could a past-life memory, if that's what it was—something he didn't believe in, something he didn't understand—make him sadder than he'd ever been in his life?

There, in a field, in the Roman countryside at 6:45 in the morning, inside a newly excavated tomb that dated back to the fourth-century A.D., was proof of his story at its end. Now, if he could only learn it from the beginning.

Chapter 3

"I call her Bella because she is such a beautiful find for us," Professor Rudolfo said, shining the lamp on the ancient skeleton. He was aware of Josh's emotional reaction. "Each day, since Gabby and I discovered her, I spend this time in the morning alone with her. Communing with her dead bones, you might say." He chuckled.

Taking a deep breath of the musty air, Josh held it in his chest and then concentrated on exhaling. Was this the woman he only knew as fractured fragments? A phantom from a past he didn't believe in but couldn't let go of?

His head ached. The information, present and past, crashed in waves of pain. He *needed* to focus on either then or now. Couldn't afford a migraine.

He shut his eyes.

Connect to the present, connect to who you know you are.

Josh. Ryder. Josh. Ryder. Josh Ryder.

This was what Dr. Talmage taught him to do to stop an episode from overwhelming him. The pain began subsiding.

"She teases you with her secrets, no?"

Josh's "yes" was barely audible.

The professor stared at him, trying to take his mental temperature. Thinking—Josh could see it in the man's eyes—that he might be crazy, he resumed his lecturing. "We believe Bella was a Vestal Virgin. Holy and revered, they were both protected and privileged. Tending the fire and cleaning the hearth was a woman's job in ancient times. Not all that different nowadays, no matter how hard women have tried to get us men to change." The professor laughed. "In ancient Rome, that flame, which was entirely practical and necessary for the survival of society, eventually took on a spiritual significance.

"According to what is written, tending the state hearth required sprinkling it daily with the holy water of Egeria and making sure the fire didn't go out, which would bring bad luck to the city—and was an unpardonable sin. That was the primary job of the Vestals, but..."

As the professor continued to explain, Josh felt as if he were racing ahead, knowing what he was going to say next, not as actual information, but as vague recollections.

"Each Virgin was chosen at a very young age—only six or seven—from among the finest of Rome's families. We cannot imagine such a thing now, but it was a great honor then. Many girls were presented to the head priest, the Pontifex Maximus, by anxious fathers and mothers, each hoping their daughter would be picked. After the novitiate was chosen, the girl was escorted to the building where she would live for the next three decades: the large white marble villa directly behind the

Temple of Vesta. Immediately, in a private ritual witnessed only by the other five Vestals, she'd be bathed, her hair would be arranged in the style brides wore, a white robe would be lowered over her head and then her education would begin."

Josh nodded, almost seeing the scene play out in his mind, not quite sure why he was able to picture it so precisely: the young, anxious faces, the crowd's excitement, the solemnity of the day. The professor's question broke through the dreamscape and jolted Josh back to the present.

"I'm sorry, what did you say?" Josh asked.

"I was requesting that you not discuss anything I am telling you or that you will see with the press. They were here all of yesterday trying to get us to reveal information we aren't ready to. And not just the Italian press. Your press, too. Dozens of them, following us. Like hungry dogs, they are. One man especially, I can't remember his name.... Oh, yes. Charlie Billings."

Josh knew Charlie. They'd been on assignment together a few years before. He was a good reporter and they'd stayed friends. But if he was in Rome it wouldn't be good for the dig: it was hard to keep a story away from Charlie.

"This Billings hounded me and Gabriella until she talked to him. What is that expression? On the record? So the story ran and the crowds came. Students of pagan religions, some academics, but mostly those who belong to modern-day cults devoted to resurrecting the ancient rituals and religion. They were very quiet and reverential. Behaving as if this was a still sacred site. *They* didn't bother us. It was the traditional churchgoers who started the small riot and all the problems. Stomping around and protesting and shouting out silly things such as we are doing the devil's work and that we would be punished for our sins. They misunderstand Gabby and me. We are scientists, no? Then, last night, I received a call from Cardinal Bironi in Vatican City who offered me an obscene amount of money to sell him what we've found here and not make it public. Based on what he offered, he—or the people who have put up the money—are very afraid of what we might have found. That's what happens when the word *pagan* is whispered in the Holy City."

"But why? They're the ones with all the power."

"Bella could add to the existing controversy over the trivial role women now play in the church compared to ancient times. It is a very popular argument and a big problem that modern religion gives women less of a role than ancient religion." The professor shook his head. "And then," he said softly, "there is the other issue. Any artifact that doesn't have a cross on it can be viewed as a threat. Especially if these artifacts have something to do with reincarnation, as Gabriella and your bosses believe."

"Why reincarnation? Because of the absolution problem?"

"Yes, imagine if man believed he alone bore responsibility for his eternal rest, that it is within his own control to get to heaven. No Father, no Son, no Holy Ghost. What would happen to the power the Church holds over our souls? Imagine the worldwide confusion and rebellion and exodus from the Church if reincarnation were ever proved."

Josh nodded. In the past few months, he'd heard variations on this theme from Dr. Talmage. His eyes returned to Bella. Even as a corpse, her intensity was like a strong wind on a beach—there was nowhere to go to escape its force. He took a step closer to her.

"Are you curious how we have certified Bella as a Vestal?" the professor asked.

"There's no question she was a Vestal," Josh answered too quickly, and then worried that Rudolfo had picked up on his slip.

From the professor's curious glance, he had. "How do *you* know that?"

He must be more careful. "I misunderstood what you said, I'm sorry. Professor, please, how can you certify that she was a Vestal?"

Rudolfo grinned as if he had not just pleaded with Josh to ask this very question. His warm eyes twinkled and he launched into his explanation with gusto. "We have written records about the Vestals that describe certain details, each of which we see here. Although this tomb does not conform to the barren type of pressed-dirt enclosure most often used when Vestals were put to death, this woman was buried alive—the punishment reserved for those nuns who broke their vows—not to starve to death but to suffocate. That's the reason for those jugs. One for water, the other for milk—" He pointed to the roughhewn earthenware. "The very presence of the bed confirms it. You don't bury a dead man or woman with a bed. Or an oil lamp, for that matter."

"Why do you think she was over there in the corner, though? Not sleeping on the cot? As the oxygen ran out it would have made her tired. Wouldn't she have gone to sleep where it was comfortable?"

"Very good, that's one of our questions, too. It's also very confusing why sacred objects were buried with her, because ancient Romans weren't like the Egyptians. Their dead were not outfitted for the afterlife. Other than the lamp and the water and the milk, we didn't expect to find anything else here."

Josh's head pounded again. "What kind of objects did you find?"

The professor pointed to a wooden box in the mummy's hands. "She has been holding on to that for sixteen hundred years. Exciting, no?"

Josh instantly recognized it. No, that was impossible. He must have seen a photograph of a similar box in a museum. Even more confusing, despite its familiarity, he had no idea what it was. "Have you opened it yet?"

The professor nodded. "To come across a fine carved fruitwood box like that and not open it? I don't know many archaeologists who could resist. It's much older than Bella. Gabby and I think it dates back to before 2000 B.C., maybe as far back as 3000 B.C., and it doesn't appear to be Roman at all, but Indian. We need to wait for the carbon dating."

"And inside? What is inside?" Pinpricks of excitement ran up and down Josh's arms.

"We can't be certain until we do more work and take many tests, but we think they are the Memory Stones of the legendary Lost Memory Tools that your own Trevor Talmage wrote about."

"What are you basing that on?"

"The words carved here and here." He pointed to the border running around the perimeter of the box. "We believe these are the same lines found on an ancient Egyptian papyrus currently in the British Museum. The same lines Trevor Talmage translated in 1884. Do you know about that?"

Josh nodded. Talmage was the founder of the Phoenix

Club—what was now the Phoenix Foundation. And Josh had read the entire "Lost Memory Tools" folder of original notes and translations that had been found behind a row of books in the library during the 1999 renovation at the Foundation.

He was given the gift of a great bird who rose from fire to show him the way to the stones so he could pray upon them with song and lo! All of his past would be shown unto him.

As Josh recited the words, a voice inside his head spoke them in another language that sounded alien and archaic.

"That's the same translation that Wallace Neely used," Rudolfo said.

"Who?" The name tickled Josh's consciousness.

"Wallace Neely was an archeologist who worked here in Rome in the late 1800s. Several of his digs were financed by your Phoenix Club. He found the original text that Talmage was in the process of translating at the time of his death...."

He continued talking as Josh recalled a flashback he'd had six months ago, on the first day he'd walked into the Phoenix Foundation.

Percy Talmage, home for the summer break from Yale, was in the dining room, listening to his uncle Davenport talk about protecting the club's archeological investments in Rome. His uncle mentioned the archeologist they'd been financing. His name was Wallace Neely and he was searching for the Lost Memory Tools.

And now, here in this ancient tomb, sitting beside the professor, another memory surfaced, but not one that belonged to him; Josh was remembering for someone in the past. He was remembering for Percy.

* * *

Percy was just eight years old the first time he'd heard about the tools. His father had shown him the ancient manuscript he was translating. It had been written by a scribe who said the tools were not just a legend. They existed. The scribe had seen them and given a full description of each of the amulets, ornaments and stones.

"The tools are important," Trevor said to his son, "because history is important. He who knows the past controls the future. If the tools exist and if they can help people rediscover their past lives, you, me—and every member of the Phoenix Club—need to ensure this power is used for the good of all men, not selfishly exploited."

Percy didn't understand just how important it was for years. And years.

Was it possible that Josh had traveled halfway around the world to come back to where he'd started? Like so many things, this couldn't be a coincidence. He needed time to work out the connections, but that time wasn't now; the professor was still talking.

"In the 1880s Neely purchased several sites in and around this area, a practice that was very common then," the professor explained. "People bought the land they wanted to excavate so they could own the spoils outright. The club went into partnership with Neely and helped pay for the excavations, which could explain why the same inscription appears in both his journal and Talmage's notes."

Josh peered down at the intricately carved wooden box clasped in the mummy's hand. In its center was a bird rising out of a fire, a sword in its talons. It was almost identical to the coat of arms carved into the Phoenix Foundation's front door. In the border, around the perimeter, he saw the markings that Rudolfo had pointed out.

"Do you know what language this is?"

"Gabriella has plans to be in touch with experts in the field. She believes they could be an ancient form of Sanskrit."

"I thought she was an expert?"

"She is. In ancient Greek and Latin. This is neither."

Josh was confused about something. "You said this tomb was intact when you found it?"

"Yes."

"So how could Neely have been here?"

"We don't believe he—or anyone else—ever worked on this site. The pages we have from his journal indicate he excavated two sites nearby but found nothing. He'd gone to work on a third site, but we don't know what happened there. His journal abruptly ended while he was in the middle of that dig."

"Abruptly?"

"He was killed. There's very little known about the circumstances."

"But you have the journal?"

"We have some pages."

"Where did you get them?"

"Ask Gabby. She brought them to me along with the grant to take up where Neely stopped."

"And now you think you've found what he and the men who belonged to the Phoenix Club were looking for."

The professor nodded. "We think so. At least some of it, but there are so many unknowns still." He pointed to a slightly discolored area on the wall near where the mummy crouched. "That was hidden by a tapestry and we don't know why. Or why we found a knife beside Bella, because typically Roman women were never buried with weapons. And why is the knife broken? What was she doing?"

Taking a long breath, Rudolfo looked down at the creature. "Oh, Bella. What secrets do you have?" The professor got down on his knees and leaned toward her.

"Talk to me, my Belladonna," he whispered in an intimate voice.

Josh experienced a flash of a completely unfounded and unexpected emotion: a white-hot surge of jealousy unlike anything he'd ever felt for any lover he'd ever had. He wanted to rush over and pull Rudolfo away, to tell him he had no business leaning in so close, no right to get so near to her. Josh hadn't known that this corpse even existed an hour before, but his recollections had taken over and in his mind he saw muscles appearing, then being covered by flesh, the flesh plumping out her face, neck, hands, breasts, hips, thighs and feet, all coming to life, her lips pinking, her eyes being colored a deep blue. The remnants of her coppery cotton robe turned white as they'd been years before. Only her long and wavy red hair remained the same—parted in the middle and braided into two ropes that hung past her shoulders.

She was a corpse now, skin like leather and brittle bones, but once…once…she'd been beautiful. A million images crashed inside his head. Centuries of words he'd never heard before. One louder than the rest. He snatched it out from the cacophony.

Sabina.

Her name.

Chapter 4

"I'm not sure you believe the story you just told me, but I believe it," the professor said after Josh told an abbreviated version of what had happened to him in the past sixteen months and how he had come to be there so early that morning. "Every time you looked at her, I could tell there was something else you were seeing. I knew there was some connection more than just curiosity." He seemed inordinately pleased with himself.

Yes, in the gloomy light, if Josh squinted, the mummy was almost a living woman crouched there in the corner, not a sixteen-hundred-year-old shell whose sleep had recently been disturbed.

A breeze from the opening to the tomb whooshed through the space, and a single wisp of a curl escaped from her braids.

She'd always been so proud of how she looked, of being well kept; how she'd hate that her hair had come undone. He could see her unbraiding it, turning it into a glorious jasmine-and-sandalwood-perfumed silk tent that covered them both as they kissed in the dark, in secret, under the trees. Her hair fell on his cheeks, his lips and twisted in and out of his fingers: it was the thread that wove them together, that would keep them from ever separating.

He didn't think about what he was doing, it happened too fast, he simply reached out and grasped the curl and—

"No," the professor shouted as he pulled Josh's arm away. "She is fragile. That she is still intact is a miracle. If you touch her, she might break. Do you understand?"

The sensation of her hair on his fingers was almost more than Josh could bear. Turning away, rubbing his hands together, he found and then focused on the ancient oil lamp, blackened with soot on the ground. It looked as if she'd pushed it as close as she could get it to the alcove in the wall, at that discolored patch of earth.

The gates in his mind opened an inch wider. Josh's head throbbed with the new rush of information. He needed to go deeper into the lurches instead of skimming them, but he could only be in one place at a time. Then or now. Not both.

Give in to it. Concentrate on what happened. Long ago. Long ago, right here. What happened here?

Josh, oblivious to the professor's warnings that he might be defiling the dig, fell to his knees and clawed at the dirt wall with his bare hands. He had something to prove. To her. To himself. He didn't know what it was—only that something that lay behind this partition would vindicate him.

"What are you doing?" the professor asked, horrified. "Stop!"

As if the dream had become reality and the reality had slipped away, Josh only vaguely heard the professor cautioning him to stop, barely felt the man's hands trying to pull him back. The man's protestations didn't matter. Not anymore.

The dirt was packed tightly, but once he dug the first few handfuls out the rest was easier to break through. The wall, which was only four or five inches thick, three-and-a-half-feet tall and three feet wide, broke apart in chunks, revealing what appeared to be the opening of a tunnel. A piece of rock ripped the skin on his left palm, but he couldn't stop, he was almost there.

A gush of cool, stale air rushed toward him.

Ancient air.

Sixteen-hundred-year-old molecules and particles filled his lungs, along with the scents of jasmine and sandalwood. He climbed in, despite the claustrophobia that reached out and grabbed hold of him and the out-of-control panic that threatened his progress. Sweating suddenly, now gasping for breath, he desperately wanted to turn around, but the pull of the tunnel was more powerful than the paranoia.

The space only accommodated him on all fours. So, on his hands and knees, he crawled forward, immediately engulfed in darkness, and sadness crushed him as if the air itself was weighted down with it. He struggled on slowly, going five yards in, ten yards in, then twenty and then twenty-five. The professor continued calling out for Josh to stop, but he couldn't: there was an end point somewhere up ahead and he needed to reach it.

He navigated a turn, gulping for air, and froze, incapable of moving. It would be easier to die now than to go forward. Picturing the dirt that surrounded him, he saw it coming loose, breaking free, raining down on him. So real was the manifestation of his fear, he could taste the grit in his mouth, feel it in his nostrils, closing up his throat.

But something important waited for him up ahead. More important than anything else in the world.

"Stop, stop!" Rudolfo yelled, his voice coming from a far distance, distorted and echoing.

Oh, how he wanted to, but he managed another five yards.

The professor's voice reached him, but more faintly now. "What if there is a drop and you can't see it? What if you fall? I can't get to you."

No, and that was one of the fears that plagued him now. A sudden break, a hollow cave beneath this one, a descent into subterranean darkness.

He sensed the energy in the tunnel and let it pull him forward. Almost alive, it begged him to come, to come deeper into its shadows, to explore what was waiting, what had been waiting for so damn long.

"Come back at least and get a flashlight.... What you are doing is dangerous...."

Of course, the professor was right. Josh had no idea what lay ahead, but he was too close now to turn back, not sure that if he did he would find the nerve to start over.

He moved forward another foot and then he felt it. Something long and hard under his fingers. Trying to identify it through touch, he examined its contours and its circumference.

A long stick? Some kind of weapon?

The surface was slightly pitted. It wasn't wood. Or metal.

No. He knew through logic and through a primordial instinct.

It was bone.

Human bone.

Chapter 5

New York City—Tuesday, 2:00 a.m.

Four months after her aunt's unexpected death from a heart attack, Rachel Palmer learned that a woman who lived in her building was assaulted on the stoop as she fished in her bag for her keys. Much to her chagrin, Rachel couldn't shake how uncomfortable she felt in the brownstone after that: always looking over her shoulder when she opened the front door, rushing up the stairs, quickly throwing the bolt behind her and never sleeping through the night. When she mentioned that she was going to start looking for another place, her uncle Alex suggested she temporarily move into his palatial duplex at Sixty-Fifth and Lexington.

Even though he never said it or showed it, she knew he was lonely—Alex and her aunt Nancy had been inseparable the way certain childless couples can be—and even though he was only sixty-two-years old, Rachel sensed it was going to be a long time before he sought the companionship of another woman.

Rachel's father had abandoned her mother when she was a child, and Alex had stepped in, becoming much more to her than an uncle. Now she was glad to keep him company and enjoy the inviolability the building's doorman plus her uncle's round-the-clock security system gave her.

Without realizing it, Rachel got used to the companionship, and in the past two days since Alex had left for a week-long business trip to London and Milan, she'd had trouble getting to sleep. Having given up for the night, she was in bed with the lights on, simultaneously watching an old movie on television, sipping a glass of white wine and reading the next morning's news on her laptop.

Tomb Belongs to Vestal Virgin
By Charlie Billings
Rome, Italy
It was confirmed yesterday that the recent excavation outside of the city gates is believed to be the burial site of one of ancient Rome's last Vestal Virgins.

"We were fairly certain that the tomb dated back to the late fourth century, specifically from 390 to 392 A.D. The pottery and other artifacts we've found further bears this out. Barring any more surprises, we believe the woman buried here was a Vestal," said Gabriella Chase, professor of archeology at Yale University, a specialist in ancient religions and languages, who, along with Professor Aldo Rudolfo from the University of Rome La Sapienz, has been working at sites in this area for three years.

"What makes this particular excavation especially exciting is that the woman buried here may be one of the last six Vestals," Chase said. "After more than a thousand years, the cult of the Vestals came to an end in 391 A.D., coincident with the rise of Christianity under the reign of Emperor Theodosius."

The noise emanating from the television disappeared. The lights in the bedroom dimmed. Rachel tried to keep reading, tried to stay in bed, feel the sheets under her hands, pillows at her back, but deep inside of her, her heart fluttered, raced; the promise of understanding gave her a physical thrill. A whole world that she didn't know anything about presented itself like an uncut diamond. All she needed to do was step forward and explore it.

Entering, she was bedazzled by a scene that glittered in hyper-realistic sunshine. Warmth surrounded her and held her, cosseting her like a summer wind. Comforted and excited at the same time. The radiance was inside her now, and she felt light, so light she was flying, moving faster and faster and at the same time aware of each sensation as if it was happening in very slow motion.

The sun burned her cheeks. The smell of the heat filled her nostrils. Her body hummed as if she were an instrument someone played. She heard music, but it didn't have anything to do with tones or keys or chords or melody. It was pure rhythm. Her heart changed its beat to keep pace. Her breathing altered to the new timing.

Then it was cold. Shivering, she peered through a glass door, through a crack in the curtains, spying on two men, both hunched over a desk.

"This is what I came to Rome for. What I gave up hope I'd ever find," said the one she knew well, though she couldn't remember his name.

Then she saw the magic colored stones and their reflections. Flashes of blue and green lights filled her with a desperate pleasure. It was a drug. She wanted to stand there and try to understand how they melded into each other, creating a hundred new shades: a rainbow of emerald melting into peacock blue melting into cobalt melting into sea green melting into sage melting into teal, into red, burgundy and crimson.

"This is important, a real find." The man's voice was hard like the edges of the stones and she felt little cuts on her skin where his words touched her. She didn't care if she bled. She wanted to be part of this moment and this pain and this excitement. It surpassed anything that had ever happened to her before.

And then it was over.

Dizzy, Rachel put her head back and stared up at the ceiling. Her skin was burning hot. How long had the episode lasted? A half hour?

She picked up her wine. No, the glass was still cold.

Only minutes?

Except it seemed so real, so much more real than any daydream she'd had before. It wasn't just an image stuck in her head. She thought she'd been sucked through time and space and had been somewhere else for a moment, not *seeing* the scene played out but *being* part of it.

Leaving her bedroom, she walked down the sweeping staircase and headed toward the kitchen. She needed something stronger than wine. She wished her uncle was home so she could tell him what had happened; it was the kind of thing he'd be fascinated by. No, nothing had happened. She must have been tired, after all, fallen asleep without knowing it, dreamed the villa and the man and the colors.

After pouring a brandy, she took a few sips, the fiery liquid stinging her eyes and burning the back of her throat, and then, instead of going back to her bedroom, she went into her uncle's den and sat down at his desk. She felt safer there, surrounded by all his books. That was when she noticed, tucked into his desk blotter so that it was hardly noticeable, a corner of newsprint.

She pulled it out.

Tomb Possibly Dates Back 1600 Years.

Rachel shivered as she read the dateline. This story had been filed two weeks ago, in Rome, by that same reporter. No, there was nothing portentous about Alex tearing out this article. He was a collector. Tombs yielded ancient artifacts. The house was filled with objets d'art. She was overreacting. It was just a coincidence.

Wasn't it?

What else could it be?

Chapter 6

Rome, Italy—Tuesday, 7:45 a.m.

Josh felt a sharp, searing, twisting pain in his middle. Taking his breath away. Stunning him with its intensity. He broke out in a second cold sweat. The pain worsened. He needed to get out of the tunnel; his panic was making it almost impossible for him to breathe. If he hyperventilated now he might suffocate, and the professor was too old and too slow to get to him in time. He needed to get out now.

But he couldn't turn around. The space was too narrow. How was that possible? He'd gotten here, hadn't he?

He sat back on his haunches and reached out both of his hands, feeling for the walls on either side. His fingers hit dirt almost immediately. The tunnel must have narrowed as it continued without him being aware of it.

The reality of the darkness descended on him. He was fully

conscious and present. The smell of the dank air nauseated him and he was suddenly, inexplicably sure he was going to die in this tunnel. Now. Any minute. In this small, narrow space that was not big enough for a man to turn around in.

A small rock came loose and pinged him on the shoulder. What if his presence caused an avalanche of stone, and he became trapped in this passageway to hell? His chest tightened and his breathing became increasingly labored. He tried a series of contortions but couldn't manage to turn.

His panic heightened.

A few deep breaths.

A full minute of focusing on one fact: he'd gotten this far, that meant he would be able to get out.

Of course. Just go backward. Don't try to turn now. Don't turn until the space widens again.

The gripping frenzy broke, the anxiety vanished and Josh became aware of a very different pain. The tunnel was filled with rubble. Small pebbles and sharp stones ripped his palms, pressed down deep to the bone in his knees. He held his hands up to his face, forgetting for a minute that there was no light—he couldn't see what he'd done to his flesh but could guess from the overpowering sweet smell of blood. Struggling out of his shirt, he banged his head on the tunnel's roof. Ripping the fabric with his teeth, he used the strips to wrap around both of his bleeding palms. There was nothing he could do for his knees.

Crawling backward was awkward and slow going, and he'd only gone a few feet when he heard the voices: the professor and another man were speaking in loud, rapid Italian. Something about the cadence made him think they were arguing.

Moving steadily, doing his best to ignore the pain, he finally reached the point where he could turn around. After that he moved faster, and seconds later rounded a curve. Ahead was a straightaway at the end of which he could see the interior of the tomb.

The professor stood in pale yellow lantern light, fists by his sides, facing someone Josh couldn't see but could hear. The stranger's voice was cruel and demanding. The professor's response was angry and defiant. No translation was necessary. The professor was in jeopardy.

Josh crawled forward another foot. Then another.

The stranger crossed in front of the tunnel opening and became somewhat visible. From his clothing, he looked like the man guarding the site whom Josh had encountered when he'd first arrived.

Nothing to worry about, then.

Except they continued to argue; hot words were flung back and forth so rapidly that even if Josh had spoken basic Italian, he wouldn't have been able to understand.

The shouting escalated and the professor tried to push the guard away, but the man stepped back adroitly and Rudolfo lost his balance, falling to the ground. The guard put his foot on the professor's chest.

It was almost impossible to crawl faster. There was too much debris in the tunnel, and despite the makeshift bandages, his wounds throbbed. But he must. This was tied to the past, a chance for Josh to right a wrong. It was inches from his reach, almost within his grasp.

A stone pierced the skin on his right knee. Involuntarily, Josh swore under his breath. Then he froze. The only chance he had to stop whatever was going on was to take the guard by surprise.

Then everything happened so quickly that he would have missed it if he'd glanced away for five seconds, but his eyes were riveted to the action. He just wasn't fast enough to stop any of it. The entire tomb was in his sight now. Far away still, but visible.

The guard leaned down, bent over the ancient corpse and snatched the fruitwood box out of her arms.

"No, no..." The professor clawed at the guard, jumping on him like an angry monkey, grabbing at him, for the box.

As if the professor were a mere annoyance, the large man flung Rudolfo off. The professor landed on the ground, close to the mummy. Too close. His arm hit her and her head fell forward—she was in danger of coming apart. Rudolfo let out an agonized scream and rushed to her side. But before he could reach her, the guard kicked her with his heavy boot and her intact form splintered at the waist with a sickening crack.

While the professor kneeled at Sabina's side, the guard opened the fruitwood box, pulled out what looked like a leather pouch, shook its contents into his hand, pocketed whatever he'd found and then hurled the box at the professor. It hit his shoulder and broke apart, the pieces flying into the air and then landing haphazardly.

Josh was only ten yards away, planning on how he was going jump out, take the man by surprise, tackle him and get back what he'd taken.

Hand forward.

Knee forward.

Hand forward.

Knee forward.

Rudolfo stood, dizzy, rocking back and forth. The guard hurried toward the ladder.

With only a few feet left to go, Josh inched steadily forward. The way the tunnel was angled he could see the whole scene, and he watched with growing dread as the professor rushed toward the opening of the tomb.

The guard had started up the ladder.

Rudolfo tried to grab hold of the man's shirt, to pull him down, to stop him.

The guard pushed the professor's hand away as if it were nothing more than an insect and took another step up.

Not ready to give up, Rudolfo took hold of the ladder's wooden dowels and tried to shake the guard loose.

Josh had two, maybe three yards to go.

The guard stopped climbing—he was halfway up now, and he just stood there, staring down at Rudolfo, and then he pulled out his gun.

The professor took a step up the ladder.

The guard's finger teased the trigger.

Josh was almost at the entrance of the tunnel, and just as he screamed an agonized "no" in warning, the gun went off, causing an enormous explosion in the small tomb and drowning out his warning. Behind him, he heard a rumble and then the sound of heavy rain. No. Not rain. Rocks. Some parts of the tunnel's walls were collapsing in on themselves. And in front of him, he saw the professor fall on his back on the hard, cold, ancient mosaic floor.

Chapter 7

The man sat in the leather chair, his hands resting on the arm pads, his fingers circling the smooth nail heads. Around and around the cold metal circles as if this one movement was enough to keep him occupied forever. His eyes were shut. The gold drapes were drawn, and the room's rich decor was cloaked in darkness.

He was satisfied to sit and do nothing but wait. Long pauses in the plan didn't bother him. Not after all this time. From the moment he'd first heard the legend of the Memory Stones he knew that one day whatever power they held would be his. Needed to be his. No price was too high and no effort was too great to find out about the past.

His past.

His present.

And so, too, his future.

The idea that the stones might work, that they could, in fact, enable people to remember their previous lives, was unbearably pleasurable to him. He fantasized about the stones the way other men fantasized about women. His daydreams about what would happen once they were in his possession elevated his blood pressure, took away his breath and made him feel weak and strong at the same time in an utterly satisfying way. And because he'd been taught to be disciplined, he gave in to the temptation of dreaming about them only when he felt he deserved the indulgence.

He deserved it now.

Were they emeralds? Sapphires the color of the night skies? Lapis? Obsidian? Were they rough? Polished? What would they feel like? Small and smooth? Larger? Like glass? Would they be luminescent? Or dull, ordinary-looking things that didn't begin to suggest their power?

He didn't mind waiting, but it seemed to him that he should have heard by now.

He had an appointment he had to keep. No, it was premature to worry. He wouldn't contemplate any kind of failure. He disliked that he'd involved other people in his plan. No one you hired, no matter how much you paid them, was entirely trustworthy. Regardless of how well he'd tried to plan for the mistakes that could happen along the way, he was certain to have overlooked at least a few. He felt a new wave of anxiety start to build deep in his chest and took several deep breaths.

Relax. You've reached this point. You'll succeed.

But so much is at stake.

He picked up the well-worn book he'd been reading last night when his anticipation of what today would bring had kept him awake, *Theosophy* by the nineteenth-century philosopher

Rudolf Steiner. There were always new books being published on the subject that mattered so much to him—he bought and read them all—but it was the thinkers of the past centuries whom he responded to and returned to so often: the poetry of Alfred, Lord Tennyson, Percy Bysshe Shelley, Walt Whitman, Longfellow; the prose of Ralph Waldo Emerson, George Sand, Victor Hugo, Honoré de Balzac and so many more who engaged, reassured and aided him in amending and revising his own ever-evolving theories. They were his touchstones, these great minds that he could only know through their words. So many brilliant men and women who had believed what he believed.

He let the book fall open to the soft leather bookmark with his initials stamped on the cordovan in gold, at the beginning of a chapter titled "The Soul in the World of Souls after Death." He'd underlined several paragraphs and he reread them now.

There follows after death a period for the human spirit in which the soul casts off its weakness for its physical existence in order then to behave in accordance with the laws of the world of the spirit and the soul alone, and to free the mind. It is to be expected that the longer the soul was bound to the physical the longer this period will last....

His right hand returned to the brass buttons on the chair. The metal was cool to the touch. There was not much he'd ever lusted after the way he craved these stones. Once he had them, oh, the knowledge he would gain. The mysteries he would solve. The history he could learn. And more than that.

He read the next paragraph, in which Steiner described how great a pain the soul suffered through its loss of physical gratification and how that condition would continue until the soul had learned to stop longing for things that only a human body could experience.

What would it be like to reach the level of not longing? A pure level of thought, of experiencing the oneness of the universe? The ultimate goal of being reincarnated?

He looked up from the page and over at the phone, as if willing the call to come. It was a simple burglary: the professor was elderly. He would be there alone. It was just a matter of overpowering him and taking the box. A child could accomplish it. And if a child could do it, an expert could certainly do it. And he was only hiring experts at every step of the way. The most expensive experts money could buy. For a treasure, for this treasure, was any price too high?

There was no reason to worry. The call would come when the job was done. The round brass buttons were warm once more. He moved his fingers over to the next two, relieved by the cold metal on his skin, and returned to the book.

Having reached this highest degree of sympathy with the rest of the world of the soul, the soul will dissolve in it, will become one with it....

If he had proof of past lives, actual reassurance of future lives, what would he do with the knowledge first? Not torture or punish; he had no desire to cause pain or sorrow. Find lost treasure? Discover truths that had been turned into lies through history? Yes, all that in time, but the first thing he would—

The sound startled him, although he was expecting it, and he jerked forward in the chair. As much as he wanted to, he didn't pick up on the first ring. He put the bookmark back in the book and closed it. Listening to the second ring, he took a satisfying breath. He'd waited for this for so long.

Lifting the receiver, he held it up to his ear.

"Yes?"

"It's done," said the man in heavily accented Italian.

"You'll proceed to the next step?"

"Yes."

"Fine."

He was ready to hang up, but the man spoke quickly. "There's something I should tell you."

He braced himself.

"We had a small accident, and—"

"No. Not on the phone. Report it through your contact." He hung up and stood.

People were fools. He'd explained a dozen times how important it was that nothing revealing be discussed over the phone. Anyone could be listening. Besides, it didn't matter if there'd been a small accident. Accidents happened, didn't they? What mattered was that the stones were almost in his possession, at last.

Chapter 8

"Are you hurt?" Josh asked the professor.

"No, stunned, not hurt."

He was on his back, lying on the mosaic floor, at the foot of the ladder.

"Here, let me help you. Are you sure he didn't hit you?"

"It was so odd, looking up into the barrel of the gun, it was like looking into the night. Except a night as big as all the nights I've ever known. As big as all the nights Bella has slept all these sixteen hundred years."

Rudolfo was having trouble straightening up; he was favoring one side of his body.

"Are you sure you are all right?"

He nodded. Concentrated. Frowned. And then looked down at his stomach.

The professor was wearing a dark blue shirt, and until that moment, in the low light inside the tomb, Josh had missed the spreading stain. But now they both saw it at the same time.

As carefully as he could, Josh pulled the professor's shirt away from his body. The wound seeped blood. Snaking his fingers around Rudolfo's back, he checked for an exit wound. He couldn't find one. The bullet was still inside him.

Meanwhile, the professor kept talking. "Good timing for you," he said. "If you hadn't been in the tunnel you would be bleeding like a pig, too, eh?"

Except, Josh thought, if he'd been quicker, he might have prevented this. Hadn't he thought this before?

"Bad timing for me," the professor rambled. "I would have liked to have lived long enough to find out if what Gabriella and I have found… Find out if what Bella has been protecting all these years…is…is…as important as we think."

"Nothing's going to happen to you." Josh put his fingers on the man's wrist, looked at his own watch and counted.

"If I'd had a daughter…" the professor said, "she'd be just like her…tough as nails…with that one soft streak. She's too much alone, though…all the time alone…."

"Bella?" Josh asked, only half listening. The professor was losing blood too quickly; his pulse was too slow.

Rudolfo tried to laugh but only managed a grimace. "No. Gabby. This find… Her find… Something no one believed existed. But she was as cool as… What is your expression… Cool as… What is it?"

"Cool as? Oh. Cool as a cucumber."

Rudolfo smiled faintly; he was visibly failing.

"Professor, I need to call for help. Do you have a phone?"

"Now we know...dangerous...what we found....You'll tell her, dangerous...."

"Professor, do you have a phone? I need to call for help."

"Did he take...all of the box, too?"

"The box?" Josh looked around and saw the pieces of it on the ground. "No. It's still here. Professor, can you hear me? Do you have a phone? I need to call for help. We need to get you to a hospital."

"The box...is here?" The idea seemed to buoy him.

"Yes. Professor, do you have a phone?"

"Jacket. Pocket."

Finding the phone, Josh checked for a signal and then dialed 911. Nothing. He stared at the LED panel. 911? Why did he think the number would be the same in Italy?

He hit zero and was connected in seconds with an operator.

"Medical emergency," he shouted as soon as he heard another human voice, hoping the words were similar enough in Italian for her to understand. They must have been because the woman said *sì* and switched him over. While he waited he wondered what he would do if the next operator didn't speak English. But that turned out to be the least of his problems.

"Yes, I understand. An ambulance. Where is your location?" the next operator asked.

An address. A simple thing, really. Except Josh had no idea where he was. He looked down; the professor's eyes were shut.

"Professor Rudolfo? Can you hear me? I need to tell them where we are. An address. Can you hear me?"

No response.

Josh explained what was going on to the sympathetic woman

on the other end of the phone. "He's not responsive. I'm afraid he's dying. And I don't know where we are."

"Are there any landmarks?"

"I'm sixteen feet under the ground!"

"Go outside, look for something, some sign, a name, a building. Anything."

"I'll have to leave him."

"Yes, but you have no choice."

He leaned down to the professor. "I'm going outside for a minute."

Rudolfo opened his eyes and Josh thought he'd heard the question and was going to tell him where they were, but he wasn't focused on Josh. Searching the room frantically, his eyes settled on the body of the woman who had died here so many years ago. Then he slipped back into unconsciousness.

Josh looked over at her, too. "Keep him safe," he whispered, oblivious of how strange a thing that was for him to do.

Even though he climbed up the ladder as quickly as he could, he didn't think he was moving fast enough. Reaching the surface, he scanned the area.

"I'm in a damn field. I see...there are cypress trees...oak trees..." He turned. "A hill behind me. About five hundred yards away there's a piece of a gate or a building, very old...."

"That doesn't help. No signs?"

"If there was a sign, goddamn it—" His voice was strained and loud.

"There is probably a road, sir. Find the road if you can," she interrupted.

"Right. Stay with me. I'll find something."

Josh jogged down the slight hill. Looked left, right. It was just a stretch of two-lane highway. To his right there was a bend blocking the view. To the left, more of the same vista: cypress tress, lush verdant fields with terra-cotta rooftops far in the background. Nothing specific to help him tell her where they were.

Someone must know where the hell this place was. Someone other than the man who lay dying in the crypt.

"Tell me your name," Josh said to the woman on the phone. "There's someone I can call to get the address. I'll call you right back."

"My name is Rosa Montanari, but I can stay on the line and connect you. Give me the number, sir."

Ninety seconds later, Malachai Samuels answered his cell phone on the second ring. "Hello?"

"I don't have any time to explain this to you, but quick, I need you to find Gabriella Chase and get me the exact address of the dig."

"I just this minute sat down with Gabriella Chase. For breakfast. Aren't you coming?"

"Put her on the phone."

"Why don't you tell me what—"

"I can't now," he interrupted. "This is an emergency."

There was a brief pause during which Josh heard Malachai repeating what he'd said. Then he heard a woman's voice, deep, silvery and anxious.

"Hello, this is Gabriella Chase. Is something wrong?"

Josh stayed on the line while Gabriella dictated the address and then while the operator ordered the ambulance. He didn't understand what was being said, but it was reassuring to know that help was on its way.

When she finished talking to the paramedics, Rosa told Josh she'd stay on the phone with him until they got there and suggested he check on the professor so she could keep the ambulance drivers updated.

Rudolfo's breathing was even shallower and he had less color than minutes before.

"Professor Rudolfo? Professor?"

His lips parted and he whispered a few unintelligible syllables.

"Mr. Ryder? Are you there?"

Josh almost forgot he was still holding the phone to his ear. "Yes?"

"How is the *professore?*" Rosa asked.

"Very bad. He's unconscious."

"The ambulance should arrive in eight to ten minutes."

"I don't know if he can make it that long. He's still bleeding. I thought it had stopped. Is there anything I can do until they get here?"

"I have a doctor standing by."

This wondrous woman had an emergency room doctor on another line, and for the next interminable few minutes, with Rosa translating, Dr. Fallachi helped Josh keep the professor alive and stop the blood loss. It would take approximately twenty minutes for someone to bleed out and die from a wound like the one the professor sustained, the doctor said. Josh judged ten to twelve minutes had already passed. It was going to be close.

From the corner, Sabina, because now that was how he thought of her, looked over at them with her sightless eyes, and under her ghostly gaze he felt the full force of his failure. If this man died, it was his fault. If he hadn't been in the tunnel, he would have been able to help Rudolfo. Instead, he'd been deep in the earth, bathed in sweat, almost paralyzed with anxiety, crawling toward some long-forgotten remembrance or some insane man's delirium.

"I'm sorry," he whispered. But only the bones heard him. Sabina's bones.

Chapter 9

One minute, Josh was cradling the professor, waiting for the ambulance. The next, the scent of jasmine and sandalwood blew past him, and he braced himself for the first stirrings of exhalation that preceded an episode. At the same time that Josh desperately wanted to stop the lurch, he also ached for it. An addict, this was his drug. It was that exhilarating. It was that horrific.

Josh had always thought that occasional sense of recognition people experience when they meet someone for the first time and feel an instant connection was nothing to pay attention to. You laugh and say, *I'd swear I already know you.* Or when you go on vacation to a town you've never been to but feel like you have been there before. It's disturbing, but you shake it off. Or it's amusing, and you mention it to a friend or spouse.

It's just déjà vu, you say, not thinking twice.

Maybe when it used to happen.

But not now.

Malachai and Dr. Talmage had educated him beyond that. That fleeting sense was a gift, a moment of unforgetting, signifying that there *was* a connection between you and the person you'd just met or the place you'd just visited. Nothing is an accident, nothing is a coincidence, according to theories of rebirth that go back through history, through the centuries, circling through cultures, changing and developing, but only attracting so much controversy in the West after the fourth century A.D. In the East, being skeptical about reincarnation would have been as unusual as questioning the wetness of water.

While he waited for what seemed much too long, trying to will the professor to live, Josh was certain he'd tasted death in that place before. He didn't know what had happened here in the past, only that he now felt he was on some unimaginable journey of repetition that was out of his power to stop.

Sitting on the ground, feeling the professor's pulse slow, he trained his eyes out the opening, up toward the sky. This way, as soon as the paramedics arrived, he'd see them.

The air undulated around him, and shivers of anticipation shot up and down his arms and legs. Even while he sat perfectly still in one dimension, he was being sucked down into a vortex where the atmosphere was heavier and thicker, where he floated like a ghost rather than walking like a man, and where he felt pleasure more purely and pain more acutely.

It began like every episode. The scene developed slowly, the way photographs appear, as if by magic, on pristine sheets of paper, swimming up out of a swirl of liquid. He was the stranger outside looking in as the scene opened before him. He saw the players and the stage. And then, in a matter of seconds, he became the person he was observing. Saw now through another's eyes, spoke in the other's voice. Was not himself. Had lost himself. Did not know there was another self.

Chapter 10

Julius and Sabina
Rome—386 A.D.

The screams alerted him as the wind blew the smell of the acrid smoke into his bedchamber. They all lived in fear of it, and most of them had been witness to some form of it at some point in their lives. Fire was their most sacred possession, and fire was their fiercest enemy.

The story of the great conflagration that burned two-thirds of the city down more than three hundred years before was still told as a cautionary tale. During the night of July 18, a blaze started in the merchants' area. There were too many structures, all made of wood, squeezed too close together. Hot summer winds fanned the flames until one by one, the stores and dwellings, some five-, six-stories high, caught on fire. For six days and seven nights, the inferno raged, and then for several days afterward, it smoldered.

The city was left in ruins.

The historian Tacitus wrote an account describing how terrified men and women, the helpless old and the helpless young, fugitives and lingerers alike, tried to escape all at once, which only added to the confusion.

Some, it was said, those who'd lost too much, or who were consumed with guilt at not having been able to save their loved ones, chose not to run, but freely gave themselves to the fire and died in the blaze. To make it worse, many who might have helped had been afraid to fight, since menacing gangs were attacking those who tried. That's where the rumors came from that Nero had ordered the fire to persecute early Christians. After all, Nero had been tormenting them for years, using them as human torches, crucifying and sacrificing them. But would the emperor destroy his own city, his own treasures?

Others blamed that great inferno on angry gods and ill luck. Still others believed the early Christians themselves started the fire to destroy the pagan city they despised. For weeks before that fated July night, in the streets of the poorest neighborhoods, early radical upstarts were passing out leaflets prophesying the burning destruction of Rome and stirring up public opinion against the old order.

Now, three centuries later, as Julius ran toward the temple, nostrils burning, feeling the heat on his face intensifying, he worried that this blaze was politically motivated. He and many of the other high priests held that these were the last days of the Roman Empire, as they'd known it. The emperor and the Bishop of Milan were seeing to that. The ideological fight between the all-encompassing pagan order and the thousands of Romans who believed in the teachings of the Jewish prophet

Jesus, or who paid lip service to it in order to curry favor with their emperor, was becoming an ugly battle between two ways of life, between many gods and one god.

Paganism was a mosaic, like the designs on the temple floors. It was made up of dozens of sects, faiths and cults it had absorbed over the years. As a result, religious freedom reigned in Rome for centuries. Why must an old faith be destroyed to make room for a new one?

Using the gray, billowing clouds as a map toward the site, Julius could tell that the fire was close to the Atrium Vestae, the house where the Vestals lived, just behind the circular Temple of Vesta at the eastern edge of the Roman Forum. The eighty-four-room palace built around an elegant courtyard had burned to the ground several times in the past. Ironic that the Goddess Vesta was the greatest threat to those who kept her safe.

As the strong orange blaze reached higher into the blackened sky, one by one they came: priests and citizens, breathing in the fumes, choking on them, but determined to save the house and ensure the fire didn't encroach on the temple. It wasn't only buildings at risk, but legendary treasures that were said to be hidden in a secret substructure under the holy hearth.

By the time Julius arrived there were two dozen firefighters, men from every walk of life who volunteered and were trained to race to the fire site and fight the blaze as soon as it was reported. One small fire—because of all the wooden buildings—could turn into an inferno in no time.

Much to his horror, Julius realized that one of the firefighters wasn't a man—but a woman who hadn't stayed back with her sisters. She shouldn't be there, it was too dangerous. But the men were too busy to try and pull her away or warn her to be careful. Even if they'd tried, he knew it wouldn't have made any difference: she would have been right back on the front line two minutes later.

Defiance was typical of Sabina, who'd been a constant challenge to the sisters who'd trained her. Although they marveled at her clairvoyance, they complained that her tenacity and willfulness weren't suited to being a priestess.

Neither was her contempt for him.

In front of others, she showed him the minimum of respect required to keep out of trouble. But when no one else was around, if their paths crossed, she let her feelings show. There were days it made him want to laugh that she looked at him with so much antagonism; others when he wanted to punish her for her impudence. It disturbed him because there was no reason for her reactions. And even less reason that despite her antagonism to him, he felt drawn to her. Admired her. Cheered her on.

As the head priestess, she proved exemplary. But unlike the other Vestals, Sabina possessed a stubborn streak, a refusal to give up all of her personality to the group, which propelled her to become one the most educated of all the nuns in recent years, studying medicine and learning how to be a healer, although it added extra responsibility to her already full life. When tired customs didn't make sense to her, she questioned them, changed them and breathed life into the old order. Even when it alienated her from the older sisters and conservative priests, she fought back bravely, passionately. Recently, the most traditional among them were applauding her efforts.

A section of the house collapsed with a loud crash. The fire was winning the battle. Sabina worked as hard as Julius did to smother the flames; she was as valiant a fighter as any man there. When their eyes met for a brief second, Julius looked away, chilled, despite the fire's heat, by the look she flashed at him. She was determined to live, which meant the fire had to die. But either she'd inhaled too much smoke or she was just too exhausted, because suddenly she fell to the ground.

Angry blisters marred her cheeks. Her robe was ripped up the side and across the front, exposing her long legs and breasts, all blackened with soot.

None of the other men seemed to have noticed. If she wasn't dead, one of them was bound to trample her to death. Julius couldn't let that happen. Leaving his post, he ran to her, picked her up and carried her lifeless body out of the way, the heat at his back becoming less and less intense until he wasn't aware of it anymore.

Sabina was heavy in his arms, and he felt the full burden of her: of her position as head of the nuns, of her complicated response to him, of her power and vitality. Finally far enough away from the fire, he laid her down on a patch of grass, allowing himself to focus on her and give in to his curiosity and his obsession—because if he was honest with himself, despite his best efforts and for no rational reason he knew, that was what she'd become.

Putting his ear to her breast, he listened for her life sounds. All he heard was his own nervous heart beating so loudly in his ears. But from her chest—silence.

No, it wasn't possible that the fire had beaten her.

Not Sabina.

He didn't realize he was shouting until the wind threw his own howl back at him.

No. Not Sabina.

She had too much energy, too much resolve.

He wanted to pray, but the grief crowded out all the words. He shut his eyes. The smell of jasmine and sandalwood emanated from her skin—mixed in with the bitter smell of the smoke—whispering to him, hinting of something he'd never had and now would never know.

By the time the other priests were his age they'd married and fathered children. They teased him about his unmarried state, not understanding it. Marriages allowed for every taste and predilection, they chided—even for men who preferred sex with other men. Why can't you find a wife?

Only to himself, only now, could he admit that he'd found a woman he wanted to wed, but of all the women in all of Rome she was one of a very select few he couldn't have.

He had been a young priest when she became a Vestal. And from the very beginning she had stood out. She was bright and curious as a young girl, then feisty and determined as an adolescent. His admiration had turned to attraction when her slim body had started to curve, when her breasts and hips teased him from under her robes.

For the past twelve years, Sabina had taunted him, then challenged him. Now, in death, she would haunt him.

Her hatred of him should have cooled his ardor. Instead, it seemed to inflame it. Alone in his own rooms, when thoughts of her would come, he'd find a prostitute. But not the lewdest, the lustiest, nor the most comely chased away the images of the virgin. Julius prayed to the gods to take away his desire. When they didn't, he ignored and surmounted his feelings... He needed to... His attention could doom her. Any congress they might have shared could be her death sentence. And his.

Her eyes were shut. Her lovely red hair was singed and blackened. Julius sat beside her on the grass, unable to get up, although the fire was still raging and he knew the men needed him. Her sisters would come and get her body later and prepare it for burial, but he couldn't leave her yet. Helplessly, he reached out and pushed a lock of hair off of her forehead. It was the first time he'd touched her. Tears coursed down his cheeks, surprising him with their velocity. Julius couldn't remember the last time he'd wept.

"Sabina." Again, a cry, not a word, still not a prayer.

And then it seemed as if the wind answered him, softly whispering his name in response. He looked down.

Her eyes were open. And upon him. And there was no anger in them anymore, but another expression: a mixture of defeat and desire.

Sabina had not perished in the fire after all.

He heard a sound that didn't fit the picture. Loud. Shrieking. Not human. No. It was the ambulance coming to him from a great blue-green distance.

She looked at him, longing and pain in her eyes.

But the siren was pulling him up, up through the murky, briny heaviness into some fresh hell.

Chapter 11

Rome, Italy—Tuesday, 8:12 a.m.

There were three paramedics. Too many people in a suddenly claustrophobic space. As much as Josh wanted to get out of the tomb, which now reeked of blood, he couldn't. Backing up, he flattened himself against the wall and watched the team go into action.

The female medic wrapped a blood-pressure cuff around the professor's arm. One of the men swabbed his other arm and stuck a needle in his vein, readying him for an IV. The third asked Josh questions in broken English.

How long ago did this happen?

When had the professor become unconscious?

Did he know the professor's family?

Did he have any phone numbers for them?

Fifteen minutes.

Five minutes.

No.

No.

He didn't know.

They worked with choreographed precision, totally focused, not seeming to notice where they were or that there was a mummified woman broken apart in the corner. But Josh kept glancing at her, checking on her.

From where he stood, he could see the professor's face, colorless and motionless. But his eyes were open and his mouth was forming words. Josh couldn't hear the words, so he moved as close as he could without getting in anyone's way. Which, in that tiny space, meant taking only two steps forward.

The professor continued whispering in Italian: the same few words over and over.

"What is he saying?" he asked one of the medics.

"*Aspetta.* Wait for her. He's repeating it over and over."

They worked on him for a few more minutes and then the woman counted—*uno, due, tre*—and together they lifted him off the ground, onto a stretcher, strapped him in, and then, in a complicated series of maneuvers, hoisted him out.

Josh followed after them.

Moving quickly, but also being careful not to jostle him, they wheeled him toward the ambulance. In the distance, the roar of a car engine grew louder. A navy blue Fiat raced up the road, dust flying in its wake. A few seconds later, it pulled to a screeching halt and a tall woman jumped out on the driver's side. She moved in a blur—pure energy—rushing toward the gurney. Josh got a flash of sunburned skin, high, wide cheekbones and windswept, wild, honey-colored hair. Her voice was a combination of authority and fear as she called out her questions to the medics. Even under stress there was a lyrical cadence to her words. As focused on her as he was, Josh didn't notice Malachai until he called out to him.

As always, Malachai was wearing a suit, despite the heat. He was so meticulous even his shoes were newly shined. That wouldn't last long now that he was on site.

"Are you all right?" Malachai questioned.

"Fine. I'm fine. But I need to talk to Gabriella Chase." Josh pointed to the woman who'd gotten out of the car. "Is that her?"

"Yes, but first—"

"The professor made me promise I'd tell her what happened, and—"

He put his hand on Josh's arm to stop him. "She's with the medics. So tell me, what happened?"

Briefly, Josh explained about the shooting.

"Were you alone with him?"

"Yes."

"You were the only witness?"

"Yes. No one else was down there. Now I need—"

"Did you see the man who shot Rudolfo?"

"Yes. Yes, I saw him. . . ." Josh pictured the scene again as if his mind had filmed it. The man grabbing the box, opening it, pulling out the dark leather pouch, throwing the box on the ground, the professor's moan, the scuffle, the shot. He stopped the pictures.

"The guard took the Memory Stones, if that's what was in the box. Shot the professor and took the stones."

"Did you get a photograph of him?"

"I was rushing to help and then it was too late."

Malachai stood shaking his head back and forth, trying to absorb the loss. They'd both desperately wanted to see the stones, to talk to Rudolfo and Chase about them, discover if they did indeed have the legendary power assigned to them. Now it appeared they'd never have that chance.

"Did you see them before they were stolen?"

"No."

"So you don't know for sure they were in the box? They could have been somewhere else in the tomb?" A faint expression of hope.

"I don't know for sure…but from the way the professor reacted I'm fairly certain—"

"I don't think you should mention the stones to the police when they get here. Don't conjecture about what was in the box."

Malachai must have read the confusion in Josh's eyes because he didn't wait for his question before answering it. "If it appears that you know too much it will make you a more likely suspect."

"But I'm not a suspect, and shouldn't they know what they are looking for? Don't they need to?"

"If they know, word will get out, it's inevitable, and the very last thing Beryl or I—or, I'm sure, Gabriella, once she knows what happened—want is for the world to know of the existence of those stones. *Especially* if they've been stolen."

"I don't know. You're asking me to lie to the police."

"About something that isn't going to help the investigation and that you didn't actually see."

"So what do I say—that I saw the guard and that I can describe him—but that I have no idea what he took? That I was too busy having flashbacks to the fourth century, where I was hanging out with the flesh-and-blood version of the corpse that's buried here?"

Malachai was astonished. "If that's true, you'd be instrumental to our understanding of what the stones are and how they work. *You'd* be vital to the solution."

"Well, there are no coincidences, right? That's what you and Beryl have been telling me for the past four months, and it looks like you're dead on. The memories I've been having—" He held his arms out to include the tomb, the woods, the hills and beyond. "All of this…it's what I've been seeing for the past year. All of this and more…"

Malachai began studying Josh, taking in his shirtless chest, dirt- and-blood-streaked face. "Are you *sure* you are all right? Your hands are bleeding."

"It's nothing but scratches. The professor is the one who's been hurt, who might not make it."

Usually, Malachai was compassionate, but from a distance. As a hobby, and to relax the children he and his aunt worked with at the Phoenix Foundation, Malachai performed magic tricks. One of them seemed to be how he suppressed his own feelings, except for a hidden, sorrowful look in Malachai's eyes that Josh could see sometimes in just the right light, as if he had been hurt badly once and never quite healed. Josh often wondered whether, if he photographed the man, the melancholy would show through. But now, for the first time, he was overwrought and distressed. "This is a tragedy. A real tragedy."

And for a brief moment, before Josh realized how absurd the thought was, he wondered if Malachai was referring to the professor's shooting or the theft of the stones.

Chapter 12

As Josh looked for Gabriella, to give her the professor's message, the crowd of bystanders grew larger. Josh remembered what Rudolfo had said about the dig becoming a tourist attraction. He looked at his watch. It was 9:00 a.m. Right on cue. The crime scene was going to be contaminated if these people trampled on it. The police still weren't there to stop them. Shouldn't they have arrived on the heels of the ambulance? Someone needed to keep the crowds back.

Scanning the gathering, he noticed a trio of nuns, two priests, a group of teenage Goth girls and a tall man holding a pad and pencil talking to one of the nuns. He had thick hair that fell into his eyes, and he brushed it away in a gesture that Josh recognized. Charlie Billings always expressed his impatience like that. Josh was glad to see him—not just because he'd always liked the reporter, but because, having been on assignment with him here in Rome, he knew Charlie spoke fluent Italian.

As Josh made his way over to the reporter, pushing through the crowd, Malachai followed him as if he needed to keep him in sight to keep him safe.

They exchanged greetings, and then Charlie, assuming that Josh was there on assignment, asked who he was covering the story for.

"I'm not here as press, I was here as a guest of the professor. But listen, I need you to—"

"Wait a minute. Do you mean you were here during the shooting?"

Josh nodded, annoyed that he'd inadvertently made himself part of the story.

"Did you see who did this? Did you get a shot of him?" Charlie glanced at the ever-present camera around Josh's neck.

"I'll give you all that later, but first you need to help me. This is urgent. This crowd could make it impossible for the police to collect evidence if they get any closer to the area around the tomb. They could be trampling evidence now. I can't speak Italian, you can. Would you talk to them and ask them to stay back?"

"How 'bout I trade you. I'll talk to them and you tell me something I can use. What happened down there?"

"C'mon Charlie—" Josh pointed "—look." The Goth girls were starting to cross the field.

"Okay, but when I'm done, I'm going to find you." He started off. "You owe me now," he called out over his shoulder.

Malachai had stepped away while Josh was talking to Charlie, but now he came forward again. "Bastard." He indicated the reporter. "But I suppose it's inevitable the press would be here."

"He's okay. I know him from way back. If I play it straight with him, he won't screw us. Listen, I still—"

Loud wailing interrupted as three police cars arrived and officers jumped out.

"The press is the least of our problems now," Malachai said. "After they figure out who's who, the police are going to want to question us. We need to work out what we're going to say about being here. This is going to be an explosive story, and I don't want the foundation to be part of it."

Yet another siren sounded as the ambulance readied to take the professor to the hospital. Josh glanced over. Something was holding them up. Now Josh saw Gabriella, fighting to get into the ambulance with the stretcher. The female medic blocked her and then, when Gabriella didn't back off, physically pushed her away. Gabriella stumbled backward, tripped and fell to the ground. Without looking back, the medic hurried into the ambulance and slammed the door as it took off.

"She needs help," Josh said, and ran toward her.

Once he reached her side he knelt down next to her. "Are you hurt?" he asked.

"They wouldn't let me go with them." She sat on the grass, eyes peeled on the vehicle as it disappeared.

"They didn't have room."

"But he's alone," she said, sounding dazed.

"He's going to get the best care they can give him." It was like talking to a child.

"Is he going to be all right?" She turned to Josh for the first time. As a photographer, he'd looked into thousands of anguished faces, but her pained expression ripped at him in an intensely personal way, which he couldn't understand.

"I hope so," he said. "Are you sure you're okay, though? That was a tough fall."

She didn't seem to understand his question.

"You fell."

She looked around, noticing where she was as if for the first time. Then, brushing off her hands, she stood up.

"I'm okay," she said to Josh.

"You sure? You seemed pretty out of it there." He handed her the knapsack she'd left on the ground, forgotten.

"I'm okay. I am. I just need to find out—"

By now, Charlie Billings had made his way over. "Gabriella?" He reached out and touched her arm. "What happened here?"

"Not yet, Charlie," she said.

Josh was surprised that she knew him, then he remembered that Rudolfo had said she'd been talking to the press.

"Not for the record, then?"

"I don't think she's up to it. Give her some time," Josh said.

"You're really racking up those favors, you know?"

Josh offered his old colleague a nod.

"Can you tell me how the professor is?" Charlie asked Gabriella, still trying to get something for his story.

"He's in critical condition, that's all I know."

Charlie scribbled something on his pad, and Josh took advantage of the moment to take Gabriella by the elbow and steer her away from the edge of the road and the reporter to her car. As Josh helped her into the backseat, Malachai, who was behind the wheel, said, "Josh, hurry up and get in. I think it would be wise to leave now and avoid the circus while we still can. Gabriella, do you have the keys?"

Focused on Josh, she didn't answer.

"I just realized who you are. You're Josh Ryder, aren't you?"

He nodded.

"You were here the whole time?"

"I was. I'm sorry."

"Where did all this happen?"

"We were in the tomb when—"

"You were in the tomb with him?" she interrupted. "This happened inside the tomb?"

"Yes."

"I want to go down to the site… I need to see it." Pushing past Josh she got out of the car. Both Josh and Malachai got out and followed her. Catching up to her before she got too far, Malachai put his arm around her shoulder and stopped her. "It's better to leave all this to the police. We'll take you to the hospital. Come back to the car with me."

"Not yet. I need to see the site first," she said, shaking free.

"Let me go with you, then," Josh said, concerned that she not be alone when she saw the blood, the broken artifacts and the state Sabina was in.

Not answering, or waiting, she took off, but before she had gone five feet, two policemen intercepted her.

The conversation appeared to go smoothly for the first three or four questions, until one of them must have asked something that agitated her, because she gestured wildly to the road, then turned, pointing back toward her car, inadvertently including Josh and Malachai in her gesture.

The policemen followed her glance.

Thirty seconds later, the two *carabinieri* approached Josh and Malachai.

"Mr. Ryder?" the younger one asked, looking at Malachai.

"No. I'm Josh Ryder."

He asked him something in Italian.

Josh shook his head. "Sorry, I don't understand."

It seemed as if he'd said that to a dozen people already that morning. The language barrier was frustrating. He wanted to tell the policeman not to waste time with him when there was a man out there somewhere who had a gun and an ancient treasure and who was getting farther and farther away, but there was no way he could communicate that.

While this was going on, the *carabinieri* had their back to Gabriella and so they didn't notice when she broke away. There were other police on the scene, busily interviewing people in the crowds, but, curiously, none of them were paying attention to the real scene of the crime—Gabriella's destination, the tomb.

Of course not, Josh realized. None of them knew that the shooting had happened underground.

The policeman, who was still trying to talk to Josh, noticed him glance away and looked to see why. When he saw Gabriella, he called out to her.

She turned. There was fierce determination in her eyes, tear marks and dirt smeared on her face, dust on her clothes. She yelled back something Josh couldn't understand and then descended into the tomb she had been responsible for discovering.

Josh's heart lurched as she disappeared. He was desperately worried for her. There was no time to wonder why he was reacting so strongly to a stranger because, at that moment, two things happened almost simultaneously: the group of onlookers broke free from the sawhorses, and all the police took off to contain them.

Josh took advantage of the distraction to race toward the crypt.

"Stop, Josh. Let's get out of here. Don't—" Malachai shouted.

"She shouldn't be down there alone," he yelled back. He kept going, not knowing if the police were behind him or not. Not caring.

He was only a foot away when he heard Gabriella's scream coming up from the ground. It was sharp and ragged, and so pained it sounded as if she were being tortured.

Chapter 13

She was on her knees in the corner of the crypt, kneeling beside Sabina's broken body, emitting a low, keening cry of grief. It took Josh a few seconds to understand that Gabriella was saying the word *no* over and over; it sounded like a prayer.

He knew he was looking right at her, but he was seeing the tomb on another day.

A flash of a white robe.

Red hair.

Dark green eyes, filled with tears.

Sabina.

He wanted to reach out into the darkness, grab the specter and make her tell him what was happening here.

Gabriella's voice, insistent, dark, brought him instantly to the present moment. "Kick the ladder out. Kick it hard and break it," she said.

"What?"

"Quick! The ladder, pull it away from the wall."

Still under the spell of his memory lurch, Josh did what she asked but didn't understand why he was doing it.

"Now snap off the rungs. Use this—" She threw him a shovel. "Please, help me, buy me some time."

Attacking the wooden ladder with a vengeance, he'd broken the top six rungs by the time the police arrived at the opening. He didn't need to understand the language this time to know they wanted access to the tomb.

"Show them the broken ladder," Gabriella said.

He wanted to smile at her clever, quick thinking, but he refrained. The man who had questioned him earlier looked from the ladder to Gabriella and then at Josh. Then he said something that caused the other officer to laugh and made Gabriella curse under her breath, "Pigs."

Josh didn't need to know what they'd said.

"You said you were down here when it happened?" she asked Josh as soon as the *carabinieri* were gone.

"The whole time. It happened too quickly for me to do anything…to stop him…."

She wasn't looking at Josh anymore, but beyond him, examining the state of the tomb. It was the first time he'd really had a chance to study her with a photographer's eyes; he noted the long neck, shoulder-length, wavy hair, full mouth and strong bones. It was her nose, aquiline with a hint of a bump, that turned a woman who would otherwise have been typically pretty into someone intriguing. She was wearing jeans and a white shirt with the top two buttons open, and Josh was shocked, in the middle of all this madness, to find himself wishing she'd left the third unbuttoned, as well.

"You said you saw who shot the professor? Who was it?"

"A security guard. Or at least he was dressed like one."

"Did you take a picture of him?"

"No, it happened too fast. I was trying to get to the professor... I wish I had."

She seemed baffled for a moment. "Why didn't he shoot you, too?"

"I was in there." Josh pointed at the tunnel, and a rush of images assaulted him: moving slowly through the space, the feeling of the dirt under his hands, the panic of the narrow space, the sense that something was terribly wrong and the urgency to get quickly to the other end.

For a second he was confused. Were these fresh images of what had happened an hour before or were they part of the mind movies?

Gabriella walked over to where he had pointed and noticed the tunnel for the first time. "What the hell is this?" She peered into the darkness. "Who dug this out?"

"I did."

"Rudolfo allowed you to do this to our site?"

"He tried to stop me but...that's why I couldn't help the professor—I was pretty far back in there."

"I don't understand. Why would Rudolfo let you do this?"

"Listen, I couldn't understand anything anyone was saying up there. I'll tell you everything that happened, but first, tell me, what did the medics say about the professor? How bad is it?"

"They won't know until they get him to the hospital. But the bleeding had stopped and that's a good sign. They said if he lives, that you're the one who—" She stopped talking, reached down and picked up something off the mosaic floor.

"Why is this broken?" Her voice shook and so did the hand that held the piece of shattered fruitwood box. "Where is the rest of this?" She was back on her knees, frantic again.

"Gabriella." Josh knelt down beside her and put his hand on her shoulder, to stop her, to comfort her, to prepare her for what he was going to tell her. Her skin felt warm through the shirt. "The security guard took what was in the box with him. That must have been what he came for. I'm guessing what that means is that he took what you and the professor think might be the Memory Stones."

Her face distorted into two expressions at the same time, something Josh wasn't sure he'd ever seen before: her eyes showed utter devastation, but her mouth set in a line of cold fury. She stared down at the pieces of wood she still held. Two seconds went by. Five. Ten. Finally she lifted her head up. All the vibrant rage and deep sadness had left her face. Only a look of resolution remained. He was surprised at her resilience.

"There's no time to talk about this now," she said. "Too much to do. The police are going to figure out another way to get down here and are going to want to know what happened." She looked back at the broken body and the wood fragments and splinters. "I need to get to the hospital. They wouldn't let me go with them in the ambulance. I'm not family, they said." She shook her head as if she was clearing her thoughts, and her curls danced. Josh thought of Sabina's curl, escaping from her braid during the robbery.

"Before I leave I need to make sure I get rid of anything that might make them ask too many questions about this area...." She peered into the tunnel's blackness. "Do you have any idea how you've corrupted this site?" She took a deep breath, then turned to him. "What made you start digging there, anyway?"

Her eyes bored into him. There was no way he could explain it all to her now, even if he wanted to—and he didn't know if he did. "I saw the discoloration on the wall and there was something about the size and shape of it that suggested there was something beyond it."

Josh wasn't sure she believed him, but she didn't press him. "Will you help me close up the tunnel? I don't want them traipsing through here. Who knows what they might disturb."

They worked side by side as quickly as they could, shoveling dirt back into the opening, packing it down, piling on another layer. Between digging this out the first time and then crawling in the tunnel, the skin on Josh's palms was shredded.

"I don't care about anything now except that when the police talk to you about what happened down here, you lie, make up something, say anything you want, but don't tell them about this tunnel. No one can go in there who isn't connected to the dig before we get in there ourselves. When they come down, somehow we have to make sure they get their samples and photos and get out. I need to seal off the site until... If you say anything, if you suggest there's a passageway here, they'll insist on examining it. No one has been in that tunnel since this tomb was closed. Anything we might find in there will be priceless. A totally unique find. Can you do this, please?" Her voice was huskier as she elicited her promise, as if even voicing it had to be done in secret.

"Since the tunnel won't help them find out who did this, no, I won't tell them."

"You promise?" She was still concerned. "Where will you say you were during the shooting?"

“I’ll say I was outside. Heard the gunshot, saw the guard running away and came down here to help.”

She nodded and went back to work.

Now both Malachai and Gabriella had asked him to lie to the police. He wasn’t eager to become involved with the investigation either, but not because he was trying to hide anything.

He wasn’t as sure about either of them.

“Josh, hurry. Please. We can’t have much time left.”

Despite his lacerated hands he went back to scooping up the dirt, packing it down and then piling on another layer, wondering if the woman who had been buried had known there was an escape route so very close by. He breathed in some of the dirt—coughed—thought about how amazing it was that no one had discovered the tomb or the tunnel for sixteen hundred years, and wondered how many secrets were buried here alongside Sabina’s heartbreaking form.

Chapter 14

The scraping sound emanated from the opening. They both looked up in time to see an aluminum ladder descending. One black loafer on the top rung. And then another as the man appeared from the bottom up.

"I'm Detective Alexander Tatti with the NTPA," he called down in better English than any of the other policemen had used. "And we have a new ladder, as you can see," he added as he proceeded to climb the rest of the way down.

"The Nucleo per la Tutela del Patrimonio Artistico protects Italy's art, finds and retrieves stolen works," Gabriella explained to Josh as she moved away from the freshly refilled alcove and got down on her knees by the mummy.

"Thank goodness you've come," she said to the detective in a voice dusted with sugar. "Thank you for bringing the ladder. I've been going crazy stuck down here for the past forty-five minutes. I need to go to the hospital. Do you know how the professor is? Do you have news?"

Tatti finished his climb with surprising agility for a man who appeared, from the lines in his face, to be near retirement age. "He's in intensive care. They won't let you in yet. So you might as well stay and help me out on this end. All right?"

She nodded.

Unexpectedly, he didn't barrage either of them with questions. Not right away. Instead, he made a slow and careful examination of his surroundings with an expression of reverence on his face. Josh liked him right then, for noticing where he was, for paying it some sort of tribute before he proceeded to defile it further.

After he had made a 360-degree circle, his glance returned to Sabina. He took six steps to her side and crouched down so he was on her level.

"How old is she, would you say?"

"We estimate she was buried here in 400 A.D.," Gabriella answered. "Or do you mean how old was she when she died?"

"I mean when she was buried and when she died. Both."

"There's little wear on the few joints that we were able to see. We're guessing about twenty-two."

"Was she disturbed during this morning's incident?"

"Yes, very badly."

"Yes? How?"

"She was completely intact when we found her. Last night when I left...it was extraordinary... Now..." Gabriella looked at Sabina. "Now she's broken apart, here and here...." She pointed to the mummy's waist, her neck and her right hand. "She had been holding on to that box. Or what's left of it."

"What box?"

Josh could see Gabriella flinch. She hadn't meant to draw the detective's attention to the broken receptacle. But now she was trapped. She pointed across the room to the splintered wood.

"What was in it?"

She shrugged. "It was sealed. We hadn't opened it yet," she lied. "Now you know everything I know. Can I go to the hospital?"

"As I said, the professor is in intensive care. His wife is with him. As soon as there is news, they will call me and I will tell you. Or if we are done sooner than that, you can go over then. In the meantime—" his accent was pleasant, giving a lilt to the English words "—you expect me to believe that you found this mummy holding on to a box and you didn't open it?"

"Yes. We have protocols. We go slowly. Everything was a surprise. One more could wait. We wanted to examine the seal before we destroyed it."

He turned around to Josh, flinging questions so fast there was no time to duck. "You are?"

"Josh Ryder."

"The man who called the ambulance?"

"Yes."

"Mr. Ryder, what was in the box?"

"I have absolutely no idea." Josh's turn to lie.

"What were you doing down here?"

"I had just met the professor, he was telling me about the find." Damn, had he screwed up? Had he just admitted he was in the tomb?

"What time did you get here?"

"Around six-thirty this morning."

"Why so early?"

"I don't need much sleep."

"I talked to Dr. Samuels while I waited for the ladder. He told me that you are from New York, that the two of you had an appointment to meet Professor Chase at the hotel at eight o'clock but that you didn't show up."

"No, I was here."

"That's what is so confusing. Why would you come here a few hours before you were going to be brought here by Professor Chase? Was there something here that couldn't wait?"

Gabriella listened just as intently as Tatti; after all, she didn't know what had happened, either.

"I couldn't sleep. Jet lag. Too much coffee. I don't know. I took a walk."

"You took a walk. Fine. You could have walked anywhere. Why here? Why didn't you wait? Why did you come here alone without your associate and without Professor Chase?"

"I told you. I was restless."

"How did you get here? There is no car for you."

"No. I said I walked."

"You walked? Walked from where?"

What was it about Tatti that seemed so familiar?

"From the hotel. The Eden. We're staying there."

"I really need to go to the hospital," Gabriella interrupted.

"Professor Chase, please. As I have said, the doctors are going to call me as soon as they know anything. This is the scene of a murder attempt, and you know the man who was attacked. You might also know who attacked him. There are also, potentially, priceless artifacts here. You are the only one who knows what they are, where everything was, what has been moved, what might have been taken if something *was* taken. You will do me more good here than you will do him there. At least for now."

Turning his attention back to Josh, he picked up where he'd left off.

"So. Yes. You said you walked here from the Eden?"

"Yes."

"You evidently like to walk."

It wasn't a question, and Josh didn't answer it. He was still trying to figure out what was so familiar about Tatti. When he realized it he almost laughed. It wasn't some memory lurch. Every one of the detective's mannerisms seemed borrowed from one of two Hollywood stereotypes, either Inspector Clouseau or Detective Columbo.

"Now, Mr. Ryder. Please." He let his exasperation show. "Tell me what the truth is about what really happened." He was a movie star playing the part of a real-life detective.

"I did tell you. I slept badly. I woke up, I took a walk."

"It's ten kilometers from the Eden, Mr. Ryder. Exactly what time did you leave the hotel?"

"I'm not sure, I wasn't paying attention. It was still dark."

"Professor Chase, did Mr. Ryder or Dr. Samuels know the address of this site?"

"No. We didn't tell them. But despite all our efforts it has been in the press."

"Yes, it has." Tatti nodded. "Is that how you found it, Mr. Ryder? From the newspapers? From a taxi driver?"

"No. No one told me. I didn't know where I was walking. Ask the emergency operator. I didn't know where I was when I called."

"She told us that you had to call someone on the phone to

find out the address. But that might be a very convenient ploy, no? You pretend you don't know where you are so as not to look suspicious."

Again, it wasn't a question, so Josh didn't give him an answer.

"Let's assume you are telling me one truth. How can you explain that truth? How can you make sense out of leaving your hotel at, say, five o'clock in the morning, and finding your way here?"

"I can't."

"What do you take me for, Mr. Ryder, a fool? What were you doing here?"

All Josh could think of was the explanation Malachai gave to the children he worked with: the five-, six-, seven- and eight-year-olds who were frightened by the power of the stories in their heads. "You are unforgetting the past, that's all. It might seem scary but it's really quite wonderful," he would tell them.

That might have been what Josh was doing there, but it was the last explanation he was going to give.

Gabriella interrupted the detective and begged him to conduct the rest of the interview outside of the tomb. "This is an ancient site that we've just begun to work on. I need to protect it and close it down as soon as possible."

Tatti promised her they would work as quickly and carefully as possible and leave as soon as they could, but not quite yet. He turned back to Sabina, and his eyes rested on her. For a few seconds, it was totally silent in the tomb. And then he asked Gabriella, once more, what she thought had been taken.

She was losing her patience. "We've been over this, haven't we?"

"We have. But I'm still not satisfied that you and the professor found this tomb, excavated it, started to catalog its contents and yet never looked inside the box. Weren't you curious?"

"Of course. But there is a protocol. To us, every inch of this tomb is as exciting as what might be in the box. The very fact that the woman buried here was comparatively incorruptible was of greater archaeological and scientific importance—even religious significance—than some trinket inside a box."

"So it was a trinket?"

She flew into a rage at that and spoke to him rapidly in Italian. Surprisingly, he seemed to be agreeing with what she said and nodded along with her tirade. When she was done, he climbed up the ladder and stayed perched there, half in and half out, as he called over the two policemen who had first arrived at the scene and had spoken to them.

Gabriella waited by the bottom of the ladder, watching him, listening to what he was saying. Beneath her anger, she was still extremely anxious. Twice, she glanced at her watch. Several times she looked over at Sabina with a curious, questioning expression in her eyes. And although Josh didn't know Gabriella yet, he knew she was wishing that the mummy could communicate, that Sabina could tell them what she'd seen, who had come down here and invaded this sacred space.

For the next few minutes, while the detective continued his discussion with the two officers, Josh struggled not to lose touch with reality and give in to where his mind wanted to go. Tried not to think. But the images were crowding in, demanding attention, refusing to go away. He held his camera up to his face and focused on Gabriella while she listened to the detective talk with his minions. From behind the lens he examined her face—the broad forehead, the high cheekbones. The intelligent eyes.

He remembered a sculpture in the Museum of Modern Art in New York, a head entitled *The Muse,* by Brancusi, made of highly polished bronze: golden, spare, cerebral. Wide almond eyes, perfect oval face.

She could have modeled for it.

Using her expressions as clues, he tried to decode the discussion the detective was having with the policemen. Several times she almost interrupted but stopped herself. Without thinking, Josh took a shot of her. The flash went off. She looked up and over at him, annoyed. Josh lowered the camera.

Finally the detective climbed back down.

"Professor Chase, I don't want to corrupt your site any more than you do. After all, my job is protecting Italian treasures. I know something about archeology, and from the look of this tomb and its location, this woman might be an early Christian martyr. She might be a saint. As we can see, she's barely corrupted." He gestured to Sabina with a flourish, trying to impress her with his knowledge. "The police understand. They will come down now and work both quickly and carefully. Luckily, this is a very small space and it will not be complicated. Then you can shut down the site until this ugly matter is dealt with. As long as you agree to give us access if we need it again."

She said, "Of course," and bowed her head for a second as if a prayer was being answered.

Then he turned to Josh. "Mr. Ryder, I need you to come with me, please. I still have additional questions for you, but we can take care of them up there."

Out of the tomb, the detective led Josh away from the clearing and closer to the line of oak trees that stood like sentinels at the edge of what seemed to be a forest. Leaning against one of these massive trees that probably had been standing since the tomb was built, since Sabina had been buried there, Tatti made Josh repeat what had happened since he'd left his hotel.

"I simply don't believe your story, Mr. Ryder," he said when Josh finished. "You walk all the way here before dawn when you already have an appointment in the morning? Why?"

"I was restless."

"But how did you know where to come?"

"I didn't."

"And you expect me to believe a coincidence like this? You think I'm stupid, Mr. Ryder?"

Josh knew how preposterous it sounded. But the truth would have sounded more like a lie.

I felt propelled here, even though I didn't know where I was going.

"If you were me, what would you do if you heard this crazy recital? Would you believe a word of it?"

What should he tell him? What could he tell him? And then he realized the truth in this case might work. "No. Probably not. But honestly, there's just nothing else I can tell you."

Tatti threw up his hands. He'd had enough for at least the time being. Grasping Josh by the arm, with greater pressure than was necessary, he escorted him over to an unmarked sedan, opened the back door, waited for him to get in and then shut the door and locked it after him.

"I won't be long. Make yourself, how do you say it? Oh, yes, at home."

Despite the open window, the detective's car was hot and smelled of strong cigarettes and stale coffee. He watched Tatti interrogate Gabriella, watched how she glanced over in Josh's direction. Again. And again. As if she was putting the blame on him, or as if she was asking him to come to her rescue and save her from any more questions.

As if she was asking him to save her.

How familiar that thought seemed.

Had someone else once asked him to save her here in this grove?

Was that his imagination? Or was it his madness?

Chapter 15

While Josh waited, he lifted the camera to his eye and looked through the viewfinder. As he snapped shots of the woods bordering the site to the right and the landscape off to the left, the sound of the shutter reverberated in his ears, like an old friend's greeting.

Right now he preferred the world framed in this oblong box, all peripheral excess and activities cut out. Reframing the image, Josh went for an even wider shot and saw a break in the line of trees that suggested an opening into the forest.

As if he were standing there, not sitting in the car, he could smell the pine sap—fresh and sharp—and feel the green-blue shadowed space undulating around him. No. He didn't want to leave this present, not now.

Struggling, Josh brought himself back, to the car, to the metal camera case in his hands. To the smell of the stale cigarette smoke.

Rome and its environs were triggering more episodes than he'd ever had before in one time period. What was happening?

He knew what Malachai would say. Josh was experiencing past-life regressions. But despite these multiple memory lurches, Josh remained skeptical. It made more sense that reincarnation was a panacea, a comforting concept that explained the existential dilemma of why we're on earth and why bad things can happen—even to good people. It was easier to believe reincarnation was a soothing myth than it was to accept the mystical belief that some essential part of a living being—the soul or the spirit—survives death to be reborn in a new body. To literally be made flesh again and return to earth in order to fulfill its karma. To do this time what you had failed to do the last.

And yet how else to explain the memory lurches?

Josh had read that even past-life experiences that seemed spontaneous were precipitated or triggered by encountering a person, a situation, a sensory experience such as a particular smell or sound or taste that had some connection to a previous incarnation.

He hadn't seen a single movie in the past five months, but he'd devoured more than fifty books on this single subject.

Something the Dalai Lama—who had been chosen as a child from dozens of other children because it was believed he was the incarnation of a previous Dalai Lama—had written in one of those books had stuck in Josh's mind.

It was a simple explanation for a complex concept, one of the few things he'd read that made Josh feel that if what was happening was related to reincarnation, then perhaps it wasn't a curse, but an enviable gift.

Reincarnation, the Dalai Lama explained, was not exclusively an ancient Egyptian, Hindu or a Buddhist concept, but an enriching one intrinsically intertwined in the fabric of the history of human origin—proof, he wrote, of the mind stream's capacity to retain knowledge of physical and mental activities. A fact tied to the law of cause and effect.

A meaningful answer to complicated questions.

Something was happening to him, here in Rome. Time was twisting in on itself in amazing detail, and the pull to give in and explore it was stronger than it had ever been. Josh put the camera down. He stared out at the break in the tree line. He could keep fighting the memory lurches or he could open his mind and see where they took him. Maybe he would come out on the other side of this labyrinth understanding why he'd had to travel its path.

Chapter 16

Julius and Sabina
Rome—391 A.D.

He left the city early that morning while the sky was still dark and sunrise wasn't yet aglow on the horizon. No one was in the streets, except a few stray cats that ignored him.

She always teased him that he was early for everything, but it was urgent now that they be careful. It was better for him to leave with the cloak of nightfall to protect him, to arrive at the grove before daybreak.

As he passed the emperor's palace, he glanced, as he always did, at the elaborate calendar etched on the wall. The passing of time had taken on a new and frightening significance lately. How many more days, weeks and months would they have until everything around them had changed so much so that it was unrecognizable? How much longer would he be able to perform the sacrifices and rituals that were his responsibility? How much longer would any of them be able to celebrate and participate in the ancient ceremonies passed down to them by their forefathers?

In the past two years he'd doubled up on his duties as fewer men entered the colleges, and now, in addition to overseeing the Vestals, he'd taken on the additional job of the Flamen Furinalis, the priest who oversaw the cult of Furrina and tended to the grove that belonged to her.

Not to the emperor.

Not to the power-hungry bishops in Milan.

But to the goddess.

Past the palace, he turned onto the road leading out of the city. A man, probably overcome with too much wine, had fallen asleep sitting up against the side of a four-story dwelling. His head was lowered on his chest, his arms by his sides and his palms open, as if he were begging. Someone had dropped food into his cupped hands. There were always poor fools on the street at night, homeless or drunk, and others who always took care of them.

Except something was wrong with this man.

Julius knew it intuitively before he understood it. Maybe it was the crooked angle of the man's head, or the utter stillness of his body. He reached down and lifted up the man's face and, at the same time, noticed how his robe was slit up the front and torn open. On his chest were the dreaded crisscrossing lines, one vertical, one horizontal, the flayed skin exposing guts oozing, blood still dripping and staining the ground beneath him a deep scarlet.

Now he could see the man's features. This was no homeless

drunk; this was Claudius, one of the young priests from the college. And his eyes had been gouged out in a final ritualistic indignity.

Julius realized what Claudius was holding in his hands: not food, but the poor soul's own eyes.

How much suffering had been inflicted on this man, and why? Julius stumbled backward. The emperor's endless thirst for power? What made it worse was that the people doing the man's bidding didn't realize he was using them and that no god was speaking through him.

"Get away. Go now," a voice whispered.

It took several seconds for Julius to find the old woman hiding in the shadows, staring at him, the whites of her eyes gleaming, a sick smile on her lips.

"I've been telling you. All of you. But no one listens," she said in a scratchy voice that sounded as if it had been rubbed raw. "Now it starts. And this—" she pointed a long arthritic finger toward the direction Julius had just come from "—is just the beginning."

It was one of the old crones who foretold the future and begged for coins in the Circus Maximus. For as long he could remember she had been a fixture there. But she wasn't offering a prediction now. This was no mystical divination. She knew. He did, too. The worst that they had feared was upon them.

Julius threw her a coin, gave Claudius a last look and took off.

Not until he passed through the city's gates an hour and a half later did his breathing relax. He straightened up, not aware till that minute that he'd been hunched over, half in hiding. Always half in hiding now.

Throughout history, men fought about whose religion was the right one. But hadn't many civilizations prospered and thrived side by side while each obeyed entirely different entities? Hadn't his own religion operated like that for more than a thousand years? Their beliefs in and worship of multiple gods and goddesses and of nature itself didn't preclude the belief in an all-powerful deity. Nor did they expect everyone else to believe as they did. But the emperor did.

The more Julius studied history the more it became clear to him that what they were facing was one man using good men with good beliefs to enhance his own authority and wealth. What had been proclaimed in Nicaea almost seventy-five years ago—that all men were to convert to Christianity and believe in One God, the Father Almighty, Maker of Heaven and Earth—had never been enforced as brutally as it was being enforced here now. The killings were bloody warnings that everyone must conform or risk annihilation.

Julius and his colleagues weren't under any delusions. If they intended to survive they needed to abandon their beliefs or at least pretend to do so. And if they were going to continue into the future they needed to relax some of their laws and adapt. But right now they had worse problems. Emperor Theodosius was no holy man; this was not about one god or many gods, not about rites or saviors. How clever Theodosius and his intolerant bishop were! Conspiring to make men believe that unless they adopted the current revised creed, they would not only suffer here in this life but would suffer worse in the next life. The danger to every priest, every cult, everyone who held fast to the old ways, increased daily. The priest he'd seen in the gutter that morning was yet another warning to the rest of the flamen.

Citizens everywhere were taking up the emperor's call to enforce the new laws, publicly declaring their conversion. But behind closed doors, other conversations took place. The men and women who had prayed to the old gods and goddesses for all of their lives still hoped for a reprieve from the new religious mandate. Yes, in public, they would protect themselves and prove their fealty to their emperor, but as modern as Rome was, it was also a superstitious city. As afraid as the average citizens were of the emperor, they were more afraid of the harm that might befall them if they broke trust with the familiar sacred rituals. So while there was outward acquiescence, even energy for a religious revolution, much of it was false piety.

But for how much longer?

The old ways would die a little more with every priest who was murdered and with every temple that was looted and destroyed until there was nothing left and no one to remember.

The trunks of the lofty trees were gnarled and scratched, the boughs heavy with leaves. The forest was so thick the light only broke through in narrow shafts, illuminating a single branch of glossy emerald leaves here and a patch of moss-covered ground there.

There were myrtle trees, cypress and luxuriant laurels, but it was the oaks that made this a sacred grove, an ancient place apart from the everyday world where the priests could perform their rituals and pray to their goddess.

He sat down on a mossy rock to wait for Sabina. There, miles outside of the city gates, he couldn't hear the sounds of soldiers training or citizens arguing or chariots rolling by. He couldn't smell the fear or see the sadness in people's eyes—ordinary people who didn't understand politics and were frightened. In the grove there was only birdsong and the splashing of water that fell from between the cracks in the rocks into the pool below. The consecrated area stretched deep into the woods, and no matter how often Julius went there, he never felt as if he saw it all or understood the mysteries that it contained. Nothing there was commonplace. Every tree was a sculptural arrangement of boughs branching off into more boughs, with more leaves than any man could count, all shimmering in a light that was always softer and gentler here than anywhere else in Rome. Every patch of ground offered a bounty of sprouting grasses, moss, shade plants and flowers.

When he was a boy, his teachers told the story of how this grove was where Diana, the goddess of fertility, assisted by her priest, had performed her duties. The King and Queen of the Wood, they were called. Bound together in a marriage, they made spring buds give way to summer flowers and then to fall fruits.

The boys snickered, glancing at each other, making up stories about what else they did up there, all alone in the woods. Joking about the bacchanals that must have gone on in the grove—sacred or not—because they all knew what men did with other men and with women. It was not secret, it was not profane.

Only the Vestal Virgins were sacred. Vestals promised a vow of chastity during their term of service and in exchange were ranked above all other Roman women and many men. Powerful, on their own, free in so many ways, they were not bound by the shackles of motherhood or the rules of men.

In exchange for that power and importance, each woman gave up her chance of a physical life with a man until after she had served for thirty years: the first decade learning, the second serving as a high priestess and the third teaching the next generation. Some thought it was a lot to ask of a woman; others didn't agree. From the time she was six, or eight or ten, until the time she was thirty-six or thirty-eight or forty, she remained chaste. Never to feel a man's hand on her skin or suffer the pressure between her legs that was natural and good. Never give in to the hot eyes of the men who came to her as a priestess but saw through the veils to the woman. Because if she did give in, if she lost her fight with virtue, there was no leniency. The punishment was grave and unrelenting. She was buried alive. It was harsh. But the Vestals were sacrosanct. And only a small percentage broke her vows.

Occasionally a nobleman did get away with seducing a Vestal. Hadrian had stolen one and made her his wife, and nothing had happened to either of them, but throughout history, as of that day in the grove, of the twenty-one Vestals who had been with a man, seventeen had been buried alive and fifteen of the men they had been with had also been put to death. The rules did not bend easily.

Although it was blasphemy and he only let himself think it for a moment, Julius thought that if they adopted the emperor's new religion, he and Sabina would be allowed to live together openly and without fear. But could they give up everything they believed?

"Julius?"

He heard her before he saw her, and then she stepped into the path of a sunbeam. Red hair almost on fire. White robes glowing. He walked to her, smiling, forgetting for just those few minutes the massacred priest he'd seen that morning and what it portended for their future. Sabina stopped a foot away and they stood apart, looking at each other, drinking each other in.

At last.

"The news in the atrium is bad. Did you know Claudius was killed?" she asked.

"Yes," he said, but didn't want to bring the full horror of what he'd seen into the grove.

"What does this mean? Another priest killed?" She shook her head. "No, let's not talk about this. Not now. There's time for this conversation later."

"Yes, there is."

"How many times have we met here? Fifteen? Twenty?" she asked.

"Why?"

"I don't know if we can build enough memories to last the rest of our lives on so few meetings."

"For me, all it took was one."

He reached her in one stride and took her in his arms as she lifted up her face to his. Bending to meet her, he pressed his lips on her lips and pulled her closer until there was no air between them, no space between them, and they just stood like that, breathing each other in.

Purring, like a temple cat, Sabina made contented noises deep in her throat. "I want you," she whispered.

Since the night of the fire, she had never been coy. While the flames blazed she had looked at Julius, openly, blatantly and finally told him that she'd known for a long time that he was her fate. That was why she'd been so hostile to him—to try to change that destiny—but she knew better now. As Oedipus learned, the more you run away from what is predetermined the more you run toward it.

But Julius was five years older than Sabina. Supposedly wiser.

Even if she was willing to give her virginity to him, he couldn't assume she understood the full weight of that decision. So he asked her that first day and each time they came together afterward, as a preamble to their lovemaking, as if they were taking vows all over again, if she was sure she understood the significance of what they were doing.

The grove was a place of rituals and sacrifices.

This was his: to always give her an opportunity to say no anew although he desperately wanted her.

"Sabina, are you sure this is a chance you want to take?" he'd ask, and wait for her response.

There were times when she laughed at him, undoing her brooch and letting her robes fall to the ground as if her defiance alone should be answer enough. Other days she took the question seriously and answered with gravitas, bowing her head and saying, "I am as sure of this as anything I've ever done. Or ever will do."

Her virginity had not been given to Julius lightly, although it had been given with pleasure. No matter how intensely they felt the pushes and pulls, spasms and clenches of each other's bodies, they never forgot that if she was found out, her punishment would be severe. There would be no grace given to her.

Or to him.

"Sabina, are you sure this is a chance you want to take?" he asked that day while she was fully dressed and they had only exchanged a dozen kisses.

Her eyes filled with tears. "I'm sure," she said, and dug her fingers deeper into his flesh.

At least for him, for now, everything that was going on below them in the city ceased to matter.

"I'll always be sure," she said, and reached for the knot of his robe, pushing the fabric away and off his shoulders until he was naked in front of her. Then she ran the flat of her hands up and down his arms, down his chest, around his waist and up his back, and though he wanted badly to undress her, too, touch her skin, and feel her naked against him, he didn't want to do anything to make her stop touching him or rush her. If only he could slow down each movement until she stopped moving altogether and, forever frozen, they could stand in the grace of each other's tastes and touches and smells. The breeze was cool when it blew over him, contrasting with the heat she had inflamed. Julius burned and chilled at the same time.

Hands on her shoulders, he pulled her yet closer, although there was no space between them, and breathed in her perfumed skin and hair: that unique smell of sandalwood incense mixed with jasmine that identified her to him as much as her face or her voice.

And then breathless, lips swollen, eyes full of shining, smoky lust, she stepped back, fumbled with her brooch, undid it and let the robe fall to the ground. Both naked now, they stood a foot apart. Touching each other with their eyes. Igniting. Feeling themselves burst into flame. Luxuriating in the heat. Not caring if this fire scorched or burned. It had already destroyed them in one way. And they'd risen from the inferno in another. Still they stood there. Touching without hands, kissing without lips, making love without entering or being entered. Trying so desperately to make the inevitable coming-together last a long time, a longer time, the longest time. He wasn't the one to make the first move; he never was. Although she'd told him over and over that this was what she wanted, he gave her every chance to change her mind. Wishing she would, praying she couldn't.

She took a step. And then another, and then they were pressed together and he felt her cool flesh against every inch of his body, feeling her as she warmed to him. As she leaned into him. As they fused. These first minutes with her were always *the* first minutes with her. It was as if they'd never been together before. As if he'd never felt any woman's flesh against his. As if the sensation of yielding skin was unknown to him until that moment. It took his breath away, made him long to take her right away, made him aware that he would rather die than ever lose her.

Kissing her, he reveled in how sweet she tasted, until suddenly her mouth was salty.

Julius pulled back only far enough so that he could look at her. As she stood there, naked among the sacred trees, the wind and the leaves making a pattern on her body, there were tears sliding down her cheeks.

After wiping them away, he took her hands and held them both in his.

"Sabina, what is it?"

She shook her head proudly, snatched her hands back, put one on him, stroking him while her other hand reached for his and buried it deep between her legs.

"Julius. Now. Please. Everything else can wait. Words can wait."

She lay down, pulling him on top of her. As he slipped inside, her legs went up around his back and locked him to her so tightly her thigh muscles felt like a vise. He tried to go slow but she was in a hurry and thrust up at him over and over and over again until he felt he was about to melt inside of her.

"This is how I want to die," she whispered between gasps. "Like this. With no room for anything else in the world but us. Just us."

It was dark in the woods, but not so dark that he couldn't see her face. He'd never forget the look in her eyes at that moment. Unadulterated happiness pierced with devastating pain. He didn't know how to describe it, or how to decipher it. The two emotions didn't cancel each other out but somehow remained distinct, coexisting in the same moment.

He would have stopped if he could, would have pulled out and held her gently in his arms, asked her to tell him what was wrong, comforted her, tried to help ease whatever anguish she was in.

Except he knew her better than that. Sabina was a high priestess. Had been an independent woman from the time she was seven years old, when she was brought into the Vestal's house to learn the ancient rituals. Now she was in the most powerful decade of the three she would spend under the Vestals' roof. She'd been trained to understand how special she was and how to deal with it. That ingrained knowledge was now part of her nature, not something she could shake off. He would not insult her by trying to comfort her when what she wanted was much more aggressive and urgent.

The final push and pull of their lovemaking was accompanied by wind rustling through the leaves and by the little exclamations each of them made, and Julius held back until he heard Sabina cry out in that tortured pleasure song that he had been waiting for. She was right, he thought as he let go, if only they could die like that. It would be kinder than what might be in store.

When they were finished, even the wind quieted. They held each other and then sat up and spread out what they'd brought with them, and although it was prohibited for any woman, including a priestess, to drink wine, they both drank and ate the cakes that she'd made.

After the small feast, she got up, pulling him with her, and they walked to the pond. This was also part of their ritual. To bathe in the water that was both warm in spots where it was fed by an underground hot spring and cool where the water rushed down from the rocks.

Underwater their hands darted like small fishes, his swimming around her breasts, circling her nipples, then slinking away to voyage between her legs, where he found a different kind of wet than the water, wet that was silkier and more slippery; and her fingers fishtailed through his legs to cup him and stroke him and make him hard again.

Julius swam behind her and slipped high up inside her, and his hands came around her hips.

"Oh, but you're greedy," she whispered.

"Is it too much?"

"No. Never."

"You want me again?"

"Again, yes. And yes again."

He laughed at her exuberance, pushing away the thought that this was prohibited. If he let that in, it would steal the orgasm that was starting from down deep, deeper than from inside him, deep from the mucky bottom. Up. And up. And up.

"Now," he whispered to her, because she liked him to tell her.

She thrust back against him and twisted herself on him, knowing exactly what she was doing and how long it would take so that she would come at almost the same time for what they both always knew might be the last time.

Afterward, wrapped in the blankets that Julius had brought, they sat side by side and he brought up the subject that neither of them had wanted to deal with—the changes that the emperor's newest edict were going to make in their lives.

"It's time for us to run away," she said. "I've been thinking about this. We can take something—one of the treasures—the statue or the stones, and just disappear somewhere where they won't care who we were before. There's no room for the three of us and our sins here in Rome."

Julius laughed sarcastically. "Steal the stones? Become outlaws?"

"We already are, aren't we?"

He hadn't heard one part of what she'd said. Or he'd heard it and it hadn't registered. Or it had and it scared him so much he'd blocked it. Because if it was true, now there would be real and visible proof of the rules they'd broken, and there would be no way of saving them. Some women might have explained it with words, but Sabina just took his hand and put it on her stomach. Her skin was warm, silken and smooth. And her stomach was just slightly rounded.

Chapter 17

New York City—Tuesday, 10:48 a.m.

Rachel was at Christie's auction house to bid on three paintings her uncle Alex was interested in buying. She'd won one, lost one and opened her phone to call him on his cell as the last of the works he wanted was about to come up. This way he could listen to the action and inform her if he decided to go beyond the limits he'd set before he'd left. After years of bidding on gemstones for her own work, she was comfortable with the auction process and usually enjoyed it. But not that morning.

The room was uncomfortable despite the air-conditioning. Not the same kind of heat she'd felt in the fantasy—because that was now what she was calling it—but it reminded her of that. It was too crowded here—it caused the elevated temperature. There were a hundred and twenty masterwork paintings for sale, and most major museum curators, dealers and private collectors—or their representatives—were present.

"Item number 45," the auctioneer intoned.

Rachel stared at the painting on the easel. It was a Bacchus, which, while not signed by Caravaggio, was believed to have been painted by his students with the master himself adding some of the detail work. Despite the lack of signature, it was breathtaking.

The colors were brilliant, the composition classic, and the features on the young god's face exquisitely rendered. The frame, she thought, was overly ornate, maybe just a little too heavy for the work. But a frame didn't matter. She couldn't stop staring.

"You're right, you must have this one," she whispered to her uncle over the phone. "It's beautiful."

"Of course it is, but there is something else, isn't there? You felt something when you saw it. You connected to it. I heard it in your voice. What is it?"

To anyone else who knew Alex Palmer, his interest in how his niece "felt" would have sounded strange. On the surface, the aspects and trappings of Alex's life proved why stereotypes existed: his wealth, sophistication, education, business acumen, art collecting and philanthropy all belonged together and painted a picture of a corporate giant with few ties to the spiritual world.

A scholarship to Harvard had put him in the same class as the son of a Goliath in the banking business. By the time both boys graduated, Ric Haslet had taken a liking to his son Christopher's best friend and become his mentor.

When Christopher died in a car accident a year later, Alex became a surrogate son. It was then that Ric became fascinated with reincarnation and came to believe that he and Alex—

based on their past lives—had been destined to meet again at this later date.

Alex remained skeptical until the day Ric related a nightmare he'd had several times in his life.

He was a captain during the Civil War, and one night he came across a young soldier, hurt and bleeding by the side of a road. Looking down at the pale man in the moonlight, he sensed that if he didn't stop the boy might bleed to death. But despite the pain twisting the soldier's features and the pleading in his eyes, the captain walked on. The boy had been wearing the enemy's colors.

In an astonished voice, Alex told his mentor that when he was in grade school he'd become obsessed with the Civil War. For his ninth birthday his parents had organized a road trip to visit several important war sites.

Walking across the Antietam battlefield, he'd become overwhelmed with sadness and broke down. When his father asked him what was wrong, Alex didn't know how to tell him what he was feeling: that he had been left to die here in this place.

It was the only past-life memory—if that was what it was, he told Ric—he'd ever had. And he'd never confessed it to anyone before.

It cemented their relationship and his future.

Rachel knew the story and understood her uncle's fascination with intuition and his obsession with past-life regression. His questioning of Rachel's feeling about the Bacchus was characteristic of how preoccupied he was—always on the lookout for moments he could collect, like the paintings on his walls, as proof that there was much we didn't understand in a dimension he was certain existed.

Ever since Rachel could remember, her uncle Alex had been

searching for proof of soul migration. He'd donated huge sums of money to the Dalai Lama, invested in obscure research and once had tried to buy a foundation in New York that was dedicated to past-life study.

Whenever Rachel questioned why he was so interested, he always gave her the same explanation. "If reincarnation exists, then I can leave myself all the things I've worked so hard for. Why should I start from scratch? I've been poor before. I don't ever want to be poor again."

But she always wondered if that was the whole reason.

Rachel had held back, as the price for the Bacchus rose quickly, reaching two and a half million dollars. Now there were only three bidders left: Douglas Martin, a well-known collector and public relations scion; Nick Loomis, curator at the Getty in Los Angeles and a friend of her uncle's; and a man sitting three rows ahead of her with his back to her.

Suddenly Rachel felt that strange humming—the same physical reaction she'd had while reading the article in the *Times* about the excavation. She fought to concentrate on the auctioneer. She couldn't afford to lose track of what was going on around her; now was the time for her to enter the race.

"The bid is at two million, five hundred thousand dollars. Do I hear seven hundred and fifty thousand?"

Rachel watched the third man's paddle go up.

"I have two million, seven hundred and—"

She raised her paddle.

"I have three million—"

Nick Loomis raised his.

"I have three million, two hundred and fifty thousand."

Rachel felt a rush of excitement. She'd never bid anything

near this amount for the stones she used in her jewelry designs. The bidding went back and forth until, at three million, seven hundred and fifty, the bid was with her.

Eyes peeled on the back of the third man three rows ahead, waiting to see if he was going to outbid her, Rachel held her breath.

He raised his paddle.

In her ear her uncle said, "Go the limit. I want that painting."

Her heart beat faster as she upped the ante.

Douglas Martin moved the price up another notch.

"I have four million, five hundred thousand dollars, do I hear—"

Rachel held up her paddle. She wanted to get this painting. She could picture herself standing in front of it, enthralled by the god's smile and seductive eyes. She wanted to touch the frame and run her fingers down the intricately carved, gilded woodwork. She wanted all of it so badly the only word she could use to describe it was *lust*.

"Four million, seven hundred and fifty thousand dollars with me on the left. Do I hear five million?" The auctioneer looked over at Nick Loomis, but the curator shook his head and put down his paddle.

"Nick just dropped out," she whispered into the phone.

"You sound nervous."

More than half the jewels she bought came from sales like this one, but she had never been this anxious. It must be the money. It was a lot of responsibility. Yes, that was it.

"We have four million, seven hundred—"

Douglas Martin raised his paddle.

"We have five million dollars with paddle 66. Do I hear five million, two hundred and fifty?" The auctioneer looked directly at Rachel now.

She had only one more bid left. She raised the paddle.

"Five and a quarter, do I hear five and a half?"

Rachel didn't breathe. She just stared at the space above the third man's head, waiting to see if his paddle would rise. To see if she'd won.

She was going to win. She was going to get this painting.

"Going once…twice."

Damn. He'd raised his paddle.

"We have five million, five hundred thousand dollars. Do I hear five seventy-five?" The auctioneer looked at Douglas Martin, who shook his head.

Into the phone Rachel whispered that Martin had just dropped out.

"So it's just you and one other bidder?"

"Yes."

And then the line went dead. Her heart lurched. She hit redial and heard electronic tones but no ringing.

She knew her uncle wanted the painting. She wanted him to have it; wanted, without knowing why, to keep it away from anyone else.

The auctioneer looked at her. The call still wasn't connecting. What would her uncle want her to do? Her uncle usually set a limit and didn't go past it. He was disciplined when it came to his collecting. It wasn't her money. She couldn't decide for him. What would he want her to do? Damn, why wasn't the call going through?

The auctioneer shook his head, understanding her dilemma but unable to postpone, and announced the sale.

"Sold to paddle number 516 for five million, five hundred thousand dollars. And now, moving on to our next lot we have…"

She got up and walked out of the room, stumbling by the time she reached the doors. She didn't usually cry, but her vision blurred with tears. Something had gone very wrong. Yes, her uncle would be disappointed—he didn't like to lose—but he had a huge collection. One more painting wouldn't matter to him enough for him to be upset with her.

Rachel's phone vibrated. She looked down at the LED readout. It was Alex, calling back too late.

"Hello? Rachel? What happened? Did we get the painting?"

"No…I didn't know what to do. I tried calling you back but couldn't get through."

"Damn it."

"I'm sorry."

"Who got it?"

"I don't know, I couldn't see him."

"What was his paddle number?"

"Why does it matter now?"

"What was his paddle number, Rachel?"

"Number 516. Uncle Alex, I'm sorry. I didn't think you'd want me to go any higher."

"It's not your fault," he said. "Don't worry about it."

But he was worried about it, she could hear it in his voice. What was it about this painting that mattered so much to him and affected her so strongly?

Chapter 18

As the stars looked to me when I was a shepherd in Assyria, they look to me now in New England.

—Henry David Thoreau in a letter to Harrison Blake, February 27, 1853

Rome, Italy—Tuesday, 4:50 p.m.

Never having been incarcerated before, Josh would have imagined that every hour spent waiting to know what was going to happen would be interminable. But the time went by even more slowly than that. If not for the church bells, he wouldn't have any idea how long he'd been in jail.

He'd been interrogated for at least an hour when he first arrived, giving a detailed physical description of the thief, glad that there was something he could tell the police that might help them find the man. But no matter how much he *was* able to tell

Tatti, it was what he couldn't tell him that angered the detective.

"I still don't understand too many things, so I think it would be wise to keep you here, Mr. Ryder. Maybe you'll think of something you've forgotten or at least decide to explain why you were at the scene when you had no reason to be there."

"Am I being held as a suspect?"

The detective ignored the question. "You know that if you are telling the truth and you saw the guard, then you are in danger. Maybe mortal danger." He spoke like a movie character again, and it was infuriating Josh. "This may not be the most comfortable bed in Rome tonight, but it is the safest."

"What are my rights here, as an American? Can I talk to a lawyer? Make a phone call?"

"Yes, of course. All in due time. Absolutely, you can."

That had been two hours ago.

Fatigue, frustration and fear mixed together in an unholy combination that left Josh nervous and exhausted and unable to sleep on the least comfortable cot he'd ever sat on. He remembered every news story he had ever read about foreigners being detained unfairly and for long periods of time for crimes they did not commit as well as the entire plots of several movies that started out with just that premise: an innocent man is imprisoned in a country other than his own.

In his case, what made it worse was that Josh knew that he'd never be able to completely exonerate himself if it meant explaining to the Italian police how he'd wound up inside the tomb at the same time that it was robbed. The lurch that sent him walking through the streets of the city before daybreak was suspicious all on its own. But to try to rationalize how he had known where to go based on some innate intuition? No. The best choice was not to say anything and sit it out, because surely by now Malachai had gone to the American embassy and asked for their help. Or he'd called Beryl and she was in the process of making arrangements to have Josh released. One way or the other, someone would be there soon. Any minute.

He stared at the four walls of the windowless, grimy cell and his mind went back to Sabina's burial site, that square underground cell that was also windowless and also a jail. Josh wished he could access his past at will. That would pass the time while he was here. He had so many questions about what he'd found out since the morning. About the tomb. About the past. Especially Julius's loyalty to a religion that punished a nun who broke her vows of chastity by death when he could instead align himself with the emperor and save both of their lives. What was it like to be so devoted? To be willing to sacrifice so much rather than betray his beliefs?

Josh thought of the image of the young priest in the gutter with his guts cut open and his eyes cut out. What proof had there been for Julius that the new religion would offer sanctuary to him or Sabina? Was it as simple as going with the devil he knew? It just didn't make sense.

The bells tolled another three hours but still no one came for him. Questions of another kind plagued him now. What kind of court system did they have here? Were you innocent until proven guilty in Italy? Without any proof, could they continue to hold him just for being at the scene? And what about a motive?

He looked around the stinking cell, the stained walls, felt the hard cot. He heard the sounds of other prisoners yelling and phones ringing. He knew he'd never sleep because if Tatti did any real investigating, he'd find out that Josh did have a motive for stealing those stones.

The next morning, it wasn't Malachai who came to bail Josh out, but Gabriella. While she watched, the policeman on duty gave him back his camera, pillbox, watch and the money he'd been carrying—everything but his passport. This he held on to. He told him in Italian, which Gabriella translated, that Josh would need to stay in Rome until they had completely ruled him out as a suspect.

"And there's another thing," Gabriella said, translating.

"Yes?"

"He wants you to know you could be in danger because you saw the man who committed this crime. You're a stranger here in Rome, you should be careful."

Gabriella grimaced, spooked by the warning.

"Let's get out of here," Josh said, turning his back on the policeman.

Stiff and sore from his workout the day before in the tomb's tunnel, as well as eighteen hours spent in the cell, he followed her out into the sunshine and was amazed at how sweet the air smelled, until he realized it was Gabriella's perfume.

"My car is a few blocks from here—parking is impossible in Rome. So if you don't mind walking, I can drive you back to your hotel," she said. "Unless you think you should stay inside and let me go get the car and pull it up. If what the *carabiniere* said is true, maybe—"

"I'll walk. No one is going to come after me in broad daylight, especially a man already wanted by the police. Now, tell me, how is the professor?" There were other questions he wanted to ask, but none was as important.

"He made it through the surgery, but he'd lost so much blood...he's still getting transfusions. At least he's stable. We'll know more in the next twelve hours."

"I wish I'd been able to prevent what happened, but I was just too far away. I'm so sorry, Gabriella."

She didn't say anything and Josh didn't doubt that she blamed him. Hell, he blamed himself. He felt awful. A man might die because he hadn't been able to get to him fast enough. And by failing him, he'd let her down. No. That didn't make sense. He didn't know Gabriella.

Except he couldn't shake the feeling that this was history repeating itself.

They walked half a block more, and he checked again over his shoulder, wondering whether, if anyone was following him, he would spot him. "They'll get whoever did this," he said, hoping it was true without having any reason to believe it.

"You think so?" her voice was laced with sarcasm. "And will he still have what he stole? You know he won't. That treasure is long, long gone. Sold, probably on the black market—damn it! I just can't believe this happened. That was the whole reason for having those guards. I knew them all. I can't believe any one of them was capable of doing this."

"For money? Come on, for money you can always find someone who's for sale."

She looked up toward the heavens as if there might be an answer there, or as if someone looking down would relieve her of her anger. The highlights in her hair glinted gold.

A few seconds went by. "Why were you in that tunnel? Why

weren't you in the tomb with the professor, where you could have stopped that man, whoever he was, from taking my stones?"

She wasn't just asking, she was pleading for an answer that would explain and justify what had happened.

He looked at her. In the sun, her eyes glittered with that same golden light. "I tried, Gabriella." He opened his hands in a gesture of impotence. The cross-hatched threads of blood and small puncture wounds had dried into dark maroon scabs.

"But you didn't get there fast enough. If you had, you might have stopped him."

You didn't get there fast enough.

Her words echoed in a crease in his mind. This *had* happened to him before. Here. In this city. Here with this woman. Or was he crazy? No, just overtired. He'd been in jail too many hours. He was starving, splattered with blood and he needed a shower.

You didn't get there fast enough.

His mind was playing tricks. He was too sensitive now to the suggestion of déjà vu. "If you think this is all my fault, why did you come get me?" He hadn't meant to sound so prickly, but he left it at that.

"Because while I was at the hospital last night, the professor woke up for a little while and I got to talk to him. He told me I should trust you. That you would help me. He said you'd talked to him—"

"Not about anything important." In the past twenty-four hours Josh had denied so many things it was becoming second nature. But he couldn't tell her what he'd confessed to the professor just before he'd found the tunnel. The time wasn't right. She wouldn't believe him. He didn't need, on top of everything else, for her to think he was a freak.

Gabriella sighed. "I know that's not true. Rudolfo told me that you confided in him and he believed what you said. He told me you saved his life. That's what the paramedics told me yesterday, too. You didn't leave his side and you were the one who stopped him from bleeding out. Like the police, I wondered if you had something to do with the robbery, and I told him that. But he said that if you had, you never would have stayed. You would have run. You would have let him die."

They had reached the end of a long block. She nodded at the church across the street. "Do you mind a detour? I'd just like to light a candle. It won't take long. Although the professor has left the formal church, he's a deeply religious man. Maybe his god is listening."

"Isn't he your god, too?"

"There's a good chance he is. It's just hard for me to settle on any one god or any one religion. I've spent my life studying different cultures, digging up burial sites, trying to understand the methods and rituals of how other civilizations honored their dead and helped them make the journey to the next life. Sometimes I think I'm a heathen according to modern-day standards and believe more deeply in some of the ancient gods I've come to know."

"But you do believe?" It wasn't like Josh to ask such an intimate question, but she didn't seem bothered by it.

"In something that's bigger than us, yes."

Despite the warm temperature, when they got to the front door, Josh felt an icy-blue mist surround him and literally push him away. The opposite of the way that the darkness in the tunnel in the tomb had embraced him and pulled him forward.

A memory dart exploded and a burst of pain crossed his forehead and circled around and back. He was sure that before this church had been consecrated in the name of Jesus Christ, it had been a different kind of holy place.

Julius and Sabina
Rome—391 A.D.

The soldier hit the marble altar with a rod made of wrought iron and smashed it. A shower of fragments hit the floor. One sailed through the air and came down on Julius's foot, slicing it open. He didn't notice. His eyes were riveted on the sacrificial stone.

What had stood for thousands of years stood no longer. For a few seconds no one moved. Not the seven soldiers who had charged this temple or the six priests who were now trying to defend it. Everyone was stunned. The nexus of prayer, for hundreds of centuries, was gone. Julius looked at Lucas, the most senior priest, and saw on his face the reality they all had to accept: no place was safe. This was the tenth temple that had been destroyed in the last six weeks.

Behind him, Julius heard loud and raucous laughter. He spun around and jumped the soldier, who, caught off guard, stumbled and fell backward. Another soldier saw what had happened and punched Julius in the face. He fell to his knees in pain so intense it made him vomit, right there in the most holy of places.

Around them shouts of anger rang out. Some men grunted, others groaned, bones broke and cartilage crumbled. Julius tried to clear his head and open his eyes, but he couldn't. He put his hands up to his face.

His fingers came away wet. He couldn't see but he knew its slickness, he recognized its sweet scent.

To his left someone screamed, "Get out. Get out now. Haven't you done enough?"

Taunts from the other side. "Heathens. You will all go to hell."

Julius tasted blood in his mouth. He rolled away, trying to get to the wall so he could use it to lean against and stand up.

"Where are the temple whores?" one of the soldiers cried out, laughing coarsely.

"The virgin whores. Bring us the virgin whores."

"Never."

Julius was surprised that the voice came from him. Surprised that he was on his feet. But despite the throbbing pain, he was. Two soldiers came at Julius at the same time. But he knew if he ducked their fists they would miss him and hit the stone.

They lunged.

Julius dropped to his knees. Above his head, he heard their bones crack and their screams. Taking advantage of the distraction, he charged another intruder from behind and pushed his fingers into his eyes.

Yelling, the soldier spun, finally falling against one of his own who also toppled over, hitting his head on one of the sharp edges of broken marble their mallets had destroyed. With four soldiers down, Julius and the other priests had a chance.

They fought fiercely and won, but when it was over, the floors were a sea of blood and bodies. There was no satisfaction, no sense of calm. There had only been seven of them today. Tomorrow others would come. And after that there would be more. The priests knew they would never win if they tried to fight them one on one. There were thousands on the emperor's side but only hundreds of defenders.

An hour later, Sabina bathed and bandaged his wounds. This was allowed—for her to go to him and administer healing salves. What wasn't was the secret that she still kept hidden under her robes. She had taken to wearing a cloak now all the time so no one noticed the small bulge, but how much longer would that work?

They'd met so infrequently in the woods, they'd been able to figure out that she was ten weeks pregnant now, and her fate tortured him. He had pledged himself to her and vowed he'd save her and their unborn child even if it meant dying in the process. The bandaging finished, Sabina gave Julius a brew of herbs to help relieve the pain.

"Maybe you should brew some for yourself," he said suggestively as he handed her the empty cup. "It's still early, they're very effective at this stage, aren't they?"

They both had been so careful. Like all women of Rome, Sabina knew how to avoid the times of the month when she was most fertile and conception most likely to occur. Plus there were the unguents and washes that she used right after they were together. But sometimes precautions failed. Then, for the wealthy who jealously guarded their estates, not always wanting to share holdings with too many offspring, or the poor who often simply couldn't afford to feed too many mouths, or unhappily married women who wanted divorces, not children, there were alternatives: either a drink made from a distillation of herbs or surgery. Although Julius and Sabina lived in an era when termination of pregnancy was without stigma, not only allowed but in certain circumstances encouraged, she wouldn't consider it.

"No. Our baby has to be born, Julius. Through her we'll always be together."

"You're wrong. The baby will only ensure we'll both be killed. What if we can't convince the priests and nuns that the laws are outdated? I know we've all been talking about making changes, but what if no one is ready by the time we are? What if I can't save you? Do you know what it will be like to suffocate, slowly, gasping for air? You can't die. Not over a child that isn't born yet."

"There are other laws, too, that matter. Laws of nature."

"You might be committing suicide by keeping this baby, Sabina," he whispered, lest anyone outside hear them.

She shook her head and put her finger on his mouth, preventing him from saying anything else.

Chapter 20

Rome, Italy—Wednesday, 11:08 a.m.

Josh leaned against the giant bronze doors on the monumental porch facing inward to the rectangular colonnaded temple, staring at the familiar way the sun filtered down from the hemispherical dome. He'd been feeling Julius's grief so deeply he could barely breathe. He was surprised that his physical reactions had crossed the divide.

The light shifted and sunbeams streamed through the unglazed oculus, creating patterns of illumination on the floors and walls of porphyry stone, granite and yellow marble. The opening also let in birds that were swooping down and then, not sure of where they were or how to escape, flying around wildly until they found a breeze and rode it out.

On the wall, Josh noticed a large plaque. The top paragraph

was in Italian, but the one beneath it was in English. He read the brief history of the church.

The Pantheon of Agrippa was erected by the Roman Emperor Hadrian between 118 and 128 A.D., replacing a smaller temple built by the statesman Marcus Vipsanius Agrippa in 27 B.C.

In the early seventh century it was consecrated as a church, Santa Maria ad Martyres.

Had he—or the man he saw in his mind—defended this very temple sixteen hundred years ago? Was he remembering for him…remembering for the dead?

From where he stood, Josh could see Gabriella in front of the side altar, lighting a votive candle with a long stick. The flame sputtered and then held steady. The glass glowed red.

Bowing her head, she knelt and clasped her hands in front of her.

Josh fingered his camera, yearning to take her picture but sensing it would be a rude intrusion to photograph this woman he barely knew, in prayer. It even felt wrong to be watching such an intimate moment, but he was mesmerized by the scene. By the serenity that hovered just above the chaos. By the beauty of her body arched over, deep in prayer. By the halo effect of sunlight glinting around her head, echoing the Virgin's halo in the painting that hung behind her in the alcove.

"You don't like churches?" Gabriella asked when she found him there a few minutes later.

Josh couldn't tell her that he'd just stood at the door to a church in Rome on a Sunday afternoon in the twenty-first century and watched what had happened in that same building nearly two millennia before, or how the horror of that past had stopped him from going inside.

In the past six months, other than Dr. Beryl Talmage and Malachai Samuels at the Phoenix Foundation, Professor Rudolfo had been the only one he'd told any of the tale to. Curious rather than judgmental, the professor seemed to accept what Josh had said without skepticism. Would Gabriella be as objective? Or would she look at him the way his ex-wife had, the way some of the doctors and therapists had, the way Josh still looked at himself in the mirror—as a freak.

Malachai had laughed when Josh told him that was how he'd felt.

"To me you are a marvel, a gift. A chance," he'd said, "for us to take our understanding of reincarnation to another level."

As they left the church, it occurred to Josh that he didn't know where Malachai was, and asked her.

"He was at the American embassy most of yesterday, trying to get them to intercede on your behalf. We talked last night on the phone and he told me he wasn't having any luck. There was some kind of summit meeting and everyone with authority was away. That's when he asked me to help. He thought I'd have a better shot with the police since I speak fluently."

"And since you're so damn attractive."

She was totally caught off guard by his compliment. So was he.

"That was fairly sexist. I'm sorry."

She shook her head. "No, it was nice."

The tension between them lifted for a minute. They were just two people standing on a street in Rome, walking in the sunshine. A guy giving a woman a compliment that she was gracious enough to take in the spirit that it was intended.

They'd just gotten into her car and she'd turned on the ignition when her cell phone rang. While she talked, rapidly in

Italian, Josh turned around and looked back at the church, watching a group of tourists go in. Lifting his camera to his eye, he studied the building from different angles and took several shots. Gabriella's back was to him; she was facing out her window. He shifted in his seat so he could see the side of her face, watch her lips move and the way the sun brought out the honey in her hair. But what he was searching for wasn't there.

After the accident he'd seen an aura around certain people's heads when he photographed them, but the strange lights never showed up in the photographs themselves. The first time he'd thought it was a camera defect and had changed the camera body and then the lenses. When it appeared a second time, he told the doctors about it. Just like the memory lurches, the lights might have been proof of neurological problems. But they never found any.

When Josh went to work at the foundation, he continued seeing the lights hovering over several of the children he worked with. Impossible to discern with his naked eye, it was only something he picked up through the camera lens: white translucent streaks radiating around the upper portion of their bodies. As if a cartoonist were indicating speed. Was it speed? Time moving at the speed of light?

He had only seen it once before that.

When Josh was twenty, his father had been diagnosed with cancer. Whatever Ben sensed about Josh's reaction, he didn't say much at first. That was his style. He delivered the news to his son in his straightforward, black-and-white way and left him to absorb it.

A few days later, they were working in the darkroom together, both of them lit by the single red light.

"I've a favor to ask," Ben said, and while they continued to develop that afternoon's shoot, he told Josh he wanted him to chronicle his illness photographically.

At the time, Josh didn't question the request. It seemed so natural. The father, a photographer, asking the son, a photographer, to capture this last event of his life. Only years later did he realize what a great gift his father had given him. A way for them to share as much time as they could together. A way for Ben to pass on every last bit of teaching about their shared craft. For them to be joined even in their unjoining.

Josh chronicled everything in those last few weeks. The slow fading. The light that disappeared in his father's eyes, lumen by lumen until there was nothing left but pain and dulled emotion. He looked through the lens and searched for the potent man he had known and loved for all of his life, but he couldn't find him in the shell made of bones and sickly flesh.

Toward the end, Josh moved back home and slept on a cot in his father's sickroom. One midnight, Josh had fallen asleep when the nurse woke him to tell him that from the sound of his father's breathing, she thought this was the end.

Josh asked her to leave them alone.

He sat in the dark by Ben Ryder's side, holding his father's hand. It hurt just listening to his raspy breathing. And then Ben woke up. Just lay still on the bed, looking up at his son and whispered, "More shots."

"Morphine?" Josh asked. Although Ben was on a drip, he assumed his father had forgotten he was no longer getting injections and needed additional painkillers.

"No." He gave Josh a weak smile. "Photographs. Of this."

A son dreams of the secret of life being revealed by a father on his deathbed. Josh was asked to pick up his camera and go to work. But it was what they did, and so Josh stood over his father and kept photographing him, not knowing if he was getting anything because his eyes were so blurred with tears.

And that was when he noticed the opalescent nimbus, like a ring of light around Ben's head and shoulders.

It was his hand shaking, it was a reflection from the bathroom light, it was something in the lens or the camera itself, it was his tears. It was nothing. It was not worth questioning.

Over the ensuing days and weeks of grief, Josh forgot about the light, and when he eventually developed the photographs, it wasn't there and he never thought about it again.

Until twenty years later when he went to work at the Phoenix Foundation and started seeing the mother-of-pearl arc of light that appeared almost like wings behind his subjects' heads and around their shoulders.

Over lunch one day, he mentioned it to Beryl and Malachai.

"That, too?" Malachai had said wistfully.

"What do you mean?" Josh asked.

"Not many people can see it. I can't."

Beryl didn't suffer her nephew's plaintive longing when it crept into his conversation. She shook her head as if he were a little boy she was displeased with, and addressed the issue without any emotion.

"We think it's a marker identifying some people as old souls."

"Have you ever seen it?" Josh asked.

"Yes."

"Through a camera?"

"No. You only see it through the camera lens?"

Josh said yes and asked her why, but she couldn't think of a reason. He asked why she hadn't written about the phenomenon in any of her papers.

"The hallmark of scientific research is reproducibility. I can put out an auger dish and grow a banana fish in it and present that as my research, but my career as a scientist would be over unless the next person who tried to do it, following my methods, could duplicate my results."

"Then I'll find a way to prove it so that if someone else follows my methods and takes a picture of the same subject it will be there for him, too."

"I don't think it can be done," Beryl said.

"I need to try. I need one absolute shred of proof. At least this has to do with something I know about—cameras, light, exposure."

Long after that lunch, Josh still wondered if the light he'd first seen years before had been his father's intact soul lifting up and leaving his tired, diseased body, starting the journey to find a new, healthy one and begin anew.

Ben Ryder hadn't been religious, and neither had Sarah, Josh's mother. Under their influence, he wasn't, either. Ben had left instructions that he wasn't to be buried but cremated and that he wanted his ashes thrown away. Like garbage. That was his wish, and Josh honored it. He knew Ben wasn't in those ashes. He was in his son's remembrances of him.

He was in his photographs.

"You just do the best you can and make the most of the life you have. Heaven," he'd once told Josh during that last year, "is just a comfortable concept to make people feel better about death."

So Josh had watched his father's energy and vitality leave and each day recorded what was left of him, but it wasn't until his work for the foundation that he wondered where his father's spirit had gone. Until then he'd never wondered if it had indeed existed as an entity that could pick up and move. Never wondered if it was in limbo waiting to be reconstituted in someone else. Certainly never wondered if he'd be the person to capture it with his camera and try to prove that it was real.

But since going to that lunch with Beryl, he did.

"I'm going back to the hospital," Gabriella said after she hung up. "The professor is worse. He might be…" She swallowed, fought for control but didn't finish the sentence.

"You said he survived the surgery."

"He did. Now he has an infection. You saved him for the surgeons, and they saved him for this to kill him."

"Let me go with you," he said.

She didn't put up an argument, and so they set off for the hospital together.

Chapter 21

The gray sedan following Gabriella's car through the serpentine streets of Rome had been with them since they'd left the church. Josh noticed it after they made their first turn.

Leaning out of his window, he quickly swiveled around, pointed the camera straight at the car, and clicked away. The car didn't slow down or change lanes.

Photojournalists know that a camera can scare all sorts of people away. Either that or it can get you killed. Josh had pulled this trick in Haiti once. While driving through an area he wasn't supposed to be in, taking pictures of the abject poverty, he'd been followed. When he focused the camera on the driver, the man had started shooting back at him.

With a gun.

But whoever was in the car behind Gabriella obviously didn't care that he'd been observed, which made Josh think he was probably the police, not someone hunting him. He decided not to tell Gabriella. She was under enough stress as it was.

* * *

Josh stayed downstairs in the cafeteria while Gabriella went up to the professor's room. Even though he wanted to see the professor, Josh didn't want to upset Rudolfo's wife and children. He was the man who hadn't been shot when their father and her husband had been, not to mention still an unlikely but potential suspect.

Finding a pay phone, he called Malachai, but there was no answer on his cell phone or at the hotel. After leaving messages explaining where he was and what had happened, Josh went into the cafeteria, bought a cup of coffee—which was far better than what they served in any American hospital—and waited.

After a few minutes, a man and a little boy came and sat down next to him. For a brief moment Josh wondered if he should be suspicious. Could this man be part of a scheme to keep him under surveillance—either by the police or by the criminal he'd seen in the tomb?

The man opened a container of milk and a packet of cookies and put them in front of the boy, who shook his head and pushed them away, refusing the treat. The man sighed, and then, noticing Josh watching, grinned and said something to him in Italian that was unintelligible except for the word *bambino.* Guessing that the man's wife was in labor and the little boy was scared of what was going on, Josh took a simple cardboard matchbox out of his pocket, emptied it of a dozen wooden red-tipped matches, and put it down on the table. He wasn't as good at this as Malachai was, but he had been practicing and was certain he could entertain the little boy and take both of their minds off of the drama going on in their lives for at least a few minutes.

During his first interview at the Phoenix Foundation, Josh had found himself unable to answer many of the questions Malachai had put to him. No doctor or therapist had probed as deeply, and despite Josh's desperate need to discover what was happening to him, he was uncomfortable baring his soul.

It was then that Malachai had pulled out a matchbox and asked Josh for a coin. Although it was a strange request, he obliged. Reaching into his pocket, he found a quarter and gave it to Malachai.

Taking it in his tapered fingers, Malachai reached under the table and tapped it once. It made a dull thud. Tapped it. Another thud. Then he showed Josh his palm: empty. He opened the matchbox. The quarter was nestled inside.

"I didn't see that happen at all."

"That's the thing about sleight of hand, you know there's a trick happening, but you are rarely looking in the right place to catch it."

"I never would have expected the director of the Phoenix Foundation to entertain me with magic tricks," Josh had said.

"What was a pointless obsession during my childhood, at least according to my father, now comes in quite handy with the children we work with. In minutes, instead of the hours it would otherwise take, the magic relaxes them, helps them open up. It's not, after all, that easy to describe your nightmares to a stranger, even for children for whom past-life experiences are not all that extraordinary." Malachai then asked Josh to tell him about the episodes that had been taunting him in greater detail. "Is there a pattern to when the stories appear?"

"Should there be?"

"There are no rules about these things, no, but sometimes there are patterns worth noting."

Josh shook his head. "Not that I can discern."

"Are they in any kind of chronological order, is there a sequence to them?"

"They're of lives that I've never lived...fantasies...dreams... I don't know if there's a sequence."

"What about your emotional reactions to them? How do you feel after a regression?"

This question silenced Josh. It was difficult to explain to anyone, no less a stranger, the overwhelming grief he felt for a woman whose name he didn't even know but whom he was convinced he had failed.

"I'm a photographer. I document reality. I take pictures of what's in front of me. I can't deal with pictures that I can't grab on film."

"I understand that completely," Malachai said. "And I can see how tough this is for you, so I only have a few more questions. Is that all right?"

"Of course. I do appreciate what you're doing.... I'm just..." It was a relief to be accepted, to have someone at last listen to his story without shaking their head and taking his temperature.

"Frustrated. I know, Josh, it is frustrating. Can you give me any idea of how long the episodes last?"

"Twenty, thirty seconds. One lasted a few minutes."

"And is it possible for you to bring them on?"

"Why would I want to?" he asked in earnest, his aghast tone making Malachai smile.

"Well, then, can you prevent them?"

"Sometimes. Thank God."

“Can you stop them once they’ve started?”

“Not always. That takes a colossal effort.”

“But it’s something you try to do?”

Josh nodded.

“While an episode is in progress, are you physically or mentally uncomfortable? Can you describe how it feels?”

Josh didn’t answer this question, either. He didn’t know how to explain it in words.

Malachai’s voice was compassionate. “You’re looking at me as if I’m a maniacal surgeon coming at you with a scalpel. I’m sorry if you feel that I’m prying—this is all pro forma for us.”

“It’s as if I’m…out of my own body.” He paused and looked past Malachai out the window at the trees in the park blowing in a harsh wind. “It’s as if I’m disconnected from reality and drifting untethered in another dimension.” He said each word as if it tasted bitter. As if it might even be poisonous.

The boy had gathered up all the matches and gave them back to Josh.

“Prego?” he asked.

Josh didn’t have to guess, he knew what the child wanted.

More distraction. More magic.

Josh didn’t blame him.

Chapter 22

Gabriella sat by the professor's bed watching the man who had been her mentor as he fought for every breath. His sudden frailty made no sense. Just two days ago they were underground, dirt clinging to their faces, sweating, doing what they both were meant to do. Except for the time she spent with Quinn, her almost three-year-old daughter, whom she missed terribly while she was away, nothing stirred her like digging out the dead and their secrets. During the past few years, Gabriella Chase's life had changed more than it had stayed the same. It was the trips back to Rome and the field outside the city gates to the excavations that had kept her sane.

There was nothing that competed with the moments of discovery. And there had been so many on this last dig. It was perhaps the proudest moment of her career when, only three weeks ago, the professor stood by her side, held his breath and watched as she brushed the first thick layer of dust off of the square object in the corpse's hand, revealing a wooden box. Another sweep exposed an intricate pattern of carvings.

"Well, look at that," Rudolfo said, sotto voce. "I think..." He peered down, inspecting the bas-relief carefully. "Yes, it's a phoenix," he said, naming the bird that symbolized rebirth to countless ancient cultures.

Her eyes met the professor's and they exchanged a look. Both of them knew the Egyptian legend dating back to the reign of Ramses III about a wooden box very similar to this one and the treasure of precious stones that the phoenix on its cover was purportedly protecting.

Neither Gabriella nor Rudolfo dared to say out loud what both were thinking—was this the Egyptian box? Here, in Rome, in this fourth-century tomb?

Patiently, Gabriella continued to brush off the remaining dirt and debris from the deep recesses of the small wooden casket, but she felt anything but patient. Typically, archeology itself destroys as it discovers; but, for the first time in her career, that had not been the case here. In fact, nothing about this dig had been emblematic of what had come before. It already had proved to be a significant find for her. Depending on what was inside this box, it might be the most important one of her career.

Normally, a site can take a decade to uncover, but this tomb hadn't collapsed in on itself. Other buildings had never been erected above it. That was one of the mysteries she and Professor Rudolfo had marveled at—how pristine this whole area had remained; how, after so many centuries, there were still parts of the world, even in metropolitan areas, where the past was so very close to the surface.

Everything about an excavation was a mystery, but, to both of them, this one seemed more mysterious than most—including the way they had discovered the site itself.

It had been snowing that Sunday morning four years before, and the old Yale campus had been shrouded by a thick white blanket. Walking across the quad, Gabriella was glad she'd gone out early. It was one of those perfect winter mornings, quiet and sparkling, and she was almost enjoying it.

Since childhood she'd been going to services at Battle Chapel, where her mother had been the choirmaster of the Beethoven Society. When she'd died, the chapel had been the only place where Gabriella could still feel her, where she didn't miss her quite so much. Maybe that was because she'd always sat without her mother beside her, or maybe it was because there, God's grace offered her some peace.

The unusual acoustical effect in the chapel that day, she later read in the *Yale News,* was a result of the heavy snow quieting the world outside and insulating the building at the same time. The singers' voices rang out like bells, pure and crystalline, and it felt as if the organ's deepest tones were vibrating inside of her body, not just in the brass pipes.

The storm had kept a lot of people away, and there wasn't much of a crowd; still Gabriella hardly noticed the priest sitting in the row in front of her. There were often visiting clergy at Battle, some who officiated, and others, like him, who just came to pray. Nothing out of the ordinary happened until, after the service ended, he approached her while she put on her coat and greeted her by name. She was surprised that he knew who she was until he explained that he'd driven up to Yale specifically to see her and that the chaplain had pointed her out when she'd walked in.

The priest introduced himself as Father Dougherty and asked if she could spare him a few minutes, and she agreed. They stayed in the chapel while everyone else left.

Gabriella could still remember how quiet it was.

The snow altered the sound of the silence, too.

Because of the storm, the interior of the chapel had been dark during the whole service, but the sun had come out and suddenly the dozens of richly colored stained-glass windows were illuminated, casting their jewel-toned shadows across the pews. Across the two of them.

Battle is a lovely building. The interior is carved from solid oak, and the walls are stenciled with complicated patterns. There is so much going on visually inside the chapel that, in retrospect, Gabriella realized she wasn't always focused on the priest's face.

He'd been so average looking. Almost too average, if that made any sense. He was at that indiscriminate age—somewhere between fifty and seventy. He wore wire-rimmed glasses. They must have been thick or slightly tinted, because she couldn't remember what color his eyes were. Or maybe his eyes were just brown. He had a very slight Boston accent.

Father Dougherty said he'd come to give her a document that had been written in the late nineteenth century. "It's stained with blood, but you can wipe it clean," he said as he handed her a manila envelope.

Inside were several sheets of rich vellum paper covered with spidery, hard-to-read handwriting. After a few seconds of staring at them in the semidarkness, it became clear what she held was torn from someone's journal.

"The diary those pages come from is safely put away," the priest explained. "It was in the possession of a parishioner who turned it over to his priest in the 1880s during confession, and because confession is sacred I can't tell you any more. I know I'm being cryptic and I'm sorry. But you really don't need to know the whole story or to read the rest of the diary, you have all you're going to need right there."

"All I'm going to need for what?"

The priest stared into the apse, an intensely meditative expression on his face, and didn't answer for a few seconds.

"If what's written there is true, you'll be famous."

"What about you? What will you get out of this?"

"I'm just the messenger. All this happened a long time ago, but my bishop believes that it's wrong for us to continue to keep this part of the document a secret."

Unexpectedly, he stood and pulled on his coat. "Just read it, Professor Chase. Do the right thing."

"What's the right thing?"

"Shed light on the darkness."

He left quickly, not waiting for Gabriella, and by the time she gathered her things and went outside, she couldn't see the black-clad figure anywhere. Just an expanse of white snow and a woman wearing a red parka trudging across the campus.

The sheets outlined directions to five separate locations that were all potential archeological digs of historical and spiritual importance, the notes said. It took Gabriella a few days to ascertain that all the sites were in Rome. Having made that connection, she contacted her mentor and partner in a recent dig in Salerno, Professor Aldo Rudolfo, who was equally intrigued. Of course he knew the general areas referred to, and he told Gabriella that just two years ago a spot nearby had been excavated, but nothing had been found.

A few weeks later he e-mailed her to say that all the sites in question were on land owned by the descendants of an archeologist who had died in the late 1800s and he was negotiating with them, hoping they'd allow a team to excavate.

It took a year, but he worked out a contract with the family and they'd finally been able to go to work.

Nothing would ever replace trowels and shovels once you got to the heart of the find, but the advanced laser and infrared surveying devices she and the professor had been using enabled them to pinpoint the exact areas to dig with more accuracy than ever before possible. The first two sites had not yielded anything of significance, only some walls, some ancient shards of pottery and glass. Typical detritus for an old field outside of the city gates.

But this site, number three, had been different.

The professor opened the box, extracted a dried-out leather pouch and untied it. The sound he made when he shone the light into it was somewhere between a cry and a shout. "Look, Gabriella, look at what our Bella is holding. It may be that you've found your treasure."

Now, with the professor lying in a hospital bed, suffering from a gunshot wound and a substantive loss of blood, fighting a critical infection, it appeared that someone thought the treasure had been worth killing for.

Chapter 23

Rome, Italy—Wednesday, 3:10 p.m.

The light changed to green, a car horn blasted and the priest crossed the street past a row of vendors, giving cursory glances at their merchandise. If he made eye contact with any of them it wasn't visible to any strangers who happened to see the middle-aged, overweight cleric. Twenty yards farther, he huffed as he climbed the few steps at the bottom of the Via Vittorio Veneto next to the Piazza Barberini and entered the dingy church of Santa Maria della Concezione.

No one at the sidewalk cafés across the street paid any attention to him as he disappeared behind the wooden doors. The church wasn't nearly as popular a pilgrimage destination as the Vatican or the Pantheon. Compared to Rome's grand and glorious houses of worship, a visit to the crypt at della Concezione was a macabre adventure, though, so it had its share of tourists. Another priest walking in didn't attract any notice.

The change from the bright afternoon to the dark interior took some adjusting to. The church was musty and lackluster except for the gold cross glinting above the nave. He looked at his watch. Stepped up to the font, dipped his fingers into the basin of holy water, crossed himself, walked up the main aisle, entered a pew, knelt down and prayed for a few seconds. Or at least it appeared that he was praying.

He was really keeping his eye on his watch. The tour, he knew from the guidebook, would begin on the hour. His heart jumped around in his chest.

After six minutes passed, he lifted his head, stared at the altar, got up and made his way to the back of the church, where the curious gathered.

The scent was different down in the crypt, but the ancient smell of dirt and moisture was not unpleasant. The smell of antiquity, he thought. A monk with a dour face escorted the six of them down a narrow corridor, through iron gates and into the five chambers of the underground cemetery that contained the remains of four thousand Capuchin monks.

But not buried remains.

Every wall and each ceiling was covered with baroque decorations made up entirely of the monks' dried out and bleached bones. Altars, chandeliers and clocks: everything a human relic.

He barely listened as the monk who led the tour droned on, explaining that *la macabra composiziones* in the series of tableaux had been made out of the bones of the dear departed monks dating back to the seventeenth and eighteenth centuries, and that the spectacle had not been created to inspire fear, but, to encourage prayer and meditation

This was not his first visit to the crypt, yet he still was amazed that the thousands of skulls, ribs, teeth, leg and arm bones, pelvises and vertebrae had lost their semblance to human remains and became the medium the artists had employed to create their spectacle.

When the tour ended, he obediently followed the other tourists up and out of the church and into the street, careful to watch the crowd scatter. No one lingered on the steps; everyone dispersed. After being certain they had all walked away, he strolled to the corner and passed the same group of street vendors he had walked by before going into the church. This time he slowed and took more notice of them.

The first sat behind a table covered with cheap Italian souvenirs: Leaning Towers of Pisa, bronze St. Peters, refrigerator magnets of the glorious Sistine Chapel ceiling. The next table had been transformed into a handbag and briefcase store. Leather goods of every imaginable shape and color were lined up invitingly, and the proprietor was doing a brisk business. The third vendor was selling cheap costume copies of very costly jewelry. Prevalent were thick gold chokers featuring facsimiles of Roman coins. There were also silver and gold ropes studded with pearls, and hanging earrings encrusted with faux diamonds. Surprising quality for street goods.

He fingered a silver necklace. Six glass gemstonelike pendants hung from the heavy links. Rubies, emeralds and sapphires.

"Gucci," the vendor said.

The priest nodded. A smile passed his lips. "Gucci? Really?"

"Good copy." The vendor spoke in heavily accented Italian. "Not expensive."

"Do you have three of these? Identical ones?"

The vendor nodded and reached under his table to pull out first one, then another and a third, each in a box with the word *Gucci* stamped on it in a similar typeface to the one the high-end retailer used. Almost but not quite exact. Close enough so that most people wouldn't notice it unless they had the real thing to compare it to.

The price was negotiated and paid. The vendor slipped the bills into his apron and watched as the priest put the necklaces into his briefcase and walked off.

Continuing down the block, he turned the corner and then entered the next café he came to, where he ordered a cappuccino in honor of the dead friars.

He put the briefcase on the bar and rested his elbows on it.

He was almost positive that no one had followed him to the church. He'd made sure of that. Certainly, no one had followed him into the crypt. And it didn't appear that anyone had been loitering nearby, watching him buy the bargain tourist fare.

The coffee was strong and hot, but he finished it quickly and went to the men's room, where he pocketed all the jewelry and put the faux Gucci boxes back into his briefcase.

Back out on the street, he strolled, stopping often to look in store windows, checking on the reflections to make sure he wasn't being followed.

If they tried to take the briefcase from him, he would put up a struggle. But he would let them have it. What he wouldn't let them have was what was in his pocket.

Chapter 24

They had walked the general area dozens of times, but Inspector Tatti had asked them to fan out this time and cover a two-mile radius in every direction. The guard who had been on duty yesterday when Professor Rudolfo was shot was still missing. The man's wife said he'd left for work as usual at 3:00 a.m. His shift was from 4:00 a.m. to 9:00 a.m. She'd packed his favorite meal—a mortadella hero and a big thermos of coffee—and gone back to bed.

He never came home.

The afternoon sun played games with the clouds, making the search much more complicated. It would be bright for ten minutes, and then shadows would fall over the whole landscape, turning an innocent rock into a man's head, a clump of tree roots into a hand.

Within the grove it was even more difficult to figure out what one was looking at. The ancient trees were so large and leafy that almost no light penetrated, so although it was only midafternoon it appeared to be late night.

The inspector in charge, Marcello Angelini, told his officers to use their flashlights if they couldn't see. They walked in formation, swinging the lights back and forth over the terrain, stopping every three or four minutes to check out a suspicious shape.

But so far they still hadn't found anything. This place was overgrown with bushes and vines. The ground was littered with nuts and seeds and pits and leaf rot from last year. Except somehow, Angelini thought, it was beautiful. It felt similar to how it was in church when there was no service going on and you could sit down by yourself to collect your thoughts and think things through.

He walked on the outer edge of the line, the last policeman in formation, showing his men that he, too, could do the hard work. When his light picked out something shiny in the shrubbery, he broke away and walked over to the spot. When he got there, he couldn't see anything but dark, glossy leaves. Maybe his flashlight had just caught one a certain way. He stepped back. Once he had some distance, he saw it. Then he advanced, keeping the light trained on that one specific spot. Yes, it was there. Silvery and shimmering.

Bending down, he reached between the leaves of the shrub and felt something cold and metallic, then something colder.

Angelini let go. Stepped back. Stared at the shrub. Let his eyes lose focus. Then he saw the abnormality in the leaf cover. Someone had sawed down the middle of the huge bush and made a hiding place deep inside, where, in the beam of the flashlight, Angelini could see the man's bloated body. Moving closer, he leaned down and shuddered. The man's throat had been slashed and his naked torso was painted with his now black, dried blood.

Finally, he thought, this was a bona fide homicide investigation. Angelini knew his boss, Detective Tatti, well enough to know what that meant: none of them would have much time off in the next few days. He was almost sorry he'd seen that damn silver watchband.

Poor man, though, he thought, and made the sign of the cross.

What had he been guarding? What was so precious this time that a man was killed for it? He'd ask Marianna when he got home. She read the newspapers; she'd know what they were digging up at this site and if it had been worth dying for.

Chapter 25

When Gabriella came downstairs from having been with the professor, it was clear she'd been crying. "He's so sick," she said as she sat down next to Josh. He bought her a cup of espresso and sat with her while she drank it. She didn't talk and he didn't pressure her to, but he had a hard time taking his eyes off of her.

Her face wasn't extraordinary, but he didn't think he'd ever get tired of looking at her. Her eyes were wide and expressive, her lips were full and she radiated a gentleness that softened her other strong features.

Finishing the coffee, she thanked him and told him he could leave if he wanted to go, but she was going to stay a while longer.

"Is he conscious?" Josh asked.

She nodded. "But he has a raging fever and the antibiotics aren't working. The doctor doesn't think he'll make it through the night. Maybe I should have lied and told him the police had found the man who shot him. That we'd recovered the stones. That might make a difference. It's such a huge find…" Her voice tapered off.

"Gabriella, I know you wouldn't talk to Beryl about it over the phone, and I know you think what you found are the Memory Stones, but did you use them? Do you know how they work?"

"I saw them, yes. But that's all… I only saw them. We thought we had time."

For the rest of the day and into that evening, Josh sat with Gabriella at the hospital. Every hour she'd go back upstairs to check on the professor's status and he'd call Malachai again, worried about where he was and why he wasn't answering.

At six-thirty, Charlie Billings managed to find Josh in the cafeteria. The policeman who had been assigned to stay with Gabriella tried to keep him away, but Josh said it was okay. He was, in fact, glad to see a friendly face, someone he knew from another time and place.

"So are you going to give me anything?" Charlie asked.

"Not yet."

"Not the answer I was hoping to hear."

"No, I guess not."

"Can you identify the guy?"

"I don't think I should answer."

"Josh, it's me."

"And you're on a fishing expedition."

"It's my job."

"It's my back."

Josh expected another round of questions and was surprised when Charlie put down the notebook and pencil. "Forget about what happened today. I ran into Emma at the bureau the last time I was in London and said something about us all getting together. She got all quiet, then told me you guys split up and that you'd taken a leave of absence. What the fuck, Josh?"

He hadn't anticipated that the personal questions would be harder to answer than the ones about the shooting at the tomb, but they were.

"I needed to go back to New York. Take care of a few things."

Charlie's eyebrows went up.

Josh ignored the unspoken question.

That wasn't good enough for the reporter. "What happened? Why New York? And what are you doing here?"

"If I tell you you're going to think I'm crazy and you're just going to have a hundred other questions."

"Questions are my stock in trade."

"I don't have answers that are going to make any sense."

"I'll take them, anyway."

Josh laughed.

Charlie knew he'd hit another wall. "Okay, forget that. You need anything, man?"

"A cessation of questions would be a good idea."

They both laughed this time, and Charlie stayed a while—being a friend this time, which Josh appreciated—and then he left to file what he had on the professor's condition and find out what he could about the police's search for his assailant.

At 6:50 p.m., Malachai finally answered his cell phone and explained that he'd been at the embassy all day, trying to work the system to get Josh released, until Gabriella had accomplished that—which he said was a miracle—and since then he'd been trying to get permission for him to leave the country.

"But I haven't had a lot of luck. The Italian authorities don't want you to leave. You were a witness to the shooting and robbery."

"As long as I'm not a suspect."

"Well, that's another problem. They're hinting that you are."

"But I gave them a description and told them everything they wanted to know."

"Everything?"

"Damn it, Malachai."

"I doubt they really suspect you—but they do want you to stay in case they find this guy. You're the only witness."

The idea of being stuck in Rome disturbed him. The haunting lurches he was having were too real, too disturbing and too confusing. Josh wasn't sure anymore if he was living in the present or the past.

"The professor is a witness."

"How's he doing?"

"Not that good."

Malachai sighed. "Why don't you get Gabriella to leave the hospital for a while and come back to the hotel and have dinner with us? She can't just sit there all day."

"I'll try. But I don't think she's going to agree to leave. And she's not in any shape to go through this alone. I'm going to stay with her."

It was more complicated than that. Josh had a sense that this was his duty, his penance to stay with her and live this vigil through by her side—and yet he knew, although he couldn't explain how, that even if he did all that, it would not be enough.

* * *

When Gabriella came downstairs at just before ten o'clock, she reported that Rudolfo had improved slightly and that the doctors had thrown her out and told her to go home.

The street was dark, and Josh looked around carefully when they stepped outside. "I wouldn't put it past the press to be out here holding a vigil and waiting for us," he said, "but it looks like we're okay." He had expected to see Charlie Billings, but he was also being vigilant. The idea that he might be in danger made him more cautious than usual, especially since Gabriella was with him. They walked to Gabriella's car, and he took her keys from her. She was drained, dazed, and in no condition to drive.

She gave him directions to her apartment in a voice that broke every few words.

The gray sedan followed them to a row of five-story apartment houses that were at least a hundred years old, all crammed onto a narrow street in the shadow of the Vatican. Josh, fairly certain by now—and relieved—that it was the police, didn't even bother to turn around and check on the sedan, he just parked.

Then, without asking Gabriella if she wanted him to or not, he escorted her upstairs. He'd told Malachai she wasn't in any shape to be alone. The truth was, neither was he.

He'd hoped she'd have a bottle of Scotch in her kitchen, but he'd settle for brandy. Glasses were where he guessed—in the cabinet closest to the sink—and he didn't measure, just poured. When Josh put the drink in her hand, she lifted it to her lips as if she were on automatic. Neither of them spoke for a while.

There weren't many personal items in the living room except

for several piles of books and a large, leather-framed photograph of a little girl, maybe three years old, smiling at the camera. Even at that age, the resemblance to her mother was apparent. It was in her eyes—the same golden-brown color. But where Gabriella's gaze was a combination of curiosity and tempered strength, the little girl's was soft and dreamy.

When she saw him looking at the picture, Gabriella came to life for the first time. "That's Quinn," she said. And now her eyes took on the same softness as her daughter's. It moved Josh in a way he wouldn't have expected.

"How old is she?"

"Almost three. I miss her like crazy."

"I bet her father is taking great care of her."

"Her grandfather and her nanny. My dad is wonderful with her."

Josh instantly regretted he'd said anything. He could tell the end of the story from the way Gabriella's face froze, as if she was stopping herself from showing any of what she was feeling. "My husband was an archeologist, too. Specialized in underwater excavations. There was a problem with his oxygen on a dive. He died three months before Quinn was born."

"I'm sorry."

She shrugged. "He was doing what he loved to do."

Suddenly her voice lacked all emotion, which didn't surprise him. Josh knew what it was like to shut down over loss, over pain, over love. He wanted to go to her but sensed it wouldn't be appropriate.

"There's some grace to the way he died, but it's not fair to our daughter," Gabriella continued. "She got shortchanged."

"I know about that."

"How old were you?" she asked.

"Twenty. I always thought that it was too soon. But compared to your daughter… I had a lifetime with my father." He suddenly missed him with a force that surprised him.

"Quinn talks about her father all the time, even though she's never met him. She tells me she knows her daddy is supposed to be gone, but he isn't, really, and one day she'll find him."

"What do you tell her?"

She shrugged. "Maybe she understands something that I can only guess at. Children can be connected to the dead in a way adults can't. They seem to know things that adults have grown out of knowing."

She took a long drink. "But you're more familiar with that than I am, aren't you? You and Malachai and Beryl?"

It was Josh's turn to shrug. He didn't feel like talking about the foundation and their work, afraid it would sound clinical in the middle of such an intimate conversation.

"Do you have children?" she asked, almost as if she'd read his mind. He didn't think he reacted, but he must have, because she immediately became apologetic. "Sensitive subject? I'm sorry."

"Don't be. I wanted kids, but my wife, now my ex-wife, didn't. It became an elephant in the room."

"Is that why you split?"

"Not really. Yes. Maybe." He laughed at himself. "I think it started the process. Emma is a reporter. We lived in England, but between both of our careers, we probably didn't spend a total of sixty days a year with each other. The glue that might have kept another couple together through a crisis had already started to dry out when we had that first one."

"*First* one?"

He didn't answer right away. He wasn't used to discussing his personal life. It wasn't that he was discomfited talking to Gabriella—rather, it was too easy. And that unnerved him.

"Am I making you uncomfortable asking all these questions? I'm sorry."

"No, I was thinking just the opposite," he said, and then told her a truncated version of the accident and the hallucinations that followed.

She listened intensely, fascinated, and she also looked at him in a way that was familiar. It was how the doctors and therapists had looked at him. Bristling, he stopped talking halfway through explaining how the hallucinations had affected him and, subsequently, his marriage.

Gabriella didn't realize he had stopped on purpose, and she asked him the next logical question. "But I don't understand. Why would your needing to find out what was happening to you upset your wife?"

Josh had expected her voice to be clinical and cold, the way the doctors' voices had been. Instead, she sounded tender. Compassionate. Maybe he'd been wrong about her. Could he take the chance that Gabriella would understand the rest of his history?

"Once it was obvious there was nothing physically wrong with me, Emma started losing patience with what she called my *obsession*. Actually, so did I, but I couldn't walk away from it. I needed to find out what was happening to me. I needed to—I still need to understand, not just whether or not I've been reincarnated, but...about my conviction that there's a woman who has something to do with all this. Whom I knew before and need to find again." He shook his head, frustrated that he couldn't explain it more eloquently.

"Does this have something to do with our dig?"

"I think so."

"With Bella?"

He nodded. "Her name is Sabina."

Gabriella shook her head very slowly, understanding now for the first time.

"You believe you knew her in the past?"

"I don't know what I believe."

"This must be very difficult for you."

It felt as if her words had reached out and embraced him, and for a few moments, he was at peace in a way he hadn't been in months.

Her cell phone rang, sounding especially loud and intrusive, Josh thought. Looking down at the LED display, she read the number.

"It's home. My father." Her voice had tensed, like a violin string pulled too tightly. She flipped the phone open. "Hi, Dad. Is everything okay with Quinn?" As she listened, her face relaxed. "Hold on." She put her palm over the phone and looked over at Josh. "He called when we were at the hospital and I promised to fill him in. I'll be right back."

Josh should have offered to leave when she got up and walked out of the room, but he wasn't ready to go. He still wanted to talk to her about what she and the professor had found in that box.

While she was gone, Josh picked up his camera and walked over to the window. He'd noticed the view before and wanted to try to capture it. A sliver of St. Peter's dome in a navy sky streaked with gray clouds. Through the lens it became an ominous scene with strangely illuminated birds swooping straight down in what looked like kamikaze missions over the spire.

Going back to the coffee table to get his drink, he passed Gabriella's desk. On top was an open notebook with a pile of photographs spilling out. With his back to the room, blocking his actions if she were to suddenly come back, it was easy enough to spread them out a little. The first three shots were various close-ups of Sabina shot in brighter light than he'd seen her the previous dawn. Josh's insides lurched the same way they had when he'd stood before her. There was no mistaking the feeling. Was it actually possible this was the corpse of the woman who had been haunting him since his accident?

No. Don't go there, Josh told himself. *Not yet. Not here. Not where you might not be able to deal with the emotional turmoil that could overtake you if you let yourself give in to it.*

The next photograph showed the carved wooden box that the security guard had thrown on the ground and broken.

Under that shot was another. Against a white background was a close-up of six glittering, multifaceted, large stones: three matching emeralds, one blood-red ruby, and two deep-blue sapphires.

He stared at them.

The Memory Stones.

On the surface of each were unintelligible markings. Nothing like any hieroglyphics Josh could ever remember seeing. No. Not true.

You've seen these before. Longer ago than you have a conscious memory. Look at them. Know them for what they are.

"What do you think you are doing?" Her voice was icy cold.

Chapter 26

The doorbell rang, postponing the conversation, or argument, that Gabriella and Josh were about to have about his snooping. She looked through the peephole, cursed under her breath, walked over to the desk, scooped up the notebook along with the photographs, and turned them over. She opened the door.

If Inspector Tatti was surprised to see Josh there, he did a good job of hiding it.

"Professor Chase, I am quite apologetic to intrude."

"Is this necessary? It's very late."

"I would much rather be home myself."

"Come in," she said, gesturing.

He walked in, nodded at Josh and took a seat on the couch. She sat opposite him, and Josh stood by the desk where he'd been caught prying.

"The guard who was supposed to be on duty early yesterday morning was found a few hours ago. His name was Tony Saccio.

He was shot, dragged into the grove of oak trees up high behind the site and left there. My men found him. Naked."

Gabriella took the news badly. After the past two days, with her mentor in critical condition and her treasure missing, this was one too many crises to cope with.

"Tony? No!" She closed her eyes.

Tatti waited for a moment and then asked her for a glass of water, not because he wanted it, Josh was sure, but rather to give Gabriella a chance to leave the room and compose herself.

After she came back with it, he drank it all, then launched into his first request: "I need you to tell me what was stolen."

"What does it matter now? It's gone."

"I need to know for whom the stolen goods would have the most value."

It was a question Josh could have answered, but it might have put him under suspicion again—it would have given the detective the motive he needed. Josh looked at Gabriella. Was she going to name him and Malachai?

"There are hundreds of thousands of collectors of antiquities. Everything in the tomb would have been of value to them," she said blandly.

"What kind of value? How much money are we talking about?"

"How much do you need to sell something for to make it worth the lives of two men?"

"You tell me."

"I don't know. It doesn't matter. It can't. I have no way of estimating what the black market value of an ancient artifact is."

"I'm sorry, it's absolutely necessary for us to know what was taken from that crypt. A full list. Exact descriptions. We need to alert the authorities here in Italy, as well as Interpol and the world's art organizations. If we don't know what is at stake and who might want it, he will slip through our fingers. We will never find our villain."

Gabriella looked into space, focused on a point outside the window, beyond the detective. Her voice was low, almost unintelligible. Tatti leaned forward to hear what she was saying.

"They appeared to be ritual objects, but we don't know their significance."

"Can you describe them?" He didn't remind her that she had lied to him before. He'd probably assumed that all along.

"We didn't have time to discover their base, but they looked like ordinary glass beads typical of the period."

"And that period is?"

"We were estimating they dated back to at least 1000 B.C., maybe further, but we hadn't run any tests yet. It was all too fast. We'd just found them." She sounded as if it just didn't matter; as if she'd used up what little energy she'd had left explaining as much as she had.

"How many?"

"How many what?"

"Of these glass beads?"

"Maybe five. Maybe seven. A handful."

"And what do you think their value was?"

Priceless. The value of my life. The value of my soul, Josh wanted to answer for her, but he didn't, stifling his voice instead with a long swallow of brandy while he listened to Gabriella tell a new lie.

"Other than the fact that they were very old—which is what made them important to us—they're only worth fifteen or twenty thousand dollars. Museum quality, of course. But they were just bits of glass, not the Holy Grail."

"Then you're going to have to tell me what else was taken. Because twenty thousand dollars is not enough of a reason to shoot two men, is it?"

She never went into any more detail than that. Over and over, no matter how many times Tatti asked variations of the same questions, she always gave him back the same answer.

Glass beads.

They had not gotten to the stage of carbon-dating them.

No idea what they were used for or what their value was.

Gabriella never glanced at Josh during the interrogation. Never acted as if she was worried that Josh might tell Tatti that she was lying, that she had photographs of the stones that she was keeping from him, never alluded to the ancient legends about the *glass beads.* Never suggested that, used with a certain mantra, these *bits of colored glass* might take you back through the veil of time to the lives you had lived before and give you a glimpse into a past long gone.

The detective pushed as hard as he could and then accepted he'd hit a wall. With a sigh, he stood up and bowed to her in a funny formal way that was familiar. Like Peter Sellers as Inspector Clouseau in *The Pink Panther.*

Tatti offered to drop Josh off at his hotel. "It would be safer for you if you had an escort."

"But I do have one, don't I? A gray sedan?"

Tatti feigned innocence, but a wrinkle appeared between his eyebrows. "As you wish."

Josh had no desire to get into the detective's car with him. The last time that had happened he'd wound up in a jail cell overnight. Nor did he want Tatti to ask him any questions that he had the answers to. Josh wasn't a good liar, although he was learning.

For instance: when your wife asks you if there is someone else, and the someone else isn't anyone whose face you have ever seen except in your unconscious dreams, it would be useful to be able to lie convincingly.

But there was another reason Josh turned the detective down. He had no intention of leaving Gabriella's apartment without getting another look at the photographs of the round objects that he was sure were not made of glass and that he was also sure, to some people, were worth murdering two men for. Or five. Or ten.

With Tatti gone, Josh expected Gabriella to thank him for not telling the detective that she was withholding information.

She didn't. Which made what he asked her all the more difficult.

"I know you think a lot of what's happened is my fault, but I'd like you to let me help you find the stones."

"How do you think you can do that? You don't speak Italian. You don't know Rome or the antiquities market. What can you possibly do?"

"Let me see the photographs, Gabriella."

"How will that be helping?"

"Malachai and Beryl have spent their whole lives studying reincarnation. There has to be some way that the foundation can help. We have money and contacts. We'll leave no stone un—" He broke off and grimaced comically at the unintended pun.

Despite everything that had happened to her in the past two days, she managed a half laugh.

It seemed he'd heard that laugh before. That he knew the cadence of it. No. He was just tired. Too tired. He was trying to force her into the role he wanted her to play because she'd been so easy to talk to earlier. Josh looked at her face, at her hair, at her high cheekbones and the slightly full mouth.

He forced himself to be honest.

No. He didn't know her. Even if he thought he was certain that her lips would burn if he kissed her, that was just normal attraction. Not something that had survived through time. He didn't care, he tried to tell himself. He caught her scent: grass and herbs and honey. Nothing like jasmine and sandalwood.

When I think of all the things I never had time to say to you…

For one terrible second he thought he had said it out loud.

What did it mean?

Where did it come from?

It was only his imagination.

Sometimes what seemed familiar only *seemed* familiar. Déjà vu does happen to people. So much had transpired in the past two days, this latest insight could just be a trick his mind was playing because he was exhausted.

Was it?

"What's wrong?" she asked, genuinely concerned.

"I'm just tired. So are you. Tomorrow I'll talk to Malachai and try to come up with a plan. Maybe we can help."

"Are you going?" Her hand went up to her throat and she fingered the simple gold chain that lay there, following the graceful line of her clavicle bones.

His own fingers twitched.

"Are you okay?"

"Yes. I'm fine." Her voice sounded a little afraid.

"You're worried about the professor. Do you want me to stay?"

She shook her head. "Thanks, but no, I'll really be fine."

He left, glad that she hadn't asked him to stay. He didn't know what might have happened, what kind of mistake he would have made, if she'd said yes.

Chapter 27

Although Gabriella had offered to call a taxi for him, Josh declined. He needed to walk, to take in huge gulps of the cool air, to stare up at the sky—at the constant sky—the one thing that would not have changed in the past two millennia. He assumed the gray sedan would follow after him, and if it didn't, he'd just stick to the main thoroughfares Gabriella had mapped out for him.

"Hope I didn't keep you waiting too long," Josh said sarcastically when he walked out of the building and saw Charlie Billings there.

"Let me walk with you?"

"Sure." Maybe it wasn't such a bad idea to have company.

"I know the guard's body was found. I know some box was taken. Or that the contents of the box were taken. That's not quite clear. Can you fill me in?"

"Why would I know?"

"You were down there."

"The professor never got around to showing it to me."

"But you've been with Gabriella Chase all day, all night. She must have told you what—"

"Listen, I know what this gig is like," Josh interrupted. "But I can't help you out. The best I can do is promise that no one else will get this story from me before you do."

"Why is everything about this excavation so hush-hush?"

"I don't know. It's not my dig."

"But you were down there. Damn it, Josh, what did you see taken? Why can't you tell me?"

"I wasn't down there."

"I didn't pressure you before, but I *saw* you coming up from the tomb."

"Because I ran down when I heard the shot, but I wasn't in the tomb long enough to catalog it. There is no story. No statement. You can count on me—if and when I have something to say to the press, I'll call you first, but you need to back off now and leave me and Gabriella alone for a while. Is it a deal?"

Billings thought about it, then stuck his notebook back in his jacket pocket. "I'll give you tonight. But I'll probably be back in the morning."

"How about the morning after that?"

"Tomorrow."

"I don't doubt it. You know, Charlie, I never knew you were such a prick."

"Of course not. You were on our side."

"Wish I still was."

"See, this is what I mean. Something is going on with you. Why the hell don't you just level with me?"

Josh thought if it were up to him alone, he might. But when Malachai and Beryl had agreed to let him study with them, he'd given his word that he would keep the foundation out of the press. And there was Gabriella, who'd asked him not to reveal the tomb's secrets. Not yet. Not to anyone.

At the next corner, Charlie and Josh parted ways. At first the streets were busy despite the hour, but then the neighborhood changed and he found himself alone in a fairly deserted piazza. He heard a loud bang, spun around, saw a cat running away from a broken wine bottle. Chiding himself for giving in to anxiety, he continued on, sticking close to the curbside and speeding up his gait. Not a single car drove by for the next two blocks. Every time he saw a storefront window across the street, Josh watched his own reflection pass. If anyone was following him, he'd see him, too, but he was alone.

According to Gabriella's instructions, he should have reached the hotel by now. Should he keep going or backtrack? Looking around, trying to figure out which way to go, he saw a reflection oscillate in a store window across the way.

There was no time to judge if he was overreacting or not. Josh sped up but kept his eye on the window. It hadn't been his imagination, or the branch of a tree blowing in the wind. When Josh broke into a jog, so did his stalker.

As he ran, Josh searched for an escape. Not a car in sight. Every storefront and restaurant he passed was closed for the night. He weaved in and out as he ran, abruptly veering to the right, then left, then left again, so as not the give his hunter a clear shot if that's what his intention was.

Suddenly he was in the old part of the city, where he'd walked with Malachai the first night they'd arrived, just seventy-two hours before. The broken cobblestones made for a tough running track, but he didn't slow down, couldn't slow down now that he remembered there was a building up ahead that connected to a hidden tunnel system. A temple.

If he could just reach its entrance without his stalker seeing where he went, he'd thwart him. It should only be another hundred yards away, to the right.... He sped up. He'd gotten a good lead...he was going to make it...just up ahead... but...where was it? There was no temple here, only ruins. What was going on? No time to stop and figure it out. If he could just find the temple, he'd be able to get away. If he saved himself, he could save her. She was counting on him. He must have gotten confused in the dark. Maybe the temple would be around the next corner...but it wasn't. Nothing was there. Worse, he'd given up his cover. He'd run right into an open theater, its shell in rubble around him. He spun around. Everywhere he looked, everything was crumbling.

Where was *his* Rome? The familiar landmarks? What had happened to *his* city? He had to get out of this exposed space where he was nothing but an easy target. Stumbling on a rock as he took off, Julius tried to steady himself, but failed and went down. Rocks ripped at his already torn hands, chewed his bruised knees. His heart beat wildly; his breath came in harsh, painful gulps. Behind him he heard footfalls and hoarse panting getting closer.

There was no way out now.

Slowly, he rose and turned around.

His pursuer wasn't wearing a toga or a robe, but was dressed in clothes that Julius had never seen before and holding an unusual metal object Julius was unfamiliar with but somehow knew was a weapon.

And then, staring at the black barrel, Julius felt a deep wrenching inside of him: a cessation, a great giving up as Josh broke free of the memory lurch to see the man who had been in the tomb with him, who had stolen the Memory Stones and shot the professor, probably with this same gun, staring at him with a satisfied smirk on his face.

Chapter 28

Glancing at her watch, Gabriella was surprised that it was 11:20 p.m. Only fifteen minutes had passed since the last time she'd called the hospital. She wanted to call again and find out if there'd been any change, but last time the night nurse had promised that if the professor took a turn for the worse, she'd phone Gabriella.

Except she was going crazy. The longer she paced the more she thought about the tragedies of the past two days: the professor's life hanging in the balance, the robbery and Tony's death. He had been such a presence at the dig, was always there in the morning when she arrived at the site with his big grin and boisterous hello. Several times when she'd worked through lunch he'd call down to tell her he was going off duty and ask if she wanted him to get her something before he went home. He'd even bought her a toy for Quinn. A doll of a Vatican guard with his high hat and yellow-and-black tights.

Tears threatened, but she fought them back. Gabriella had learned, first when her mother died and then when her husband had been asphyxiated, tears didn't do a damn bit of good. Emotions were something to be endured, not indulged. Sometimes when she thought about Quinn she bit down on the inside of her mouth until the pain distracted her from the overwhelming fear—the floating fear, she called it—that she could not control what would happen to her baby.

Gabriella had spent her life with the dead, and she wasn't scared of joining them, but she couldn't bear any more loss in her life. Especially not her precious child. And yet, tragedy was too accommodating. Accidents were always waiting. A runaway car careened down a street. An errant germ passed from child to child at school. An internal time bomb was transmitted from parent to child through DNA.

No, no, no. She wasn't going to fall prey to this perverse, masochistic indulgence. If horrors were going to come, her worrying now wouldn't stop them. She should get out of there. Take a walk. Stop at a café. Have a glass of wine. Anything but sitting, waiting and thinking or, worse, obsessing.

She brushed her hair, picked up her bag and walked toward the door, and then her cell phone rang.

Mrs. Rudolfo was crying. The professor was worse. His fever had spiked and he was delirious. The medicine wasn't controlling the infection. Would she come?

Yes, Gabriella said. Yes, of course, she was on her way.

The man in the gray sedan watched Professor Chase come out of her apartment, run to her car and get in. He turned on his ignition, and twenty seconds after she pulled out, he did, too, driving far enough behind her so he wouldn't be too obvious.

The man in the black SUV who had parked much farther down the block saw Gabriella drive away, too, but he didn't follow her. All he did was punch a number in on his cell phone and wait for someone to pick up.

Across the street, inside the apartment building that Gabriella had just left, her landlady sat in the living room of her ground-floor apartment, knitting a sweater for one of her grandchildren and watching an old Fellini movie on television. She was close enough to the telephone so that when it rang, Camilla Volpe picked it up on the second ring. She said hello, listened, nodded, said, *sì, sì, sì,* began to say something else and then heard the man she was speaking to hang up. Reaching for a key ring that sat in a green glass bowl on her entry table, the landlady went out her front door.

Her knees hurt as she climbed the stairs. Her arthritis was acting up, but she was tired of going to doctors and waiting in sitting rooms. There wasn't any miracle cure for getting older. She remembered her grandmother's hands when she reached her nineties, gnarled and spotted with heavy ropes of veins in bas-relief.

Reaching apartment 2B, Signora Volpe opened the door as if it was her right to do that. And it was, wasn't it? If someone she had rented one of her apartments to was doing something illegal, it was her duty to help the police catch her, no?

There were always stories in the papers about archeologists raping Rome—finding ancient artwork and smuggling it out of the country where it rightfully belonged. If the American woman was doing that, it was her responsibility to help the police.

The detective on the phone had told her the proof he needed

would be in the black notebooks Gabriella Chase wrote in and in the photographs of the site.

That was what she was supposed to look for: black notebooks and photographs. That was all they wanted.

Methodically, Signora Volpe went through the piles of papers on the desk. She could feel her heart beating. She was like one of those actors in the movies her husband liked to watch when he was alive, sneaking around, spying on people. She was sixty-two years old and she had never set foot in a police station. Now she was cooperating with a detective and playing private eye. As scared as she was, she was also a little excited. Exhilarated, really. After all, she was helping to prevent the theft of a national treasure.

Under a pile of papers and magazines, Signora Volpe found a notebook. And, yes, it was black. She picked it up. What luck to have found it so fast! Underneath that was a pile of photographs. Glancing at the one on top, she saw a small, cavernous room. Old and dusty, but with the most glorious painting of flowers on the wall. Could they steal a wall painting, she wondered?

Taking a plastic bag from the pocket of her housedress, she shook it out and carefully put the photos and the notebook inside.

Detective Metzo had told her to look on the bookshelves, too, and in the bedroom. She hurried through the task. She'd been inside the apartment for several minutes. What if the American woman came home suddenly? She'd need to make up a story that someone complained about, what? Not noise. Maybe a gas leak. Yes, a gas leak. That would be perfect. But she wouldn't get caught. Detective Metzo had given his word that he'd honk his horn if he saw her tenant. Three times. Quickly. That would be her signal. So far it had been quiet.

No, there was nothing in the bedroom. The search was over. She'd found what he wanted in the living room. A dozen photographs and a notebook.

Now for the next part.

"Why can't I just come downstairs and give you what I find," she'd argued with him when he'd explained what he wanted her to do.

"It has to look like a break-in, Signora Volpe. Please." Metzo had started losing patience.

She did understand. She and her husband, dear Jesus, keep his soul safe, had worked so hard to restore this building. It hurt her to do this, even this one small thing. But she was protecting a national treasure—possibly, the detective had said, a treasure of importance to the church and the Holy Father. Pride was a sin. She would have to confess on Sunday that she had hesitated over this small act.

She took off her shoe and held it.

She couldn't do it.

She had to.

Inhaling, then holding her breath, Signora Volpe smacked her shoe against the window, the one that looked down on the alleyway. The glass shattered and, a few seconds later, hit the pavement below with a sound that reminded her of church bells. That gave her courage. It was a sign. But the next part was going to be more difficult. It was one thing to break glass that was simple to replace. It was much more upsetting to hit, hit, hit the wooden frame until it split and fell apart. And then hit it from the outside, while she leaned out the window, trying not to look down on the alley, not to see the glass shimmering in the moonlight.

When she was done it looked just like a robber had broken in. That's what it was supposed to look like, Metzo had told her.

When she asked him why, he'd put his fingers to his lips in a mock hushing gesture and told her that he wasn't at liberty just yet to discuss police procedure. And then he had given her double what it would cost to replace the window and the wooden frame and had promised a nice bonus if she found what he was looking for.

She tried not to think about the wood being more than a hundred years old and that she'd never be able to replace the frame exactly. But, she thought as she dropped the plastic bag out of the window as instructed, she *was* doing her job, helping the police. What was some old wood if she could save that lovely flower wall in the photograph or a precious relic? Leaving the apartment, the worst of it behind her, she felt a little righteous.

After all, she'd made a noble sacrifice.

Chapter 29

Josh heard the gunshot. Saw the blood. Smelled the iron and smoke. He watched the man he recognized as the thief tumbling toward him, eyes wide with surprise, lips pulled back from his teeth in a silent scream.

The body fell on top of Josh, pushing him to the ground, spilling blood on him, wetting his clothes, the stink of it getting into his nose.

Hearing footsteps, Josh lifted his head and, in the distance, saw the back of a man, the shooter, retreating into the darkness, disappearing into the night.

What had happened? He couldn't remember it all. Yes, yes, he could, he'd been running in the present and had run right into the past, his past. Or so it seemed.

Josh looked down at the body of a man who had wanted him dead, who was now dead himself, and then up, up at the sky. Up at the moon. Sixteen hundred years ago, the same moon might have been hanging just as low, illuminating these same marble buildings and making them gleam the same way. But then they were intact, not stumps. Stars shone for millions of years. It was the people—the transients, and the corruptibles and what they created—that changed.

Shaky, he rose to his feet and started to walk away from the man, away from the blood. He needed to get back to the hotel so he could call the police, tell them where they could find the body. But first he had to find a way out of the wreckage that stretched on and on, reminders of the people who'd lived and died and left nothing but this rubble—and their memories that lived like tapeworms inside him and the other poor suckers. He was, they all were, just hosts for uninvited guests. Wandering through the deserted, emptied-out world, all he could do was keep walking, shaky and stinking and bloody, until he could find the perimeter of this ancient wasteland.

He didn't understand why he was still alive. Had the mastermind behind the robbery decided that the thief was the greater liability? Had the robber threatened his boss, blackmailed him, made new demands? Or did Josh know something that was important to the unraveling of the puzzle that surrounded the stones? If they really were the ancient memory tools, was he the one who could unlock their secret based on information hidden in his deeper memories? Was that why he'd been spared?

But what if the stones were never found? They'd been a last hope, a promise—albeit a far-fetched one—of a possible path to discoveries. If he could compile histories for Julius and Percy, and of the other ghosts he saw in flashes, he'd be able to do the necessary research to prove beyond any doubt that he'd lived those lives.

In the sky among the stars, Josh imagined he saw the emeralds, sapphires and that one ruby he'd glimpsed in Gabriella's photographs. They gleamed and twinkled, teasing him about a quest that now seemed farther away than those pulsars and quasars.

No, he was being naive. They were merely gems men had imbued with mythical attributes: legends, not actual conduits. There was no way they could connect him to his previous incarnations—if there really were such things as previous incarnations

It was illogical and absurd. It was magical thinking. It had to be.

But then, why was it happening again? And it was—he could smell it.

Powerless to stop it, he wasn't sure he even wanted to. Josh had too many questions, and far too few answers.

Chapter 30

Julius and Sabina
Rome—391 A.D.

The scent of acrid fumes roused him. In the distance, lit by the moon, a winding plume of black-gray smoke rose up, reaching toward the stars. He got up and began to walk, then run, toward the fire, but by the time he reached its source, it didn't matter. He was too late. The damage to yet another temple had been done, and the structure was destroyed. With the awful scent in his nostrils, Julius turned away and started back, pushing himself to hurry despite the sudden exhaustion that had overcome him while he stood there staring at the charred and blackened mess. Their world was turning to ash.

He had an assignation to keep, and even if he hurried now he was still going to be late. He hoped Lucas wouldn't worry.

Passing through the area of ancient ruins, he turned to the

left. With each step there were fewer and fewer crumbling walls around him and more new marble structures. And then, out of breath, he reached the small grove of cypress, olive and oak trees.

Entering the cool, green copse, Julius inhaled the woody scent. Even here, this far away, it was tinged with the stench of fire. For another five minutes he walked through the thicket and emerged on the other side, at the edge of a well-tended cemetery, where his mentor, Lucas, the Pontifex Maximus, waited.

They exchanged greetings, spoke of the fire, and then began to stroll, heading down the center aisle, passing elaborate funeral monuments to their most illustrious citizens.

They were walking with the dead. It was what they had been doing every night for years. Late, when everyone else slept, Lucas and Julius met by the entrance to the Campus Martius near the Tiber and set off together. With everything changing around them, there was something comforting about being in a place where nothing could ever change. Long ago these souls had moved on, and all that was left were stone-cold monuments to remind those still living of who they had been and what they had done.

It was easier to be in the past than to imagine the future. But that was what the two men had to do. It was their responsibility, their holy mandate. They arrived at the mausoleum where Augustus was buried and, as they always did, both stopped and stood silently, honoring the statesman.

The structure was a wonder of rising concrete concentric circles faced with white marble. Between each two circles a perfectly shaped cypress was planted. Two Egyptian-style obelisks stood sentry at the entrance. In the center was a circular burial chamber where a bronzed Augustus, forever strong and powerful, rose on a column. There were other funerary urns inside, too, housing not only Augustus's remains but those of his relatives and friends: the remnants and debris their souls had left behind.

From that spot, several tree-lined paths radiated out toward gardens and the rest of the cemetery. Each night that they walked there, Lucas and Julius took a different direction. By now they knew them all but still alternated.

"There is news from Milan," Lucas said over the sounds of the rushing river.

Julius nodded, waiting for him to continue. Reports from Milan were never good. He breathed in and tried to force himself to take some pleasure from the clean scent of the evergreen shrubs that adorned this space while he prepared himself for the news.

"The night air is good for my cough…you don't mind walking farther, do you?" Lucas asked.

That was code that the elder priest was concerned about spies and that they should wait to talk until they reached the temple that stood in the clearing, where no one would be able to get close enough to hear them.

There were too many trees here for them to take any chances. Branches heavy with foliage were good hiding places at night. It would be so simple for the emperor's men to be waiting, listening, trying to learn their plans so they could foil them.

If anyone was watching, they were just two priests who were enjoying their sojourn just as they always had. For years they'd taken late-night expeditions, discussing religion and politics, trying to solve the world's problems. Now that world was losing all semblance of order and small familiar rituals like this one were greatly comforting.

In the far distance, both men heard a scream, followed by shouts. They searched the night sky, looking out into the darkness. Nothing at first. And then flames shot up, tingeing the horizon with their orange glow.

Somewhere yet another inferno was consuming a midnight meal. The fires were hungry in Rome that summer. More buildings were destroyed than in the last six years combined. And not just to arson. It was all part of the changes. People were uncomfortable and scared, and so the men drank too much wine each night and the women were not as cautious with the hearth fires as they needed to be. Accidents happened.

But not at the house of the Vestals or at their temple. Sabina had been proactive, cutting back all the foliage near the house, keeping guards on duty at night, having buckets of water at the ready at all hours of the day and night.

Watching the illumination light up the sky, Julius remembered the night five years before when he thought Sabina had died in the fire. He shivered although it was warm out. Since then, she'd freed the priestesses from many archaic rules, modernizing several rituals in an effort to help the nuns be perceived less as "others" and blend into society with greater ease.

No matter what strides she had made, though, she hadn't done enough. One law, very much still in place, was soon going to prove her destruction.

And his.

Julius blamed himself. He should have been stronger. Should have cut it off before this happened. But he'd become too arrogant, tempted fate one too many times and finally lost—it was a lesson in hubris, but one he was learning too late.

What is it about man that he is so drawn to exactly what he is not supposed to have been?

Rome was not a provincial town. Like all men, priests were allowed carnal pleasures. There were brothels to visit and lusty sexual games to play. He could revel in the perfumed body of any woman he met or luxuriate with any man of his liking.

The only person he'd ever desperately wanted was the one forbidden to him. How could he have been so bold as to take the chances he took when the punishment for their coming together was death?

He knew the answer. It would be a worse death for them to be alive and not to be together. To walk the same earth and never touch, never whisper about what mattered to them, never sink into the ecstasy that their bodies offered them.

The long, silent part of the walk over, Lucas and Julius came out of the far end of the cemetery and into the clearing. A temple, with a rounded dome supported by a dozen fluted columns, stood in the center of a field of flat grass, surrounded by a garden that contained only low-lying plants. There were no trees within earshot.

Nevertheless, they circled the temple.

"I don't think we've been followed," Julius said.

"We have plans to make," Lucas said once they settled down under the temple's tiled dome. "And soon. The rumors are that the emperor has a new initiative."

"A harsher one?"

He nodded. "The bishop from Milan has been here and they have worked out the next phase of the cleansing."

"Do you know what this one will include?"

"All forms of pagan worship will be completely banned, including private religious rites, though we know there's no way to enforce this. The emperor will decree that no sacrifice will be permitted anywhere in the city, including inside our own homes. We won't be allowed to light votive candles, burn lamps, offer wine or incense, or hang wreaths to our genius or to our household gods—Lars and Penates. All of these will be treasonable offenses, like the divining of entrails or burnt offerings.

"Even tying a ribbon around a tree or adoration of a statue will be outlawed and, I was told, will be punishable by property loss. And worse. This decree will sanctify our destruction in the name of their god."

"How much longer before all this is written into law?"

"A month? Two? I'm afraid that in less than a year there won't be any temples standing. There won't be any of our priests left."

Neither of them spoke for several minutes—Julius because he was stunned by the enormity of the changes; Lucas because he was depleted by repeating them.

"We can't give in," Julius said. "We need to fight back."

"We're outnumbered by thousands."

"You're giving up?"

"I'm talking to you. I'm trying to figure it out. I just don't think we have any chance of taking them on in hand-to-hand combat."

"Outsmarting them, then?" Julius asked.

"If there is a way."

"At least we can protect our relics from the looters. Safeguard them so that once this is over and we are back in power we can restore them to where they belong. Then we can leave."

"When this is over and we are back in power? You're optimistic. I'm not so sure, Julius."

"Then we'll start over somewhere else and wait. This emperor won't live forever. His successor can snap his fingers and reinstate our religion as quickly as Theodosius has made the new religion the law. This isn't about lofty ideals. This is politics, and politics are capricious."

The Pontifex nodded at the younger priest in a way that made Julius think of and remember his father. "Of course you're right. There's always a chance. But when you're smart enough to combine politics and religion in the way the emperor has, you don't just change laws. You change people's minds. Theodosius is playing on our citizens' fear of the unknown. In each new speech he reminds them that only by honoring him and his new religion will they be ensured a place in the afterlife. That if they don't, they will be damned to hell—a hell he describes as more horrific each time he speaks of it. He's succeeding in terrorizing everyone. Every citizen is frightened, not just for what will happen to them when they are alive, but what's going to happen to them and their loved ones after they die. People are afraid to disobey him. By combining the new religion with the secular law he has increased his power tenfold."

A warm breeze wafted over them. Julius wished they could use it to blow away the changes that were threatening their way of life. He took in the familiar landscape, wondering if the future would be kind to this place of peace or if the cemetery would befall the same fate that some of the temples had already endured.

There was some movement in one of the cypresses in the distance. But the wind had died down. Julius touched the Pontifex's arm and nodded his head toward what he'd seen.

A few seconds later, the branches moved again.

And then, in another tree, a branch swayed.

In whispers, Julius and Lucas assessed the situation.

How many spies were there, waiting for them to leave the safety of the temple? What was their mission? Were they prepared to attack, or was this just a sortie to find out what they could about the priests' plans?

"Should we risk it?" Lucas asked, nodding toward the escape hatch that was all but invisible in the complicated tile floor unless you knew where to look for it.

"If they already know we're here and then we disappear, they might discover our underground tunnels. We can't risk that. We're going to need those tunnels to get out of Rome if it comes to that."

"You're right. We'll wait. Even if it means staying here till morning. There will be enough people out and around then that we'll be safe. Our city is still not at the point where it's acceptable to murder two high priests in broad daylight. At least, I hope not."

The rest of the night passed slowly. Even after there was no obvious movement, the two men were too cautious to leave the safety of the temple until daybreak, so, in whispers, they strategized.

As a plan evolved, it became obvious that if they were cautious and quick, there was a possibility they could save what was precious to them to rebuild their religion in another land—and perhaps, one day, resurrect it in Rome.

Each sacred treasure must be entrusted to one priest or one Vestal as befitted his or her rank, who would, when the time came, sneak it out of Rome. Traveling alone or, at the most, in pairs, they would all rendezvous at a central location far outside the city and then, as a group, find a safe haven.

"Who should we entrust the Palladium to?" Julius asked. "It has to be a priest." The sculpture of Athena, her right hand carrying a raised lance, her left a distaff and spindle, was over three feet high. "It's too heavy for any of the Vestals."

Carved from wood, colored with paint made from powdered lapis lazuli and malachite, and decorated with gold leaf, she astounded everyone who looked upon her. The artist had somehow been able to imbue the immobile face with both compassion and strength. That and the history of the statue made it one of their most historic treasures: the powerful replica had been rescued from Troy by Aeneas and was purported to assure the ongoing safety of Rome. She was their luck. Without her blessing on their journey, the superstitious among them would fear for their success

"I think Drago should take it," Lucas said, naming Julius's brother.

"He'd be honored."

Next, the Pontifex assigned the two other wooden statues in the repository along with the provisions for the household gods, the Penates—ashes of unborn calves, mixed with the blood of horses from chariot races.

A half hour later, they had reached the end of the list. There was only one treasure left, and there was no question that Lucas himself would be responsible for that. Why hadn't his mentor delegated any of the objects to Julius? Despite his efforts not to be, he was disappointed. Why had he been shunned? There was only one reason he could think of.

Somehow, Lucas had found out about Sabina and knew that Julius might not live many days after his lover if it was discovered he was the father of her child. Law dictated that the man who committed the crime of taking a Vestal's virginity also be punished by death. Right now, though, dying was an abstraction. Not being given one of the sacred objects to save was a real humiliation.

He looked out at the horizon to the faintest dusting of golden morning light. Julius knew he was behaving like a child, allowing his personal feelings to interfere with monumental issues that threatened their way of life. They were facing a crisis the likes of which none of them could imagine, and he was jealous of his own brother and his fellow priests because they had been given more responsibility?

"We can go soon to start another difficult day," Lucas said, nodding toward the dawn. "But there's still one more treasure."

In the penus—the Vestals' inner storeroom and the best protected room of the house—a carved box containing the Memory Stones was reported to be buried under the floor. The exact location was a secret that had been passed on from one generation of elders—the head priest and priestess—to the next, and after so many centuries, some thought the stones were only legend.

"You believe they're real?"

"I believe they are there. What their power might be, I don't know. No one has seen them in hundreds of years."

"But you know where they are?"

Lucas smiled. "I know where they are supposed to be. So does the head priestess."

It was said that every time there had been a fire—and there had been many—the reigning Pontifex had made sure the Vestals' house had been resurrected identically to the old structure so that the penus remained in the same spot. In this way the treasure could be found if it was ever deemed appropriate to dig it up.

Months ago, in the sacred grove, Sabina had told him that they should steal those stones and run away. As head priestess, she knew where the spot was. He remembered that day now—how he had left the city that morning fearful, thinking that the threat they were under couldn't be worse. How they had made love in the shadows of the trees and bathed in the pond. How he'd found out she was carrying his child. Carrying a baby and a death sentence. All in one.

"You will, of course, take the stones," Julius said.

Lucas shook his head. "Anyone who guesses what we're planning will presume I'll take responsibility for the most precious objects, which is what I want everyone to think. That's why I'll disappear first. There will be chaos. Rumors will start that I've taken the stones. Next, the Vestals and senior priests, everyone except for you, will flee. All remaining suspicion and conjecture will go with them. By then our treasury will be empty. It will appear everything of value is gone. No one will suspect the greatest treasure remains behind. That's when you'll go."

For a moment the pressure lifted. Lucas had anointed him. His skin tingled and his head swam with the idea that he was going to be the first man in so many years to touch them.

According to the legend, the stones had been part of a cache of treasures dug up in Egypt during the infamous grave-robbing siege of Dynasty Twenty, where they had been discovered in

Ramses III's coffers. Next they became the property of the Nubian King Piankh/Piye of Kush, who came from Sudan, conquered the various kingdoms of Egypt, and founded the Nubian dynasty. Stolen from that king by a deposed member of Egyptian royalty, the stones next were given to Numa Pompilius, the second King of Rome, as a tribute by the prince who had requested sanctuary.

When Numa received them, it was well known that the stones were an ancient aid to remembering past lives. But the mystery of how to use the stones had been lost long before. Visibly, each was inscribed with symbols, but no one in Numa's court had been able to make sense out of them. He offered a large purse as a prize, and scholars traveled far distances to try their hand at interpreting the markings. Failure only made Numa more determined to unlock the stones' powers.

Yes, he wanted to know the secrets of his past so his soul could find peace, but he was also desperate to use the tools to garner power and wealth, to find all the treasures and mysteries that had long been lost to civilization.

Each year he increased the size of the prize, and by the time of his death, the award was rumored to be one full quarter of his wealth—but still no one could decipher the markings on the stones and unleash their powers.

Numa Pompilius believed, as many did, that after he died he would one day return in another body to live and rule in Rome again. If he couldn't learn from the stones in his present lifetime, he wanted to ensure he'd have a second chance in the next. So, shortly before his death, he announced that he'd appointed two women, Gezania and Verenia, to protect the sacred hearth and make sure its flames remained burning so that Rome would be assured the benefit of fire. He named the priestesses Vestals after the goddess, Vesta; gave them honors and great power; decreed they would remain pure and set up rules of progression so their order would continue far into the future.

But guarding the fire was only the cover for the real reason Numa ordained the women: their holy contract with him was to guard the sacred stones after his death. He also made it a crime, punishable by death, for a man to take a Vestal's virginity. If, he thought, he could make men fear the women, it would keep them from entering their inner sanctum; thus, the stones would remain safe.

It was one thing to keep the men away from the women. It was yet another to guarantee the women would not invite men into their house. So Numa not only made their virginity sacrosanct, he ordained that a Virgin's punishment for breaking her vow of celibacy would be her own slow death by suffocation.

Numa's last act of caution to ensure that his precious hoard would remain untouched until his rebirth was to start rumors that the stones were cursed and that anyone who even tried to find them would be afflicted by unforgetting everything that was meant to stay forgotten and be haunted for all the days of his life with waking nightmares.

All these years later, that curse still hung over the stones. Romans were superstitious people. No man had invaded the Vestals' house. Even those virgins who, like Sabina, broke their vows and gave in to love or lust, did so outside the residence.

As far as anyone knew, the stones, if indeed they had ever existed, were buried there still.

Like Julius, Lucas stared out into the sky, watching the pale orange and light blue morning emerge.

"How soon do you think we should leave?"

"Seven or eight weeks. No longer if we want to be safe."

That was close to when Sabina would give birth. It would be dangerous to leave just when the baby was due. Either they needed to leave before or wait until well after.

Soon it would be bright enough for him and Lucas to venture out from the safety of the temple. In the few minutes left to them, Julius knew he had to tell his mentor and friend the truth. Sabina had been able to hide her growing secret under the more voluminous cloak she now wore all the time, but that was becoming more and more difficult. If they were going to try to escape, instead of Sabina going into hiding at her sister's house, which was one of their plans, he needed Lucas's help, not his umbrage at being kept ignorant.

Will he understand and protect us? What if he won't? I can't be afraid. I have to trust him, take the risk and confide in him. If I am going to save Sabina I must have Lucas's help.

"I can't go if it means leaving Sabina behind."

Lucas didn't say anything for a few seconds. Julius felt the first rush of fear.

"You're like a son to me. I've known you since you were a child. Did you think I didn't know about you and Sabina?"

Julius was momentarily stunned.

"But you never said anything."

"What was there to say? Would you have listened to me?"

Julius almost smiled—but there was more to tell him. And he was sure Lucas didn't know the rest.

"And I can't just walk out of the city with her and my child by my side and the stones in my pocket."

Lucas nodded like a condemned man accepting a sentence.

"The worry of that possibility has kept me up many nights." He was silent for a few moments, thinking. "Everything is falling apart around us. The times are confused. Maybe we can use Sabina's pregnancy to our advantage. It might be just the thing to make it appear that we are following the rules when in reality we will be smashing them to pieces."

Julius felt the first stirrings of hope he'd had in months.

Half an hour later, the two priests walked down the steps of the temple out in the open. Without incident they reached the cemetery's summit and the large bronze statue of Augustus Caesar. His shimmering shoulders looked powerful enough to hold up the world.

Lucas gestured to him as they passed by. "There were a hundred years of civil war before he took over. Maybe you're right about the tides turning again in our lifetime."

They all knew what their first Roman emperor had done. They were the lucky recipients of his efforts. The currency system, highways, postal service, bridges, aqueducts and many of the buildings that he had built still stood. The greatest writers: Virgil, Horace, Ovid and Livy, whose works were still read, all had lived in Caesar's reign.

"Under his rule we wouldn't need to run and hide," Julius said.

"We're going to take this into our own hands now, we're going to survive."

"And when—"

The force of the first rock, coming from such a distance, threw Julius off balance. The second felled him.

"Julius? Julius? Can you hear me?"

It was an effort to make sense of what Lucas was saying.

"Julius?"

He forced himself to open his eyes and instantly felt searing pain over his right eyebrow.

"You were hit. You're bleeding badly."

Lucas leaned over the younger priest, peering into his face anxiously. But to Julius, he was going in and out of focus. He closed his eyes.

"Julius?"

His head throbbed.

"Julius?"

This time he opened his eyes and kept them open.

"What happened?"

"They must have been waiting for us the whole night, waiting in the trees to cut us off."

Julius fought off a wave of dizziness. The thicket of cypress where the men must have been hiding was a perfect camouflage. Of course, two or three men could stand within the curtain of their heavy foliage and appear invisible. If you didn't know they were there you would never guess to look for them.

When Julius was a boy, his father used to draw complicated pictures for him and then ask him to find the hidden bird or donkey or urn. He'd stare hard at the drawings, studying the spaces between the spaces, and sure enough, in the places where you didn't expect them, in the shapes of the emptiness, was the hidden object.

Hiding in plain sight, his father had called it.

That's what the rock throwers had done.

And that's how he and Lucas were going to save Sabina. They were going to use the shapes of the emptiness.

Chapter 31

Rome, Italy—Wednesday, 11:55 p.m.

Leo Vendi, the driver of the black SUV, left the plastic bag from Signora Volpe under the front passenger seat, got out of the car, locked it, hid the keys on top of the right tire, walked two blocks west where his motorcycle was parked, climbed on, turned his key in the ignition and sped away. He didn't think about waiting to see who was going to show up and claim the bag of papers the old lady had thrown down from Gabriella's apartment. It was late and he was tired and hungry. Leo was a pro, and if someone wanted papers left in a bag, in a parked car, in a residential neighborhood, he would deliver exactly that.

A quarter of an hour later, while Leo was eating a plate of pasta and drinking a good but cheap red wine, a man named Marco Bianci approached the black sedan, casually picked up the keys, let himself in and drove away. After he'd driven a dozen blocks he finally allowed himself to look in the passenger seat at the bag—it looked full. That was good. He hated to disappoint clients, and he'd already had one serious mishap on this job.

All that was left now was to meet the priest in front of St. Peter's after the first mass of the morning. Marco would stay in the car until then; he didn't mind. He didn't want to risk having anything happen to his bounty. The priest was going to pay him well for his trouble.

"You deserve to be generously compensated. These are crimes against our Lord, our Christ," the priest had said. "It seems like a small thing—a broken window, a pile of papers—but it's not. It is blasphemy against the will of God. Our very entrance to heaven is at risk."

Marco had bowed his head and Father Dougherty had blessed him. Then he had taken the American priest's money and arranged how the deal would go down.

Chapter 32

It is the secret of the world that all things subsist and do not die, but only retire a little from sight and afterwards return again. Nothing is dead; men feign themselves dead, and endure mock funerals and there they stand looking out of the window, sound and well, in some strange new disguise.

—Ralph Waldo Emerson

Rome, Italy—Thursday, 7:20 a.m.

Josh woke up to the ringing of the telephone but didn't answer it. The ancient vista of Rome and the conversation with Lucas were more real to him than the bed he was sleeping in. So was his headache. No, it was Julius who'd had a headache, in the dream. Josh couldn't also have one in reality.

Turning over, he tried to get back to where he'd been. There were urgent decisions Julius and Lucas still needed to make, dangers that had to be thwarted. Josh tried to conjure the landscape that had been so clear in his mind only minutes before. The orange-pink sky. The statue of Augustus. The tall cypress trees. And the problem that needed to be solved: how to save Sabina.

Was there any way to get back, or had he lost his mental grasp of the membrane that held him tethered to the dreamscape? He rubbed his eyes—the movement hurt his hands. He opened them and looked down. The scratches he'd gotten in the tunnel had scabbed over the day before. Now many of them, too many of them, were freshly opened.

Fresh blood oozed from the angry lines.

In a rush he remembered the recent past, the scene hours before, being hunted and then his hunter being hunted.

Brushing his hair off his forehead, he was careful not to touch the two-inch gash there. But there was no gash. That was part of the memory lurch. Josh was going mad. How could there have ever been any doubt? This was not some crisscrossing of who he was now and who he had been in a past life. This was his imagination spinning out of control, caused by the trauma incurred during the terrorist attack being exacerbated now by new violence. Of course it was, and the sooner he could get out of Rome and away from the endless flashbacks, the better.

No. Stay. Solve this. Save her.

He felt as if he was being wrenched through a hole in a wall that was far too small for him. Why was he chained to another time and place and to people who were long since dead? Josh didn't have an adequate way to describe the agony of being forced back to the present when every ounce of your soul says you need to stay in the past. When you are so certain that the people you love won't survive without you. If Julius didn't come for her, Sabina would think she had been abandoned. She would think she was unloved.

There is no "she." You're a lonely man whose imagination is spinning out of control.

Josh's body ached as if it had been battered. Josh's body. Julius's thoughts. His skin was so dry it felt like sandpaper. His eyes were burning, his hair was dirty, the muscles in his legs felt as if he'd run a marathon. The smell of fire was inside his nostrils.

Insanity was frightening. Josh didn't want to analyze and dissect what was happening to him anymore. He just wanted it to cease. He wanted to return to a time before the accident, with recollections that started when he was four years old and got his first camera and he and his father went out into Central Park in the snow so that he could take his first roll of pictures.

The only way to break this spell was to get out of bed and into a shower. But not even the cold water pelting his body did anything to shake the sense that he was only half awake, that part of him had been left behind in that netherworld with Sabina.

Fuck. Fuck. Fuck. This was nuts. There was no woman named Sabina. There was no past. There was only his brain, corrupted by some invisible trauma that had not yet presented itself clearly enough to be diagnosed.

Certainly, Josh had read hundreds of Malachai's and Beryl's reports of children who remembered their past lives with such accuracy that the foundation had been able to find historical proof of some of what they'd lived through. However, all the cynics said that if there was evidence, it was logical to think it had been planted rather than remembered.

Sometimes, yes. But over and over? With thousands of children? To what end?

Those kids had been tortured by their past lives. You could see that in their eyes, hear it in their breaking voices. There was no monetary gain for them or their parents. None of them or their families had ever gone public. Other than the Phoenix Foundation helping the child put the disturbing scenes to rest, not one of the three thousand children Beryl and Malachai had helped had ever tried to cash in on their experiences.

So why couldn't Josh accept that what happened to them was what was happening to him? Why wasn't it possible that something had gone terribly wrong long ago in Rome, and now, all these centuries later, he was remembering what he was not meant to remember through some accident of metaphysics?

What if this woman whose mummified body had been discovered by the professor and Gabriella *was* named Sabina? What if there had been a Roman priest named Julius whose fault it was that Sabina had suffocated to death in that small, narrow space? Wasn't that the kind of horrific event that might have karmic repercussions that would reach through time to demand retribution?

But even if he believed it all, what the hell was he supposed to do?

He turned up the water. Made it hotter.

How do you avenge a death that took place in the year 391 A.D.?

You find the body her soul now inhabits and make it up to her.

Wasn't that the thought that had been plaguing him since he woke up from the accident in the hospital?

Somewhere a woman was waiting for him and he wouldn't be himself again until he found her.

He'd been so confused and obsessed with the idea of this woman it had shredded his already-damaged marriage.

Somewhere a woman who once shared Sabina's spirit was waiting for him to help her and get it right this time.

Lust does not explain itself. There's no logic to the powerful hunger that can interrupt any single moment and render you almost helpless. Standing in the shower, water dripping off him, trying to make some sense of his messed-up life, the last thing he expected to feel was overwhelming naked need for the woman's skin—for Sabina's skin.

Leaning against the cold tiles, he shut his eyes. He tried, but failed to stop himself. His body didn't care what his mind dictated. He wanted to find her. Wanted to smell her and taste her and bury himself high up inside of her. He wanted to know her again and disappear with her into that place where passion dissipated every bit of fear and existential panic. It didn't matter if their joining ultimately doomed them. Being together was worth dying for. All that mattered was that they were connected, that their bodies crashed together again and obliterated all the pain of living in an unfair world. That for a few minutes they could find some ecstasy to succor them through the bleakness and the blackness.

In the shower stall, back up against the wall, the imaginary love-making inflamed him. He was burning up, igniting, flaring and soaring: he was with her for what always felt like the first time.

He allowed himself to say the word—her name—moaned it out loud as his blood surged through his veins and her curls fell on his face and his chest, and the jasmine in her hair scented the steamy air, and he clutched her thighs as they wrapped around him and pressed himself deeper and deeper and deeper into her, and for a time he believed it was her muscles that moved him forward, forward, forward.

Out loud, in the cry of release, came her name again.

Sabina.

The sound of the final note of a sad song played on the strings of a harp. A long, solemn note, lasting, lasting, lasting and then gone.

Chapter 33

The phone was ringing when he came out of the bathroom, and this time Josh answered it. Malachai apologized if he had woken him up, and asked Josh to meet him for breakfast in a half hour in the hotel's restaurant.

"We have plans to make," he said.

The same phrase that the Pontifex had used in the dream.

Plans to make.

"Josh? Are you there?"

There was a basket of bakery-fresh rolls on the table along with tiny dishes of jewel-colored jams and jellies and a plate of butter balls, but Josh ignored the food as he told Malachai what had happened the night before: how he'd been chased, how the thief had been shot, how the shooter had fled and about the elusive dreams of ancient Rome that had amalgamated with his waking nightmare.

Malachai, his face set in angry lines, asked Josh if he was all right. Yes. If he was sure he didn't need to see a doctor. Yes, he was sure. If he'd called the police and reported the crime. Yes, last night when he got back to the hotel. If he'd slept at all. No, not much. And then a dozen more exacting questions about what had happened.

Josh explained it all, including how the lurch had broken through and how Julius had tried to help Josh find a hiding place. When he'd finally finished answering all of Malachai's questions, he had one of his own.

"I want to know how you and Beryl authenticate the cases of reincarnation the foundation investigates."

"Why do you want to know that now?"

"I can't just keep wondering if Julius and Sabina existed. I need to find out for sure."

Malachai put down the roll he was buttering and leaned back a little in his chair. "We use all the historical data available to us. And when there isn't any we do everything we can to make sure that the child we're dealing with hasn't been coached and that his or her parents aren't trying to exploit the child. It's one of the benefits of our training as psychologists."

"But how exactly do you know these kids haven't been pre-programmed or spoon-fed their stories? Or that they're not making them up, influenced by what they've seen on television? Children understand what they hear way before they can speak or articulate for themselves. Maybe their parents believe in past-life experiences and talk about them in front of the kids—even when they're babies or toddlers."

"Maybe. We're not dealing with material objects that we can examine in concrete terms. Sometimes, we just have to trust our training, our experience." He picked up his coffee cup, sipped at it and put it down. "You're not done yet, are you? You always have more questions than I have answers."

"There's one case Beryl wrote about where a mother was convinced her daughter was a reincarnation of an earlier child who had died at a young age."

"I remember that."

"Maybe the mother was so bereft she invented the idea that the new baby had the soul of the dead daughter, and..."

Malachai pressed his lips together, just enough for Josh to notice.

"What is it?"

"Nothing, go on," the psychologist encouraged.

Josh wondered if something about the case had been a problem for Malachai, but he took the man at his word and proceeded.

"Maybe the mother told her little girl stories about the other daughter and the child intuited that she would make her mother happier if she took on those attributes and reenacted those stories. There are always other ways that these kids could have learned...that I could have learned the stories I'm seeing?"

"Of course there are other ways."

"Can all of this be wishful thinking?"

"Yes."

"That's your entire answer?"

"For now. We can go back to that if we need to. What's your next question?"

"The majority of the foundation's cases come from countries and cultures where reincarnation is part of the belief system. Why is that?"

"It's far easier for people to come forward when they know they won't be ostracized. In India, a child talking about her past life will be taken seriously. In America that same child will be told she's 'making that up.' Most people in our country can't and don't recognize past-life memories as such when they hear them, because they aren't yet aware of the possibility that's what they are." Malachai leaned forward.

"If we are going to discuss possibilities, we need to also address the one that reincarnation does exist. Let me ask you something. In the Old Testament, Moses heard voices telling him what to do. If that wasn't a metaphor—and many people believe it wasn't—then was Moses insane or did he have psychic ability? I'll give you another one. Christianity is built around Jesus being resurrected. Millions of people believe this as—pardon the pun—gospel. But what does that say about the apostles who witnessed it? Did someone who had died reappear in front of their eyes? Or was it a mystical experience? Was it wish fulfillment? Or did it really happen? I could go on and on, Josh. Almost every religion is based on experiences that scientists can't explain. Is everyone who believes wrong?"

"No, but believing may be a panacea."

"Of course it could be, it can be. You're not the first one to use Occam's razor reasoning on me. Given two equally predictive theories, choose the simpler. Yes, certainly, that's one way to deal with this."

"I just want objective proof."

"I know. You want a photograph of auras. You want to see angels dancing on the head of a pin."

"Don't patronize me."

Malachai sat back in his chair. "I'm sorry if that's how you perceived it. It's just as frustrating to me as it is to you. I thought that by now you'd experienced enough that you wouldn't be susceptible to this kind of parsing."

Before Josh could respond, Inspector Tatti arrived at their table. He wasn't expected; he hadn't called. He just showed up, pulled out a chair, sat down, waved to a waiter and ordered an espresso.

"To what do we owe this pleasure?" Malachai asked with a tone Josh didn't think he was capable of. "And how did you know where to find us?"

"I called both of your rooms. The concierge said he had not seen either of you leave. He was kind enough to phone up here and confirm you were having breakfast. It is early still, so it was logical reasoning." He looked pleased with himself as he took a sip of the coffee the waiter had just put down. "Professor Rudolfo died this morning."

Josh's reaction was instantaneous. He thought of Gabriella finding out and fought the urge to get up, go downstairs, hail a cab and rush to her side. She shouldn't be alone now. This was going to hit her hard. Of course, she'd blame him. Perhaps he deserved it. In effect it *was* his fault. He hadn't been quick enough. He'd been in the damn tunnel when he should have been in the main room of the tomb.

Malachai told the detective how sorry he was and there was no question his sympathy was heartfelt. He suddenly looked exhausted. This was a great blow to the foundation.

Josh wondered which of them felt worse. Which of them was more desperate for proof that reincarnation existed? The stones had held out hope that the robbery, and now the professor's death, had destroyed. The stones were once again legend, as much a fable as they had ever been.

"You didn't come all the way here just to tell us that, did you? What is it, Detective? What else do you want from us?" Josh asked. He was sick of talking to the police.

When he'd gotten back to his hotel the night before, he'd called Tatti, who had sent two officers who spoke passable English to the hotel to take his statement about the shooting while at the same time *carabinieri* had gone out in search of the body.

"Josh is too upset to follow the rules of polite conversation," Malachai apologized for him. "Last night was quite an ordeal, as I'm sure you can imagine. What did you find out about the man who was chasing him?"

Tatti looked up from under his lashes to stare at Josh through narrowed eyes. Instead of Clouseau, he was channeling a Pacino-type, hard-edged cop. "Nothing conclusive yet, but this is now a triple homicide and we still are in the dark about certain pieces of critical information."

"Of course you are." Malachai's voice had returned to soothing.

Josh wasn't listening anymore. Back in the tomb, he watched Professor Rudolfo fall to the ground, smelled the graphite, the blood, felt it, wet and sticky on his fingers, then saw the man who'd pulled that trigger, falling forward last night, now spilling his own blood.

"Mr. Ryder?"

He looked up. "Yes?"

"Is there anything else you can tell me about what happened in the tomb or what was taken?"

"Haven't we gone over this?"

"Yes. And now we need to go over it one more time. Will

you tell me where you were, what you saw and what it was that was taken?"

Josh repeated everything he'd told Tatti two days before.

"And you didn't see the beads?"

"No, but Professor Chase saw them. Isn't she better equipped to help you with this than I am?"

Tatti ignored the question. "How did you know that what was inside that wooden box had been stolen?"

"Because afterward, I saw the broken box on the floor and made an assumption."

"But you did not see what was in the box?"

"No." It was the damn truth. How he wished he had seen the stones.

The detective stopped to take a roll, break it apart, spear a ball of butter, spread it carefully with his knife, spoon some of the jelly onto his plate and transfer that to the roll. The inappropriate operation complete, he took a bite, chewed slowly and washed it all down with coffee. Then he resumed the interrogation.

"The two of you work for a foundation in New York, is that correct?"

Josh nodded. Malachai said yes.

"And in our first interview you told me that you, Mr. Ryder, are a photographer and you, Mr. Samuels, are a psychologist. But neither of you was very forthcoming about that, so I had one of my officers do some research and I found out what you photograph and who you work with." His eyes glittered with his cleverness. Oh, he was proud of his skill at detection. Josh badly wanted to burst his bubble and tell him anyone could have found that out online in less than two minutes.

"And..." he said, leaning forward, "I'm now certain that there is a connection between who you work for and what was taken in the crypt. Otherwise, why would you be in Rome? Why would the story of the discovery have brought you here, if not because it had something to do with the field you both study?"

Josh didn't answer—it was a rhetorical question, and the last thing he wanted to do was give the detective additional information. Malachai must have been thinking something similar, because he didn't respond, either.

"Tell me, this reincarnation that you study, isn't it antireligion?"

"Hardly," Malachai answered. "Leaders of all Western religions have conveniently forgotten that until sixteen hundred years ago reincarnation was part of all theologies, Judaism and Christianity included. It's not very threatening to the Jews and they don't preach against it, but it is very dangerous and threatening to the Church because the notion of karma steals power from the institution. Only the clergy can give absolution and offer you heaven, they say. It's unthinkable that man could be in control of his own soul, lifetime after lifetime, and achieve nirvana without their help."

Josh was becoming more and more agitated. This was taking too much time. He wanted to get to Gabriella. "What does the subject of reincarnation have to do with your inquiry, Detective?" he interrupted.

"I think reincarnation has something to do with what you expected to see in the crypt. Mr. Samuels, would you care to go first? I don't want to play games. What did you come to Rome to see?"

Malachai had a photographic memory. He'd been studying the field of reincarnation for more than fifteen years. He was obsessed with death and dying rituals, legends, myths and religious services and beliefs. For the next few minutes he regaled the detective with tales relating to bodies that had been buried without any embalming and yet had survived more or less intact. He explained the importance of these incorruptibles to certain religions that regarded such phenomena as miraculous.

"For instance, did you know that in the Catholic Church such a body is often one of the signs of sainthood?"

"Of course I know that. I live in Rome. I am Catholic." The detective nodded, but he was becoming impatient. "How is all this connected to why you are both here?"

Malachai gave him a surprised look. "Naturally, we came to see the body." As if there had been nothing else in the tomb other than the body. "For anyone interested in past-life experiences, these bodies hold endless fascination."

Tatti seemed disappointed. "Is that the only reason you two were here?"

"Yes. We had heard about the woman's condition."

"You didn't know anything about what was found in the tomb other than the body?"

Malachai shook his head. The detective turned to Josh.

"And you are sure you saw nothing when you were down there that might have been worth taking—worth killing a man for?"

"I'm sure."

Josh knew he'd been curt. He didn't care. Malachai could be the diplomat. He didn't want to sit here and be interrogated anymore. He'd had more than enough of the annoying detective. Gabriella shouldn't be alone.

"Detective," he said, "I really think you need to be talking to Professor Chase. Not us."

"I agree with you. But Professor Chase can't help me any longer."

"Why not?" Josh's mind reeled. The stones were missing. Rudolfo was dead. If something had happened to Gabriella…

Tatti plucked a second roll out of the breadbasket and was going through the endless process of dressing it first with butter, then jam, taking his time answering, waiting to see what reaction he raised from the two men opposite him. He took a bite, swallowed, and then took another. A dollop of ruby jam fell onto his white china plate.

Josh forced himself not to react, not to repeat his question and not to get up and grab the detective by his suit lapels and make him answer.

"We don't have proof of whether she left Rome on her own or if something has happened to her. We're checking the airlines now."

"Do you mean she's missing?" Josh asked.

The detective took another bite of his roll, chewed and swallowed. "Until we find her, yes, exactly. She's missing."

Chapter 34

Two *carabinieri* were on their way out of Gabriella's building when Josh and Malachai got there. Inside, they found the landlady standing in the hall beside a partially opened door, watching the last of the activity with a curious expression on her face. In broken English she answered Josh's questions, telling him that she hadn't seen Gabriella in several days and didn't know what had happened to her.

"I think maybe she just went home," she said. "No problems. Just home." She kept looking past him into the hallway, up the staircase, as if she was making sure all the police were gone.

"Is there a reason you think she went home?" Malachai asked.

"Why you two asking me all these thing? I already talked to them." She motioned to the empty hall the uniformed men had just passed through.

"Because she was here at eleven last night when I left, and if she went out after that you might have seen her go," Josh said.

She was slowly closing the door, inch by inch, as she spoke. Unmistakably wanting to get rid of them. "Not that late, no. I no see anything."

"We'd like to take a quick look around her apartment to see if she left a note for us," Malachai said, trying to press money into her hand, but she pushed him away.

"I can't let you in. The *carabinieri* told me. There will be trouble if I let anyone in."

Somewhere in the building a telephone rang. A baby cried. The hallway was hot and Josh was sweating. He could smell garlic.

"We won't disturb anything," Josh insisted. While Malachai was hoping to find something about the stones, Josh was anxious to find anything that might explain Gabriella's disappearance.

Signora Volpe backed up, shaking her head, and without any further response, closed her door on them. Josh started knocking on it, despite hearing her turn the lock.

"All we want to do is look around," he shouted.

Malachai pulled at his arm. "Come on, let's get out of here. She's not going to let us in, and we don't want to be here if the police come back."

"I don't care if they come back. Something's going on, Malachai, and I want to know what it is. What if..." He couldn't think it, much less say it, but he feared the worst.

They walked out onto the street. The gray sedan was there. Had it been there when they arrived? Josh wasn't certain.

"Wait a minute. Tatti had that car following Gabriella ever since the professor was shot. It was here when I left last night."

"If Tatti knows where she is, and he didn't tell us, he must be trying to trap us."

"Or to see who comes to her apartment for the same reasons we're here," Josh suggested.

"Well, the last thing we want is to give Tatti any additional reasons to suspect we are involved in the robbery, now that he's about to give us the go-ahead to leave Rome," Malachai warned. "Let's get out of here."

At the end of their breakfast, after the unsatisfactory interrogation, the detective had surprised them by returning Josh's passport and saying they were both free to leave the country, though he hoped Josh would agree to return if there was a trial. Malachai had immediately booked the only seats for New York that were available at such short notice, but they weren't on the same plane.

"Tatti will change his mind in a heartbeat about either of us leaving if he thinks we're holding back information or are involved as anything other than innocent bystanders," Malachai said as they walked down the street.

"You go home, then," Josh said. "I'm staying. At least until I find out where she is."

"Why does finding Gabriella matter to you that much?"

"Maybe she was seen at the site," Josh said, ignoring the question because he wasn't sure what the answer was himself.

"Josh? What's going on?"

They'd stopped for a light on the corner.

"I don't know. I can't explain it. It's just a feeling I have—" He broke off, too embarrassed by what he had been thinking to say it out loud.

Malachai guessed. "Do you think Gabriella is part of your past?"

There were no cars passing. It was quiet in the street, but Josh's whisper was still hard to hear.

"Maybe."

They found a taxi and gave the driver the site's address. As they passed through the center of the city, Josh stared at the large, pitted, gray stone stumps that seemed to fill in and rise up as tall, proud, shining columns in front of his eyes.

"My brother was murdered not far from here," he said morosely as they passed by the ancient coliseum.

"Your brother died in Rome?"

There are a few moments just as you're falling asleep, Josh thought, when, already half in a dream, you blurt out words or phrases from inside your slumber. Speaking wakes you up and you realize you've been spouting gibberish. The moment was like that for Josh.

"I don't have a brother."

"You just told me your brother was killed not far from here."

Josh couldn't focus on Malachai's voice; a tornado of fractured images was swirling in his head.

"Give me a second."

He'd been overcome so quickly he hadn't noticed the jasmine and sandalwood, but yes, it was in the air. He felt the current tugging at him, despite it being such an inopportune moment. He didn't need to be a victim of his memory, he *could* control it. But he had to choose, then or now. If he stayed in between he'd get sick. He could feel the first sparks of the migraine. Shutting his eyes, he focused on the litany Dr. Talmage had worked out with him and repeated the mantra silently:

Connect to the present, connect to who you know you are.

Josh. Ryder. Josh. Ryder. Josh Ryder.

They'd gone another two blocks when Malachai shifted in

his seat slightly and subtly turned his head, glancing out the back window.

"I think we're being followed," he said.

"By the gray sedan?"

"Yes, and I don't like it."

"It's just the *carabinieri*."

"How certain are you of that? What if it's someone sent by whoever has the stones, who thinks we know their secret or someone who has a problem with the foundation and is looking for a way to implicate us in this mess? We have enemies, you know. We're not very popular with the Church. The Catholic Church, especially. And we are in Rome."

"The professor was saying the same thing about the Church down in the tomb before...before he was shot." Josh looked out the window. After a moment, he continued. "He told me the site was getting its share of protesters from religious groups. I saw a few of them there that morning."

Outside the taxi the scenery changed as they got farther from the city and deeper into the countryside. "You know," Josh said, "if it is some crazy group, and if they killed the professor, Gabriella could have been their next target."

Chapter 35

> It is a strong proof of men knowing most things before birth, that when mere children they grasp innumerable facts with such speed as to show that they are not then taking them in for the first time, but are remembering and recalling them.
>
> —Marcus Tullius Cicero

It was raining at the site but not hard enough to discourage the crowd of three or four dozen sightseers and protesters. The grass was matted down and muddy from having been trampled. A patrol car with two officers inside sat by the side of the road like a warning sign.

Malachai and Josh circumvented the throng, trying to get a glimpse of the field and the entrance to the tomb, but the wooden lean-to was gone. On the spot where the makeshift structure had stood above the hole in the ground were flat wooden planks.

The tomb had been closed.

Josh's chest tightened. He had known loss before, but never a deprivation that was tied to so much promise.

"Hope hangs on too long sometimes," his father had told him once. They were in the darkroom. The illness had not yet felled the tall, strapping man. Josh was still in denial about the looming disease that would change both of their lives so drastically.

"With it goes possibility," Ben continued. "We can manage the darkest nights and the longest drops as long as we think someone might be waiting for us with a lamp to light our way or with a net to catch us when we fall."

Josh felt the air undulate around him and shivers shoot up and down his arms and legs. Once again, while he stood perfectly still in one dimension, he was being sucked down into that vortex where the atmosphere was heavier and thicker. He was back in the darkness, in the tunnel, unable to breathe, the panic gripping him and not letting go.

"Did you know that suffocation is supposed to be one of the most painful ways to die?" Josh asked Malachai, who put his arm around the younger man's shoulder and led him away from the field and from the crowd, toward the grove of trees beyond and behind the site.

The rain had let up. Indicating a log, Malachai said, "Sit down. You're white as a ghost. What happened to you back there?"

Josh heard his own voice as if it was coming up from underwater, miles down deep. "I couldn't breathe. For a second everything went black and I couldn't get a goddamned breath. I was on my hands and knees in that tunnel again, in total darkness, and I couldn't get out fast enough."

"Was it then or now?"

Josh shook his head. It might have been either. It didn't matter.

They sat quietly for a few minutes while Josh concentrated on the present. On where he was now. His name. The date. The time. Where the clouds were in the sky.

"I'm okay now." He stood up, but instead of heading back where the taxi was, he found himself walking toward the forest.

"Where are you going?"

"There's a stream back in here. I need to wash my face. It's healing water. I'll feel better."

Malachai stared at him the same way he had in the cab when Josh had mentioned his "brother's" murder, the way he had stared at him in his office the first day they'd met when Josh had told him a young man named Percy had once lived—and died—in the building that now housed the foundation.

"Did you walk out there the other day with the professor?"

Josh shook his head.

"How do you know what's there?"

"I've seen it." The implication was clear; he didn't need to explain it.

"How much of it do you remember?"

"More than I could back in New York. Since we've been in Rome, whole scenes from the past have been playing out in my mind."

"So you haven't walked here yet?"

"No."

"Can you tell me what we'll find, other than a stream?"

Josh shut his eyes. "Giant oaks, a pond where we bathed, a clearing covered with pine needles. A rock with a crevice in the shape of a crescent moon."

They had hiked for a quarter of a mile when, in the leafy shadows, they came up to the oaks and then the brook.

Kneeling down, Josh scooped up water and washed his face. Then he dipped his hands back into the rushing water and this time drank it down.

"What do you know about this place?" Malachai asked, amazement and curiosity mixed together in his voice.

"It was a sacred grove. A holy place and one of Julius's responsibilities. It's also where..." Josh stumbled over his words, not because he cared how he sounded but because it was still too new and too raw and he didn't trust himself to be able to talk about it without becoming emotional. Confronting these images was complicated enough without acknowledging the maelstrom of feelings they aroused. Yes, of course, the pictures that showed up in his mind were interesting, worth discussing, curious, but the loneliness they triggered, along with the guilt and the eternal longing, were unbearable.

"What's happening?" Malachai asked.

"Someone I can't see or talk to has control over me and is force-feeding me his poor, sick soul."

Next to Josh, solemnly, Malachai bent down to the water, made a cup with his hands, filled it with water and, with his eyes closed, drank it as reverently as if it were holy water and by ingesting it, he might have a vision, too.

Josh turned away.

He knew how desperately Malachai wanted to experience what he had and how much the older man envied his affliction, and it shocked him to see him like that instead of in control, clever and razor-sharp.

Coming out into the clearing, they headed back toward the

crowd for a last look around for Gabriella, even though Josh knew that with the tomb shut down, she wouldn't be here. It was a last futile effort.

A *carabiniere* was approaching, and when he met up with them he spoke quickly in Italian. From his tone and his gestures it was clear that he was chastising them and ordering them off the premises.

"We only speak English," Malachai said.

The policeman pointed toward the barricades where the field ended and the cars were parked. "Go now, please."

"We were leaving, anyway," Josh muttered, not caring what the cop picked up from his inflection. They walked back toward their waiting taxi. Everything was wet and muddy and the whole place bothered him now. He just wanted to get away. From the tomb, from Rome, from the fucking insane thoughts inside his head.

When they were three feet from the barricades a little girl of six or seven, with curly black hair and olive skin, broke free from her mother and ran right up to Josh and, throwing her arms around him, broke into tears.

Her mother came running after her, shouting her name, which was Natalie, but the little girl ignored her, holding tight to Josh as if she was trying to keep him tethered to the ground.

"Do you speak English?" Malachai asked the mother.

"Yes. Yes, I do." She had an accent but spoke very well. "I'm Sophia Lombardo." She wore jeans and a leather jacket, and she had the same black hair as her daughter and very blue eyes that were filled with concern.

"Natalie," she said as she put her hand on her daughter's shoulder. She murmured something to her in her native tongue.

The little girl jerked her shoulder away, and against his legs Josh felt her whole tiny body stiffen and her arms grip him.

"Is she all right?" Malachai asked.

"We were watching on the news this morning the report about the tomb and the terrible accident, and she became very agitated and said she wanted to come here. I said it wasn't possible—she had to go to school and I had to go to work—but she became hysterical. She never has tantrums, this was different. My husband and I became worried. I'm not a mother who gives in, but she was so upset, in so much pain, all because of the news report." Sophia was bewildered by her daughter's reaction.

"I think I can help her. Would it be all right if I talked to her?" Malachai asked. "Does she by any chance speak English?"

"Oh, yes, she is bilingual. Her father, he is British."

Malachai crouched down on his knees so that he was eye level with Natalie, murmuring in the soft, singsong voice he used with the children. "Don't be afraid, Natalie. Don't be afraid. Not you."

With each word, the sobbing slowed, and when she was calm he asked, "Tell me what's wrong. Why are you so upset?"

"She..." The sobbing started anew.

"It's all right. Go slow. I can help, I promise."

"She was...my...sister...."

"Who was, Natalie?"

"I'm not Natalie," said the little girl, who was still gripping Josh's leg.

"Who are you?"

"Claudia."

"And how old are you, Claudia?" Malachai asked.

"I'm twenty-seven."

Chapter 36

Sophia Lombardo interrupted before Malachai could stop her. "She's always played this little game that she's a woman named Claudia."

"For how long?"

"Ever since she could talk."

Malachai looked at Josh above the child's head and then back to the little girl. "So you are Claudia?"

She sobbed. "Yes."

"And what happened to your sister?"

"She was in the tomb. She was not supposed to die at all...but she did...and she never saw her baby again."

"That's very sad, and I'm sorry," Malachai said very seriously. "Was the baby all right?"

The little girl nodded her head and the curls went flying. "I took care of the baby."

"That was very good of you. Is there anything I can do to help?"

The child looked at him with some confusion. Whatever spell she'd been under broke. She let go of Josh's leg, backed up and looked down at the ground shyly, as if she were suddenly embarrassed.

"Do you remember what we just talked about, Natalie?" Malachai asked her.

She nodded.

Josh felt his camera on his chest. He wanted to look at this child through the lens, but he didn't want to scare her. He caught Malachai's attention and pointed to the Leica. Malachai whispered his request to her mother, who nodded.

"Can I ask you two or three other questions?" Malachai asked. "It would help me a lot and it might help you, too. I know many children who remember being other people. I know how to make it hurt less."

Natalie looked up at her mother, who nodded yes.

"Okay," she said quietly.

"And would it be okay if my friend took your picture? It would mean so much to me."

She looked up at Josh and beamed. The idea of him taking her picture appealed to her.

"So, do you hear Claudia's thoughts often?" Malachai asked.

"Once in a while. Mostly when I am going to sleep," she said.

Josh focused. It was there. The iridescent white light streamed off her shoulders and arced into the atmosphere, dissipating as it fanned out.

"It's wonderful that you can do that. Is there something that Claudia needs you to do for her?"

The blue eyes lifted to him, and in them was gratitude. Not

a child's appreciation. It was the look of a full-grown woman who had suffered profound loss.

Josh took her photograph before she answered Malachai, while she was just still looking at him, absorbing the offer. For a few moments he felt more like himself than he had in days. The camera connected him to who he had been before the accident. Holding equipment, doing his job, everything else fell away. The music of the machine, its clicks and whirrs, steadied him, and the disjointed zigzags of dark emotion that had been weighing him down for days lifted. In the viewfinder he could see that Natalie was relaxing, too. Keeping up a steady stream of easy dialogue with Malachai, she seemed to have forgotten the anguish of only a few minutes ago. Josh had seen this before. Malachai connected to the children he worked with in a way that really did seem like magic. Communicating with them about their pain, frustration and disturbing hallucinations, he almost always was able to soothe them.

It was a gift, Josh had told him.

Malachai had answered that if it was, it had come out of grief and wasn't worth the cost. When Josh had pressed him to explain, he'd shrugged it off. "I learned about sadness when I was too young for such a lesson, so I relate to what these children are going through."

He didn't explain what kind of sadness.

Josh and Malachai walked with Natalie and her mother back to their car. Sophia put some music on the CD player, sat Natalie in the front seat with a doll, and then stood outside with them and asked what had just happened.

Malachai stepped away with Sophia to explain, and Josh focused his camera on Natalie again. The haunted look in her eyes disappeared as she concentrated on undressing her doll and redressing her in what looked like an ancient Roman costume. The mother-of-pearl nimbus was still there.

"Natalie, come down and say goodbye like a big girl," Sophia said after she'd finished talking to Malachai.

Natalie climbed out of the car, shook Malachai's hand and thanked him. He pulled a small silk frog out of their handshake and delighted her with it as a gift. "How did you do that?" she asked, starry-eyed.

"It's magic," he smiled.

Josh hadn't seen the trick coming. He was never looking in the right place at the right time.

The little girl turned to Josh to show him the toy. As soon as her eyes rested on him they filled with tears and the smile disappeared from her face.

Malachai knew what had just happened before Josh did. "Natalie?" he asked.

She shook her head.

"You're Claudia now?"

"Yes. And my sister…my sister…" She was crying hard now and couldn't get the words out at all.

"What happened to your sister? It's okay to tell me. Maybe I can help you," Malachai said, but Natalie was focused on Josh, who leaned down to her level.

"What was your sister's name?" Josh whispered.

"Sabina," she said. "And she can't breathe."

The small voice was a child's, but in his ears the one word sounded like a volcanic explosion spewing forth and burying him under its white-hot lava.

"That was a long time ago, Claudia. She's at peace now," Malachai said.

Natalie was still looking up at Josh. “We loved her so much, didn’t we?” she said to him.

“Yes, we did,” he whispered, shivers creeping over every inch of his skin.

Chapter 37

Rome, Italy—Friday, 3:25 p.m.

Josh collected the bouquet of flowers, bottle of wine and two giant stuffed animals that he'd asked the concierge to procure for him while he was packing and got into the waiting town car he'd ordered. He had a pilgrimage to make on his way to the Fiumicino airport.

The stop was only a fifteen-minute detour, but he gave himself an extra ninety minutes so he wouldn't need to rush.

Under a grape arbor, the girls were having what appeared to be a tea party with their dolls, but they stopped to stare at him as he got out of the car with the gifts and started up the walk. They didn't recognize him, but then he hadn't expected them to. It had been more than a year since he'd come to their house after the funeral on what must have been the saddest day of their lives.

"Mama! Mama!" the smaller of them called as she ran ahead to announce the visitor's arrival. As he approached, the elder sister, Dianna, eyed him suspiciously and positioned herself to the left of the door almost as if she were, ironically he thought, standing guard.

Tina greeted him warmly and then told both her daughters that it was all right and to go back outside—or at least that was what Josh thought she said with his limited knowledge of Italian. Cecelia made a move to leave, then stopped, turned around and asked her mother a question. Tina laughed, reached into a cabinet, pulled out a box of cookies and handed it to her.

"She is too smart and knows just when I am too busy for an argument."

Sitting at the kitchen table while Tina fetched a vase and filled it with water, Josh asked how she was doing. She used a combination of gestures and accented English to tell him that things were getting better, blushing a little when she said it.

"I'm glad for you. And for the girls, too. To hear their mama laugh sometimes."

Arranging his flowers, she pushed an iris in front of two pink tulips. "I think about him every morning, every night and ten times between, but I don't always cry. What surprises me, though, is how sometimes I still forget. One of the girls will do something and I'll think that I can't wait till Andreas gets home from work to tell him."

"Sometimes I still pick up the phone to call my father to tell him something—and he died almost twenty years ago." He frowned. "I'm not sure that was the right thing to tell you. I'm sorry."

"No, it is fine." She positioned the vase in the middle of the table and then offered Josh wine or coffee. He said he'd love some coffee and she turned on the espresso machine.

"And you? You are better, too, no?" she asked.

"Yes. Much better, thank you."

She turned away from her preparations and faced him, studying him for a few moments. Then she shook her head. "Not all better, though. It's still in your eyes. I know what happened that day only from being told. I didn't actually see it. I think in some ways you have it worse."

Andreas Carlucci had been the security guard at the checkpoint right outside the Vatican, who had been caught in the blast that had almost claimed Josh's life. The two of them were at the same hospital, in rooms next to each other. Tina had stayed at her husband's side during the week he fought for his life, and every evening before she left to go home to her girls, she would stop by to see Josh. Swimming in and out of his drug-induced haze he would look up and see her, an angel standing by his bed, her long black hair framing her face, head bowed, eyes closed, whispering a prayer for his recovery.

Josh was released the day before Andreas's funeral, and although he was still dizzy and in constant pain, he'd gone to pay his respects. It was the first time, but not the last, that he'd wondered whether, with two children and a wife, it might have been better if Andreas Carlucci had been the one to make it.

The same thought occurred to him now, watching her as she poured the coffee.

"It was nice of you to come and visit," she said as she handed him a cup. "Are you in Rome for work?"

He nodded. "My first time back."

"How was it? Did you have any—" She broke off, not sure of the words in English. "Backflashes?"

"Flashbacks?" He smiled but avoided the question. "Do you and the girls need anything?"

She shook her head. "We have his pension, plus I have gone back to work part-time. My parents help me out with the girls, who like having them around."

"They look wonderful. I was thinking, before I leave, would you like me to take pictures of them? Of all three of you?"

Josh photographed the two girls and their mother in their garden with the afternoon sunshine shining down on them. At first the children were shy, but after he gave them their stuffed animals they relaxed and started having fun, laughing and posing and losing all inhibitions.

"Do you have pictures of our father from before the accident?" Dianna asked him suddenly.

Josh hadn't thought she knew who he was.

"I do, yes. I have several."

"Can we have them, please?"

"Of course. I should have thought of it before now," Josh said, including Tina in his response. "I'll send them as soon as I get home."

And then Dianna picked up her doll and resumed playing with her sister.

All the shots Josh had taken in the seconds before the bomb exploded featured Andreas arguing with the woman who turned out to be a suicide bomber, insisting she let him inspect the baby carriage. No one in the family would get much joy from seeing how aggravating his last conscious moments had been.

"One minute they're playing, the next inconsolable and then back to playing. Kids bounce back so fast," Josh said to Tina as she walked him out to the waiting car.

"I think it's because they aren't afraid of grief the way we are. . . ." Her eyes filled with tears.

"I'm sorry. Maybe my coming here wasn't a good idea after all."

"No. It was a very good idea. And a very kind one. I am glad to see you. So what if I cry? I always knew that Andreas's job was dangerous. I was afraid that if he died, I would die, too. Now that I've found out I can live without him, I am not scared of so much."

Josh didn't know what to say. But Tina did. She took both his hands in hers, bowed her head, closed her eyes and intoned the words that had sounded like music to Josh when he had first heard them in his hospital room as he swam in and out of the pain medication, and sounded like music to him still.

Chapter 38

Flight 121 left Rome two hours late, at four-thirty in the afternoon. During takeoff, the seventy-year-old man in seat 29B sat hunched over his worn Bible, reading page after page of the Book of Genesis. The man next to him gave him a few curious looks and then tried to ignore him, but every once in a while he looked back. When the plane had been airborne for forty minutes, just as dinner was served, an announcement asked Mr. Meyerowitz to identify himself. At first he was startled to hear the voice saying his name in front of all these people. He felt his heart lurch inside his rib cage. Then he remembered he'd ordered the kosher meal and this was routine. He turned on his seat's call button, and minutes later a sweet-looking brunette with very red lipstick brought him a boring and bland dinner of dried-out chicken and watery vegetables.

When she came to take the tray away, he was polite and circumspect to her.

"Would you like some coffee, Mr. Meyerowitz?"

He wanted to tell her he wasn't hard of hearing and that she didn't have to lean forward and articulate so carefully, but instead he just nodded. "I would very much like some tea. With sugar."

After he finished his tea, the man took a break from the Bible to nap, but he slept fitfully. Under the blanket he gripped his briefcase, and he kept waking up to look at his watch and check the time.

It wasn't doing any good to keep checking. They would land when they landed. If he was a magician he'd make the flight take one hour instead of eight—but he'd still be just as nervous. If he could just relax and concentrate on being calm. He was prepared. He knew all the rules and regulations. Nothing would go wrong. Closing his eyes again, he focused on lowering his heart rate and evening his breathing. Within minutes his nerves had smoothed out.

The plane landed on time, and he shuffled through the airport. He felt dirty. His long black coat, baggy black pants and white shirt were wrinkled and smelled stale. Being unkempt displeased him, and the way people stared at his clothes, beard and peyos was annoying to him. Orthodox Jews often drew sidelong glances even in New York City, despite there being such a large population of them there, but it was still unsettling to feel eyes following him in the line, staring at the hair on his face and at his clothes.

But the visibility would work in his favor; he knew that. It was just that he preferred the pristine priest's cassock as a disguise.

The immigration line took more than an hour, even though

he was an American citizen with a valid passport. Everyone around him looked sleepy. Although he was wide awake, he faked one yawn, and then another, going over his mental checklist of all the possible questions and his answers. Yes, he was prepared.

But he was also worried. He couldn't help it.

Too much had gone into this plan. Too much depended on it.

Too much had gone wrong already.

Finally it was his turn to go through Customs. He presented his tax declaration along with his opened briefcase to the man in uniform whose name tag read Bill Raleigh.

"Will you open this pouch for me?" Raleigh asked, pointing to a navy felt bag after reading the customs declaration.

Meyerowitz opened it and pulled out six smaller felt pouches.

"Open this one," Raleigh said, pointing.

Like a mantra, Meyerowitz kept thinking one thought over and over as he unwrapped the stone and laid it out for inspection.

The United States has no import duties on loose gemstones.

The United States has no import duties on loose gemstones.

The United States has no import duties on loose gemstones.

He was pleased his fingers weren't shaking. Anyone's would, he thought. Even if they hadn't done anything wrong. Just being questioned was nerve-racking. But Meyerowitz stayed calm. He hadn't expected any problems. He knew the rules. Only gemstone imports from certain countries were prohibited, and from his passport it was clear he had not been in Myanmar, Cuba, Iran, Iraq or North Korea.

He laid the sapphire gingerly on a yellow pad in his briefcase.

Raleigh barely glanced at it as he next pointed to a small white envelope. "And that packet along with your receipts?"

Meyerowitz opened it, pulled out a folded sheet of tissue paper, unfolded it and revealed seven small loose diamonds, each less than one and one-half carats. Then he reached into a pocket on the inside of the briefcase and withdrew two sheets of paper that constituted the invoice for all the stones.

"And what is in these pouches?"

"Those are fake pieces I picked up in Rome. Good quality. My brother-in-law does costume. I wanted him to see."

"Can you open them, please?"

He shrugged. "Why not?" he said as he opened them and pulled out cheap imitation Gucci necklaces with their faux precious stones.

Despite the law, despite the fact that everything was in order, something concerned the customs official enough for him to call over a supervisor. It took the second man thirty seconds to complete his walk across the room, and by the time he reached them, Meyerowitz's heart was beating so hard in his chest he was worried they might hear it. He focused on relaxing himself. Any sign that he was overly concerned would be detected by the trained guard.

There is no reason to worry. There is nothing illegal about what you are doing. Breathe. In. Breathe. Out. They are just being cautious. They fear terrorists and check random people constantly. This is routine.

But what if Interpol has put out a report? What if someone is looking for this cache of jewels? What if the precious gems and diamonds didn't disguise the real treasures? What if he said the wrong thing? What if they confiscate the stones? No, remember, no one has seen the stones but the two professors. The police don't necessarily know what they are looking for.

"Are you Mr. Irving Meyerowitz?"

"Yes, I am."

"Your profession?"

"I am a jeweler."

"Where do you work?"

"Here. Here in New York. On West Forty-Seventh Street. Number ten."

"And what was the purpose of your trip abroad?"

"It was a buying trip."

The official was square-faced with pockmarked skin, and smelled slightly of tobacco. His fingers were thick and stubby and also graceless as they examined the dozen gems and the papers.

Meyerowitz tried not to contemplate the possibility that something was going wrong or the power of this petty official who was capable of ruining everything.

Behave normally.

"Is there a problem?" he asked with a slight irritation in his voice. This was in character. Who wouldn't ask this? He hadn't done anything wrong, after all. He was acting within the law; he knew that.

"Just a minute, please." The guard read the rest of the receipts.

He read the man's name tag. "Mr. Church? I don't understand what the issue could be?"

"Do you have anything else to declare?" Church asked.

"No. Just what is here."

"Do you have—"

There was a loud noise behind them. Everyone turned. A man had tripped over a suitcase and fallen onto a metal cart. He seemed to be hurt; blood poured out of his nose. He screamed out in pain. Everyone looked over—Raleigh, Church, all the people in line. No one was paying attention to Meyerowitz anymore. He wanted to grab the gems and run out of the terminal. But that would be foolish.

Church gave quick instructions to Raleigh as he walked off toward the accident. "Let him through."

Outside, Meyerowitz tried to walk slowly, not to rush, not to draw any attention to himself as he headed for the taxi stand where he got in line, cursing over how long it was. He wished that he'd hired a car to greet him. But that would have left too much of a trail. A limo driver wasn't like a taxi driver. A limo driver would pay too much attention to the old man. He'd remember where he dropped him off. As it was, Meyerowitz would need to take one cab somewhere that he could use a men's room so he could change before feeling safe enough to take another to go home.

It wasn't until he was safely in the cab that he allowed himself to wonder what had alerted Raleigh? He went over every step of the interrogation again. All routine. No, it couldn't have been anything he'd said. Was it something he'd done?

He shifted in the seat, smoothed out his black coat, felt the coarse wool, thought about how glad he'd be to get out of these foul clothes. And that's when he realized his mistake.

It was Friday night.

Remember the Sabbath and to keep it holy.

No Orthodox Jew would travel on the Sabbath.

How could he have been so stupid?

Chapter 39

New Haven, Connecticut—Saturday, 11:19 a.m.

Gabriella Chase sat on the floor of her office, surrounded by a maelstrom of books, papers and wet leaves that were blowing in with the wind and the rain through the open window.

She'd thought she'd feel safer at home, thought that she'd left the fear on the ground in Rome when she'd boarded the plane to bring her back. And in fact, last night, sleeping under the same roof as her father and her daughter, she had felt as if the worst of the crisis was behind her. But now, looking around her, at the clear signs of the intrusion, at the details of the chaos, she realized she'd been wrong. There wasn't anywhere she could go that would be safe until whoever had done this had found what he wanted.

Unless he already had.

The wind picked up and howled. The window. She needed to shut the window. But she wasn't sure she could get up yet.

"Professor Chase?"

She twisted around. Two men in campus security uniforms were standing at the door. She recognized the older one but couldn't think of his name. How was that possible? He'd been working here since before she had.

Think.

Think.

Her eyes, usually bright with curiosity, were dull and her hair, usually wild but winsome, was tangled and matted.

The guard she knew walked over to her. "Are you all right?"

She focused on him and his question. "Yes. I'm fine, Alan." Yes, that was his name. Alan. And the other guard was Lou.

With a bang, the window crashed into the sill.

The noise alarmed Alan and almost made him jump, but Gabriella seemed unaffected.

"It does that," she said in a bland voice. "I keep meaning to have the janitor fix it." She was still sitting on the floor.

Alan put his arm around the professor's back and helped her up. She was so easy to lift; there was no resistance. As he led her to the chair behind her desk, she started visibly shivering. After she sat down, he looked around, found a sweater on the back of her door that had been far enough away from the window to still be dry, and draped it around her.

"Professor Chase, what happened here?" Lou asked. "Can you tell us?"

"I don't know. I was in the library. I just got back five minutes ago." She looked at her watch. Shook her head. "No, almost fifteen minutes ago. Everything was like this. All over the place. Blowing everywhere. I tried to catch the papers. All my papers. Years of papers. The window must have been open awhile.

There's water on the floor. I didn't see it and slipped. I hit my knee on the desk..." She brushed her damp hair back off her face.

"I don't imagine you know yet if anything was taken," Lou said.

She shook her head. "No. I don't know. I can't—" She indicated the mess around her. "It's such a mess. I don't know where to start. But I'm okay. Really."

"I think we should call the New Haven police and report this ASAP," Lou said, and opened his cell phone.

Ten minutes later, Officer Mossier, a very serious but baby-faced policeman showed up with his partner, Officer Warner, an older cranky veteran.

Mossier took out his notebook and started asking Gabriella what had happened since she'd come back to the office.

"Was the door locked when you got back?"

"Yes."

"Had it been locked when you left?"

"Yes."

"Were the windows locked when you left?"

"I don't know."

"Do you normally lock the windows?"

"No...not often."

"What about today?"

"I'm not sure."

"Do you have any idea what's missing?"

"I have years of files in this office." She gestured to the soggy mess of papers littering the floor. "But I don't know why anyone would want them."

"Do you have a disgruntled student from last semester? From the summer session?"

"No. Yes. Well, there are always students who are upset by marks they get on papers, but there's no one I can think of who would be this upset...." She shook her head and hair fell onto her face. She pushed it away again. "No, no student that I can think of."

"What do you teach?"

"Archeology."

"You go on digs?" Mossier asked.

Gabriella nodded.

"Now, that's something I always wanted to do. Go on a dig. I've done some spelunking and always thought that—"

Warner interrupted. "Was there anything you had in here from a dig? Any antiquities? Something worth breaking in for?" He looked around at the shelves, which were mostly filled with books and framed photos.

"Nothing of any value, no. Some shards of pottery, some pieces of glass, but debris, mementos, that's all. Nothing of real value..."

Mossier didn't seem to pay attention to how she'd let the rest of the sentence drift off, but the senior cop did.

"We'll write this up. Ask around and find out if anyone witnessed anything. In the meantime, I'd like you to try to put your papers back in order in the next few days, and if you notice anything amiss, will you let us know?"

"Yes."

"Are you all right? Would you like us to drive you home, or to the hospital?"

She nodded. "No. I'm okay, but thank you."

"Is there anyone we could call to come and get you? I don't think you should be alone just yet," Mossier said.

She nodded. "My father."

* * *

It only took Professor Peter Chase less than ten minutes to get to his daughter's office. Rushing in, he ignored the police and went straight to Gabriella.

He was an older man with heavy jowls, a thick head of white hair and intense, and alarmed, dark eyes. "What happened?"

As soon as she saw him she started to cry. Not loud sobs; rather, tightly controlled, quiet weeping, but the tears fell quickly, wetting her cheek in a matter of seconds.

Peter pulled out a handkerchief, gave it to her and put his arm around her. Over her head he looked at the two policemen and asked them if they'd stay for a few minutes longer since he had some questions he'd like to ask them. "I'm Professor Chase. I'm Gabriella's father," he said, forgetting for the moment that they'd called him at Gabriella's request. "Have you figured out what happened here?"

Warner took over. "Not yet, sir, but we're going to do the best we can to find out."

"And in the meantime, what are you going to do to protect her?"

"We're going to do everything we can to figure out what happened here," Officer Warner repeated.

"Do you have a daughter?"

"Yes, sir."

"Hold old is she?"

"I have two. One is twelve, the other is fifteen."

"Would that be a good enough answer for you if this happened to one of them? *Everything we can to figure out what happened here?* What about telling me how you're going to protect her?"

"If you knew how seriously I take my job, you'd know that it is enough."

"Can't you put a detail on her?"

"Not unless someone has threatened her, sir. I wish I could."

"So do I, damn it." The professor tried to stare him down and intimidate him, but the officer wasn't flinching. It was a standoff. Finally Gabriella broke the silence.

"Dad, let them go. I'm not in danger. No one wants me. Just something that they thought was in here."

"How do you know that?" her father asked.

Officer Warner was on the threshold but turned around, alerted.

"I don't know it for sure. But it certainly appears that way, doesn't it?" She looked from her father to the two policemen. "I appreciate your help. Will you let me know if you find out anything?"

Warner didn't leave.

It looked as if he was waiting to hear Gabriella's answer to her father, but she wasn't going to talk in front of him.

"Thank you," she repeated to Warner.

The cops had no choice. They left.

Once the door closed after them, the elder Professor Chase repeated his question. "How do you know that no one is after you?"

He waited. In the silence, he faintly heard two sets of footsteps retreating.

"Gabriella?" he insisted.

"I know because the same thing happened to my apartment in Rome. Someone broke in the last night I was there. That's why I left."

"Why didn't you tell me that before now?" her father asked, his voice straining.

She shrugged.

"Was anything taken in Rome?"

"A notebook. Some photographs."

"What the hell have you gotten yourself mixed up in?" her father asked.

"Something very old, Dad. Something very powerful. Or at least that's what we think. What we thought. No, not we… me… Rudolfo is gone… What I think."

Last night, once she had checked on her daughter, once she had changed into jeans and an old, comfortable sweatshirt that had belonged to her husband, and poured herself a vodka and tonic, once she'd filled her father in on what had happened in Rome—or at least most of it—she'd gone into the room that doubled as her home office and library combined and rifled through a drawer, looking for a card that she'd kept there for the past three and a half years.

Nervously she picked up the phone, noticed her hand was shaking and hung up. She'd thought about making this call before but had never followed through. As curious as she'd been, she hadn't wanted to risk the dig and who knew what might happen if she contacted the priest who'd brought her the site plans. After everything that had gone wrong in those past few years, it had felt so good to be excited about something again, she hadn't wanted anything to spoil the thrill of the excavation.

But that was all over now.

Several times after that snowy Sunday four years before when Father Dougherty had first given Gabriella the papers in the Battle Chapel, Rudolfo had wanted her to get in touch with Father Dougherty and plead with him to show them the rest of the journal.

There are so many unanswered questions, Rudolfo had said.

Now there were more. Too many more.

Her hand shook as she dialed the number. The phone rang three times before it was answered by a friendly voice who identified himself as Father Francis and asked how he could help her.

"My name is Gabriella Chase. I'm sorry to call so late, but could I talk to Father Dougherty, please?"

"Father Ted Dougherty?"

"Yes."

"Oh, he's no longer with us."

"Can you tell me where I could reach him?"

"Hopefully in heaven, my dear. Father Dougherty died."

"Oh, I'm sorry. That's terrible. When did he die?"

"Let's see, it was seven, no, it was eight years ago now."

"Eight years ago? Are you sure?"

"Yes, of course. I gave him last rites myself."

Chapter 40

New York City—Saturday, 8:10 p.m.

When Rachel Palmer arrived at the opening gala at the Metropolitan Museum, the building was ablaze with spotlights as tuxedo-clad men and women in chic evening gowns moved up the grand staircase. The flag flying above the stone entrance announced the show: "Tiffany Jewels—the First Century."

Inside, Rachel stopped in the entranceway to the American Wing, mesmerized by the three-story gallery decorated for a party. Candles flickered and cast a soft glow, the air was scented with the roses that graced every table, and a six-piece orchestra filled the room with cool jazz. Waiters in formal attire passed trays of champagne and canapés.

Rachel stopped in front of a huge marble sculpture that she'd seen a hundred times before but had never really noticed. Two men were fighting, caught in a clash of wills. Her eyes traveled over their sinewy thighs and arms, their twisted torsos and their pained but proud expressions. She sucked in her breath and held it for a moment.

They were so powerful. She longed to reach out and run her fingers down their satin skin and feel the well-defined muscles. By her side, her fingers itched. She looked at their groins, which were modestly desexualized, and yet she thought the marble men were more arousing than any of the flesh-and-blood men she had met in the past few years. She felt the oddest surge of physical excitement. She had a strong desire to kiss their marble lips and see if she could bring one of them to life. What would happen if she stepped up on the pedestal and did that? Probably be arrested, she thought. Her eyes dropped to the bronze placard beneath the white marble sculpture.

Struggle of Two Natures of Man
George Grey Barnard (1863-1938)
Marble, 1894
First called "I feel two beings within me,"
the work represents the forces of good and evil.

Her heart raced inside her chest and chills raced down her back as she reread the date. 1894. But why the shiver of fear? What had happened in 1894?

A waiter passed with a tray full of glasses, but she let him go by. She wanted a drink—not the silly champagne they were serving, but a real drink. Walking toward the bar, she saw a man lounging there, his back to her.

He was instantly familiar although she couldn't place him. She examined the long, lean body, the way he slouched, as if he was at home in the rarefied museum. Something about him made her angry. She wanted to get away from him, and at the same time, she was afraid of losing sight of him.

A couple strolling by obscured him, and by the time they passed by, he was gone. Rachel looked around, but he really seemed to have vanished.

Panic rose in her like bile.

No. She couldn't lose him again.

Again?

That didn't make any sense.

"What would you like?" the bartender asked, not looking up, not particularly interested in his next customer. It was a fancy gig, not a local bar; he wasn't required to make conversation with these guests.

"The best Scotch you have. Two ice cubes. No water. Please."

It was the "please" that made the bartender stop for just a minute, to look up, to smile at her, to take his time, to enjoy pouring her a drink, just the right amount with exactly as many ice cubes as she asked for.

Six more people descended on the bar. He handed Rachel her Scotch and regretfully attended to the other requests.

The couple standing next to her was talking about an article that would appear in the next morning's *New York Times.* Clearly, they were curators.

"Rudolfo was buried today, did you hear?"

"It's a real tragedy."

"Still no word on what was stolen?"

"No. There are rumors pagan objects were found that could be of major significance."

"Any specifics?" the woman asked.

"None. But the last time he was interviewed a reporter asked Rudolfo if it was true that the objects might challenge some basic precepts of Christianity. He came back with, 'I'm a very religious man, I certainly hope not.'"

Nearly every ancient excavation included jewelry, and Rachel had often taken inspiration from Roman, Greek and Egyptian finds, but every time she heard about the treasures at this site she reacted strangely, as if it were imperative that she see them.

Feeling dizzy, she held on to the bar. Something they'd said had struck a chord that resonated within her. The hum started. Her body throbbed. She shut her eyes. Colorful flashes strobed behind her eyes. No, she couldn't let this happen here, or now, and so, forcing her eyes open, she looked around to center herself.

She should leave before it was too late, she thought.

Too late for what?

This was crazy.

Sipping the Scotch, Rachel heard the sound of ice in her glass clinking against the crystal and wondered why it sounded threatening. The first taste stung the back of her throat, the second went down more smoothly, and as she took a third she scanned the crowd. Her eyes settled on the man who had been by the bar, who looked so familiar.

"There you are," her uncle Alex said as he came up behind her and kissed her softly on her cheek. He was in his early sixties but looked younger. Impeccable in his tuxedo, he exhibited no signs of jet lag or fatigue from his recent trip.

"I wasn't sure you were going to make it," she said.

"I couldn't miss this opening," he said warmly, and asked the bartender for the same drink his niece was having.

A patron of the museum, he was also on its board of directors, and several pieces from his wife's collection of Tiffany jewels were on display that night. "Nancy would have loved to see this," he said, surveying the room, a twinge of melancholy in his voice.

"Yes, she would have."

They both sipped their drinks. "Have you seen Davis yet?" Alex asked, his voice slightly huskier than normal.

"No. But I'm sure he'll find me sooner or later."

"And that bores you?"

"Do I sound bored?" Rachel tried for a smile but it didn't mask the lackluster look in her eyes.

"You do, dear. Are you?"

"I suppose so, but I'll live."

"You might as well be one of these stone sculptures," Alex mused out loud. "Immune to falling in love. No one has ever made your eyes shine the way a stunning unset gem can."

"Stop worrying."

"One day you will stop believing in the possibility of heroes, accept the reality of the people you meet, deal with their limitations and learn to make the best of it."

"Why should I do that? You didn't. Aunt Nancy didn't."

Alex chortled. "I see Davis over there. Let's go and congratulate him."

The curator stood in front of the facade of the Long Island home of Louis Comfort Tiffany, which had been transplanted to the museum in the 1980s. He was talking to a man whose back was to them, the two of them framed by the wisteria-festooned stained-glass arch.

Although she could only see the other man's back, Rachel

knew it was the same man she'd been noticing all night, the one she was tying to find and at the same time trying to stay away from. But how could she recognize him just by the way he stood and the tilt of his head when she didn't know him?

Rachel's instinct was to turn and walk away, but she was nothing if not logical, and this irrational thought was an anathema to her. So, arm in arm with her uncle, she approached.

"Rachel Palmer, Alex Palmer, this is Harrison Shoals," Davis said, making the introductions.

Rachel was in front of the warm light; it rocked her, and she heard the humming. She focused on her uncle. He looked slightly displeased, but he wasn't acting as if reality was breaking apart and fragmenting.

"Actually, Mr. Shoals and I have met before," Alex was saying as he thrust out his hand to Harrison, who shook it. "Nice to see you again, Harrison." But he didn't sound as if it was nice at all. He turned to Rachel. "Harrison is the dealer who won the Bacchus from us at the auction." From his tone, he still regretted it.

Rachel reeled as she processed this information. This was the man who had bought her painting?

"It's a pleasure to see your generosity on display," Harrison responded in a charming, polished voice.

"I'd be a liar if I didn't admit that one of the pleasures of collecting is showing off how smart you were to buy when you did."

Rachel heard their conversation louder than it was. The phrase, *a liar,* reverberated in her head, and she was still thinking about it when Harrison turned to her and offered his hand.

With what seemed like an excruciating effort, she reciprocated. His eyes were a frosty green, the color of the sea in the winter. And then their fingers met.

Alex and Davis were discussing the jewelry on display, which the curator was trying to convince the collector to permanently loan to the museum, and she didn't think either of them noticed the surprise on Rachel's face or the confusion on Harrison's as they touched.

The searing heat soldered their flesh together. It was so real and immediate that both of them, at the same time she found out later, thought of the phrase "spontaneous combustion," but neither said it out loud.

Harrison Shoal's eyes looked worried. For her? For himself?

Rachel felt a gut-wrenching pull so strong, she wondered if she had stepped forward, but no, there was still a good twelve inches separating them.

Then that damned humming returned. She tried to fight it. To hold on to her equilibrium. To stop herself from slipping into the warm void. To resist. Her vision clouded, just for a second. When it cleared it was as if the tears that had filled her eyes had been blown away by a wind.

The room was darker than it had been only moments before. The candlelight shimmered with a phosphorescent glow. The atmosphere grew warmer, and the scent of the roses intensified into a heady perfume that made her dizzy. It was becoming hard to breathe, harder still to stand up.

The song the band was playing segued into a slow, seductive waltz. The air undulated and wavered, and it seemed to Rachel she was looking through a blaze.

This man was dancing with her, and where his arms touched

her body she felt she was being indelibly marked by his fingertips. As he moved her around the room, her body screamed where she was in contact with him.

People around her were talking in Italian. She wasn't in the museum anymore. This was a grand palace in a foreign country. She could see the tips of her shoes; they weren't the silver sling-backs she'd put on earlier that evening but kid boots, and her gown was now rose-colored and swept the floor. She felt air on the back of her neck where her hair was pinned up…but she never wore it up.

"We must keep the secret for a while longer. Will you promise to do that? Otherwise, it might be dangerous."

Suddenly frightened, she nodded.

He spun her around and the room streaked by, a haze of colors. And then she blinked and everything—the lights, the music, the scent of the flowers—returned to the way it had been before. She touched her own cheek, needing to understand the sudden fever she felt, but her skin was cool to the touch.

Chapter 41

> But it sometimes happens that the Angel of Forgetfulness himself forgets to remove from our memories the records of the former world and then our senses are haunted by fragmentary recollections of another life. They drift like torn clouds above the hills and valleys of our mind and weave themselves in the incidents of our current existence.
>
> —Sholem Asch, The Nazarene

New York City—Monday, 7:15 a.m.

The sky was gray and menacing—matching Josh's mood. Leaving his apartment on West Fifty-Third Street, he walked four blocks uptown, and entered Central Park through Merchants' Gate at Columbus Circle and continued north, waiting for some of his anxiety to lessen. For the past four months, before his trip to Rome, this morning walk to the Phoenix Foundation had been one of the few things that calmed him. A few hundred yards in, he stopped and breathed in deeply, smelling the freshly cut grass and the heavy humidity, but his sense of unrest didn't lessen.

What had happened in Rome had put him in danger—danger that might have followed him home and had raised too many questions. Where were the stones? What were they capable of? Why had the thief been killed? By whom? What had happened to Gabriella?

While he was still in Rome, he'd tried to reach her but could only get the number for her office at Yale, and although he'd left messages there, he hadn't heard back. He'd tried several more times since returning home but still hadn't made contact, which had exacerbated his anxiety.

Josh hurried past a row of weeping pine trees that stood like ominous sentinels along the paths. He was rushing, but didn't have to. The foundation was only a mile's walk, at this rate he'd reach it before eight, which was still too early to start making phone calls and locate her.

At West Drive near Strawberry Fields, Josh turned right toward the bridle path, a rarely used area of the park with little pedestrian traffic since so few people went horseback riding, especially on a weekday morning. If he had the time, Josh always took this detour so he could walk by the Riftstone Arch.

In the mid-1800s, when Fredrick Law Olmstead had sculpted the park out of rampant woodlands, he'd brought in several architects to work on the project. One of them, Calvert Vaux, had built Riftstone in 1862 using Manhattan schist stone and created one of the park's few bridges that appeared to be a natural arch. Big outcroppings of boulders, tall trees and overgrown shrubs concealed the brick supports that held it up, and the sloping hillside on either side obscured its elevations.

When he was a kid, Josh had visited every area of the park, including this one, but rediscovering the arch on one of his first walks to the foundation, he'd discovered it was now a trigger. Walking here in the past few months, he'd had several lurches that threw him back to the late nineteenth century and into encounters with a young man named Percy Talmage who'd often come here with his sister, Esme. First, as children, to play and later, as young adults, to get away from the untenable atmosphere in their home. Unlike Josh, they didn't walk through the park to find the arch. The Talmages reached the Riftstone Arch by way of a hidden passage built into the rocks that led to a tunnel connecting the park to their home: the building that now housed the Phoenix Foundation.

At their first meeting, Malachai had been taken aback when Josh told him he knew about Percy and Esme. Beryl less so. When it came to past life experiences and present-life incidents there were no coincidences. But then, when Josh had described the tunnel, even she had been astounded. There was nothing on record or in the architectural drawings of either the mansion or the park that included the secret underground thoroughfare that had collapsed on itself sometime in the early 1920s and had been closed up.

Several times, Josh had tried but failed to locate the entrance to the tunnel somewhere near the arch.

Percy's memories of being there with Esme, though, were not as difficult to find.

* * *

Malachai was on the phone when Josh stuck his head in his office doorway, but he motioned for Josh to come in and sit down.

While he waited for the call to end, Josh noticed an antiquarian book lying on the large partners desk, light from the green glass lamp illuminating the gilt lettering on the cover: *Breakthroughs in Translife Detection.*

Opening it, he almost thought he could hear sighs escaping. How long had it been since these pages had been exposed to the air?

Breakthroughs in Translife Detection
By Christopher Drew
First Edition
1867
Ackitson and Kidd Publishers
New York City

The first page had extensive water damage, but Josh had no trouble reading from the introduction.

In the history of mankind, never before has there been a less spiritual age. Never before have we paid so little attention to the soul. Never have we been more obsessed with the material world and less connected to the metaphysical one. The result is a generation of unhappy men who disguise their melancholy with the quest for power and material wealth.

The questions of who we are cannot be asked without first asking who we were. Not to do so is to walk away from the past knowledge that has future implications. What this book aims to do is help the reader to discover his past so that he can—

"I'm sorry that took so long," Malachai said as he hung up. "How was your trip back?"

Josh filled him in and then asked him the same question.

"I took a sleeping pill and dreamed about gladiators." Malachai smiled, and without asking poured Josh a cup of coffee. "You look like you could use this."

Josh sipped at the steaming liquid, not caring if he burned his mouth. Malachai was right. He did need it. "We shouldn't have left Rome," he said in a tense, strained voice. "If we'd stayed we might have been able to get a lead on who orchestrated the robbery and where the stones are, and find out from the detective where—"

Malachai interrupted, "We were strangers in a strange land, Josh. Two men were dead. You were in jail for twenty-four hours. You were the only witness to two homicides. Your life was in danger there. We're damn lucky we got out as fast as we did and they didn't keep us there—or you there—as a material witness."

"We gave up too fast."

"Didn't you hear anything I just said? Someone killed the professor and stole the stones, and you saw him."

"I saw a shadow and then I saw that shadow killed."

"But who killed him? And why? The danger is still out there, Josh. "

"A possible threat isn't as disturbing as the idea that we've lost the stones. I need to know who I am, who I was...and I thought I was going to finally find out. God, I'd kill to get those stones."

"I'm glad you didn't say that in front of Inspector Tatti. We never would have gotten out of the country." Malachai stared at him.

"You don't think I had anything to do with the robbery, do you?" Josh was astonished.

"Of course not. But knowing how tortured you've been, if you believed that the stones would free you from your nightmares, I could imagine stealing them might be a solution."

"Well, I had nothing to do with it."

"How *did* you know where the tomb was that morning?"

Did Malachai doubt him, too? The police had. But they couldn't find any evidence that tied him to the crime. That's what Tatti had been looking for while Josh had been in jail. One shred of proof. For an insane second Josh wondered if, during those early morning hours when he'd wandered around Rome in a trance, he'd gone into a psychotic state and arranged for the robbery—or, worse, gotten hold of a gun and committed the crime himself. Maybe he only imagined being in the tunnel, imagined watching the guard shooting the professor. If he could hallucinate the sequences in ancient Rome down to tasting the water and smelling the air, could he go into a fugue state and commit a heinous crime? Had his mind twisted on itself? Had his desperate desire to find answers pushed him over the thread-thin line that separated the psychopath from the sane?

He wanted to go back to his office and start making phone calls and find Gabriella. He barely knew her; the urge to talk to her and check on her wasn't reasonable, but it was authentic.

As he stood up he knocked his shin on the bronze ormolu dragon-shape foot of Malachai's desk's leg.

"Damn that beast," he said as the pain momentarily discomforted him.

"What did you say?" Malachai asked pointedly.

"I hit my shin on the corner of the desk. It's nothing."

"No, you said something when you hit your foot, would you mind repeating it?"

"I don't know what..." Josh thought for a second. "Oh, yeah. Odd phrase. God knows where I picked it up. *Damn that beast.*"

While Malachai's face remained unruffled, his voice belied his astonishment. "The dragon ornamentation on the left lower leg of the desk sticks out an inch farther than the one on the right and lines up precisely with most people's shinbone. In the past century it was a family tradition of sorts to say *Damn that beast* if you got whacked."

"Great. Another bizarre coincidence. My life is just full of them."

"No, Josh. You know by now there aren't any coincidences in reincarnation. Everything is part of a greater plan."

"I'm trying to remember that."

"This hasn't been easy for either of us, has it? We both want the stones so very badly. I wonder which of us wants them more—you, because you think they will help you figure out a past you can't understand, or me, because I believe they'll help me prove a present I'm the only one who understands."

Malachai never discussed himself except cryptically. While Josh had learned some of the man's past from being around him and Beryl for four months, he still only knew the most basic things. His parents had a child before him who had died at a young age. Malachai was born two years after the little boy's death. From what Josh had gleaned, his father had never gotten over the death of his elder son.

Growing up in Manhattan, Malachai had gone to the Horace

Mann School until the tenth grade, when he moved to London with his socialite mother after his parents divorced. He returned to America years later in 1980 with a degree of Doctor of Clinical Psychology from the University of Oxford and went to work with his aunt at the Phoenix Foundation. Never married, he was often linked to different women in the gossip columns—usually wealthy daughters or second wives of successful businessmen. Malachai's mother had died; his father was still alive and healthy at eighty-seven, but he was estranged from his son.

Everyone had ghosts.

"I need to get back to my office and find Gabriella. I need to know what happened to her and if she's all right."

"I know what happened."

"You do? Is she all right?"

"Yes. She's back in New Haven. She left Rome of her own accord, just as we guessed."

Josh sat back down. "So Detective Tatti was playing with us when he suggested she was missing. What a little bastard. Have you talked to her? Do you know why she took off so suddenly?"

"Right after you left on Thursday night, she got a call that the professor's condition had worsened. While she was at the hospital, her apartment was burgled. That's what all those policemen were doing there the next morning. Frightened, she decided it wasn't safe to stay in Rome and decided to come home, but it appears the trouble followed her back. Her office at Yale was burgled Saturday."

"Was she hurt?"

"No, she's fine. At least physically. She's frightened, though. I think we should go up there and talk to her. Gabriella knows more than anyone alive about those stones. Her scholarship might help us find them."

"Do you know who she or the professor discussed them with besides you and Beryl?"

Malachai shook his head. "Very few people. All of them trustworthy. A curator at the Metropolitan Museum. One at the British Museum. The heads of the archeology departments at both their universities. Neither she nor Rudolfo wanted to go public until they knew what they really had. Neither of them wanted a media circus. They were right."

"But that doesn't mean that there aren't other people who found out. Workers at the site could have overheard conversations, or caught a glimpse of what was in the box and guessed. Gabriella's or the professor's cars or apartments could have been bugged. There are a hundred ways that the information could have leaked, despite their being careful."

"You're right, of course." Malachai twisted the gold cuff links he always wore. They were ovals engraved with the same design as in the bas-relief on the front door—phoenix birds, each with a sword in its right talon.

"How much money do you think the stones are worth?" Josh asked.

Malachai picked up a deck of cards and shuffled them. Shuffled them again. They made a smacking sound like water hitting the shore.

"It might not have anything to do with money. Not if someone inside the Catholic Church is behind the robbery."

"And do you think that's possible?"

"You saw the nuns and priests protesting at the site," Malachai said as he shuffled the deck again. "Wicca, witchcraft, pagan religions, reincarnation. Each one chips away at the omnipotence of the Church at a time when they can't afford it. No, they wouldn't want the stones to surface—not to mention do their magic. If it was the Church, we'll never find them and they'll never be for sale."

"Do you think that's what happened?"

"I don't know, but I'm determined to find out. You think I'd admit defeat this easily? After all these years? When we were so close? Absolutely not. We've simply moved arenas. The stones were stolen—either for someone in the Church, or for a specific collector, or to sell on the black market. I've already put the word out that we're willing to pay for any information that leads to an answer. Rest assured, if the stones are for sale, I'll pay the price. Give up? Not yet. Not ever if I can help it. I want those stones."

He shuffled the deck yet again. "That's why we need to see Gabriella. She can help us. Can you call her and find out when she's free? We can take a drive up to Yale tonight or tomorrow. Just get on her calendar. Make it clear that we can help each other a tremendous amount...."

"You spoke to her—why didn't you ask her yourself?"

"She was with her little girl and didn't want to stay on the phone. Besides, I think she'd be more receptive to you asking."

"Why?"

"I'm not the one who thinks she's might be my long-lost *inamorata*."

"Neither am I. There were no memory darts, nothing that would lead me to think she is." Although, he thought but didn't say, he had wished it.

"Really? Nothing? I thought I sensed a bond, a spark."

"How much are you prepared to pay for the stones?" Josh changed the subject.

Malachai put the cards down on the leather-topped desk, fanned them out and said, "Pick one."

Josh went to reach for one, then changed his mind and chose another.

"Five million," Malachai said before Josh turned it over.

When he did, the card was the five of diamonds.

Chapter 42

Josh's insanity, or whatever it was, didn't wait for an invitation. Nor did it care that it was unwanted. Being at its mercy left him in a state of low-level anxiety. Knowing that at any time, for reasons he didn't understand and had no control over, he might be zapped by a lurch, kept him on edge. There was no warning, just as there was no way to cut a lurch short, or bring one on. He hoped Malachai was right, but he had his doubts. That, plus jet lag, exacerbated his state of mind that morning. He didn't want to sit in the foundation and wait; he wanted to see Gabriella right away and find out about the burglary in Rome and the one in New Haven, find out if she was really okay. But when he called, he still got a recording.

Just before ten, he felt a migraine coming on and swallowed two pills that were supposed to stave off the brutal headache. He rubbed his temples. It was quiet in his office—too quiet. Before his head injury he always had music playing. Jazz singers, old-fashioned crooners he'd heard growing up or driving rock. What had been keen appreciation had in the past sixteen months turned into a necessity. Silence exacerbated the lurches.

He pulled out a pair of headphones he kept close, but he was too late. The jasmine-and-sandalwood scent that precipitated an episode was in the air. He was spiraling down toward flickering candlelight. Pleasure and excitement bubbled up inside him.

And then fear. The present disappeared and he slipped back more than a hundred years into the past.

Women in low-cut gowns and men in tails mingled, chatting and sipping cups of punch or flutes of champagne that a white-gloved waiter was handing out. Old-fashioned music edged into his mind. There was a long table against the wall being used for a buffet of delicacies: pyramids of oysters, bowls of glistening caviar, dishes of olives, platters of roasted meat and fowl.

Percy Talmage refused the champagne, asked the waiter to bring him a glass of port, and made his way through the room, listening to snippets of frivolous conversation and gossip. Only his uncle Davenport, who stood in a corner with Stephen Cavendish, appeared to be having a serious discussion. Inching closer, Percy was careful not to draw attention to himself. He'd learned the art of being invisible and was quite good at spying on his uncle. A few years before, he never could have imagined he'd be capable of the deceptions he now practiced daily. The hidden passages his father had the architects build into the house for his own amusement had become as familiar to Percy as his own bedroom, and the magic arts he and his father had studied as a diversion were now invaluable tools. It had been all the rage to play parlor tricks, and his father had delighted in them. How surprised he'd be to learn about the way Percy was using them now. His breath caught in his throat. He still missed his father even though it had been eight years since he'd died, but this wasn't the time for grief. The dossier of evidence he was building was growing fat. He didn't understand what was going on, but he knew that he was getting close, just another few pieces to the puzzle and then he would be able to—

"How on earth do you think a nineteen-year-old girl is going to protect our investment, Davenport? I expected more from you than this," Cavendish growled.

"Don't make the mistake of underestimating my plan. In its simplicity is its genius."

"It's not a plan, it's a folly. Blackie is a dangerous man."

"But he's also a man with one particular weakness, and that's what I'm taking advantage of."

"Does your wife know you've thrown her daughter to the wolves—or, in this case, wolf—on our behalf?"

Davenport leaned forward and murmured a response that Percy couldn't hear, but the lurid laughter that followed chilled him.

They were discussing Percy's younger sister. Esme had left for Europe several weeks before to study painting in Rome for six months with a private instructor. Along with the teacher, Davenport had arranged a villa and a chaperone—in the guise of his elderly spinster sister. He'd even reassured their mother that Titus Blackwell, who would be in Rome supervising the club's archaeological dig at the same time, would look out for her.

What did this new piece of information mean? How did it fit in with everything else Percy had learned? When the answer came to him he felt stupid. Why hadn't he connected Blackwell's presence in Rome with his sister's trip before now? He had seen the financier talking to Esme at parties, but everyone talked to Esme. She was vivacious and funny. Yes, she flirted, but it was innocent. Wasn't it? Esme couldn't be involved with Titus. With a married man.

But the expression on Davenport's face had suggested something else.

Could Esme be in love with Titus?

Was that what the cryptic comments in her letter referred to? She certainly was happy in Rome, and she had always been an iconoclast.

Percy backed away from the conversation. He would get his sister home even if it meant going to Rome himself. This was one too many travesties in a string of betrayals that Davenport had brought upon his own brother's family, his legacy and his home.

As a young man, Trevor Talmage had founded the Phoenix Club in 1847 along with Henry David Thoreau, Walt Whitman, Fredrick Law Olmstead and other well-known transcendentalists. But their original mission—the search for knowledge and enlightenment—had been abandoned in favor of a single-minded quest for power and wealth when, after Trevor's death, Percy's uncle Davenport had usurped everything, including his brother's marriage bed.

And now he was using his niece and had embroiled her in his treacherous plans.

What kind of danger was she in?

Percy sipped the port that had once been his father's drink of choice. Now he was the only man in the house to touch the amber bottles imported from Spain. Uncle Davenport had laughed at his nephew's choice of drink, asking him how he could ingest that sweet syrup. That was fine with Percy; it pleased him that his uncle would never touch the reserved stock. This particular shipment had been exceptional and there were at least three bottles left.

Another sip. And then a stab of pain. The sickening twist in his stomach he'd had several times in the past few days. Sweat broke out on his forehead. He needed to lie down, in his own bedroom, away from the crowd and the music.

On his way out of the ballroom, Percy saw his uncle watching him with dark, sparkling eyes. Examining him. He must see that Percy was ill; surely, he could tell that from where he stood. But he wasn't making an effort to come to his aid.

And then Percy doubled over with pain.

When he opened his eyes, he found he was in his bed; his teeth chattering, his forehead burning and his stomach cramping in pain so intense he was whimpering like a dog.

His mother, her skin so pale she looked as if she'd been sculpted from marble, sat beside him, wiping his face with a damp towel, ignoring the tears that were coursing down her own cheeks.

Percy fought against the spasms, trying to form words. If only he could catch his breath and get a reprieve from the attack long enough to tell his mother what he'd discovered.

"Davenport, he's trying to talk," his mother said to his uncle. The man's hand came down to rest on her shoulder; Percy saw bony fingers and a gleaming wedding band.

"Poor, poor boy," he said.

She was leaning down, her face only inches from his.

"What is it, Percy?"

He tried to speak, but all that escaped was an agonized moan. His eyes shut against the unbearable cramps.

"He's getting worse. We're losing him."

Percy forced open his eyes—at least he could warn her with a look—but it wasn't his mother's face he saw. It was his uncle's, peering down at him, his steel eyes glittering with victory.

"Mother..." he managed.

She bent over him again, pressing a cool, cool cloth to his forehead. She was crying.

"Josh?"

He reached up to touch his mother's cheek. To wipe away her tears.

"Josh?"

Like a stretched rubber band snapping back to its original shape, Josh rebounded. But for a few seconds he was overwhelmed with pathos, watching his mother's pain.

No. Not *his* mother. Percy's mother.

"Are you all right?" Frances asked. She stood in the doorway to his office with a takeout bag from the deli up the street. "I brought you some breakfast," she said, smiling. She knew he never remembered to pick anything up for himself and had taken to getting him whatever she got for herself.

He focused on her, tried to clear his head. It was all a riddle inside of an enigma, and he was at its center. Lost.

Chapter 43

New York City—Monday, 10:50 a.m.

The rash of articles in the news regarding the opening of the Vestal Virgin's tomb, the shooting, the two murders and the theft of ancient artifacts had apparently triggered trans-life episodes in men and women all over the world. People who'd never experienced anything like them before were having odd, disturbing hallucinations and looking for someone to talk to. Because the Phoenix Foundation and Josh Ryder were mentioned by name in the articles—no thanks to Charlie Billings—there was a steady stream of calls from early that morning that continued into the afternoon.

Fielding requests from adults who wanted help with apparent past-life memories was part of Josh's responsibility. He'd explain what Malachai had first explained to him when he'd shown up: the foundation has a long-standing policy not to work with adults. They were simply a research facility that documents childhood cases of past-life experiences. Adults, Dr. Beryl Talmage felt, had too many years of stored visual imagery that could have been processed and confused with memories. And then Josh offered the names of counselors who could help with meditation techniques to control the callers' episodes.

But the conversations he had that morning were more difficult for Josh; he understood all too well how dazed and desperate the callers were. He was personally involved now.

Many of them described scenes that fit like jigsaw pieces into Josh's own puzzle. One man said he was having dreams of being a farmer in some ancient country when a fire razed his house and killed him and his brother. A second was having flashbacks about being a high-ranking soldier in a time he couldn't exactly identify but that was in the early days of Christianity, and the methods he'd used to quell the crowds that he was supposed to control were brutal and unsettling. A woman remembered creating mosaics on the floors of temples and said she was going to try to draw what she saw and send them to Josh.

He was deeply affected by the idea that if reincarnation was possible he might have crossed paths with some of those people in their earlier incarnations. He wanted to help; he wished he could meet with each one of them on the off chance that they would know something he didn't, shed some light on the dimly lit scenes that hovered in his mind and teased him.

Yet, as fascinating as all of their stories were, and as tempted as Josh was to break the rules and agree to work with them, he didn't. It wasn't his choice to make. Beryl and Malachai were adamant: the foundation did not work with adults. He'd been the only exception in years. So all he could do was commiserate and offer the names of the recommended meditation coaches.

At lunchtime, he finally talked to Gabriella, and, while she insisted she was fine and agreed to see him and Malachai that night for dinner, he could hear stress and tension underlying her words. Her tone left him feeling uneasy; and so, at three-thirty in the afternoon, he decided to rent a car and drive to New Haven early.

Downstairs, as Josh walked through the conservancy toward the front door, he heard a woman's angry voice. Turning the corner into the reception area, he saw her. Wearing a pale pink suit and high-heeled shoes, she stood in front of the receptionist's desk, bedraggled and distraught. Without thinking about what he was doing, Josh lifted his ever-present camera up to his eyes and saw—through his lens, around her head, emanating out from her shoulders—shears of light that made him shiver. For a moment he didn't breathe, afraid even the slightest movement would alter the spectral effect.

Sensing someone was looking at her, the woman turned. Josh lowered the camera. And met her eyes.

The sensation only lasted a second. It wasn't déjà vu. She wasn't someone who seemed familiar. This time there was no doubt. Josh knew, so fucking deep in his gut that it couldn't go any deeper—they had known each other before. During that other time where Josh's memory held back more than it gave up.

As he walked toward her, she opened her mouth in a surprised O and Josh knew she recognized him, too.

They faced each other, the air around them stilled, the traffic noises outside filled in the silence. Her eyes—red from crying—showed astonishment. "Do we know each other?" she finally asked. "You seem so familiar."

"I'm not sure."

Then she frowned a little. "No. My mistake. I thought…" She shook her head.

Josh took in her damp hair, the creased skirt and the rivulets of mascara on her face that either her tears or the rain outside had caused. He looked at Frances, who shook her head in exasperation.

"What's going on?"

"I've explained our policy. She won't leave without getting an appointment."

"It's all right. I'll take care of this." He turned from Frances back to the woman. "I work here. I'll try to help you. But first why don't you come inside and dry off."

The woman was silent as she followed Josh through the door and down the hall. He gave her a sideways glance, noticing how intently she was examining everything they passed. The paintings, the chandeliers and the rugs. As if there was something about them that she didn't understand. Before he could question her, she started chattering nervously.

"I can't believe how upset I got down there. Or that I started crying. I'm not normally like this. I never fall apart. Except lately." She was flustered. "I'm sorry."

Josh shook his head, dismissing the apology. "What happened?"

As they walked up the staircase she explained, and at the same time, continued to explore her surroundings.

"The receptionist asked how she could help me, and then, once she heard what I wanted, she said that they—that you only deal with children. I said I understood, but asked if there wasn't someone I could talk to, anyway. Maybe get a recommendation for another place that could help me. Miss Ice Cube told me someone to call, someone named…" She paused, trying to remember. "Someone named Jack Ryder or Joe Ryder handled that, and I asked if I couldn't just see him."

They'd reached the landing and Josh made a right toward his office. "This way."

As she walked, she picked up the explanation where she'd left off. "Your receptionist made it clear that it wasn't possible to see him without an appointment but that I should feel free to call. I got angry. She asked me to leave. We played verbal ping-pong for a while, and that's when I burst into tears. And as I said, that's just not like me. But then, I haven't been myself for the past few weeks. I just don't know what to do."

His office was in the mansion's turret. She stood on the threshold, cocked her head and stared at him. "What the hell am I doing telling all this to a perfect stranger? I really am losing my mind."

Know her or not, Josh recognized her desperation.

"I'm Josh Ryder. Maybe I can help you."

The rain had stopped, the sun had reappeared and pastel light spilled into the circular aerie through the green, violet and blue stained-glass windows. The woman's gaze darted around the room and rested on the window seat. Patches of colored light created a pattern on her pale jacket and her face.

"Would you like some coffee? A towel?"

She looked down at her wrinkled and wet clothes, as if noticing them for the first time.

"A towel, yes, and a bathroom?"

When she returned a few minutes later, her hair was

brushed, the rivers of mascara had been removed and she'd cleaned herself up.

"Thanks. I needed that."

"Feel better?"

"Much."

"Would you like to sit down?"

As he'd guessed she chose to perch on the window seat.

"So, what brings you here—" He realized he didn't know her name and asked her what it was.

"Rachel Palmer."

"Nice to meet you, Rachel," he said, wondering in another part of his mind if it really was the first time they'd ever met.

"I'm having...I don't know what to call them...hallucinations, I guess. I don't understand what's happening to me."

"It's very disconcerting, I know."

She looked at him gratefully. "You believe me? You don't think I'm crazy?"

"Of course I believe you. That's what we do here. Believe the unbelievable." Josh smiled.

"But it's all so crazy."

Josh nodded. Not surprisingly, this was how most conversations with those burdened by inexplicable memories began.

"Don't worry. I'm not at all judgmental. What's so crazy?"

"In the past week I've been to my own doctor, who couldn't find anything wrong, and a psychiatrist prescribed an anti-anxiety pill—but this isn't anxiety. I'm normally very stable. The hallucinations aren't in the present. They're not even here in New York. But in Rome. And I'm not me...I'm someone else. They're like dreams, but I'm awake. Or it seems like I'm awake. Isn't that insane?"

That morning, several callers had mentioned Rome. Each time it had raised his hopes that someone else out there might have more information about the past, his past, than he did.

"It's not insane at all," he said, "and I know about the referral syndrome and the prescriptions. They didn't help, did they?"

"Not at all."

"Can you describe the hallucinations themselves?"

Josh's encouragement helped, and she continued. "I've been a jewelry designer for years, but for the past few days, maybe a week, the colors of the gemstones seem to be affecting me in some bizarre way. As if they're hypnotizing me. My body begins to hum…." She broke off. "Even I can't believe how stupid this sounds."

"No, it doesn't, at all."

"Are you going to be able to help me? I can't stand this." While she'd been talking to him, she'd nervously been picking at her cuticles. Now one of them started to bleed. She didn't seem to notice.

"I can't promise you that I can help, but I'll listen, and then we can figure it out."

Listening wasn't breaking the rules, was it? Damn it, he didn't care if it was. He wanted to know who she was. Rachel Palmer was the first person he'd met whom he sensed he'd known before. Long before. When he was someone else. The little girl in Rome, Natalie, had known him, but he hadn't connected to her. Was it possible that Rachel was the incarnation of Sabina? No, without knowing why, he was almost certain she wasn't.

"Nothing like that can happen just from touching someone's hand, can it? A room can't change. You can't remember an incident that you don't know occurred, can you?" Rachel asked after she finished describing the auction at Christie's, the painting, the stranger who days later turned out to be Harrison Shoals and whom she was drawn to despite, or because of, the strange effect he had on her.

"Many people think everything you're experiencing is entirely possible."

"I know my uncle Alex does. He's been fascinated with reincarnation for years. But I never paid much attention to it before. Do you believe it's possible?"

"It doesn't matter if I do or not. What matters is that you're disturbed by it."

"And now we're back to where we started. Will you help me figure this out? I'm scared. It's not just that I'm not in control anymore, but I have this urgent sense that there's something I'm supposed to be learning from all this. That there's something I need to do now, to prevent...a tragedy. Now. Oh, shit, I sound like an idiot again."

"No. You don't. Not at all."

She looked at Josh full on. The sound of water rushing in filled his head, he smelled jasmine, tasted honey. It was a lurch, happening here in front of this woman and he couldn't stop it. He felt as if he were slipping. He fought back. He couldn't lose control now. Focusing on the feeling of the wooden chair arms under his fingers, he pushed up through the blue sea, caught hold of the sound of Rachel's voice and hung on to it like a life preserver.

"Can you help me?"

"I want to..." Josh heard his own voice coming up through the water—he didn't know how many seconds later.

"Yes, please, please." It was a cry, plaintive and so very familiar.

He stood and walked to the window to get away from her pleading eyes. Pleading not just for her, but for whoever she had been before.

No, he couldn't do this. He would drown in this woman's eyes if he worked with her. How could he do anything for her when he still hadn't helped himself?

"I want to. But I can't."

"What is it you do? Why can't you do it with me?"

"Either through simple meditation techniques or through hypnosis, we make it possible for the children who come to the foundation to reach their deeply buried past-life memories and bring them to the surface. To remember. Then we can look at the issues and work out why these particular memories are pinging them, disturbing them."

"So do that with me."

"I would, but the foundation's policy is to only work with children."

"But you said you understood…I'm desperate. I've met a man I feel bound to after knowing him only a few days. Since meeting him the flashes have become more frequent and more intense. I decide not to see him because it's so upsetting and feels dangerous, but then I can't seem to stay away. Oh, great. Now I sound like some stupid lovesick teenager as well as a crazy lunatic."

"What do you mean by dangerous?"

"I have a feeling of terrible dread. That something is going to happen to us. Or that it already has happened. And I'm frightened." She was worrying her cuticles again.

"I need to get to the end of this weird story that's unraveling," she continued. "I need to find out who I was before. Please, you have no idea how hard this is for me."

He felt a wave of sympathy for her.

Since his last trip to Rome, Josh's own lurches had been more frequent and intense. Never before had he felt such an urgent need to find out if reincarnation was legend or fact. The idea that Sabina's soul had been reborn into a new body that was here on earth, an idea that had haunted him before, now tortured him. He shouldn't be doing anything but trying to find her, even if that meant he'd be flying into the eye of a storm. He had the same apprehensions as Rachel. Would he and the woman who had been Sabina repeat the damage they'd done to each other? And why, instead of excitement, did the idea of that potential rendezvous fill him with dread?

Since coming to the foundation, he'd heard those fears from several of the older children Malachai and Dr. Talmage worked with. He'd seen the manifestation of their agonizing need to resolve their past, expressed in the haunted look in their eyes. He saw it in the mirror. He saw it in Rachel's eyes now.

She lifted her hand to wipe away fresh tears and exposed her bracelet. It was a circle of thick gold links—too massive for her fragile wrist. Hanging from the links were oval gems in vibrant colors that picked up the sunlight coming through the window and reflected it back, momentarily blinding Josh.

He could barely breathe for the intense scents of jasmine and sandalwood that overwhelmed him. He blinked. The lights were gone, so was the feeling and the smell. All that was left was Rachel, staring at him, imploring him with fearful eyes.

Chapter 44

Dr. Talmage sat behind her desk so the wheelchair was invisible. When she was seated like that, there was nothing to suggest she had MS. Her timeless grace, forged with determination and intelligence, reminded Josh of a John Singer Sargent portrait in the Metropolitan Museum of Art.

A pediatric surgeon who also had a Ph.D. in religious studies and another in psychology, she'd retired from the medical profession thirty years ago, when she was just thirty-five, to work with her father at the foundation. At this point, she was renowned for her work with thousands of children who had had past-life experiences.

"I know how much you want to work with this woman, but no, Josh." Dr. Talmage was thin to the point of brittleness, and her legs might be too weak to support her, but when she spoke her whole being took on a power and strength that belied any illness. "We just can't take on the responsibility," she said with a finality that suggested she was done with the conversation.

But Josh wasn't. He'd help Rachel himself, outside of the foundation if he thought he'd had enough training. But what if he tried to hypnotize her and something went wrong?

"It's not the responsibility that's the problem. It's that you care more about being accepted by the scientific community than you do about helping people," he said, not only continuing the argument but exacerbating it.

"You have no idea what you're saying."

"Yes, I do."

She wheeled out from behind the desk and over to where he sat. Two bright spots of red had appeared high on her cheekbones. "You don't come in here and lecture me about how I run the foundation. You haven't ever presented a paper in front of your colleagues and heard people snickering behind your back. It took me twenty-five years to reach the point where I'm tolerated…where my papers are read. So, no, you're right. I don't want to work with adults who think they were Cleopatra in a previous life. Do you know how many people out there have delusions of past-life grandeur? How do you propose we figure out who's on the level and who is just a little bit psychotic?"

"The way you did with me."

"*I* didn't take you on as a patient, my nephew did. All I did was agree to open my library to you in exchange for your making a photographic report of the work we do. You're not my *pet project*."

Josh winced but didn't falter. "You're right. You haven't helped me. And that's another crime. You are a fucking living encyclopodia of reincarnation theory, but you sit there like some Buddha, not saying a word, offering cryptic koans about letting the water reveal its secrets in time. In what time? In whose time?"

The frustration that he had been living with every single day for sixteen months was too close to the surface. He wanted to go see Gabriella. He was tired. Jet lagged. He had witnessed two murders, had been in jail, had been—as Malachai kept pointing out—might *still* be in danger and was still remembering the pain and suffering and fears of people who had died long before he, Josh, had even been born. If anything, his confusion was greater than it had been before he came to the foundation. Today he'd sat face-to-face with a woman who, from every sign, was experiencing the same thing he was, and all he could offer were some useless platitudes.

"You came here and knew things about us and about this house that no one else could possibly know. You wanted to study what we study. You wanted to learn what we were learning. That's what you asked for and that's what my nephew and I have been giving you. As an intern, Josh, not as a patient. There's a difference. You weren't in trauma, you weren't phobic to the point that it interfered with your ability to function. You didn't need extreme measures."

"But this woman might."

"We've tried what you're asking and were burned time after time. Between the lawsuits, the liars and the ridicule, we made a decision. We don't work with adults. And as long as you're here, you won't, either."

He didn't respond.

Her dog, Cleo, a five-year-old dark gray Basenji—a breed

that dated back to ancient Egypt—trotted over to her and licked her hand. Beryl petted the top of her head. "I don't like being pushed, Josh."

"I know that."

"So why are you pushing me?"

"Because I think this woman is connected to the stones in some way. People are dead, Beryl. Three of them. Murdered. And it's because of what you and I and Malachai think was in that tomb. If we're right, we can't afford to risk losing one piece of knowledge. There's too much we don't know. There's so much we need to know."

"I can't take chances with our reputations. I'm sorry. I really am."

"With all you know, you don't have any flashbacks yourself, do you? You and Malachai. You don't know this kind of hell, and I hope you never ever discover what it's like. Because if you do, this decision will haunt you. I swear it will."

After leaving a message for Malachai to meet him at the Town Green restaurant in New Haven at seven, Josh left the foundation—glad to get away from there after the argument with Beryl—rented a car and headed out of the city. He was anxious to see Gabriella, even if he wasn't sure why.

It was raining again, and the storm intensified the farther Josh traveled out of the city. The wind blew leaves mercilessly across the highway, and traffic was heavy on the Hutch and then on the I-95. Thunder cracked and bolts of lightning lit up a purple-gray sky. Tree branches flew, making the ride seem treacherous. By the time he got to Stamford, he'd passed three accidents. Five by the time he got to New Haven.

Parking the car in a spot he found after driving around the block twice, he hurried across the quad toward the building where Gabriella worked.

The campus was almost deserted, partly because of the rain, but also because the summer session had ended and the fall semester hadn't yet started. The gloomy day made the emptiness disturbing.

Reaching 51 Hillhouse Avenue, Josh walked inside, appreciative of the dry interior, glad to be leaving the worst of the squall behind him.

When Gabriella opened the door and saw him, the right corner of her mouth lifted in a small smile. Behind her, Josh glimpsed a tall, gray-haired man.

"I'm a little early—I thought we could have a drink. Unless you're busy?" Josh asked.

"No. That would be nice. Come in," she said, and introduced him to her father, Peter Chase. The two men shook hands as the elder professor inspected Josh, frowning when she explained how she knew him.

Peter turned back to his daughter. "If this isn't going to take long, I can wait for you downstairs and we can get a bite to eat before my faculty meeting tonight."

"Thanks, but I'm having dinner with Josh and Dr. Samuels. Remember?"

"You are still getting over the shock of what happened here. I think you need to come home where it's quiet," her father insisted.

"I think the quiet might drive Gabriella crazy, Professor Chase," Josh said.

Peter frowned.

Was it because Josh had butted in and was claiming to know his daughter that well? Or had contradicting Peter Chase been presumptuous?

Josh was surprised himself. Not that he'd interfered, but that he'd had such a strong sense of what the night would be like for her if she went home. The sound of the rain. A sleeping child. An empty bedroom. A melancholy night. No. It would all only increase her anxiety.

"And how the hell do you know what my daughter needs?"

Gabriella winked at Josh. "He's right, Dad. The last thing I need is to sit at home and overthink what's been going on. I'll be okay."

"I'll cancel my meeting," Peter offered.

She shook her head. "Absolutely not."

"Well, okay, but I'll be home by nine," he said gruffly.

"Don't rush because of me."

"I don't like the idea of you driving at night in this storm."

"I'll follow her home in my car, Professor Chase. She can leave her car there and then I'll drive her to dinner and back." He wasn't sure if this made Gabriella's father more or less upset. Obviously, it was safer, but he still didn't look happy.

"Go ahead, Dad, don't be late for your meeting. I'll be fine. Josh will take care of me." She kissed her father good-night and he left, but not without giving Josh a long, hard stare that he'd probably been torturing men with since his daughter had gone out on her first date.

On the way to the restaurant Josh asked her distracting questions about Quinn, and Gabriella seemed delighted to relate the ordinary day-to-day events that are small miracles when your child is almost three years old. Speaking about the little girl, she seemed to relax and the restive tenseness disappeared from her voice.

"How is it having your father live with you?"

"It's been good for him and for Quinn."

"And for you?"

She didn't answer right away. "It's important for Quinn to have a man around, and I never could go back and forth to Rome if it wasn't for my father." There was something she wasn't saying, but Josh didn't press her.

"I thought you told me you had a nanny."

"I do. I've had a few nannies, but I wouldn't be comfortable leaving Quinn overnight without my father being there, too."

"Why a few nannies? Are you difficult?"

There were so many other things he wanted to ask her, but he knew she wasn't ready for his questions yet.

"Very difficult," she said in a teasing voice.

He liked the way it washed over him and lifted his spirits.

"I can't imagine that."

"And I can't imagine *that*." She laughed.

That was an even better sound.

If the laughter resonated inside of him, if it made him realize that he'd been waiting since the first time he met her to hear her laugh like that, if it gave him real pleasure to know that he'd alleviated some of her stress and had brought her to a more relaxed place, he chose not to think about those things. They were dangerous thoughts for a man determined not to get involved until he'd found the answers to some very difficult questions for himself.

"My father still thinks I'm seventeen," she said.

"Yeah, he looked at me as if you were seventeen."

"He did?"

Josh nodded.

"Oh, I'm sorry."

"No, you're not."

"Actually, it was easier when I was seventeen. My dates expected that look then."

Josh took notice that she had, in an oblique way, put him in the category of her dates, and it made him inexplicably happy.

He'd stopped at a red light. Its ambient glow warmed her face and lit up her long hair with fiery highlights. She caught his glance. Her eyes were a light, lovely gold, the color of fall leaves. The rain pelted on the windshield, beating down in a steady, comforting rhythm. What if he kept driving? Drove all the way back to Manhattan? What if he took her to his apartment and made them both drinks and put on a John Coltrane CD? What if he told her that he had *wanted* to be put in that category and understood why her father glared at the men whom he thought might be interested in his daughter?

No. Stay away. You're not free. Not really. You're haunted.

Out of the corner of his eye he could see her left hand in her lap. He wanted to reach over and take it. Feel her skin. Learn the landscape of her bones. See if what he sensed was all on his side or if she felt it, too.

You can't touch her—touch anyone—until you've figured out why the past and the present are colliding.

The restaurant was on Chapel Street in an old Victorian building that had been renovated down to the crown moldings and tiled floors. The weather had kept a lot of people home, so they had one of the smallest of the four dining rooms to themselves. In the hour before Malachai arrived, they discussed their lives before Rome as if by some silent agreement they'd decided to avoid the one subject that was loaded for both of them and enjoy their time alone.

He'd ordered a Johnnie Walker Blue Label and she'd asked for a vodka and tonic with lime. In the soft lights her skin glowed and her hair reflected the light. Josh stopped himself from reaching out to touch her. He liked watching her face when she talked, how the shadows played off her strong bones, how the right corner of her mouth always lifted slightly more than the left when she smiled—and how, more than once, when he looked away and then back, he caught her starting at him. In a not-altogether-unpleasant way.

When Malachai arrived, Josh was sorry to see him. He watched Gabriella's face to see if she was, too, but he couldn't read her expression. They all exchanged pleasantries, and after ordering a Campari and soda, Malachai asked Gabriella about the robbery in Rome and the one in her office. What had been taken? Did the police have any leads?

Josh watched as her face fell and her body language changed. She looked as if Malachai had just wrenched her back to the recent past. He regretted that he couldn't have prolonged her respite, and his.

She started with the last night she'd spent in Rome and explained how she'd come home from the hospital, late, after the professor had died, to find her window broken and her papers ransacked. "They took one of my notebooks that had some freehand maps I'd drawn of the tomb, some notes on the excavation and a batch of photographs of the mummy. But I don't know why anyone would want those things. If the tomb hadn't been robbed, if the professor hadn't been shot, it might have made sense, but since the stones had already been taken, I don't understand."

"And that's when you decided to leave?" Josh asked.

"It was so unnerving. I'm a single parent—I couldn't risk my safety and stay. I called the airport, booked the first flight out the next day, packed a bag and checked into a hotel for the night. So much about this dig has been disturbing right from the start. There are always stories that excavations are cursed, but this is the first one I've worked on that really might be."

"What do you mean, right from the start?" Malachai asked.

"I didn't spend any time thinking about it when it happened, but the way I discovered the site was very strange."

"You're the one who found the site? For some reason I thought Professor Rudolfo had," Malachai said.

"No. I did. And I think how it happened is tied into the stones being stolen and the professor being killed, and why someone broke into my apartment last week and my office on Saturday."

While they ate, Gabriella told Josh and Malachai the story, starting with the priest finding her in the chapel at Yale. While she started recounting the first two digs, her fatigue and fear faded as she relived the excitement of those early days in Rome.

"So you didn't find anything at either of those sites?" Josh asked.

"No. Both were dead ends."

"So you moved on to the third site?" Malachai sat straight up in that slightly formal way he had, his eyes focused on Gabriella.

"Yes..." Her words trailed off.

"And that was where you found the Vestal and the stones?" Malachai asked.

"Yes."

"Are you going to go back?"

"To Rome?"

"Back to finish working on Bella's tomb?"

Josh wanted to correct him. It was Sabina's tomb. But he let it go.

"I don't know. I'd need to find another archeologist to work with me now that..." The sadness had slipped back into her eyes and she looked tired. "And if I go back, I'd want to take Quinn with me."

"Is that a problem?" Josh asked.

"Right now it is, because of Bettina."

"Bettina?" Malachai asked.

"She helps me take care of Quinn."

"Is she leaving?" Josh asked.

"She's an aspiring actress, and her plan is to go part-time and try to get some work on the stage once Quinn starts school this fall. She wouldn't delay that to go to Rome with me for six months, and I wouldn't take Quinn away from home with all the stress that will bring without having someone she knows and trusts with us. So I can't think about returning before I work out those child-care issues."

Malachai leaned forward yet farther. "You must go back. It's imperative. You have a destiny with Bella. And with the stones."

"The stones..." She shook her head. "I don't imagine I'll ever see them again."

"How far did you get in substantiating their history or translating the engravings?" Malachai asked as he lifted his glass to his mouth.

Josh noticed how, even when he drank, his eyes didn't leave Gabriella's face while he waited for her response.

"Not far. There wasn't time. We'd only just found the tomb. Those are the kind of details that we'd typically wait to deal with after we'd finished the excavation."

"Can you work on the translations without the actual stones from your photographs?"

Why was he badgering her? Josh wanted to stop him, to make him be quiet, to give her some time. He wanted to wrap her in his arms and offer her a safe harbor. He wanted too much. All things he couldn't have. Gabriella, the stones, proof of what was happening to him.

"I guess I can, but it seems pointless now."

"It's not. The foundation is determined to find the stones. They matter to us probably as much as they do to you. And when we've secured them we're going to need to know how to use them."

Now she was puzzled. "Do you think they have some power?"

"Going back to the beginning of the Phoenix Club, my great-great-great-uncle was certain they weren't just a legend, but had properties that could induce past-life memories. I don't know if I believe that, but I can clear up one mystery. I'm fairly certain the papers your priest gave you have something to do with my great-great-great-uncle's research and efforts."

"How so?"

Malachai poured what was left of the wine into his glass, took a sip and described the group of wealthy industrialists, artists and writers who financed an archeologist in Rome at the end of the nineteenth century who thought he had found a clue to where the stones were buried.

"What was his name?"

"Wallace Neely."

Gabriella nodded vigorously. "Neely owned the site the tomb was found on. Rudolfo negotiated with his heirs. He was a very promising archeologist who had several successes but died tragically when he was only thirty-three."

"Do you know how he died?" Josh asked her.

"He was killed in Rome a few days after he announced that he had made a marvelous discovery." As she said it, she realized the coincidence.

"He was murdered?" Josh asked, astonished.

Now it was her turn to be stunned. "I hadn't realized… it's history repeating itself," she said, her voice a whisper.

"Did you know this?" Josh asked Malachai.

"Some of it, but I didn't put it all together until now."

"Do you know what discovery he made?" Josh asked Gabriella.

"No one knows. Rudolfo and I were sure he must have cataloged his finds, but his records have long since disappeared."

"Maybe he was killed for what he discovered, too," Josh suggested. "If that happened then and this happened now—"

Malachi interrupted. "Things are not always what they appear to be. Remember that." He reached out to Josh's ear and pulled out a silver dollar.

Gabriella looked confused.

"It's his hobby," Josh told her. "Making magic."

"It's not just a hobby," Malachai corrected. "It's the preferable way to live your life." He laughed. "Making magic," he said, repeating Josh's exact phrase.

Outside the restaurant, Malachai said good-night to both of them, and Josh drove Gabriella home. The rain had stopped, but the trees still dripped and the roads glistened in the lamplight. After he pulled up in front of the lovely Tudor house on a quiet tree-lined street, Josh got out and began walking her up to the front door.

"You don't need to—"

He didn't let her finish. "Yes, I do. I want to make sure you get inside and are safe and sound before I leave."

"It's nice of you to watch out for me."

Josh heard her words as if he was underwater again; it took an extra second for them to get to him. Holding her glance, he tried to read it. He was sure it only took a few seconds of real time, but he didn't perceive it that way. It seemed to take ages to work through the pathos and foreboding in her expression and get to the longing.

He was so focused on her, the smell of jasmine and sandalwood crept up on him and he didn't have time to fight the lurch because he hadn't felt it coming.

Chapter 45

Julius and Sabina
Rome—391 A.D.

The crowds lined the streets and watched as the procession moved toward the gates of the city. To them it was tragic drama, it was sport, it was spectacle. For the first time in forty years, a Vestal Virgin was going to be buried alive for violating her vows.

Sitting atop her funerary bed, which rested on a cart held aloft by six priests from the college, Sabina let her eyes follow a woman who walked along the dray, a baby in her arms, keeping them in sight every second of the long, slow march.

The dust rose up and got into the priests' nostrils, clouded their eyes and coated their skin. It was too hot to be walking this distance, too hot for them to be carrying this woman, so hot it was inflaming the crowds, whose voices rose to the heavens with their jeers and curses.

Julius feared that even on this holy procession, there would be violence. In the last month the emperor had issued a proclamation commanding citizens everywhere to encourage all remaining pagans to convert.

"Encourage" meant different things to different people: more temples had been plundered, more priests had been attacked during religious services, more fires had been set and more buildings had burned down to their stone foundations. Romans who had prayed to pagan gods months before, now, either out of true faith or to curry favor with the administration, came at holy men with weapons. With every priest they subdued, the greater their control and power grew. That was what religion was about now: power.

Each night, Julius and Lucas had continued to meet and plot in secret, often joined by Julius's brother and fellow priest, Drago. This procession was part of those plans.

Nine weeks before, Sabina had stopped trying to hide the pregnancy. She would be buried alive as custom and law dictated, one week after her child was born, in a tomb they had built in the hills near the sacred grove.

No one knew that Julius was the father, so his punishment had not yet been meted out, and he'd been free to work on the tomb. They'd made a show of its construction: bringing in artisans to create an elaborate fresco and a detailed floor mosaic.

During the past week, as they put the final touches on her resting place, Sabina had sat nearby, nursing, cooing and smiling at her baby. But she wasn't the only one watching. There were spies everywhere. In fact, Julius was counting on them. So the digging was carried out during the day in plain sight of the bystanders who came to watch.

It had been so long since a Vestal had been buried alive, the citizens of Rome found great symbolism in the upcoming event. With the last Vestal's death would come the death of the old ways.

But once everyone had left and the sun had set, late each night under cover of the deepest darkness, there by the sacred grove, where Sabina and Julius had been meeting as lovers for so many years, where he had found out she was carrying the child who would be her death sentence, he and his brother worked on the secret of her grave until their fingers bled.

Pagans believed that after they died their souls were reborn and given a chance to right the wrongs they had done in their last life. As long as Julius could move the earth with his hands, nothing was going to stop Sabina from having a chance to be reborn in this life.

From her perch on the funerary dray, Sabina looked from her child to Julius, who walked on her other side. Now her eyes glittered with unshed tears. They'd be saying goodbye to each other soon. Their life together, the way they'd known it, would end. There would be no more meetings in the grove, no more nocturnal swimming in the pond. Julius wouldn't see her skin dappled with the moonlight under the oak trees that had sheltered them and hid them for so long.

Tomorrow both of them would start the next step of their journey.

He smiled up at her. *Courage,* he mouthed to her, knowing she couldn't hear him with the crowds jeering and shouting.

Courage, my love.

In her lap, her hands were empty. She was not allowed to carry anything into the tomb with her. The box was tucked inside a girdle, its bulge covered by her robe, its edges digging into her ribs: her dowry for her next life. The most treasured of all the treasures was going into the grave with her. For more than a thousand years the Vestals had stood guard over the sacred fire and what had been hidden under its hearth; it was only right that Sabina would guard it in her next life, as well.

They had arrived at the tomb. It was time.

She looked over at her sister and the baby she'd entrusted to her. Leaning over, she kissed the child's soft cheek. "I'll see you soon, my little one." Then she looked at her sister. "You remember what to do?" she asked Claudia, who nodded, too overcome with tears to speak clearly.

"If the worst happens, the treasure is worth a fortune. Neither of you will ever want for the rest of your lives."

"Don't talk like that…nothing is going to happen. It's going to work out." It was dangerous to say anything else.

Sabina put her arms around her sister and her baby and held them, feeling her daughter's little fists beating on her chest as she struggled to reach for her milk.

Finally Sabina let them go.

Julius and Lucas helped her off the dray and down into the tomb. Quickly they went over the plan—knowing the crowd was outside, and if they spent too much time underground it would be suspect.

Lucas left first, climbing up the wooden ladder.

Julius took Sabina's hands.

"Sabina—" he whispered.

She shook her head. "No, shh." She put one finger to his lips. "There's all the time in the world for us, you'll see." She sounded so sure of herself, he thought. So certain. But the tears running down her cheeks belied her optimism.

She stood up on her toes and kissed him, hard, on the mouth, trying to say everything that she couldn't articulate with words. Julius tasted salt on his lips but didn't know if it was her tears or his.

Chapter 46

New Haven, Connecticut—Monday, 10:18 p.m.

"Are you all right?"

His heart was ripped open. He was overwhelmed with sorrow and wanted to go back. To her. To Sabina. To their child.

"Josh?"

Gabriella's voice was coming from far away, and he knew he needed to follow it. Feeling the awful wrench of leaving, he panicked as Sabina's face dissolved in a great blue-green wave and he reached out for her.

"Josh?"

It was taking too long to reconnect to the present. He should say something, but he couldn't find the words yet. He nodded. Took a deep breath. "I'm fine." He was shocked to see his hands on her arms. He'd reached out for Gabriella? The confusion only intensified when he realized he was glad he had. He wanted to be holding her. It felt right.

"Are you sure you're okay?"

"I have lousy timing," he said.

"What do you mean?"

"Because…because you've had a horrific few days, because too much has happened, because it's late."

"No, I'm okay, Josh," she said, and from the way she looked at him, she didn't seem to be thinking it was too late.

They were in the shadows, protected from the street and from the glass windows on either side of the door where her baby-sitter or her father might be watching. Josh pulled her closer and kissed her. It was immediately intense. Too intense. He let her go.

"It's been a long time for you, too, hasn't it?" she whispered.

He nodded, and this time she kissed him.

The world fell away and he stopped thinking. He gave up the dream of Sabina for just these few minutes. His nerve endings came alive and his blood warmed. It felt so damn good to feel her body pressed against his, to know she was responding the same way he was.

And then the rain started again.

They separated, and she had a pleased but still hungry look in her eyes.

That was when he realized that hers had been kisses that he'd never had before. There was nothing familiar or known about the smell of her or her taste or the way they fit together. Her hair was soft on his cheek, but he'd never felt it before. He kissed her again. Fell into a darkness that was deeper than the night sky. Her fingers gripped his arms and she leaned far into him. A sadness started at the center of his pleasure, and the two emotions did battle. Giving in to one meant giving up on the other.

Josh had wanted her touch to be familiar to him. For so many nights and days and weeks and months, the search for proof of reincarnation, his past and the woman who inhabited it, had haunted him. Now Gabriella would haunt him, too, tantalize him as something he couldn't allow himself to have. But for now, for one night, he could feel her skin on his skin and hear her breathless *oh* as sensations overwhelmed her. It wouldn't hurt anyone, would it? If, just for a few minutes, he hid inside her kiss?

The rain was falling and the wind was blowing, swirling around them, an embrace outside of their embrace, cocooning them in a whoosh of cool air that separated them from the rest of the world.

And then the sadness won the battle with the pleasure, and Josh let go of her. He couldn't stay. He couldn't do that to either of them.

Chapter 47

New York City—10:30 p.m.

Rachel arrived at Harrison's apartment after walking up and down the block outside his building, fighting with herself for almost fifteen minutes about whether or not to meet him as planned. The sound of his voice on the phone, inviting her over, worked on her like a magnet. It was so damn stupid, but she'd never felt that kind of pull to a man before. Her uncle teased her about it and she regretted confiding in him. Maybe she should stop being afraid, give in and see where it took her. Chalk up her fear to naiveté—certainly not with men, not with relationships, but with love.

As she paced she mentally listed off all the reasons she'd logically be drawn to him: he was an art consultant who dealt with paintings, sculptures, antiques and jewels for collectors. All beautiful things. He reeked of taste. Of culture. He was good-looking. And perhaps more than anything else—even though it made no sense—Harrison was elusive. She couldn't quite reach him—not the secrets of him that she sensed were many and were buried deep. And Rachel found that more attractive than she would have imagined.

Upstairs, Harrison greeted her at the door with a chaste kiss on the cheek that was somehow erotic because of the way he held her upper arm so tightly. As if he was holding back, but barely.

"I'm just finishing up a meeting. Come in, it won't take too long."

Rachel thought he was going to leave her in the living room while he returned to his office, but he brought her with him.

His apartment was both his home and office. Smart and sleek, decorated in tones of gray with silver accents, the penthouse boasted large floor-to-ceiling windows that looked out over a nighttime city that sparkled like diamonds.

Harrison poured her a Scotch just the way she liked it: expensive and neat. He gestured to a chair to the left of his desk while he returned to the phone call he'd interrupted to let her in.

She sipped the drink, caressed the seat's baby-soft leather and tried to keep her eyes off of him. At one point, he caught her staring and smiled.

After a few volleys of conversation that referenced an expensive painting, Harrison opened his top desk drawer and pulled out some papers, and in the process Rachel spotted a very small black gun.

The crazy sensations assaulted her. The humming and the music that wasn't really music lulled her, pulled her from the sights and sounds of his office in that moment and took her somewhere else. Instead of sitting in the glass-and-chrome library looking out over the city, she was suddenly in a wood-paneled library with windows that faced a hillside. On the wall were Renaissance paintings, good ones, and the man who sat at the desk, exactly where Harrison had been sitting minutes before, was someone very different.

He was attractive, but in his fifties. No jeans and Armani jacket, but rather some kind of formal, old-fashioned suit. And they weren't alone anymore. Standing to the other side of the desk was a poorly dressed young man with mean eyes and greasy hair.

The man who had taken Harrison's place looked at her seductively. On the desk in front of him, on the tooled-leather blotter, a small black revolver gleamed in the lamplight. He never looked at it while he carried on his conversation with the thug, but it was a bigger presence than any of them.

"We can't be responsible for a robbery, can we? In fact, we should offer a substantial reward for any information leading to the capture of the thief or the thieves." He nodded knowingly.

She needed to get away. From both of the men. From the gun. But she felt trapped, as if time had turned into metal straps that were holding her back. She tried to speak, but it felt like she was pushing rocks out of her mouth. All that she managed was a mangled cry, and then everything changed back to the way it had been before, except for the panic she was experiencing.

Harrison was worried. Solicitous. Talking to her softly, asking what he could do, how he could help. Rachel asked him why he had a gun, and he convincingly said he needed protection with all the paintings and jewelry that he brought in and out of his office. It made sense. But the feeling that she was in danger, in a very real way, stayed with her even as she sat there and drank with him and talked with him.

When he reached for her again and kissed her, she was surprised to find herself moving toward him, not moving away. Wary but pulled by a curiosity and force she didn't understand. How could the darkness in him and the shadows that surrounded him work like an aphrodisiac?

When, smoothly and expertly, he proceeded to seduce her, she didn't stop him.

With his head on her breast, whispering to her, touching her so lightly his fingers felt like feathers on her skin, she convinced herself that she was being crazy. That there couldn't be anything wrong with a man who could make her feel that way. And then it happened.

A quick flash.

The other man had taken Harrison's place again. *He* was making love to her now. But not as gently. Not as carefully. He was greedier, hungrier. In the background, distracting her, were colors—but connected to what? She couldn't tell. She saw the deep verdant emeralds, night-sky blues and rich-wine reds, all so beautiful she couldn't stop looking at them, not even for the man who was inciting pleasure and pressure between her legs. But what were they? She tried to focus, to figure it out...and then she was back in the present, with Harrison, as he brought her to a finish that shook her whole body and she slipped back into the colors and vanished inside of them.

Chapter 48

It was two o'clock in the morning. The window was open, and the breeze offered a soothing embrace. One lamp shone down on the desk, but the rest of the room was shrouded in darkness. He'd had the idea that he would try to block himself off from his reality and create a separate physical existence for this experiment.

The six stones were laid out on a deep blue velvet cloth that covered the blotter. The emeralds, sapphires and ruby glowed.

It had been written that these jewels would open up a doorway from the present to the past, but all the ancient texts alluded to the magic process in elusive terms. He felt as if he were adrift on the sea in a boat that kept him afloat, but that he did not know how to steer.

Every religious ceremony has specific steps. Just as a Mass was not an arbitrary group of prayers and actions, there was a set of steps attached to these stones, as well. A process. Instructions. But what were they?

Professor Chase's papers hadn't revealed anything. Neither the notes that had been taken from her apartment in Rome, nor those that had been stolen from her office in New Haven. There was no indication that she had any idea what the markings on the surface of the stones were. He needed her to translate them.

If she could.

Chase was renowned for her knowledge of ancient languages. Of course she could—or she'd know who could. She was his key to how to harness the stones' power: a dangerous, awesome power.

Weren't the highest echelons of the Church worried about the magic of the stones? And for good reason. If man discovered that Nirvana was within his reach—if it was in his own hands, not in the hands of God—what authority would the Church hold over him?

He had waited a long time, but the wait was almost over. From the first step of the plan, years ago when he got the diary excerpts to Gabriella Chase and Aldo Rudolfo, he'd patiently waited, and now those seedlings were mature trees that would soon bear fruit.

There was a lot to do now in a very short period of time. He sighed. It was a long and deep expression of desire and fear and trepidation. He hated involving other people. Risking the safety of innocents was an affront to his morals, but he was out of choices.

Three men had died so far, and he'd have to live with that forever. Blood stained his soul. Would probably stain it deeper before this quest was over. But didn't all great efforts require sacrifice?

He'd give the gods one last chance to reward him before he moved on to the inevitable and heinous next step.

Separating the six stones into two groups, he held the emeralds in his left hand and the sapphires and the single ruby in his right. Shutting his eyes, he focused on the feeling of them, the sensation of their edges biting into his flesh. There were so many historians, so many collectors, so many religious men who would pay him all of their fortunes for what he was holding, but no amount of lucre could entice him to give up this treasure.

Concentrate, he told himself.

Concentrate on the stones.

He knew how to pray. He knew how to meditate. He knew the power of emptying your mind of minutiae and letting nothingness come to the forefront. That kind of meditation was not a miracle. Not holy. But it had always had a mystical and magical effect on him. It took him away, it settled his ghosts.

The Father. The Son. And the Holy Ghost.

He almost laughed at the perfection of the phrase in this context, but instead concentrated on wiping his mind clean.

First the cleansing.

Then the emptiness.

Stay with the void.

Experience the hollowness.

Now let the colors swim.

Blood-red slipping into ruby, turning scarlet, soaking up darkness and developing into a royal purple. Then reversing it. Seeing the purple, adding light to it so it transformed to lavender, then rose, then blanching the color so it tinged to pink, pushing in light so it was the merest pale, blushing white. Now reversing the process, pushing some color back in, graduating the roseate tone to vermilion, dissolving it to dark wine-red, burning it into inferno red, sliding the embers into sunset's glow and then a glowing torch's orange.

He was deep into the meditation.

See yourself. See who you were. Know who you were.

He repeated it.

See yourself. See who you were. Know who you were.

There was a blue-blackness now like a cold night sky. He swept through it. It was the sky over every country, every age. The answers were there, deep inside the galaxy, he knew that, now to just reach for them.

What was the secret of the stones?

Nothing came to him. No words, no sensations, no knowledge.

What was the secret of the stones?

Again, nothing.

His eyes opened, then his hands, and the stones spilled out onto the velvet cloth. The colors flashed at him, teasing him, promising him more than he might ever know unless he took action.

He'd tried it every other way; now he had no choice.

He turned his eyes to the computer screen and with weary fingers typed in a name, sure that at some point the young woman had been online and left her footprints in cyberspace. It only took seconds for the invisible vaults of information to open and give him what he needed.

Yes. Perfect. He had his key. She'd take him inside, where he'd find a very different treasure. One he could use to trade with: a life in exchange for information.

For mere words.

For sounds that meant nothing out of context.

It wouldn't be hard for a mother to make that choice.

Would it?

Chapter 49

Finding myself to exist in the world,
I believe I shall, in some shape or other, always exist.
—Benjamin Franklin

New York City—Tuesday, 2:00 p.m.

The next morning, Rachel Palmer had sounded so distraught on the phone that Josh agreed to meet her. She suggested the American Wing at the Metropolitan Museum of Art. He always felt at home and comfortable there. Josh was a city kid, and he and his father had spent endless afternoons at the Met over the years. But Rachel's anxiety was pervasive and cast a pall over the afternoon.

"If someone is here, watching me," Rachel said as they walked through the sun-filled gallery, "this doesn't look very suspicious."

"Who would be watching you?"

"I'm going to sound paranoid."

"I won't take it personally."

She smiled. "My uncle Alex."

"He's having you followed?"

"I think so."

"Why?"

"He thinks I'm in danger."

"Well, isn't that what you think, too?"

"Yes. But his reasons are specific. He's done some research and uncovered a scandal or two surrounding some artwork and jewelry Harrison's bought and sold over the years. It's worrying him, although it's nothing out of the ordinary, considering the business he's in. It makes me think he's not telling me everything he knows about Harrison."

She stopped in front of the big, hulking marble sculpture of the *Struggle of Two Natures of Man*.

"He's changed so much since my aunt died. I know that happens, of course, but this isn't just mourning."

"What else could it be?"

"Alex is obsessed with reincarnation. Always has been. You know he tried to buy the Phoenix Foundation a long time ago? Anyway, it's been much worse since my aunt's death, and then I made the mistake of describing what happened with Harrison. Now Alex believes I'm experiencing past-life memories and is obsessed with the idea that Harrison could be dangerous. And although I haven't told him, I think he's right."

"You've had another episode?" Josh asked.

She sighed and described going to Harrison's apartment the night before, seeing the gun and spiraling backward. "But there's nothing specific I can tell you. I don't know who the men were. Or where we were. Nothing, really—just pictures and a few phrases."

They'd left the American Wing and were strolling through a series of galleries filled with religious artifacts. He noticed a huge ivory cross, a triptych of the Annunciation and birth of Jesus, and a glass case of reliquary objects. Josh had been there before so often they were all familiar.

"The problem is that no matter what I tell myself, and how determined I am to stay away from him, I feel drawn to him. As if this is out of my control. And I don't like being out of control."

"I'm sure you don't," he said as they passed over the threshold into the hall of Arms and Armor. Gleaming silver knights—their spears held aloft, banners flying above their heads—sat atop stationary horses in their own elaborate silver mesh suits.

"My father and I used to come to this hall when I was a kid… It's been years since I've been back," Josh said, remembering being here with Ben. It was magical then and still was, because, while everything around him had changed and altered, these knights were still there, in position, lifelike and waiting to hear the call to battle that would never come.

It was a different kind of stepping back in time, a safer kind, and he half expected to hear his father's voice, so Rachel's caught him by surprise.

"Here's the deal, Josh. How much would you charge to hypnotize me and put me through a series of past-life regressions so I can get to the bottom of this mess?"

"It's not a question of money. The foundation only—"

"What? Kids' pain is more important?"

"No, but—"

"This morning he drove me to work," she interrupted again. "When I was getting out of the car, I looked down. My shoes were old-fashioned boots with tiny buttons running up the front, nothing I've ever owned or worn. And the car had turned into a horse-drawn carriage. Harrison was wearing a morning coat."

"And then what happened?"

"I heard my name called, and it was all over."

"Which name?"

"What do you mean?"

"What name did you hear?"

"Rachel. What name could I have heard?"

"Your name from the past."

"So you believe me?"

"I believe that you are seeing what you say you are seeing."

"And you'll help me?"

He shook his head. "I told you that the foundation—"

"I'm not asking to work with the foundation. I'm asking to work with you."

They both turned as two boys—between eight and ten—ran wildly into the gallery, shouting as they pointed out the swords and shields and helmets to each other.

"I want to be that one," screamed the smaller.

"And I'm that one."

"We're knights!"

"What are we going to fight for?"

"To kill the bad guys!"

The children who'd described their past-life experiences to

Malachai and Beryl never explained how they knew when someone they met in the present had been someone they'd known in the past. And they didn't doubt their feelings. Children didn't need to be convinced. They didn't need to educate themselves about the concepts of reincarnation in order to believe that what they were feeling was real. They didn't become obsessed by the philosophy of their nightmares; they just experienced them.

Rachel turned away from watching the boys and back to Josh.

There was something there. He felt it. Almost impossible to detect, but palpable. And different from what he expected. Since the accident, he'd come into contact with many women, and he'd looked into their eyes—the way he was doing with Rachel—searched for some glimmer of familiarity, and waited; but she was the only one with whom the connection existed. And persisted. She wasn't Sabina, but she was someone he'd known.

Selfishly, he realized that he wanted to work with this woman and find out if his life and hers intersected. Where they intersected. What it might mean to him, how it might help him.

"It's happening," Rachel said in a soft, low voice.

"What?"

"My body is humming and I hear that far-off music, but it doesn't have anything to do with tones or keys or chords or melody. It's pure rhythm."

"Where are you?"

"With you. In the museum, of course."

Josh wasn't sure if she was in the present or the past. Before he could ask, she said, "Can we go? Isn't it time for tea?"

"Tea?"

He knew what was happening.

"Yes, of course. Where would you like to go?"

"Home," she said, surprised, as if he should have known that. "Where else would we go?" She seemed to know him so well. But who was she seeing?

"To a coffee shop? A hotel?"

"Delmonico's."

"I don't know where that is."

"Of course you do. Why are you teasing me?"

"I wasn't. I haven't heard of it. Is it nearby?"

She blinked and shook her head as if she were trying to find focus. "You haven't heard of what?"

"Delmonico's."

"What's that?"

Josh knew then for sure that whoever had suggested tea hadn't been Rachel Palmer.

Chapter 50

New Haven, Connecticut—3:06 p.m.

Carl watched the house from across the street. Inside the rented car, slumped down in the driver's seat, he appeared to be talking on a cell phone, but in fact it wasn't turned on, so to anyone who noticed him, he looked like he was parked for a benign reason.

Taking his eyes off the house, he checked the cheap drugstore watch that irritated his wrist. The nanny should be getting home anytime. He'd followed her to the park, watched her talking to the other nannies while the kids played with one another, and, when she got up to come home, he'd taken off so he'd be here waiting for her. He preferred sustained surveillance before he started a job, but he hadn't had the luxury. He'd gotten the call at three in the morning, which gave him far too little time.

He'd wanted to complain that it was no way to start a job, except the money was too good. How could he afford to turn that much down?

"Not this month. Hell, not this year," he said out loud. If you're going to feign being on the phone, you might as well be on the phone.

Narrowing his focus, he concentrated on the street from one end to the other. There wasn't a soul coming or going, and no sign of activity in any of the houses. Carl closed the phone and shook his head as if he had finished the call and was disturbed by it. Easy enough to fake—he just imagined he was listening to his wife. Damn, he was getting antsy.

This was the one part of the job that sucked: waiting to make the initial contact.

He'd been at attention from the time he left his apartment at six that morning, when he'd taken a train from Grand Central to Thirty-Third, and from there to Hoboken, New Jersey, where he rented the car. The woman behind the counter barely looked at him as she went through the process of setting him up. He made small talk with her, asking what part of Maine she was from. She told him Manchester and seemed a little surprised that he'd guessed. But Carl had an ear for voices and accents. He only had to talk to someone once to recognize them the very next time he spoke to them. Only had to meet one person from a region of the country and then he'd be able to identify it again.

He didn't tell her that, though. It might make him too memorable. Instead he told her his wife's family was from there.

Altogether he was pleased with his effort: he'd looked and acted normal enough to be completely unremarkable. For this

Job he'd become a middle-aged man of medium height with a slightly bumpy nose, glasses, sandy hair and mustache, wearing nice slacks and a sports jacket that had seen better days but was by no means shabby. He enjoyed building a disguise. As the layers and wigs and contacts and makeup went on, he'd disappeared into the man he was becoming, so that by the time he was ready to go, he couldn't recognize himself in the mirror.

Opening the phone again, Carl pantomimed talking while mentally going over the plans one more time. There was no such thing as being too careful. What he always had to be prepared for—the one thing he could never be prepared for—was the unexpected. At that moment, he saw movement at the end of the block. There she was! Coming around the corner, pushing the stroller, she was ambling slowly, disappearing twice in the shadows cast by heavy maple trees.

Carl waited until she was closer, then shut the phone, patted his pocket, felt his wallet and detective's badge, got out of the car and crossed the street.

"Excuse me, you're Miss Winston, aren't you? You work for Professor Chase?"

The woman was in her early twenties. Short and sweet-looking with round, bright eyes that had suddenly become cautious. He glanced at the stroller. The little girl was sleeping. Perfect.

"Yes, is something wrong?"

He pulled out the badge and his identification.

"I'm Detective Hudson. I'm going to need you to come with me."

"Why?"

"I can explain everything once you get in the car."

"Did something happen to my parents?"

"No, there's absolutely no reason to panic."

"I didn't do anything," Bettina whimpered, and the little girl stirred. That wasn't good. He didn't want her to wake up now.

"Of course you didn't. Please, Miss Winston." Very gently, he put his fingertips on her elbow and moved her toward the curb. "But I do need you to come with me across the street. My car is over there." He pointed.

"Right now? Can't I go into the house first and—"

Leaning down toward her just enough to be inclusive but not enough to suggest intimacy, he spoke in a grave voice. "Mrs. Chase has received a letter threatening her child, and after the recent robbery in her office, we don't want to take any chances. We want to get you and Quinn someplace safe."

"That's just horrible." Bettina's fingers tightened on the stroller, and she pulled it closer. "Why would anyone want to take Quinn? What does that have to do with—"

"We'll explain everything, but right now I need you to come with me."

As he led her across the street toward the car, Carl could feel Bettina trembling slightly. Good. If she was nervous, this would be easier. He opened the door for her and she looked inside.

"I can't—we need the baby seat."

Damn, something he'd missed. This was the problem with a job that involved a child; he usually avoided them. There was too much information that wasn't intuitive to him.

"Can you hold the stroller?" she said. Before he could answer, she had run back across the street toward the car parked in the driveway. As she opened the back door, he looked up the street and then down in the other direction. The road was clear, the sidewalk still empty, but it was taking too long for her to unclip the seat, and the little girl was stirring. Then, just his luck, a silver sedan turned onto the block.

From this distance it looked like Mr. Chase's car.

Bettina had gotten the seat out and was coming toward him. Carl rushed to meet her, grabbed it and went to work strapping it in. Out of the corner of his eye he watched the car looming closer. He fumbled with the baby seat. The sedan turned into a driveway halfway up the block. He breathed easier.

After strapping Quinn in, Bettina started to get in beside her. "I'd like you up front with me, so I can explain everything to you without twisting around."

After they were both inside the car, he turned on the ignition and was pulling out when he saw a second car, an SUV, turn the corner at the opposite end of the block. In the shadows cast from the tall elm trees he couldn't tell if it was black or dark blue. Mrs. Chase had a dark blue Jeep. Which way to go? Risk passing the car or make a U-turn and risk the driver seeing his license plate. Carl made the U-turn. Checking the rearview mirror, he still couldn't tell what color or make the car was from this distance. If it was her, she was hours early. Was she close enough to see the plates? Probably not. Besides, she wouldn't be paying attention. A car driving down the street wasn't suspect in itself. Even if it was Mrs. Chase and she found the nanny out, she wouldn't question that right away. Not yet. Not for a few hours.

"Do you have a cell phone?" Carl asked Bettina.

"Yes."

He made a right at the corner. No one was following. "Can I have it?"

"Why?"

"Procedure."

She took it out of her purse and handed it to him. He opened it, shut it off and slipped it into his pocket. "I don't understand. Why do you need my phone?"

He didn't answer. She stared at his profile. Looked around at the car. Noticed now for the first time that there was nothing in it. Totally empty. And that struck her as odd. Didn't detectives practically live in their cars?

She'd learned this kind of thinking at drama school. The details of a character brought him to life.

"Can you tell me why you need my phone?"

He didn't answer.

And that didn't make sense, either. Why wouldn't he tell her? He was there to help her and Quinn and Mrs. Chase.

"Oh, God," she said in a voice that quaked with fear. "You're not the police, are you?"

Chapter 51

New York City—Tuesday, 4:30 p.m.

One day Josh would understand why he rushed back to the foundation, borrowed Malachai's car without checking if it was all right, and drove out to New Haven without calling Gabriella to make sure she'd see him.

Later, Beryl Talmage would give him two different explanations. Rationally, she argued that, having recently been in jeopardy, he was overprotective of everyone he cared about and of course he'd want to check on her.

But intuitively she thought the strong karmic bond that Josh shared with Gabriella propelled him to her.

As soon as he saw the front door to Gabriella's house wide open, adrenaline surged through Josh, and he raced inside, afraid of what he was going to find.

She was leaning against the staircase wearing a damp

raincoat, her umbrella and pocketbook at her feet, a sheet of paper trembling in her hand.

"Gabriella? Are you all right?"

She looked up. Her golden eyes shone like glass; all other color was drained from her face. Her lips were pale except for one drop of blood where it looked like she'd bitten herself.

"What's wrong?"

"My baby..."

"What?"

All she could do was repeat, "My baby, my baby..."

Josh took the paper from her.

Quinn is all right. We don't want to hurt her, but we will if you call the police and report her disappearance. As soon as you translate the Memory Stones and can tell us how to use them, your child will be returned to you unharmed. Leave your cell phone on.

Right now this is just a nightmare. Don't let it become reality.

"When did you get this?"

"I just got home. Just now. It was in the mailbox."

"Did you call the police?"

She shook her head. "I won't. I can't risk her life. Didn't you read it?"

"You need to—"

Gabriella interrupted, her voice low, like the growl of a feral cat. "I can't. I'll do whatever these people want. She's my heart. Don't you understand?" Veins in her neck were standing out, showing the strain in every word. "These...these must be the same people who killed Rudolfo. I can't take a chance. They're *killers,* Josh."

She was shaking violently so Josh reached out, pulled her close and held her, feeling every one of her tremors along his whole body. She continued talking, almost as if she didn't know she was in his embrace.

"I'll find someone to translate the markings. I know everyone in the field. I'll find out what they say. I'll figure it out now. Tonight. Then by tomorrow I'll have Quinn back, won't I?"

She was becoming frantic, and Josh was worried that she might become hysterical.

"We need to call the police," he said.

She pulled back suddenly, her face set in anger. "No! If you aren't going to help me do this my way, then get out. I need to save my baby. Don't you understand?" She was screaming.

The longer they waited to call the police, the colder the kidnapper's trail would become. "Gabriella, listen to me, you said this yourself, they are killers, and—"

Ignoring him, she kept talking, too quickly, too loudly. "I can't. All I can do is what they tell me to do. I can't do anything else. If you don't want to help me, then just get out. Get out!"

"I do want to help you," Josh said softly, trying to soothe her, but she wasn't listening to him. "Of course I want to help you," he repeated. This time she heard him. She took a breath. He'd broken through.

"How did you know what happened? Who told you?" she suddenly asked.

"No one. I don't know. I had this crazy feeling…it doesn't matter. C'mon, sit down, let me get you some water. Let's talk about what to do."

He led her to the couch where she did as he asked and sat down, and then popped up immediately, running toward the stairs. "I need to see if she has her bear...." She took the steps two at a time. "Her father gave me the bear when I was pregnant. She knows it's from him and she never goes anywhere without her bear. She never does...."

Josh followed her into the baby's room while she frantically searched in the bed, under the blankets and in the toy chest. He knew why she was looking for it. If Quinn took the bear, then she was alive when she left the house.

"It's not here," she said, managing a heartbreaking smile through her tears.

Chapter 52

New York City—Tuesday, 5:50 p.m.

Alex cut a branch off the miniature ficus tree. The bonsai had been another passion that her uncle and aunt had shared. Now the care and feeding of the dozen ancient trees scattered through the duplex was left to him alone and he treated it with the sacredness of a visit to his wife's grave.

Rachel stood in the doorway to the living room, not wanting to interrupt her uncle, but he'd said he'd wanted to leave at six. She watched him minister to the one-hundred-and-twenty-year-old tree that stood only eighteen inches high and, as she did so often when she was with him, wished there was some way she could help ease his grief over losing his wife.

Putting down the pruning scissors, Alex stepped back and inspected the tree's silhouette and, satisfied, set to picking up the clippings and tiny leaves he'd just cut off.

"Uncle Alex?" she called out softly.

He turned. The sadness etched on his face only lasted a few seconds before he pulled the curtain on his emotions and his expression returned to the equanimity he usually exhibited. Her aunt had once told her that Alex was so successful in business because he was a master of deception. "He can hide everything he's thinking so no one knows what he's doing. Even me. And I must say it's very disconcerting."

"Is it time to go?" he asked. "I'm very much looking forward to this."

Fifteen minutes later, as they walked around the Albert Rand gallery, Rachel was glad she'd agreed to come. It would have been a shame to miss this private showing of master drawings that included a Tintoretto, a Raphael and the prize: a Michelangelo sketch.

Even the sophisticated upper echelons of the art world who often paid little attention to what hung on the walls at an opening were swooning over these rare finds that had come from an estate and were being seen by the public for the first time in more than a hundred years.

She stood in front of the Michelangelo, studying the rough drawing of a hunched-over naked man, his back to the artist in a pose that seemed a premonition of one of the slave sculptures.

"It's amazing, isn't it?" Harrison said, coming up behind her, putting his arm around her waist and pulling her into him. She hadn't known he was going to be there, and now shivering with erotic tension, she leaned back against him, feeling that conflicting excitement and fear that he produced in her.

"Treasures like this, which have been hidden away for so long, have a special aura surrounding them. It's almost as if they are animated, they know that finally they are being seen and they shine—like you do. What a pleasant surprise to see you here, Rachel."

She turned around and smiled at him. "I didn't know you'd be here, either."

"Did you come by yourself?"

"No, I'm with my uncle."

She wasn't sure but she thought that Harrison's eyes narrowed slightly at her uncle's name. That didn't really surprise her. Despite the pleasantries they'd shown each other the first time she saw them together at the Metropolitan Museum of Art that first night, both men, in private, had made it clear to her how much they disliked and distrusted the other. It was yet one more complication that troubled her.

Harrison looked at the drawing again, not aware of her consternation. His sensitivity and devotion to art was one of the reasons she found him attractive.

"Think about it, before tonight, for more than a hundred years this drawing was a secret that almost no one knew existed."

Rachel felt the first stirring of friction as the humming began and the terra cotta of the artist's crayon spiked into oranges and yellows and reds and crimson curls that fanned out into an arc of colors that pulled her into its current. The noises in the room faded away. She felt as if she were getting smaller and smaller, almost disappearing. Nothing *here* was translating into *there,* except for one feeling, the pressure of his arm around her waist.

Chapter 53

Rome, Italy—1884

Standing in the garden, looking out over the city, leaning against him, feeling his arm encircling her waist, Esme was relieved that his depression of the past two weeks was lifting. Blackie, who had been so attentive and wonderful to her since she'd first met him months ago in New York at one of her uncle's soirees, had changed so much recently, becoming temperamental and distant. She'd been planning on ending the affair if his moods continued. His exuberance now was more of a relief than the breeze that was cooling off the intense Roman heat.

She was glad Aunt Iris, her chaperone, had retired early for the night—-as usual—so she could be alone with her lover. *Her lover.* She still thrilled at the idea.

Not many of the women in New York society whom her mother preferred her to spend time with would dare to be with a man this way. But the group *she* preferred, whom she studied painting and drawing with, flaunted being avant garde, considering it de rigueur to break the rules and defy convention if you were a true artist.

"And to think, before today, for more than a thousand years this treasure was a secret that almost no one knew existed."

Blackie, a mature and very successful railroad magnate and twenty years her senior, was acting like a child, laughing and kissing her and asking her if it wasn't the most wonderful news she'd ever heard.

For the past few weeks he had been complaining bitterly that he'd been fooled, that in fact, all of the members of the club had been and that Wallace Neely must be robbing everyone blind.

How different a man becomes when he's accomplished what he's set out to do.

"Tell me what he's found," she said after they'd left the terrace and sat down inside to cups of the bitter but wonderful Italian espresso that she'd become addicted to.

"The tomb is very small, which doesn't suggest it was the burial place of someone important. And yet, it holds one of the most important treasures that have been found in the last century."

"Did you actually see it?" she asked.

"No, but Neely is bringing it here tonight. He didn't want to—he has his protocols—but I told him we weren't having a celebration dinner without the objects that we are celebrating."

"Have you telegrammed the members of the club to let them know?"

"That can wait, at least until I've see seen the objects. Touched them," he said, looking down into his hands as if he was already grasping it. "They say this treasure holds the secret to past-life regressions."

She didn't understand his or any of the club members' preoccupation with the study of transmigration of souls. All of them had such extraordinary, successful present lives, why did it matter to them who they were before? If there was a "before." Wasn't it enough that they had everything they wanted and were the most influential men in New York? In America, some said.

Even her brother, Percy, had been obsessed with this excavation in Rome, but unlike the others, it was because he feared the imbroglio that would erupt if the archeologist found what he was looking for—what they all wanted him to find. She had received disturbing letters from him that summer. With a shaky pen he filled page after page with his suspicions regarding their uncle, now also their stepfather, and concern over her own well-being. He was often ill, he'd written, with sudden and violent stomach problems that the doctor couldn't diagnose. The letters had arrived regularly until three weeks ago when they suddenly stopped. Maybe, she'd hoped, he was traveling. Maybe on his way to see her in Rome, to convalesce here.

"Aren't you curious to find out who you were in the past?" Blackie asked.

"Jesus was resurrected. Mother says that's all I need to know about the dead coming back to life."

"But you are a little curious, aren't you?"

"Maybe a little."

He laughed and pulled her to him and, in the late afternoon sunlight filtering through the drapes, kissed her full on the mouth. The pressure of thinking he'd been wrong about the dig must have been preying on him, she thought. It had been too long since he'd made love to her.

His lips traced a line from her mouth down her neck while he harshly pulled down the bodice of her lavender dress, exposing her breasts. She shivered. He licked the skin around her nipple, and when the breeze blew in through the windows it felt cool where it was wet. Cupping both her breasts, he held them as if they were precious jewels. "You are so lovely," he whispered, then leaned in and kissed her mouth.

Blackie was married and had three children and claimed that until he'd met Esme, he had never taken indiscriminate lovers just to prove his prowess. He had a moral code that he'd adhered to, unlike so many other men of his class and position.

She'd laughed at that and had called him an ethical criminal.

And this was when she was happiest with him, when he fought and lost against his principles. She loved to watch him become powerless in her thrall. Men really had so little control, although they thought just the opposite.

"You make me into a heathen," he told her, his words thick with passion. "A pagan," he shouted. He pointed to the windows. "Out there are ancient Roman temples where the true pagans once worshipped," he whispered, "but I worship you."

The archeologist arrived at the villa in an understandably upbeat mood. A small man with sunburned, weather-beaten skin and tousled brown hair, he wore an ill-fitting suit that was badly in need of an ironing and shoes that needed to be shined. Dressing and grooming himself took too much time away from his beloved vocation. Wallace Neely, Esme knew from the previous times they'd met, couldn't carry on a conversation unless it had to do with ancient Egypt or Rome and the work he did on digs. That night it didn't matter; no one wanted to discuss other things. Blackie put on quite a show, bowing to him and plying him with the wonderful wine and rich food the villa's staff had laid out. He entertained Neely the way he made love to her, holding back on the climax until he couldn't bear it any longer.

And then when Neely was relaxed and Blackie couldn't wait, he asked Esme if she'd excuse them. Before she could protest, he took Neely into the library.

Watching him close the double doors behind him, she stomped her foot in frustration. He didn't think he could stop her from seeing this so-called treasure, did he? Not after she'd suffered through listening to him worry about it for all these months.

Aunt Iris would scold her for going outside bare-armed, but Iris wasn't going to know. She was already upstairs, retired for the night.

From the terrace, looking through a slit in the library curtains, she watched as Blackie lit a second candelabra and brought it over to the desk. The flames illuminated the archeologist in chiaroscuro as he bent over and opened an old leather sack, unfolding it, corner by corner. Then, just as he exposed its contents, Blackie stepped forward to get a closer look, blocking the cache from her view.

"This filth is what we've been waiting for?" Blackie asked derisively.

He reached for the discovery, then his goblet, and poured his wine over whatever he was holding, right there in the library, not caring he was ruining the desk's fine leather top.

"No, no, you can't. That's not protocol." Neely reached out to grab Blackie's arm but Blackie shoved him away with a violence she'd never witnessed before. Now she could see what he was looking at: a fistful of gems, wet with wine and glistening in the light, shining like pieces of broken stained glass.

Neely, having regained his balance and some of his dignity, stepped up to the desk. "I insist, Mr. Blackwell." He put his hand out. "You've compromised our find. Please give those back to me."

Ignoring the small man, Blackie continued to stare down at the emeralds, sapphires and the single ruby. Each stone was almost as big as a walnut—they must be worth a fortune—precious gems that large!

"Mr. Blackwell, let me have the stones back. I insist."

Straightening up, smiling as if nothing untoward had happened, Blackie returned the stones to Neely.

Hurrying, Esme rushed back inside in case they came looking for her in the parlor where she was expected to be. And where she was, but just barely, when the two men returned. Blackie with a calm expression on his face, Neely with his lips set in a hard line.

"Before you leave, let me make a final toast to you and your find with a glass of port, Wallace. It's a night to celebrate, not to be churlish." He turned to her. "Dear, may we have some of that fine Madeira?"

Fetching the wine, she thought of her brother for a moment. Port was his drink of choice. How she wished he was here, so she could tell him what she'd just seen, how Blackie was acting, get her brother's advice.

For the next hour, as the professor discussed pagan religious beliefs, burial practices, Christianity in the fourth century, the tomb he'd found, the methods he'd be using to date the treasures and translate the markings the wine wash had revealed on their surface, he drank, and Blackie kept the port flowing—continually refilling Neely's empty glass while only topping off his own.

Blackie seemed to hang on to Neely's every word, even when those words became slurred. By the time the archeologist had talked himself out it was well past midnight and the man was quite inebriated.

"Let me help you up, old chap. I fear it's time for you to go home," Blackie finally suggested.

Staggering to his feet, tightly clutching his parcel, Neely tried to straighten out his jacket but only managed to twist it worse. He looked ludicrous as he stumbled to the door.

"Will he get himself back to his rooms all right?" she whispered to Blackie. "Shouldn't you take him back with you to your villa? It's so late and dangerous on the roads, I really—"

Blackie gave her a severe, silencing stare; his light blue-gray eyes looked icy cold. Never before had he been so dismissive of her. Between the curt look and his brutish behavior to Neely in the library, she didn't quite recognize him. Tonight, for the first time, she'd seen a part of his soul she didn't like very much. For all his declarations of love, she'd glimpsed, in that fraction of a minute, how unimportant and expendable she was. Worse than that—how unimportant and expendable everyone was to him. The moment broke open so wide and so deep, so quickly, a wave of nausea came over her, and she was sure she was going to get sick right there. How could she have been this wrong about him? How could she love someone who didn't deserve it? No, she must have misinterpreted the look he'd given her.

As Blackie helped the professor out, she went upstairs to her bedroom, where she sat down at her desk, picked up a pen, dipped it in the inkwell and started a letter to her brother. She'd tell him everything that had just happened, he'd explain it to her. But she didn't feel well. Putting the letter aside for later, she walked out onto the balcony, hoping the breeze would restore her.

It was there two or three minutes later that she heard voices and looked down to see Blackie escorting Neely out of the house.

"Good night, Professor. Job well done."

Neely gave a small bow from the waist and tottered off toward the carriage that was waiting for him in the driveway.

Blackie turned and headed toward the villa. Wasn't he leaving also? Had he left something in the library? Did he want to say good-night to her? She was afraid to go downstairs. What if she saw that look in his eyes again?

Below her, the tipsy archeologist swayed as he waited for his driver to come around and help him into the carriage.

"But you're not my man," Neely said, in a thick voice loud enough for her to hear.

Not responding, the driver grabbed Neely by the arm and pulled him forward. It was a strange dance the two of them did. The drunk archeologist leaning in, groping for support, then pulling back, while the driver held on, not letting go. A glint of moonlight reflected off the driver's silver coat button, no, not his button, something he was holding as he pulled Neely closer.

For a moment the two men were fixed in position. Motionless. An owl hooted far off in the woods. There was no other sound. And then, slowly, Neely collapsed, sinking down in what seemed like slow motion.

It was disturbing but not that unusual. He was drunk, after all.

The driver reached down. Good, he was going to assist Neely. But he was handling him so roughly! Shaking him. Neely wasn't moving. He let him drop. What was going on? And then the driver kicked him! What was he doing? He kicked him once more and when Neely still didn't move, the man plucked the satchel out of Neely's hands, hurried to the carriage and swung himself into the seat, turning his back on the archeologist's broken and bleeding body, which lay on the grass in the front of the villa.

"Help him!" she shouted out.

The driver cracked his whip.

"Someone, please, help him!" But her voice was drowned out by the sound of the horses' hooves filling the night.

Chapter 54

New Haven, Connecticut—Tuesday night, 9:55 p.m.

Gabriella spent the next half hour trying to get through to Alice Geller, an expert in ancient languages who taught at Princeton University, and who, Gabriella was sure, would be able to read the markings on the stones. She called her every ten minutes, becoming more frustrated and panicky as time passed.

"When Alice gets home and gets the messages, she'll call back," Josh reassured her.

"I can't wait. I'm not waiting. I'm going to drive up there and bring her the photos."

"Wouldn't it be faster if you e-mailed them?"

"She doesn't have a computer at home, and I can't wait till she goes to the office tomorrow."

"Okay, then I'll go with you."

Three hours later, Josh and Gabriella reached Princeton, New Jersey. He'd insisted on driving, hoping to use the time to convince her she should call the police, but she was as relentless as the rain, repeating that all that would do was put her daughter in greater jeopardy. She made him promise he wouldn't tell anyone.

"If you'll call your father and let him come home and be with you."

Peter Chase had left early that morning to give a series of lectures in Spain. "He has a heart condition," Gabriella said. "This is the kind of news that could kill him while he's thousands of helpless miles away. He dotes on Quinn." She stared out the window and was silent for a minute. "Besides, there is nothing he can do to help. There is nothing anyone can do to help except translate the markings."

Alice took one look at Gabriella when she opened the door and wrapped her friend in a hug. Josh was afraid that the physical comfort was going to break her.

"What are you doing here this time of night?" Alice asked as she ushered them inside. "I've been so worried since I heard what happened in Rome. You must be devastated."

Gabriella's eyes filled with tears, but she shook them away. "I can't describe how horrible it's been."

Josh knew how true that was. He put his arm around her, and together they followed Alice from the front hall into the living room.

Tall and big-boned, Alice was wearing several layers of clothes, all their edges showing, like hints of secrets. Her home was as eclectic as she was, a showcase for the ancient art and artifacts she'd collected during her long career. While Alice made them all tea, Gabriella stood in her kitchen and explained that she needed help with a translation that was critical to an excavation she was working on. Alice wasn't buying that that was the whole reason, but she obviously cared for Gabriella and knew her well enough not to push.

They all sat down at the kitchen table with their mugs. Gabriella spread out the assortment of photographs she'd brought with her.

Alice inspected the shots that Josh remembered seeing in Gabriella's apartment in Rome. Damn. Why hadn't he realized what this was about when he heard about the second break-in? He could have warned her, and she would have been able to keep her daughter safe. Of everyone, Josh should have known how desperate someone would be to get this information. He knew how desperate he was, didn't he? And he didn't want to use the stones for power or money, only to prove what seemed unprovable.

"It's difficult to see some of the edges of these markings. Do you have any shots with different lighting?"

"No." Gabriella's panic was close to the surface. The calm was a facade.

"That's okay." Alice left the room and came back ten seconds later with a magnifying glass.

A few minutes went by, then a few more. Slowly and methodically, Alice examined each photograph. The rain splashed against the windowpanes in a steady pattern. Neither Josh nor Gabriella spoke.

"If I could just shine a light under one of these..."

"It's my fault. I should have taken tighter shots. I should have lit the stones better."

Alice touched Gabriella's arm. "Second-guessing yourself is never very productive." She looked back at the photos. The waiting was so difficult for Josh, he could only imagine what torture it was for Gabriella. He took her hand and held it.

"I haven't seen anything like this before. It might be a form of Sanskrit, but I'm just not sure. It might be Indus...and if it is...I'm not going to be of much help. I haven't worked with that language at all. Almost no one has."

"No one?" Gabriella's voice shook.

"Let me make some phone calls."

"Now? Will you call now? I need you to do that."

"Well, it's late, and I don't know if..."

"Please, Alice. This is very important." There was no mistaking the plea. The desperation in Gabriella's voice sent chills down Josh's spine. It was the sound of a mother's passion.

He watched Alice react. It didn't matter if it was conscious or unconscious, she bowed her head for a second as if prayer was the only possible reaction to Gabriella's voice.

Chapter 55

Denver, Colorado—Wednesday morning, 8:24 a.m.

The call came a few minutes after they landed at the airport. The flight attendant had just announced that they could turn on their cell phones while they taxied in to a gate. Gabriella pulled hers open, said a frantic hello, and then listened, rapt, not moving, her eyes focused on the seat back in front of her.

For a few seconds she didn't say anything, and then, "Please, tell me, how is Quinn? Why can't I talk to her? Where are they? Yes, yes, I'm trying…I'm on the plane still—"

Whatever the man on the other end of the phone said, it frightened her and she looked around to make sure no one was paying attention to her. "No. I won't. No. I understand." Her voice was lower, painfully controlled.

"But why can't I talk to Quinn?" she whispered.

Pause.

"What if I can't? Friday is only... What if it takes longer?"

Her voice was laced with fear, her eyes were closed and her fingers gripped the small silver cell phone so tightly it looked as if they might snap.

"Wait... Hello? Hello? Please, don't—"

The line must have gone dead.

Panicking, she shut the phone, then opened it, located the incoming call and hit Send.

While she waited, Josh wasn't sure she breathed. Beads of sweat popped out on her forehead and her eyes filled up, but her expression remained one of fury and force.

"I can't get him back."

"Damn it, Gabriella, let's go to the police."

"No. No." She was wildly hitting the redial button.

"It's not too late. They know how to—"

She interrupted. "Don't you understand? I can't take that chance. You know who these men are. You know the professor is dead. That Tony is dead. Christ, you were almost killed. I can't take the chance that—" Her voice broke, and for a few minutes she stared out of her window, quietly sobbing.

"Did you talk to Quinn?" he asked when she was calm again.

"No, but he played me a recording of her and Bettina. He said they're both fine. 'Safe and sound' was what he said. But he's only giving me until Friday to get the translations. Only three days to figure out a mystery that's more than three thousand years old."

Josh had a fleeting image, like an old, scratchy mezzotint, of Sabina handing her baby to her sister, but it flickered and disappeared like a candle snuffed out. He looked at Gabriella, watching grief overwhelm her again, knowing there was nothing he could do. He wanted to comfort her—at least offer some solace—but the door had just opened and they needed to go; they had a second plane to catch.

They were in Denver to catch a plane to Salt Lake City, to drive to San Rafael Swell to meet with Larry Rollins, an archeologist both she and Alice knew, who, it turned out, had recently made significant breakthroughs in Indus. They'd tried to contact him only to find out he was on location, unreachable by cell phone or wireless technology. If they wanted to talk to him to enlist his help, they had no choice but to go to him.

"If Rollins can't help… What am I going to do if he can't help? I think I'm going crazy, Josh. I don't know how to hold on."

He wondered how many times in the past twelve hours he'd tried but failed to find a way to give her succor. He just wasn't well versed in issues of faith and didn't know what to offer up. In the midst of the world's brutality, he had seen grace in the tiny dot of an airplane coming to bring supplies to a bombed-out village, glimpsed hope in the eyes of a soldier when he made it back to camp after a mission, witnessed mercy in the way a nurse bent over a wounded man and for a moment made him forget the hell of his pain. But faith? Prayer? The world Josh had lived in for the past dozen years had not wanted for either, but he had never been sure what good they had done. Gabriella was the one who went to churches and temples, who lit candles, kneeled in pews, who prayed to every religion's god, and still she was suffering. What could he say?

"You know how to believe, you know how to pray. You need to believe and pray that Rollins will help."

Chapter 56

Scranton, Pennsylvania—12:15 p.m.

"Come on, baby, eat some grilled cheese," Bettina said to Quinn. "It's good. Look." She took a bite herself and gagged. She was too scared to be hungry, but she had to eat, she knew that, just like Quinn did.

"It's cold," the little girl complained. "Can you make it hot?"

"No, this is a new way to eat it. Come on, please?" She was pleading with the child as if the one bite would be a sign, as if Quinn eating would mean they were going to get out of this alive. "Please?"

"'Kay," the girl said, and took a bite. She chewed and then wrinkled her nose, but she was eating.

Bettina glanced over at Carl, who sat in the easy chair in front of the door reading a paperback book. The curtains were drawn, but she could see a strip of light slipping in under the dingy motel-room curtains. She'd stopped trying to figure out where they were—he never opened the drapes—but she was still trying to listen for some signs of activity beyond the walls of this room, although he kept the television on all day and all night and it was impossible to hear anything outside with the constant noise.

"Now, drink some milk."

"Warm."

Bettina made an effort to smile. "The sandwich is too cold and the milk isn't cold enough, huh?"

Quinn laughed, which, in this pathetic place, was a miracle.

At least it was still daylight. Bettina dreaded another night. She started sweating just thinking about the heavy blindfold he'd wrap around her head and the feel of the handcuffs he'd clamp on her wrists again. But it was the rag that he stuffed in her mouth that terrified her most. He'd told her it was all necessary so he could get some sleep. He needed to sleep, too, didn't he?

She'd lain there last night, uncomfortable, scared, barely able to swallow, sick to her stomach and had tried to recite her parts from plays she'd acted in, but the feel of the cotton on her tongue made her gag; the rough fabric on the blindfold scratched her eyes and the constriction of the cuffs kept her conscious. She should be tired, she thought; the only actual sleep she'd gotten in the past thirty-six hours was when she drifted off without knowing it while Quinn napped.

Bettina looked around the room one more time, hoping she'd spot something important. But there was only the big bed with sheets and a quilt that smelled of mold, a dresser with one of its drawers missing, a cheap mirror, a fake wood table and two big chairs, one of which he had commandeered, the tiny bathroom with its stall shower, two tiny bars of soap and thin terry-cloth towels. There was no phone, just a jack. But there must be a phone somewhere. Carl must have unplugged and hidden it. All she needed was five minutes to search, find it and just—but he never left her alone without incapacitating her.

"Just another sip of milk, baby."

"And then cookies?"

"And then two whole cookies."

At least he'd gotten the right food. He'd asked her for a list and gone out while she was supposedly sleeping. The second she heard the door close she went to work, trying to push the blindfold off by rubbing her forehead against the mildewed pillows, managing only to dislodge it enough to let in some light. And had gotten a nasty sheet burn on her cheek in the process.

He'd noticed the mark when he untied her and asked her what it was. She shrugged. Every time he came close to her she held her breath, afraid, for some reason, to smell him, yet at the same time trying to get up the courage to lean forward and bite him, to throw him off guard for just long enough that she could get the gun out of his waistband. But then what? What if she bumbled it and just wound up annoying him more? What would he do to her then?

The news came on the television, and Bettina hoped that there would be something on about her and Quinn missing. They did that all the time on the news. There was that Amber Alert.

"You think you're going to see yourself?" Carl shook his head. "Be careful what you wish for. The only chance you've got at getting out of this is if she *doesn't* go to the police. I've got my instructions. Word gets out..." He shook his head, knowing he was scaring her by what he wasn't saying.

The newscaster was discussing a new bill that the Senate had just passed. Why weren't they showing Quinn's picture? Her picture?

His phone rang and she felt herself jerk. His ring-tone was a few bars of a really popular song from the seventies or the eighties that her parents used to listen to sometimes. She knew that if she ever got out of here, those few bars of melody would torture her whenever she heard them again.

"Everything is fine," Carl said. There was a pause. Bettina tried very hard to hear the voice on the other end so maybe when this was over she could help the police, but all she knew was that it was a man calling.

"What time?" Carl was drawing a circle with his finger on his pant leg while he listened. "Yeah. Got it. Listen, I—" The man must have interrupted. "Distract them how?" Pause. "What do you mean, start a fight with you?" Carl frowned. "But if you take my gun away from me I won't be able to—" He paused. "No. I don't like that. I'm not some fucking actor in a cop show. No way. I'm not gonna stand there long enough for you to act like some fucking hero. No fucking way. This isn't how we planned it. I take the package and give up the kid. You meet me later where we said and I give you the pot at the end of this particular fucking rainbow." Another pause, this one a longer one. "Okay, okay, don't get your panties in a bunch." Pause. "Yeah, but first tell me, where is my fucking money? We agreed it would be deposited beforehand. I don't give a shit how the hell this comes down, you *understand* that? This part of it is my way or no way. The kid is a pain in the ass, anyway, and—"

Another pause, and then without saying another word, Carl snapped the phone shut.

"And now for the weather—" Carl quickly switched the channel. "We can't have you knowing where we are."

Why not? Even if she knew what state they were in, how would that help?

"Another cookie," Quinn said, oblivious to everything going on around her.

"You've already had two." Even under so much pressure, Gabriella's rules were ingrained in her. What the hell difference could another cookie make now? "Here, hon."

Quinn took it. Took one bite. Put it down.

"What's the matter?"

"Go home now." She looked scared.

Of course she was aware of the tornado of tension that swirled around her. "I know, honey. We'll go home soon."

"I don't like it here. It's like Mommy's nightmare."

"How old is that kid?" Carl asked.

"I told you, she's almost three."

"So how does she know things like that? Her mommy's nightmare?"

It was the first time since they'd gotten in the car that he'd exhibited any curiosity about either of them. Up to now it had been either *shut up,* or *tell me what she eats,* or *put your hands behind you.* Maybe he was getting bored. Maybe she could lull him into a conversation. Then what?

He was waiting for her to answer.

"Only children can be much more precocious than other kids. They pick up on a lot of adult conversation. Things you don't realize you're saying, they hear and remember."

He frowned.

Oh, no, did he think she meant that after this was over Quinn might be able to describe him? Her heart started racing.

Quinn had been listening; she knew some of the words the grown-ups had used. She looked at Carl. "Do you remember a lot?"

"Enough."

"What's enough?"

"I remember enough things."

"From before or from now?"

He considered the question, then turned back to Bettina. "Get her to quiet down. Isn't it her naptime or something?"

She pulled Quinn into her lap, reached over for the little girl's teddy bear and put it in her outstretched palms.

"Story?" Quinn asked. This was the ritual at home. Bear in arms, one story, and then sleep.

"Yes, honey, story." The problem was, Bettina was too frightened to think of a single story except for crazy ones about what was going to happen to them and what would make him use his gun and why his eyes were dead. She'd studied faces for her acting classes.

Bettina's teeth started chattering. It had been happening on and off since they'd arrived. It wasn't that she was cold; it was a manifestation of her fear.

"Stop making that noise," he grunted at her.

"I…can't."

"Yes, you can." He didn't raise his voice. All he did was move his hand one inch closer to his waistband where the gun was. He'd done this off and on since yesterday, as if he were training her like a dog, to respond and obey.

She put her forefinger in her mouth to try to stop her jaw from moving of its own accord.

Quinn stared at her. "Tina, are you sick?"

"Yes, baby, a little."

Quinn reached out and put her little hand on Bettina's forehead. "No temperature."

Bettina grabbed her hand, kissed it, pulled her closer and hugged her, whispering, "Everything is going to be okay, Quinn. We'll go home soon."

"Soon?" the toddler asked.

Bettina nodded.

"I miss Mommy."

"I know, sweetheart."

Bettina hated herself. Hated that she was so damn scared. So stupid. First for getting in the car and then for not coming up with a single idea of how to get them out of there. It was all her fault.

Her teeth started chattering again.

"I said quit it," Carl barked.

"She's scared," Quinn said in a brave little voice, staring right at him.

"I've had enough of her jabbering," he said to Bettina. "You'd better make her go to sleep now, because if you can't, I will."

Chapter 57

> The tomb is not a blind alley: it is a thoroughfare. It closes on the twilight. It opens on the dawn.
>
> —Victor Hugo

San Rafael Swell, Utah—Wednesday, 1:10 p.m.

The only entrance to the section of the canyon called the Lower Sphinx was a slit in the boulders, and the path beyond it, through the sensuous, undulating rocks, was treacherous. In some places it was so narrow they could only walk sideways. Gabriella was managing it fine, but Josh, because of his claustrophobia, was fighting back a full-blown anxiety attack: he was shaking, sweating and dizzy. Each step was an exertion that took his breath away.

Their descent was guided by a student who worked for Larry Rollins and who kept up a lively chatter about where they were and what the different formations meant. Gabriella walked behind him, and Josh was at the rear. He watched her, seemingly unafraid and resolute, trudge on. Intellectually, he knew that the pull of saving her child was driving her, but it didn't take away from how impressive she was. He watched her, sleek and graceful like a cat, climbing down the ladder that led to the next level, down into the earth, into a deeper part of the canyon. She looked back at him only once, holding his eyes for a beat, and then she followed the guide into the darkness.

"Wait!" he called out too late for her to hear him.

Seeing her disappear down into the hole had made his panic worse. He didn't know why he had called out to stop her or what he'd wanted to say to her, only that it seemed he would have just this one chance, and after that he would lose her again. He shook his head. It didn't matter, not now; there was no time to analyze it.

He climbed down after her, certainly not as surefooted, or as calm. He was in good shape but this wasn't a smooth path around the reservoir. Where the ground here wasn't rocky it was muddy, and sometimes the puddles hid hazardous outcroppings that could trip you if you took the next step too fast.

What made this dangerous trek so frustrating as well as frightening was that these canyons were a pilgrimage that every serious photographer hoped to make one day. So as much as Josh knew how urgently they needed to reach Rollins and get his help, as much as he was fighting his paralyzing phobia, he desperately wanted to stop and shoot the underground landscape.

They were still on earth, but they might as well not have been. This was not a familiar or known environment. For thousands of years, rushing waters had charged through these rocks, year after year sculpting the sandstone into waves of warm orange and red. Looking at them, you could envision the currents, running, running against the rock, wearing it down, year after year, until finally they had changed the face of the stone. And until Rollins had found a series of ancient drawings and markings deep inside the gulch, there had been no evidence that ancient people had ever explored them.

Only the first quarter of the Sphinx canyon was open to visitors, the guide continued to explain, but they were headed for the second section. More danger lurked there than the snakes that hid in the shallow pools or the shards of rock that could slice open your skin if you fell on or brushed up against one. If it started to rain anywhere nearby, the canyons were known to flood.

In 1997, a group of hikers had been trapped and drowned in nearby Antelope canyon. A year later, three others had drowned in the Sphinx.

Rollins had been coming here for two years to study a group of caves that were highly decorated with animal figures and markings that turned out to be an ancient language never before seen. Since he had finally cracked the code, six months ago, his work was going faster.

Now, Josh thought, he and Gabriella were bringing him a new puzzle, but he wouldn't have eighteen months to decrypt it.

He wouldn't even have eighteen days.

Gabriella slowly sidled forward. The rocks rose up around her, enclosing her; amber light shone down on her, bathing her in earthy underground colors. This was inner space, as foreign and fantastic as if they had shot off a rocket and arrived on another planet.

Absorbed by the wonder of the geography, Josh automatically reached for his camera, but there was no time to shoot this scenery. He continued on.

Would Rollins be able to decipher the markings on the photographs Gabriella had brought? He was, Alice had said, their only chance. That was why they'd flown from New York to Denver, then to Utah, rented a car, driven more than a hundred and fifty miles, and now, half a day later, were wending their way toward him.

They'd reached another drop, and as they descended, spiraling deep, deep into the earth, the darkness was relieved only by the pin lights on the helmets they wore. Although they'd been at it for an hour, Gabriella still moved at a steady, strong pace that Josh had trouble matching.

One hundred and ten minutes after entering the Sphinx, the guide delivered Josh and Gabriella to Rollins, who knelt in a twelve-by-twelve grotto examining a small wall drawing, one in a series of over a hundred, with a magnifying glass.

After they'd greeted each other and Josh had been introduced, despite everything on her mind, Gabriella managed to ask Rollins about his discovery. She didn't look away or fidget while he explained what they were looking at, but Josh knew that she was churning inside. Listening without hearing. Counting the seconds until Rollins would finish explaining his recent work and she could ask him for the help she had traveled so far to find.

Finally, Rollins asked to see the photos. Opening her backpack, Gabriella pulled them out and handed them to him. Readjusting his torch, he peered down. Time passed slowly as he pored over the glossies for at least five minutes. Meanwhile,

Josh lifted his camera to his eye to shoot his surroundings. Moving around, looking through the viewfinder, he examined and photographed as much of the area as he could. He was shooting the drawings and panning to the right when he caught Gabriella in the frame.

He hadn't looked at her through the camera since that day in Rome in the car. It hadn't been a conscious decision. Or at least he didn't think it had. Maybe he hadn't wanted to be reminded that there was no aura. But now he focused on her.

Looking hard.

But what he hoped to see still wasn't there.

Josh leaned against the wall of the Sphinx canyon. Why couldn't he stop wanting this woman to be *the* woman? Why was he still searching for a clue that she might be? No matter how hard he looked, there was no glimmer of light around her head or resting on her shoulders. What surrounded so many of the children Beryl and Malachai worked with, what had bounced off of Rachel just a week ago, what had shone like a nimbus around his father twenty years before, wasn't there.

In his father's case, Beryl had suggested the light was the shadow of his present soul preparing to move on. With the children, she suggested the light was the shadow of another soul, the residue of a past life, fighting through the barrier of forgetfulness to make itself heard or felt in its new human vessel so that this time the wrongs of the past would be righted and the soul would be at peace in the next life.

He changed his focus and moved in tighter on Gabriella's face. No, the chimera he had spent the past twelve months trying to reproduce with his camera as proof of reincarnation wasn't hovering over her or anywhere near her.

In the library at the foundation, Josh had read about efforts to photograph auras as far back as 1898 when electrography was first invented. He'd seen Yakov Narkevich Yokdo's early examples as well as others, many of which were obviously darkroom manipulations. In the 1940s Seymon Kirlian invented a process that involved photographing his subjects in the presence of a high-frequency, high-voltage, low-amperage electrical field and produced what looked like multicolored auras. But Josh didn't just want to photograph biological energies—he believed he was seeing evidence of the souls of men, women or children who had died tragic or violent deaths and had unfinished, unresolved lives. That's what he yearned to capture on film.

"This is some puzzle you've brought me," Rollins said. Gabriella turned, and Josh put the camera down. Rollins was still talking. "But I think I've found a clue.

"These markings here are numbers from the Harappan language," Rollins said. "And these are Indus script. Alice was right."

Gabriella's facial muscles tightened.

"What's wrong with Indus?" Josh asked.

She looked as if she was going to cry, but she explained as if she were in a classroom, giving a lecture. "Indus was the first major urban culture of South Asia, covering an area that now includes some of Afghanistan, large parts of India and most of Pakistan. There is a very large cache of writing samples from the mature period, which was from 2600 B.C. to 1900 B.C., but there's been no significant developments deciphering the language in the last seventy years."

"That was true until last year," Rollins said as he bent down over the photographs again. "But I've been working on it, with Parva in India, and we've made some breakthroughs."

It was as quiet in Rollins's cave as it had been in Sabina's tomb, Josh thought, and the idea of that day blew over him like a chill wind.

Rollins looked up. "I'm sure that one of the symbols on each of these stones is a number. In Harappan, numerals were represented by vertical lines, so look at this... and this..." He pointed, and first Gabriella and then Josh leaned down and inspected the photographs.

"Do you know what numbers?" Gabriella asked.

"Parva and I haven't yet found a vertical-line numeral sign denoting eight, but we think the language is base eight, and we know the symbols from one through seven. There are additional signs for higher numbers, but they're not germane to what I'm seeing here. Looking at these markings, I'd say we're looking at stones numbered 4, 1, 5, 7, 3, and I just can't read this last one, it's too faint."

"I should have brought bigger blowups." Gabriella's voice was pained.

"It wouldn't have mattered. I can't do the translations here. Parva and I have determined that Indus is logophonetic." He turned to Josh to explain. "Meaning, the script has signs for the language's phonetic values as well as signs for meaning. So far we've identified more than four hundred symbols. I don't have them all in my head. To do this I need to be in my office on the computer."

"But you think you'll be able to tell me what they say?" Gabriella asked, her voice straining.

Rollins unscrewed the cap on a bottle of water and took a drink. "Yes, I'll be home in another week or so and will—"

"I only have until Friday."

"Gabriella, what is this about?" Rollins asked. "Does it have something to do with Rudolfo's murder? With what you found in Rome? Were these stones in the Vestal's tomb?

She looked at Josh as if she was hoping he would make the decision of what to tell Rollins for her. Josh couldn't stand the pain he saw in her eyes.

"Larry, we can't explain now without putting you in danger, but it is absolutely urgent." He'd never tried so hard to convince anyone of anything.

"We'll leave now. I'll get started as soon as I get home."

"We can go with you to San Jose. Stay in a hotel," Gabriella suggested.

"There's nothing you can do to help. I need to sit in front of a computer for about two months. I know, I know, you don't have two months. Don't worry. Go back home, Gabby. At least you'll be with your dad and Quinn. I'll call the minute I make any headway."

Gabriella trembled at the sound of her daughter's name.

A gust of wind blew dust around them. Amber dust that reminded Josh of Rome. He felt the first stirrings of an episode, heard a woman crying and could faintly smell jasmine.

Sabina, heavy with the weight of their baby, sat on the floor of the temple. The sound of crickets was the only noise. It was the middle of the night, and no one else was awake. They had put out the sacred fire, which in itself was a blasphemous punishable act, but they didn't care about that. They were already facing a far worse punishment.

After the area cooled enough, they'd started digging out the hearth to find the treasure that had supposedly been hidden there for so many centuries. While they dug, Sabina told Julius how the stones had been passed down from Vestal to Vestal—stories that even he, as one of the highest-level priests, had never heard.

"Maybe we could try to use the stones before we hide them and see if we've been together before."

"You don't know that yet?"

In the midst of their fear and panic, she stopped to smile at him, and he leaned in and pressed his lips to hers.

"Do you know how to use them?" he asked.

"There's a mantra."

"A mantra?"

"Sounds that you need to repeat, in a certain order, that facilitate a mystical, meditative state that will draw out past-life memories."

"What are you saying about a mantra?" It was Gabriella's voice, Sabina's face. The past and the present were superimposed on each other, and he was caught between them, knowing he couldn't stay in both dimensions. Turning away from Sabina, he focused on the sound of Gabriella's voice, broke free of the lurch and found himself in the canyon, only in the canyon.

"Josh? You said something about a mantra." Gabriella was waiting for him to explain.

"The markings could be a mantra…a string of words…or sounds," Josh said.

"Can you sound out any of the symbols?" she asked Rollins.

He tried. Failed. And then tried again. "No, that's not right." He tried once more. It wasn't a word. Instead it sounded like a dissonant note of ancient music that might have been sung out early in the morning to call the holy to prayer. The syllable came out soft and rounded and hung in the air, reverberating, echoing in the narrow space where they all sat surrounded by sandstone and topaz-tinged light.

It was possible that no one had made that particular sound in more than three thousand years, but none of them had the time or inclination to consider the historical spiritual significance of what was happening.

A little girl was waiting for her mother to save her.

"It's going to be tough to get all this translated by Friday," Rollins said.

"You'll try, won't you?" she asked plaintively.

"Of course."

"When you figure it out and call us, don't read the sounds out in order," Josh suggested to Rollins.

"Why?" Gabriella asked.

"In case. . . ." He held her gaze. "In case it works, Gabriella. If this is real and any of us speak the sounds in order, we might be affected. It's a long shot, just a guess. But there could be something about the sounds that none of us understand. We can't take any risks."

Chapter 58

The first leg of the long, arduous journey back to New York was exhausting—the reverse underground trek, the drive and then the plane ride to the Denver airport. They were walking toward the gate for the last part of the trip when her cell phone rang. Flipping it open, she said hello and waited. Josh could hear that it was a man on the other end of the phone but not make out any of the words.

"Yes, yes...but first, is Quinn all right? Tell me about Quinn."

Gabriella closed her eyes for one brief second, then opened them in an expression of relief, looked at Josh and nodded. He took her by the elbow and moved her away from the crowd over to the windows where it was quieter.

Josh watched her gnaw her bottom lip. If this was like the last call, she'd hear a recording—a few words from Bettina, a quick sentence or two from her daughter—and then receive instructions from the nameless kidnapper.

He looked at his watch. They only had ten minutes left to get to the gate and board the plane, and it was the last one out that night. But she was still on the phone, and then she laughed. It was such an utterly joyous sound it sounded almost obscene and was followed immediately by tears. She was working at not breaking down.

"No. I don't know yet." Pause. "Yes, by Friday. Where am I supposed to go?" She listened, nodding. "No, of course I won't bring the police." Pause. "Can I have someone drive me, though?" Pause. "How do you know he's not a policeman? I don't know. How do I know Quinn will still be alive?" Pause. "Yes. I have the phone. It's with me all the time. But please don't—" Gabriella shut her eyes and slumped against the wall. The hand holding the phone dropped to her side. "He just hung up," she said to Josh, her voice drained of emotion.

"What did he say?"

"He…he's going to call sometime on Friday to tell us where to meet him." She bit her lip and although her eyes shone damply, no tears spilled out. "That's when he'll tell me where to meet him. But Josh…he…" She took a deep breath as if to swallow her hysteria. "He knew where we were. That I'd…that I'd been to see Rollins. But *I* never told him. Never told him Rollins's name. I never told him where we were going or who we were going to see."

"You're sure?"

"Yes. I'm sure. Right before he hung up, he just said he hoped Mr. Rollins was as good as his reputation. We need to call Larry now and warn him," Gabriella said as she opened her phone, punched in a number, and waited. "No answer. That doesn't necessarily mean anything worse than he's out of range, does it?"

"No. Of course not."

But she couldn't let it go. "If he's hurt..."

"He's not hurt, Gabriella. Listen to me. If this lunatic is still waiting for you to get him the answers, it means he can't get them on his own."

This logic becalmed her.

Josh checked his watch. "We should get to the gate now." But when they reached it, they found out that the plane had just been delayed for forty minutes. "Let's get some coffee." He didn't want her just sitting there staring at the clock; even drinking weak, lukewarm coffee afforded something to do.

"Do you think he's listening in on my telephone calls?"

"Too complicated to set up."

"Do you think we're being followed to make sure we're not going to the police?"

Involuntarily Josh looked around. After Rome—where they'd been followed not just by the police but by the assassin and thief who himself was assassinated—he knew if someone wanted to get to you they could. Of course Quinn's kidnapper could have someone trailing them.

Josh led Gabriella to a table and then got in line, bought two coffees, two muffins and two apples, and set them down on the Formica table.

"You need to eat something," he said.

Gabriella didn't reach for the food, only the coffee. She took a sip and then asked, "Did *you* tell anyone where we were going?"

"Only Malachai. And he might have told Beryl. All this madman had to do was search the Internet for archeologists who specialize in ancient languages. There can't be too many, right? You, Rollins and Geller would come up in the first ten results."

Gabriella seized on his explanation, clung to it and, for a second, looked almost relieved. Then the momentary comfort was gone. "It was just a dig, another excavation and now...how many people are in danger because of me? Because of the stones? Rudolfo's dead. The security guard is dead. My daughter and Bettina are missing. Alice may be in danger. Now Rollins—and he has a wife and three kids. Everyone who comes in contact with me is in danger now. You should warn Malachai and his aunt that they could be at risk. And you—you especially, Josh."

"Stop now." He wiped the tears from her face and brushed a stray strand of hair off her forehead. "We're going to get through this and come out of it fine. All of us. You and me, and especially Quinn. Whoever has the stones is using Quinn to force you into giving him the information he needs but doesn't want to hurt her. Or Bettina. Or Rollins. I know he didn't intend for Rudolfo to be killed. I saw that happen. The thief was on his way out. He was running away. He never would have shot Rudolfo if the professor hadn't gone after him."

But he could tell from the expression in her eyes that she couldn't believe him, and he didn't blame her.

For the next half hour there was simply nothing to do but give in to the tedium and wait. Gabriella took a thousand deep breaths and looked at her watch an equal number of times. Josh took a few minutes to check his phone and saw he had three messages.

Two were from Malachai asking what was going on with Rollins, what they'd discovered and when they'd be back. The last message was from Rachel, but as he started to listen to it there was an announcement that their flight was boarding, so he only heard snatches of what she was saying.

"Another flashback... Blackie and another man...in Rome and was killed. Please, Josh. Just consider what I'm asking. Please." Her anxiety was so familiar, and so was the way she was acting as if she were his responsibility. But how could that be possible? He'd met her only three days ago.

The plane ride back to New York was uneventful, and Josh was thankful that Gabriella could find some escape in sleep. He'd spent a long day looking into her eyes and seeing too much pain.

"When you look into the eyes of someone you're photographing and glimpse a terrible suffering, don't turn away," his father had once told him. "It's a gift to see into the depths of grief, because only when you realize that someone can be in that much pain and still function, speak civilly, shake your hand and tell you how nice it is to meet you, do you understand why you can't ever give in or give up. There's *always* another chance, another day. That's the miracle of the human spirit. Take on the pain, Josh. Give it its due. That's the only way to beat it."

His father's face in sleep, when he was dying, had been as serene as Gabriella's was now.

Josh tried to sleep, too, but he couldn't stop thinking that there was some clue to what was happening that he was missing. Something kept bothering him. What was it?

Pulling a notebook and pen out of his knapsack, he wrote out the list of numbers that Rollins had translated—1, 3, 4, 5, 7—and left an *x* for the one he hadn't been able to read. Even if the missing number was a 2 or a 6, the numbers still didn't fall into a logical sequence.

Why would six stones be numbered that way?

His head was pounding and he felt the first hint of a migraine. Reaching into his pocket to grab the pillbox, his fingers brushed against his cell phone. There'd been no time to call Rachel back in the midst of Gabriella's ongoing crisis. As much as he wished he could help Rachel reconcile Harrison with the man in Rome—

Josh stared out of the window, into the deep black sky. Black without any hint of color. Black...was that the name of the man she'd mentioned? Black? No. Blackie. The name was familiar, but he couldn't remember why. Shutting his eyes, he leaned his head on the window and let his mind go blank. There was something, but it was so indistinct, like a whisper, he couldn't grab hold of it.

Blackie?

He was sure now he'd heard the name before Rachel had used it. Black? Blackie? Blackness? Blackwell? Yes. That was it.

It wasn't a name Josh had ever heard before, he was certain of that. But it was a name that Percy Talmage knew. Titus "Blackie" Blackwell had been one of the members of the Phoenix Club and the man who'd gone to Rome to oversee the archeologist who was—the rest exploded in a burst.

Percy's sister, Esme, had gone to Rome. She was Blackie's lover. Was it possible Rachel was remembering Esme's life? That *she* was Percy's sister? Suddenly it all came together; a swirl of colors and shapes that finally settled down into a recognizable image.

"What's wrong?" Gabriella asked.

"I thought you were sleeping."

"I woke up a few minutes ago. You look like you saw a ghost."

"Is it at all possible that the tomb had been opened before, a hundred years ago?"

"No."

"What if they'd used that tunnel I found?"

"No, that was undisturbed, too. We'd have some evidence. Why?"

"What about the box of stones? Could that have been opened before?"

"How, if the tomb was closed? No, that box was sealed shut. It definitely hadn't been opened in over a thousand years."

Then there were no other possibilities, especially if Rollins was right about the numbers on the stones.

"There aren't six stones," he said.

"What?" Gabriella said. "I don't—"

He didn't let her finish. "Listen to me. You and Rudolfo didn't find all of the stones. I can't believe I didn't figure it out before now. There is another set of stones…another six stones that must have been buried in a different tomb. One that Neely did find. Altogether there are twelve stones, Gabriella. That's why the numbers are out of sequence."

He watched a light flash in her eyes, then watched it go out.

"No. That can't be true. Don't you realize what that means? If you're right? If we give this lunatic Larry's translation he'll know there are twelve stones and think that Rudolfo and I found them and hid them and this horror won't end. If we try to give him a phony translation and it doesn't work—"

"Gabriella, this man has to know that he's dealing with a legend, and—"

"Maybe you're wrong. The numbers could mean something else. Why wouldn't all the stones be in one place?"

He put his arm around her shoulder, encircling her grief and frustration with his arm. He wished his palm could wick up her pain, that he could absorb it into his own body, his own skin.

The moment wasn't familiar. Gabriella's grassy, citrusy scent wasn't, either. But how he felt? That was different. He shut his eyes against the onslaught of emotional memory. He had shared a grief like this once, with the woman he had lost. It was one of the silken threads that wove them together in the past and through time. Julius and Sabina had faced the unknown fate of their unborn child, and had ached over it in each other's arms.

"What am I going to do?" Gabriella asked.

"You're going to give this lunatic all twelve stones, along with a full translation."

"How?"

"I'm going to find them for you."

Chapter 59

New York City—Wednesday, 2:00 a.m.

"I feel so helpless," Gabriella said to Josh as they walked out of the terminal. "Everything is out of my control. I can't even help you with this next part."

The car service she'd called from New Haven was waiting for her by the curb. The driver took her overnight bag, placed it in the trunk and opened the door for her. She held on to it, looking so worn out, Josh thought, the only thing that was keeping her standing was the car's support.

"Will you call me tomorrow? As soon as you know something?" she asked with a tremor in her voice.

"I hate that you're going home to an empty house. I wish you'd called your father and asked him to come back from his conference."

"Why? So he could sit and worry with me?" She was hesitating, not quite ready to get in the car, waiting for something.

Josh took her hand. Her confident stance and the courageous glint he'd seen in her eyes when he'd first met her at the dig in Rome were gone.

How could a figment, a fragment of a woman he didn't know, matter to him as much as this woman might? As much as she already did? Flesh and blood versus a concept of destiny? He was a fool.

"I'll be up there as soon as I can."

"I'll be all right. You don't need to—"

"No. I don't *need* to. We're past words like that, Gabriella."

She blinked back tears, found some hidden reserve of strength and stood up straighter.

Josh was relieved. He needed to know she'd be okay, that she could take care of herself until he could get back to her, because it was urgent that he find Rachel and take a journey with her now—one that didn't involve cars or planes but that might take him much farther away.

Thursday, 10:05 a.m.

Josh walked up the stone steps toward the Metropolitan Museum's main doors, where Rachel was waiting for him in her uncle's office. She looked anxious; she was smoking a cigarette and had deep circles under her eyes.

She greeted him impatiently.

"What's wrong?" he asked when he saw her.

"I didn't tell you over the phone," she said, sipping from a cup of steaming coffee. "I am definitely being followed, and I—"

Josh stopped listening. He wondered if Rachel's tail had been following him and Gabriella, too, if there was another connection to all this that he'd missed.

"No," she said. "No one could have followed you. How would they know you out of the tens of thousands of people who come to the museum every day?"

How had she had known what he was thinking?

She always knew. You two were like that.

The answer came from Percy, across the years. Josh shook his head, trying to shake loose the voice.

"What is it?" Rachel asked.

"Nothing."

"I'm sure it's my uncle, but I don't know why. He's being so obsessive about my flashbacks. Instead of being worried about me, he's pressuring me to explore them, to go to a hypnotherapist. He's even found someone he wants me to see...and I will if you won't help me. But I want you to do it. I trust you. That's another crazy thing...that I trust you. I don't really know you. But if you won't help... I have to do something, especially now..."

"Especially now? Did something else happen?"

"Yes, but it's very confusing. I can't figure it out, but it's important.... Someone died, Josh."

"Who?"

She paused. He waited. She looked into his face, fastened her dark blue liquid eyes on his.

"I think I did. I think I died."

Chapter 60

Rome, Italy—1884

Everything changed after Wallace Neely's murder.

The playful lover who had taken her swimming at midnight in the villa's pool, had filled her bed with rose petals and had her serenaded by a La Scala singer, was gone, replaced by a nervous man who had become obsessed with buying art. During their last week in Rome, they met with half a dozen of the city's best dealers and Blackie bought a Botticelli, a Rembrandt, a Tintoretto and a Velázquez.

It seemed to Esme that he was collecting other treasures to make up for the one that he'd lost, but when they had dinner he didn't want to discuss the paintings. He didn't even appear interested in the history of the masterpieces he now owned. When she asked why he was spending such a fortune on artwork if it wasn't important to him, he told her that it was a good investment. She knew he was depressed over the robbery and murder and worried about what the Phoenix Club's reaction was going to be when he told his fellow members. He had, after all, come to Rome expressly to watch over their excavation, and he'd failed.

Esme was relieved when he finally told her he was going to book his passage home and asked if she wanted to go with him. She was glad to get out of Rome early. Her grand tour had ceased to be an adventure. She was worried for her brother and missed her mother. She had nightmares about the archeologist's murder. Her painting lessons weren't going well; the teacher wasn't as qualified as he was supposed to be, and she preferred the Art Students League in New York. But worse than all that was that whenever Blackie touched her now, she grew cold and slightly afraid.

They set off on their transatlantic journey the following week, and once they were at sea her spirits rose a little. They'd be home soon.

The second night out, as they were leaving dinner, Blackie surprised her. "I bought a gift for you in Rome before we left. Would you like to see it?"

"Of course." She was intrigued, despite her recent misgivings.

Inside his cabin, Blackie used a small gold key to open one of his three trunks. He rifled through the hanging clothes, finding and then pulling out a well-wrapped rectangular package approximately two-and-a-half feet wide and almost four feet tall.

Using his mother-of-pearl pocketknife, he cut the strings and slit open the rough wrapping, revealing a package covered in finer paper, which he gave to Esme to unwrap.

She had studied art with a passion since she was twelve, and she knew there were hundreds of thousands of paintings in the world. Her teacher had once told her that of all those, maybe tens of thousands were breathtaking. Of them, thousands were masterpieces. Of those, perhaps a mere hundred or two hundred exhibited the rarest of talents—the ability to use a simple brush and pigment and re-create life. To present a moment of human suffering or madness or ecstasy and offer it up as a mirror. To show man how brutal he could be, how sublime, how passionate or how profound. Only a few dozen painters could make you forget for a moment that what you were looking at was not flesh and blood—that the coal eyes would not blink, that the pink lips would not part. Caravaggio was one of them. And so, Esme thought, the painting she was looking at must be one of his.

It depicted a young and sensual god whom she recognized from other paintings of his that she'd studied. Bacchus was creating havoc, invoking sex and debauchery, delight and deceit. The grapes hanging above his shoulder were so real, Esme was sure she could pluck one and eat it. The god's smile was so lascivious she was certain he'd blink at her any second.

All the color in the room was sucked up into the vortex of energy the painting imparted. She'd never held anything so amazing. When she gasped, Blackie gave her the first real smile he'd offered since the night Neely had died.

"What a treasure," she whispered.

"You, dearest Esme, have no idea." There was a glint in his eye, a sly look she knew. It foreshadowed a surprise of another kind: a sexual one.

He reached out and took her hand, not kindly, not as an apology, but rather as an invitation to a wicked evening of games that the god in the painting would approve of.

Esme wasn't sure how she felt. She still remembered what she'd glimpsed of his soul in Rome. But didn't he seem so much better now that they were on their way home?

With the Caravaggio Bacchus looking on, he pulled her close and whispered in her ear that he wanted her naked. That he wanted to see her flesh pucker in the cold and then make her burn.

His erection pressed against her thigh, and she assumed he was going to make love to her right there and then, but once she was undressed and positioned the way he wanted, on a chaise lounge, legs slightly spread, leaning on her side, facing him, he returned to the painting—but what he proceeded to do next made no sense.

He removed the canvas from its fancy frame and set it aside, almost as if he didn't care about it. Not care about a Caravaggio? Next, using his pocketknife, he jammed the blade into one of the frame's joints. When he'd loosened it, he moved on to the next one, and then the next.

"What are you doing—"

"Don't fret. Just watch."

With the gold frame disassembled, he inspected each arm, up and down, prodding, pushing, searching for and finding what he was looking for. He touched a small notch. Then, using the edge of the knife, he unscrewed the threaded wooden pin.

A spring creaked.

A hiding place was revealed.

Reaching in with two fingers, Blackie pulled out a white tissue-paper package, unwrapped it and held it up.

More extravagant than the gold frame or the rich oil paint, the emerald glittered and gleamed. He reached inside again. He retrieved a second package and unwrapped a sapphire. Another. Then two additional emeralds. Finally, a single ruby.

These were the stones from the tomb that she'd glimpsed through the window the night Neely had been robbed, and killed.

Esme was afraid to breathe.

Leaving the gilt frame in pieces—holding the stones loosely, the way a boy might hold a handful of marbles—Blackie looked down at her. The only noise was the stones hitting one another as he shook them.

"Now lie still."

Humming, he reached out with one finger and drew invisible *X*'s on Esme's body. Six of them. And then taking one stone at a time, he placed each in a row, starting with the hollow space where her clavicles met, down the flat area between her breasts, one in her belly button and then a line of three following her hip curve.

"Don't move," he whispered. Grabbing a silver oval mirror off the dresser, he angled it so that he could show Esme her own body, decorated with the gems.

Nothing made sense to her anymore. How had he gotten these? Why were they hidden in the frame?

"Look," he commanded.

In the mirror she saw the stones sparkling on her skin. Blackie picked up the ruby and held it to the light. "I'm going to move this one to your lips. And we are going to make love. If you can keep your mouth closed, and keep the ruby right there, no matter what I do to you, I'll give it to you. I'm betting on myself this time. No matter how good it feels, Esme, you must keep silent, you must keep your mouth closed," he said as he placed the ruby on her lips.

The gem was cold and surprisingly light for its size. Esme held her head still. She couldn't say anything, but she could try to figure out what had happened and how her lover had wound up with these stones.

Had he found the thief and paid him off? Why hadn't he told her? Had he told the members of the Phoenix Club? Did her brother know?

She felt Blackie's breath between her legs and the pressure of his fingers as he pushed her thighs farther apart.

Of course she could keep silent, she thought as his silky hair brushed against her skin. After all, she wasn't susceptible to him anymore. He might be evil. She *wouldn't* respond to him.

He was between her legs, blowing gently on her nether lips.

Hot air, hot, hot air.

Nothing. She felt nothing.

He did it again.

She focused on everything but how it felt.

He blew on her again and again.

Esme arched her back.

"Don't move," he whispered.

She felt his words against her and it was an even more arousing sensation. Words being spoken into her. Words gliding inside her, disappearing into her darkness.

"If the ruby falls off, you lose," he joked, and went back to work, teasing and tempting her with such dedication she wasn't quite sure what his motivation was—to make sure the ruby stayed in his possession—or that she did?

Chapter 61

Esme woke up sometime later in Blackie's bed with a blanket thrown over her and no sign of him. She walked out to the sitting room and found him putting the painting back together. Rejoining the last arm of the frame, all the stones hidden again.

"Where did you get the stones, Blackie?"

He looked up, startled.

And in that one second, when he had not expected to see her and so had not pasted on a benign expression for her benefit, she saw what she'd seen that night at the villa when he was getting Neely drunk and she'd questioned him about it.

There was a coldness to his gaze. Anger. Dismissal. No remnants of their recent passion remained. How could someone's eyes be so empty? So distant?

"Where did I get what? The painting? I bought it in Rome. One of the days you were off being fitted for a gown."

"No, the stones."

"I picked them up from a dealer, too."

The ship moved through a calm sea that night and the sound of waves breaking against the boat was not loud enough to muffle his disingenuous tone.

She became aware of what she really had known since she'd first glimpsed the stones.

"You arranged it...you got him drunk. You're responsible for Neely's murder...aren't you? You did it to get the stones. To keep them from the club... You're going to keep them yourself?"

"I think I underestimated you. I knew you were bright, but I didn't think you would figure all that out. But you're not bright enough. I also overestimated you. I never thought you'd be so foolish as to involve yourself in something that isn't any of your affair."

"You had a man killed!"

"No. That was an accident. I had a man robbed."

"But he died."

"Stop acting so shocked. What would you have me do? I needed to accomplish something. Was I supposed to pray for Providence to send a solution?" Blackie returned to wrapping the frame. "Why don't you put on some clothes, darling. They are serving midnight supper on the upper deck. Aren't you hungry? Wear the blue frock and the sapphires I bought you. Don't take all this so seriously. I didn't have anyone killed. Neely's death was an unfortunate accident." It wasn't an invitation; it was an order, and she was afraid to ignore it.

They went to the bar, where Blackie ordered champagne and caviar, which they served with blinis, finely chopped onions and thick sour cream.

Esme couldn't eat anything, but he gorged himself. The champagne, however, was a different story. Esme wanted to get drunk. She wanted to stop focusing on this man and her uncle and to stop worrying about her brother.

Blackie kept refilling her glass, and she kept drinking it down.

When she realized that he was pouring for her the same way he'd poured for Neely the night he got him drunk, it was too late, she was already feeling the champagne.

After the bottle was emptied and all the blinis were gone, Blackie took her arm and walked her out on deck. It was very late by then and no one was around. The sky was studded with glinting stars that circled back deeper and deeper, and for just a minute Esme could almost see the dimensions of the space up above her.

The water was rougher than it had been earlier, and a series of swells beat against the side of the ship. The wind had picked up, and it howled around them.

"I wish you hadn't found out." He put his arm around her waist.

In the moonlight, Esme watched the now-heavy clouds roll in. She was sad when they covered up some of the stars. Another wave hit. The ship was huge; how big were these waves?

In a surprising moment of passion, Blackie grabbed Esme and pulled her to him. She felt his hardness on her thigh. And then she felt another hardness pressing into her ribs.

This one was metal, not flesh.

Despite the champagne, she knew what it was without having to look. She had seen it before in his possession; its image and shape had been burned into her consciousness.

This was not Blackie, her lover, who was holding her. It was Blackie, the thief...the thief he'd always been.

Esme put her arms around his neck and held on to him tightly, pretending that she was embracing him back, that she didn't know what was going to happen. And then, when she felt his finger start to move on the trigger, she quickly reached down and tried to twist his hand around so the shot would enter his rib cage, not hers.

She didn't hear the sound over the pounding waves and the wailing wind but she felt the sting. Reflexively, she grabbed on to Blackie and held tightly. As she held on to her lover she could see in his eyes that this hadn't been easy for him.

At least she had that.

The mountainous waves beat against the ship endlessly, it seemed, filling the air with foam and spray. In the sky she could see the eyes of the Caravaggio god, and he was smiling and winking at her. Or was it just a star breaking through the storm clouds?

Pain radiating from Esme's side saturated her senses.

He was so sorry, he said. It was all a mistake. He was going to take her back to the cabin and call the ship's doctor and save her after all. His voice sounded very far away.

Just then, the ship listed hard to the left and Blackie shifted, sliding into the railing. The deck was slippery. With her blood? Ocean water? He was having a hard time both holding Esme and keeping his balance. Another massive wave hit. Blackie slithered backward, then righted himself. She was a heavy, dead weight, dragging on him. Good, she thought. Good. She didn't want to be light for him; didn't want this to be easy.

A crack of lightning.

Bright white light shone in his eyes.

Malevolent eyes. Not her lover's eyes. She could read his eyes and knew they were not going back to the room. No, he had no intention of saving her. That had been another lie. The last lie.

He leaned up against the railing, trying to keep his balance.

The ship listed to the starboard side.

Then reversed.

He managed to get some traction and lifted her up, and she knew then what he was planning. The water was going to be cold. But at least then it would be over. The pain would be gone. She still had one arm around his neck, and now she reached up with her other arm and pulled his head down toward her face with a force that she hadn't had a moment before.

"One last kiss," she whispered.

He kissed her, whether it was out of pity or real emotion or guilt didn't matter; she needed those few seconds to get a better grip on him—not realizing he was using them to get a better grip on her.

With one last, great effort, fighting against the swaying ship, trying to keep his footing, he lifted her up and moved closer to the railing, then he leaned over and let go.

A last great wave buffeted the boat. The wind gusted and sprayed them with a shock of cold salty water. He lost his footing. She held tight around his neck.

They were both flying through the air, holding on to each other, neither of them letting go, not now, not in death, lovers of a sort to the last: they disappeared from the bow of the ship on a night that had started out with a calm, calm sea.

Chapter 62

New York City—Thursday, 10:50 a.m.

"You're going to go to sleep now, Esme. And when you wake up, you'll be Rachel and remember what happened, but you won't be afraid. A part of your mind has always known this story. You just didn't have conscious access to it. When you wake up you'll know that there are things you need to work out, but you'll be confident that you can do what needs to be done. You'll be able to put the memories into perspective. You'll remember what you've seen when you wake up, but you won't be afraid. You're not Esme. Harrison Shoals isn't Blackie."

Josh watched her face while she slept. The dark lashes resting on her cheek. Her red lipsticked mouth closed tightly around the last word she'd said. There was no eye movement, just the rise and fall of her chest as she breathed.

"Rachel…"

She didn't move.

"Rachel...when I count to three you are going to wake up and feel totally refreshed and clearheaded."

He waited nervously. This was what Beryl Talmage had warned him about. He'd exposed Rachel to a new image of her soul in another body in another time, and it was going to be hard work to align the two separate selves.

"One. Two. Three."

Rachel opened her eyes and looked right at him. Her lovely face was in repose, framed by chestnut waves. There was nothing there to suggest she was in any kind of distress.

"Take your time. You remembered a lot."

The way the darkness descended on her face, it was as if he'd suddenly pulled the sun out of the sky. Her eyes clouded, her mouth pursed and she bit the lipstick off her lips. Her hands twisted in her lap. It only took twenty or thirty seconds for her to remember most of it.

"He killed me, didn't he?" Rachel asked.

"Not you. A woman named Esme."

"He shot me and I died?"

"He shot Esme. It happened a long time ago."

"And he died, too, didn't he? I was holding on to him and he was holding me out over the railing and the ship was listing badly and I had my arms around his neck and I pulled him down with me."

"Not you. Esme."

"Was he the man who is Harrison now?"

"Not exactly. Just like Esme is not really you. Let me show you." Josh took a mug off the desk and filled it with water from the bottle he pulled out of his backpack. Standing, he held out his arm, opened his fingers and let the mug fall to the marble floor, where china smashed into a dozen fragments and the water pooled.

She stared at him as if he'd gone crazy. "What are you doing?"

"We—you and I, everyone—our bodies are the mug. Our souls are the water. When you break the mug, the water spills out, and while it does change its shape, its properties remain the same. What was in the bottle, then in the mug and now there on the floor is all the same water. You still can see it. I'll get down on the floor and soak it up with a towel, but it will still be the same water that was first in the bottle in one configuration and then was in the mug in another and then on the floor in yet another. That's how reincarnation works. Our souls find new bodies, and along the way we change, the same way the water picks up dust and particles and molds to the shape of the new vessel that holds it."

"But what do I do now that I know that Titus Blackwell killed Esme?"

"Use the information to help you understand your anxiety about Harrison. Examine your fear of who he is now versus who Blackwell was then, find out if your emotions are grounded in the present or the past."

"To what end?"

"So you can get it right this time, in this life. End the cycle. Not repeat the past."

"Repeat it literally?" Her face had drained of color. "If I find out something illegal about his business practices do you think he could kill me to keep me quiet?"

"I'm not a magician or a fortune-teller. There's no rule book to this stuff. We're learning as we go along. I could spout hours of philosophy and theory about the concept of reincarnation, but it would be just that, theory and philosophy, and I don't think that it would help much right now."

She frowned. "I know you can't tell me this, Josh, but based on what you've seen other people go through, what are the chances that this *is* history repeating itself?"

"The idea that someone who killed you once will kill you again is too pat. This is subtler than that. It's about the emotion behind the action. If greed was what made Blackie kill in order to protect his secret, then it's possible greed is the emotion Harrison is wrestling with now and that it will affect your relationship with him somehow."

"I can't breathe in here," she said as she propelled herself out of her seat and walked quickly out of the room.

Josh followed Rachel down the hall and to the elevators. She jabbed the button, once, twice, waited, jabbed it again, and then took off for the stairs. He stayed with her down four flights, then through a hall filled with giant primitive sculpture that loomed up and seemed to tilt wildly as he sped by and into the main lobby.

He couldn't let her go off on her own. Not so soon after coming out of the trance. People everywhere stared, surely thinking he was in pursuit of her for all the wrong reasons. All he hoped was that no one would try to stop him before he caught up to her.

"Rachel!"

She didn't turn around, but kept going, out the front doors, down the granite steps, onto the sidewalk, where she turned right, ran half of that block and then took another right into the park.

He finally caught up to her inside the playground at the Eightieth Street entrance. She was bent over next to the sculpture of the three bronze bears, trying to catch her breath, and when he called her name this time, she looked up and he saw the tears streaking her face. Behind her, a half a dozen kids climbed on a jungle gym. Shrieking and laughing, they challenged one another to go higher.

"I'm sorry. I just got scared," she said when he reached her side.

"I know."

"Can we take a walk?" Her voice sounded young and vulnerable.

He nodded, and they took the path that led past the playground toward a wide expanse of green lawn where dogs were chasing one another while their owners looked on. At the fork, she didn't hesitate but took a left, and for a few seconds they were in darkness as they passed under a bridge. On the other side, she got her bearings, made a move to go right, then changed her mind and turned left.

The route she had chosen was the one he was familiar with, too.

"There's so much I don't understand. Why is this remembering happening now? Why not last year. Or two years ago?"

"I think you responded to what we call a trigger—an event that jump-started your memory."

"What kind of event?"

"You told me the first time you experienced a flashback you were reading... Do you remember what you were reading?"

"About the excavation of the Vestal Virgins' tomb in Rome in the paper." She stopped and turned to him, stunned. "Reading about the tomb was my trigger. And the second time it happened I was at the Met, and those curators were discussing the robbery and the murder of the professor in the same tomb.... Josh, is it the same tomb that Neely discovered?"

"I don't know that for sure, but I don't think so."

"What did they find?"

"They found the Memory Stones."

"The same stones that I remember?"

"I'm not sure."

As they walked under shadows cast from heavily leafed oaks and linden trees, Josh told her the story in greater detail than the newspapers had reported it.

"Is that why you agreed to see me that first day?" she asked when he was done. "Because you wanted to use me to help the other archeologist...what's her name?"

"Professor Chase. And no, that's not why. It couldn't have been, you didn't tell me about the stones until today."

"But it's why you agreed to meet me today and hypnotize me."

"Rachel, listen, someone's life is in danger and it's imperative that I find the stones that Blackie took."

"I don't know where those stones are."

"When you were under you told me about the painting Blackie had bought Esme. Do you remember that?"

She considered this. "Yes. Of course, the painting..." She was seeing it in her mind. "The young Bacchus." And then her face dissolved into a mask of horror. Something was terribly wrong. Something she couldn't process.

"What is it?" He hoped his guess was right.

"That's the painting that Harrison is brokering. The painting that he bought at the auction. The same painting that Blackie gave Esme. The one my uncle wanted so much and was so angry I didn't get at the auction."

They'd reached an overgrown part of the park called the Ramble, where it was easy to forget that you were in Manhattan in the twenty-first century. Instead of skyscrapers there were boulders as tall as the trees, and instead of traffic there was only birdsong and the sound of rushing water.

"Help me, Josh. This is all much too much to process. It's coming at me too fast…."

"I will, but we don't have a lot of time."

"Is it possible the stones are still with the painting?"

"If no one knew about them but Esme and Blackie, and they both perished on the ship, then yes," Josh said.

"Do you think Harrison knows about the stones?"

"I don't think so."

"What about my uncle? He's purchased several paintings from the Blackwell's estate. Actually, every painting that the estate has put on the market. Josh—" Her eyes were wild, and she was overwhelmed with the flood of information.

"What if I help you and they find out? If my uncle finds out? Or if Harrison finds out? This could be just the thing that sets him off. If I go with the reincarnation theory, that we keep coming back until we get it right, then what if he's not ready to do it right? Why shouldn't I walk away from him now? Never see him again? Protect myself?"

"Maybe you should."

"Can I, though? Can I just walk away from him, never see him again? Will I avoid whatever this is leading up to? What happens to me if I just walk away from Harrison and my uncle and from you?"

"I'm not psychic. I've been searching for answers just like you have. I can only tell you the theory."

"It's better than nothing. Explain it to me."

"If you buy into reincarnation, then you buy into fate. So if you try to run away, like Oedipus did, you might escape from what you perceive as the danger only to come face-to-face with the real danger at the end of the journey."

She looked down as she stepped over a large felled tree trunk covered with lichen. "No, I'm sorry. I can't do this. I'm not stupid enough to walk right into a potential minefield."

"I can't blame you. My problems aren't yours to solve."

They walked on in silence for another few hundred yards. She was leading them west now, toward an exit. The path looped around and then sloped down. At the bottom, Josh realized he knew this spot. They were right under the bridle path. He hung back a few steps; he didn't want to be the one to choose which way to go, not now. She'd chosen the route. He had assumed the path she'd taken had been somewhat arbitrary, that she'd certainly been too upset to plan a course. But on some level, some part of her must have known where she was taking them, because there were no coincidences and they had arrived at the Riftstone arch.

"Do *you* believe in fate?" she asked.

Standing in its shadow, he looked at the bridge. "I don't know what I believe."

She followed his glance and stared at the rough-hewn stone structure. Almost as if she was in a trance, she walked up to it and put her hand out, touching the rock with her fingertips.

"Josh, do you have lurches, too?" she asked as she turned around to face him again.

"For the past year and a half."

"What was your trigger?"

"I was in an accident."

"Were you hurt?"

"Yes, I was almost killed."

"Where do your flashbacks take you?"

"To Rome. Ancient Rome."

She stared at him quizzically. "But that's not the only place, is it?"

"No, it's not."

She was still staring at him as if she was trying to see through him. "The humming…" she said. Then frowned. Shut her eyes, opened them. "Esme had a brother. Did I tell you that?" Swaying slightly as if she were dizzy, she reached out for one of the supporting boulders that held up the arch. "I think they played here. She was worried about him when she was in Rome. She thought he might be sick because he'd stopped writing—did I tell you that when I was under hypnosis? Did I tell you about my brother?"

"No. Do you know his name?" He waited, not aware that he was holding his breath.

"Percy."

Her voice sounded extremely loud, and it seemed to Josh that the word "Percy" echoed, bouncing off of the stones. The scent of jasmine and sandalwood blew down over him, and he braced himself. This was no time for a lurch, but now that he sensed it coming, he ached for it. An addict craving his drug. The air undulated around him, and shivers of excitement shot up and down his arms and legs and wrapped around his torso. He wasn't moving, and yet he had that same feeling, as if he was being sucked down into a vortex where the atmosphere was heavier and thicker. He turned around and saw his sister, Esme, standing high up on the highest rock, laughing and shouting to him to come and look at what she'd found. *"A man's gold pocket watch. Someone must have lost it. Look how it shines."*

No. He wasn't Percy. He was Josh.

"Do you remember it here?" Josh asked, unaware he was even speaking out loud.

"Is this where we found the gold watch?"

"Yes."

Rachel's eyes were wide with wonder.

"Do you believe that you were my brother?"

"I think so."

"It would be nice, wouldn't it, to think you were. That I found you again."

He nodded.

"What happened to him? To Percy, do you know?"

"He was poisoned by his uncle."

"Uncle..." She hesitated, thinking, remembering. "Uncle Davenport," Rachel said, slightly in awe of what she was realizing. But she was calmer. He could see it in her face, sense it.

"Josh, I don't want to put my life on the line for some legend that may or may not be true and that has nothing to do with me. Except I have this crazy feeling that I'm supposed to be doing this. I'm not making sense again, am I? What if I've gotten involved with... What if Harrison... Christ, if this reincarnation stuff is true and if he and I did this dance before, then we know what's going to happen next. He's going to kill me."

"Or you're with him so he can make the past up to you."

"Which is it?"

Josh felt another twinge of responsibility for her. Was it because of the sibling bond someone named Percy and someone named Esme had shared?

"You have to help me. I don't know what to do," she cried.

"I can't do that."

"You have to."

What if she was right? What if she did need him to tell her? If that was part of this. The two of them finding each other. Not just him finding Sabina. But Percy finding Esme. He'd failed to protect her in the past but maybe he'd be able to protect her in the present.

"You love Harrison, don't you?"

"Does that matter?"

"Yeah, it does. Nothing happens by mistake. If we go by the theories, and if you love him, you need to give him a chance to do the right thing this time."

"Walk right into this fucking fire? Who will save me this time if everything goes wrong again?"

There are no rules of engagement, Josh thought. No list of suggestions for how to deal with past-life experiences and present-life situations. Those who believe in reincarnation do not suggest that scenarios will ever repeat themselves exactly. But they could. We are products of our instincts. We can be dragged away from something that is dangerous only to turn around and return to it the minute we're free to. Maybe she needed to live this out. Maybe, Josh thought, he was full of shit and should encourage her to get away from all of them, even him, as fast as she could.

"I'll be there with you. I'll make sure nothing happens."

Rachel looked at him with a sudden trusting smile and he felt, deeply felt, what those two people named Esme and Percy—who had lost their father and lived under the same roof with a vicious man named Davenport and a mother who didn't have the strength to stand up to him—what that brother and sister had meant to each other so very long ago.

"Even if I wanted to do this, to help you find the stones, to see if they're actually still there after all this time, I'm not a magician. I can't steal the painting out from under him."

Josh considered Malachai, who was a magician. All his tricks were done in plain sight. "No, of course you can't. I'd never ask you to steal the painting—I don't need the painting—I just need five minutes alone with it. It wouldn't take longer than that to take the frame apart, would it?"

Chapter 63

Josh and Rachel went to a coffee shop to plan what to do next. It was two o'clock in the afternoon on Thursday, and in less than twenty-four hours, Gabriella would need to have a lot of answers for the man who was holding her child captive.

After they'd fleshed out the next steps, Rachel used her cell phone to call Harrison and put the scheme into motion, and Josh went out into the street to call Gabriella.

Answering on the first ring with a stressed hello, she sounded both relieved and disappointed at the sound of his voice. Briefly, he explained what had happened and what he was planning to do.

"You can't do that, Josh. I can't bear being responsible for you, too."

As much as he believed her, he knew part of her didn't mean it. It was what she should say, but no one mattered to her the way Quinn did, and nothing would ever matter to her again if anything happened to Quinn.

"I'll drive right up to New Haven as soon as I'm finished in the city—and Gabriella..."

"Yes?"

"I'm sorry for leaving you alone this long."

"It's okay. I've been online with Rollins most of the day, working on the translations. Be careful, Josh—" Her voice broke on his name.

He winced, and even after he'd clicked his phone shut, he was still hearing her, seeing her in his mind: the way her light brown, almost-gold eyes flashed, and how she pulled her wild, honey-colored hair off her face whenever she thought hard about something.

Should he have told her about the possibility there was a second set of stones? Had it been cruel to have raised her spirits if, in fact, they didn't exist?

When he returned to Rachel, she was still on the phone. He couldn't help but hear her strained conversation.

"I don't understand. Either he's made an offer on the painting or he hasn't." Pause. "Well, then, let my client see it—the worst that will happen is that you'll have a second offer to use as pressure." Pause. "Good, we'll be there in less than an hour." She smiled, but the smile was twisted with disillusionment.

The doorman of the apartment building on Park Avenue and Seventy-Ninth Street asked Josh for his name so he could be announced.

"Barton Lipper."

They had planned carefully. Barton Lipper was a client of Rachel's who lived in Maryland. A recluse, he ordered pieces of jewelry from her every four or five months. An Internet search brought up stories about the man's billions, but no photographs.

The sunglasses Josh wore, despite the setting sun, hid his eyes, and he was grateful for their opaqueness. A man can see when you are lying—especially if the man was himself a liar. He didn't know for sure that's what Harrison was. That he sold paintings that often had questionable provenance did not, in itself, brand him as a criminal. Sotheby's and Christie's had, over the years, sold paintings of questionable provenance, too. And in this case, the School of Caravaggio painting had never been stolen. The estate of Titus Blackwell had inherited it and it passed from generation to generation until six weeks before, when it had appeared on the market for the first time.

The question was, had it ever been taken apart?

The elevator man, who also wore white gloves, looked straight ahead while Josh watched the numbers light up on the board. It seemed as if the ride was taking too damn long. Finally, the bronzed doors opened.

"It's Penthouse A, on your right, sir."

Inside, Terry, a young woman, greeted Josh, who introduced himself as Barton Lipper. Escorting him to the salon, she told him that Rachel Palmer wasn't there yet, but that Harrison would be with him in just a moment.

The room had a double-height ceiling and no windows. Three of the walls showcased oil paintings from the eighteenth and nineteenth centuries. The fourth was empty except for a carpeted platform that sat like a small stage, waiting for the performance to start.

Terry asked Josh if he'd like anything to drink. He asked for water and she left to fetch it. A few moments passed. Josh didn't get up to inspect the paintings around him. He didn't need the distraction; he wanted to concentrate on what he was there to accomplish.

A few minutes after Terry returned with the water, Harrison came in. He was tall and imposing, physically a good match to Rachel's stunning looks.

"Mr. Lipper. It's a pleasure," he said, and offered his hand.

The handshake was quick.

"Rachel called a few minutes ago. Her taxi is stuck in rush-hour traffic. Though, every hour in New York is now rush hour. In the meantime, would you like to wait for her or look at the painting?"

"I'd like to see the painting. I'm on a tight schedule."

Harrison disappeared, returning a moment later with a framed canvas he held gingerly with its back facing out so that Josh couldn't yet see the painting. Harrison placed it on top of the uppermost step of the carpeted platform, stood in front of it, shielding it as he adjusted it, and then stepped back.

Rachel was right. This was not a masterpiece. It was a feat. A luminous, absorbing re-creation of reality, so intensely alive and powerful that within seconds of looking at it you forgot it was a flat surface covered with a mix of oil and pigment. This was a world unto itself. That it had been created by a brush and paint, that it was not a living, breathing man somehow frozen in that moment, seemed impossible.

"Amazing, isn't it?"

"Yes. It makes everything else—" Josh searched for something to say "—just a painting."

Harrison nodded.

Josh rose and walked toward it. He'd planned on using these

initial moments to look at and familiarize himself with the frame. He'd spent a half hour earlier taking apart four of the paintings on Rachel's walls. At best, if everything went right, he was only going to have a few minutes alone with this one, and he needed to be quick. But he couldn't focus on anything but the sensuous eyes, the voluptuous mouth and the invitation implicit in the Bacchus's gaze.

"Mr. Shoals?" Terry was at the door.

"Yes?"

"Rachel is downstairs. She's tripped on the sidewalk getting out of the cab. She'd appreciate it if you would come down."

"Oh, no, this is my fault. She's here because of me—let me go," Josh offered, trying for sincere concern.

"No, that's not necessary. These things happen. I'll leave you with Bacchus. I'm sure you'll be in excellent company."

Josh's heart was pounding so loudly he worried Terry might be able to hear it and come running. He took the painting off the stand and turned it around. Some of the energy drained from the room. Now it was just rough canvas and four pieces of wood mitered together.

Rachel had seen the back of the painting when she'd inspected it at the auction house and had explained that removing the painting from its frame would be a simple procedure.

All he had to do was pull out the four clips that secured the canvas to the wood.

He fumbled as he worked out the first clip, but did better with the second, and his speed improved with the third and fourth, so in less than sixty seconds he had the canvas safely put aside and stared at an empty gold baroque frame.

Working more quickly, almost recklessly now, not caring if he chipped the wood or gold leaf, he took the frame apart, remembering how Esme had described this process while Rachel was under hypnosis.

Josh inspected each arm, up and down, prodding, pushing, searching. Nothing on the first arm or second. He was running out of time. Just as he picked up the third, he heard sounds outside. Was that Rachel? Already?

The third arm looked the same as the first two.

Yes, the sound was Rachel, asking for something. Water? It didn't matter. He picked up the fourth arm and found what he was looking for.

Digging at it with the edge of the smallest of the tools he'd brought with him, he tried to pull it. No. It wouldn't work like that. He looked closer. Where the grain of the wood ran left to right was a small ridge.

Maybe...

Using the edge of the knife, he unscrewed the threaded wooden pin.

A spring creaked.

A hiding place was revealed.

Josh was afraid to breathe.

The room around him had closed in. There was nothing but the piece of wood and the hollow space inside of it. The glorious painting wasn't there. There were no people outside. He tipped the wooden arm over and shook it.

Chapter 64

"What are you doing?" Harrison asked. He stood by the door, trying to hold back his anger.

How much had he seen? What was he thinking?

Rachel laughed. The sound of light crystal. Of water splashing. "You know, Barton, you can't just take apart a painting without asking."

Josh shrugged. "I can if I'm considering spending this kind of money for it. I always look at paintings out of the frame. Frames are a distraction, to say the least."

Rachel had schooled him on this just an hour before. Many collectors insisted on seeing the canvas out of the frame to inspect it. If he used this excuse, it would be plausible.

"But you took the frame apart?"

"To judge its authenticity."

Harrison was kneeling down, inspecting his painting. His eyes swept the surface from right to left and then back again, ignoring Josh and Rachel, and the wooden arms on the ground.

"What were you really doing?" he said as he picked up one of the arms and looked at it.

Josh didn't know how long Harrison had been standing behind him. Had he seen something? What would Harrison do if Josh tried to leave? Was he in danger? Was Rachel? She'd told Josh that Harrison had a gun. Was he carrying it? Probably. If you are showing a four-million-dollar painting to someone and you own a gun, you probably don't leave it in a drawer.

"It's a beautiful painting. But the frame is inappropriate," Josh said.

Now Harrison looked at him as if he was insane.

"Who cares about the frame? The painting is a Caravaggio."

"It does appear to be from the *school* of Caravaggio. But the frame isn't original." Josh knew the comment was irrational. That was the point. He needed to convince Harrison he was eccentric and make the disassemblage convincing. He had what he'd come for, and it was time to leave.

"Thank you for showing it to me." He nodded and walked to the door. Put his fingers on the knob. Turned it. He was about to open the door when—

"You're not going to want to do that, Mr. Lipper."

The gun was a snub-nosed revolver, icy-black and compact. And it was trained on Josh.

Chapter 65

"Why don't you sit down and show me what you put in your pocket when I walked into the room."

"Harrison, don't be ridiculous. Don't you realize who you are accusing of—"

"Rachel, please. Now, Mr. Lipper, what did you put into your pocket?" Harrison was trying to keep his eyes on Josh and look around the room at the same time. When he realized he couldn't, he opted to watch Josh and asked Rachel to take inventory.

"Is the Fabergé letter opener on the desk?"

"Yes, of course. Harrison, there's no way that Mr. Lipper would take—"

"There should be a small frame next to that, rubies, enamel."

"It's here. Put down the gun," she said. Her voice was shaking and Josh thought that was okay. It would make sense to Harrison that Rachel, with one of her clients being held at gunpoint by her lover, was nervous.

Harrison's eyes had not left his face, but Josh still couldn't read his expression, couldn't get a bead on him. "Mr. Shoals. I can show you what you saw when you walked into the room, but to do so I'm going to need to put my hand back in my pocket."

He nodded. "Fine. Do it slowly."

Josh reached into his jacket pocket and found the box of breath mints, wrapped his fingers around it and pulled it out. He was taking a chance, but he'd learned from watching Malachai do his magic tricks that most of the time, people don't know what they've seen because they aren't looking in the right place.

"This is all it was. I'd be happy to wait while you inspect the rest of the treasures in the room, but honestly, I didn't take anything of yours."

This was the truth, and Josh knew his voice presented it as the truth. He knew his face showed it as the truth. The stones had never belonged to Harrison. As Josh suspected, he had not even known they existed.

Harrison picked up the box of mints, shook it and listened to the slight rattle. He returned it to Josh and lowered the gun.

Rachel ran over to Josh's side as fast as she could, considering she was limping convincingly. "I'm sorry, Mr. Lipper." She'd apologized, but the look in her eyes was gratefulness. That was when Josh realized that she was going to be all right now. She'd come to understand how her past was warning her about her present and what she needed to do with the information.

Josh waved her off, as if to say it was nothing and he didn't blame her. She was gathering up her bag and her jacket.

"Where are you going?" Harrison asked her.

She looked at him, held his eyes, shook her head. "You pulled a gun on him! You could have shot him. I don't belong here. This was all a mistake." She walked to the door, to where Josh was waiting for her.

"What kind of game is this, Rachel? Did your uncle put you up to this? What kind of scheme are the two of you planning with the Bacchus?"

"My uncle? What does he have to do with any of this?"

"You didn't know he's the client I mentioned? Oh, please, don't insult me. I just want to know what's going on."

"You have to believe me, I didn't know… I had no idea. My uncle's been talking to *you* about buying the Bacchus?"

"He's determined to own it. But we're at an impasse over— No, I'm not falling for this. You must know. *I'm* the one who's being played for the fool."

"Harrison, it doesn't matter to me whether you believe me or not, but my uncle has no idea I've been here today."

"Rachel?" Josh said in a quietly insistent voice. "We need to go."

She walked through the door that he was holding open for her. Josh let her pass, then, just before he walked out, he turned and looked back at Harrison Shoals. "The frame isn't an original—you should do something about that."

"The frame is unimportant." Harrison shook his head, incredulous.

"Not to me. An original frame would have been quite a treasure," Josh said, and walked out.

Chapter 66

Downstairs, they quickly got into the town car that Rachel had come in and kept waiting so they could leave right away, in case Harrison tried to followed them or harassed them.

"Where to, miss?" the driver asked. "Home?"

She looked at Josh. "Where should we drop you?"

In his left pocket was the box of mints. In his right pocket, the stones pressed against his thigh, teasing him. Shoals had seen him put something in his pocket, but he hadn't focused on which pocket. Josh had bluffed, and it had worked. That's the thing about sleight-of-hand that Malachai had taught him. You know there's a trick happening, but you are rarely looking in the right place to catch it. He wanted to tell Malachai what a good teacher he'd been.

He had to rent a car and get up to New Haven, but first he needed to pick up his photographic equipment. Josh wanted to light the stones so that every mark was perfectly clear and distinct before they e-mailed the pictures to Rollins. He also needed to wrap up the stones carefully before he drove up to see Gabriella; they were too precious to be rolling around in his pocket.

"I'm going to the foundation, but let me drop you off first. Where are you going?"

"I guess back to my uncle's."

"Is there somewhere else you can go? I'm not sure that's a good idea. Not yet."

A veil of worry clouded her eyes. "You don't think my uncle would—"

"I don't know, and that's why I want you to go someplace that is completely neutral. Just for a few days, until we can make sure."

"I thought this was about me and Harrison, Esme and Blackie."

"It was—it is—but...isn't there someplace else you can go, just for a few days? I promise I'll help you figure all this out as soon as I can. In the meantime, you have to stay safe."

"It's not possible that my uncle has anything to do with this. He's not a violent man."

"I'm sure you're right, but I don't want you to take any chances. You're safe now, Rachel. I want you to stay safe."

She gave the driver the address of her closest friend and turned back to Josh. "If I am safe it's because of you. Harrison pulled a gun on you. Over a painting. How could I have been attracted to him?"

"You're not the first person to be seduced by power."

She smiled ruefully, "No, I'm not. Esme was, too. That's why I need to figure all this out. So it doesn't happen again."

When the car pulled up in front of Rachel's friend's apartment on York Avenue and Eighty-Eighth Street, she leaned forward, threw her arms around Josh and hugged him.

"You're in danger, aren't you?" she asked.

"No, this isn't about me."

"But you're the one taking all the chances. Please, be careful. Okay? I just found you."

Fifteen minutes later, Josh opened the door to the foundation's basement, which had been turned into a state-of-the-art, temperature-controlled library, and where he stored his equipment. He shut the door behind him and was just going to pull the stones out of his pocket when he saw Malachai standing on a ladder, inspecting a row of books on a high shelf. He turned at the noise. "Thank goodness, Josh, I was so worried," he said, and climbed down. "Where have you been all day? I expected you to come back or at least call after your plane landed."

On the large table in the middle of the room, Josh noticed a dozen dusty books were open to various pages. They were all titles from the mid 1800s on different methods of inducing past-life regressions.

"How did it go with Rollins? No, first tell me, how is Gabriella?"

"In terrible shape. And all alone. I wish she'd call her father so he could be with her. But she's stubborn. I don't know how she's holding it together. Panicked about her daughter, working with Rollins, trying to come up with the damn mantra."

"Are they getting the translations done?"

"Rollins is still stumped on a few markings, but he should meet the deadline."

Using an index card, Malachai marked the page he had been studying in one of the books and shut it. "Imagine what it would be like if the mantra worked. To be able to remember who you'd been before, not just fragments, but the entire story. To push back the curtains of the present and peer into the past. Have you considered the man who will wind up owning the stones? He'll be one of the most powerful men on earth, Josh. Damn it, we should have had them here." His eyes narrowed. "We were so close."

"Haven't you ever considered that it's all just a myth, and that the mantra is nothing but a collection of sounds that doesn't do a thing?"

"Still not a true believer?"

"I need just one thing in black and white. If I could have just photographed one aura, captured it on film..."

"Finding us here at the foundation, where Percy once lived? Knowing about the tunnel into the park? What about the little girl at the site of the excavation in Rome? Those weren't proof enough for you? What kind of magic was that, then?"

"The story of the tomb was all over the television and in all the papers. Natalie could have heard people discussing it anywhere. As for the tunnel, I had spent hours in your company before that happened—you could have hypnotized me."

"Without you noticing? I think not. And have you forgotten that you're not a good subject? As for Natalie, yes, she could have heard that a woman's body had been found in the tomb, but how would she have found out her name was Sabina? The same name you came up with. A name no one else had even whispered. Pulled it out of thin air?"

Josh shrugged. "I'm sure I was thinking about her name at some point. Maybe it was ESP. Maybe it's all been ESP."

"Or maybe it's reincarnation. Beryl and I believe we've heard proof over and over. Living proof. You, Josh, you're living proof. But if we had the stones in our hands we'd be able to convince even the nonbelievers." Malachai's eyes were shining with the possibilities. "People like me, who've never been able to remember, would be able to look back and find the answers to help them go forward."

Until that moment, Josh had planned on taking the stones out of his pocket, showing them to Malachai and telling him about Rachel remembering Esme's life and death on the ship. But the hunger in his mentor's eyes worried him. What if he snatched them away and wouldn't let Josh have them back? What if he was more desperate than the man who was orchestrating all this madness?

No, wouldn't anyone do the right thing in those circumstances? What were a handful of emeralds and sapphires in exchange for a child's life? Even that particular handful of stones. But proving reincarnation had been Malachai's work for much longer than it had been Josh's distraction. Knowing for sure would explain his life, but for Malachai it would be vindication of a life devoted to that one subject.

Men are monsters all.

Who'd said that? Percy? Yes, Percy, discussing his uncle Davenport Talmage, the man who had poisoned him and sent his sister to her death. Esme...who died as a result of her uncle's greed. Rachel had an uncle, too.... Was it possible that Alex was just as greedy and more involved in all this than anyone had guessed?

"Have you thought about tomorrow?" Malachai said, interrupting Josh's conjecturing. "I want to go with you. Follow you and Gabriella. The two of you can't do this alone. What if something were to go wrong?"

Chapter 67

Josh arrived at Gabriella's house just after eight that night. He didn't notice until he'd followed her into the living room and she was in the light, but in the past fourteen hours, so much life had been drained out of her. It wasn't just how pale she was or how deep the hollows were under her eyes. Gabriella seemed to have faded, the way old snapshots do. She tried for a small smile at seeing him, but it turned on itself and wound up being an anguished grimace. Even the room exhibited her anxiety—there was a coffee mug precariously close to the edge of a table; an apple with a single bite taken out of it that had already turned a soggy brown; a sweater that lay trampled on the floor where she must have just dropped it when she took it off and never bothered to pick it up.

Neither of them spoke. She was waiting to see what he'd found, and he was in a hurry to show it to her, believing his discovery would at least offer her a whisper of hope. Her eyes never left his hands as he opened his backpack and pulled out the manila envelope. She held out her palms as if she were a child begging for food, and, one by one, he placed each stone into her cupped palms: an emerald, an emerald, a sapphire, an emerald, a sapphire and a ruby. Clutching the gemstones to her chest as if, together, they made up her baby, she sank down to the floor and wept.

Sitting down beside her, Josh took her in his arms, held her and just let her cry. But in less than five minutes she was back on her feet, determined and again in control.

"We must photograph these…right away, and e-mail them to Rollins. He's waiting. It's taken him all this time to get the other six done. I don't know…if he can do this…it took him twenty hours to do the first half…. What if these are different markings, and he can't—" She stopped herself, biting her bottom lip, which by now was badly bruised.

"I brought my equipment. I can set up in your dining room and get the shots done in less than ten minutes." It wasn't relief Josh saw in her eyes, only a lessening of panic, but at least he could give her that, he thought.

After Josh shot the stones from several angles and downloaded them onto Gabriella's computer, she e-mailed the file to Rollins. Within fifteen minutes, he called to let her know he'd gotten them, had been able to open them, and was ready to get to work.

After she hung up, she looked more depleted than she had when Josh walked into the house.

"Something wrong?" he asked.

"He said the marks are different on these stones. None of

them repeat from the first group. It's going to take him the rest of the night and into the morning to decipher them. If he can do it that fast..." Like so many of her sentences lately, this one didn't end but just faded out.

"He'll get it done, Gabriella."

"Will he?" She shook her head vigorously. "You don't know. Neither of us does. I can't stand it. Being out of control like this is the worst part. I want to do something... She's my daughter, and I want to do something to save her..." Gabriella ran her fingers through her hair, which was by now a tangled disarray of curls. "Oh, God," she moaned. "I want to do something. Anything..."

"I know. And you have. You found the one person who can help you, and he will. Listen to me..."

She hadn't been looking at him, but now she turned and faced him. He'd seen the expression in her eyes when he'd been in the Middle East photographing the mothers of children who had been unwitting victims of terrorist activity. It was a different expression of grief than he beheld in the faces of the mothers whose sons or daughters had been soldiers. In those deaths, the mothers had clung to their children's heroism with a tenacity that was like the silken threads a spider weaves: so fragile-looking, but so impossibly tensile and strong.

"Why don't you take a shower? I'll make us drinks and something to eat. You haven't eaten anything since last night on the plane, have you?"

"You can cook?" She was almost smiling.

"Surprised?"

"Yes, for some reason."

"Well don't expect anything Cordon Bleu, but if you have some eggs I can—"

"You know, I don't think I can eat anything."

"It's not a choice. You need to eat or you won't be any good to anyone tomorrow. So point me toward the kitchen."

On the way he told her Malachai was going to follow them in his car the next day, in case anything went wrong.

"What if they have someone watching us? What if they see him?" she asked, her voice tight with new tension.

"He'll be very careful. It's safer this way. What if something were to happen to me? Then you'd be alone with this monster." He reached out and touched her cheek. "Go ahead. Go upstairs."

She didn't go, not yet. "When this is all over…when Quinn is back home…back with me, I'll find the words to adequately thank you."

The end of this ordeal still seemed far away. Ahead of them was an arduous path through a war zone where, he hoped, at the end was a little girl he'd never seen who would be reunited with her mother.

While Gabriella showered, Josh poured himself a few inches of Scotch and sipped it as he gathered the ingredients for eggs and toast. Now that he'd delivered the stones and Rollins had started on the translations and he was alone, he felt the full impact of what had happened to him that day. Meeting with Rachel, hypnotizing her, hearing her heart-wrenching rendition of Esme's past—Esme, Percy's sister, a woman it seemed he was somehow psychically tied to—lying his way into Harrison Shoals's gallery, taking apart the painting, finding the Memory Stones and stealing them, only to have a gun pulled on him. At least he'd been able to help Rachel break her ties to Harrison, a man who, if there was such a thing as destiny, was far too dangerous for her to have in her life. But there was still the question of Rachel's uncle. Was Alex a threat to her? Worse, was he a threat to Gabriella and Quinn? Should he call the police while Gabriella was upstairs and tell them about Alex—

His cell phone rang. He looked at the readout, saw it was Malachai and answered it.

"I wanted to check on you both. Is there anything new?"

"No."

"What about the mantra? Will she have the mantra for the stones in time?"

"I think…listen, Malachai, you should know this—there are twelve stones."

"What?"

"There are twelve Memory Stones, not six."

"How do you know that?" His voice was tense.

"We'll explain it to you when you get here tomorrow."

"No. I don't think so. Not after everything we've been through. I'd like you to explain it now."

Josh had never heard that edge in Malachai's voice, but it didn't surprise him, so he explained what had happened.

"When did this happen? I just saw you. Why on earth didn't you tell me this before? Do you have them, Josh? Are they in your possession?"

Josh looked into the dining room where the stones were all still laid out on Gabriella's glass table. Light shone down on them and up through them, illuminating them from within. They glowed like underwater sea creatures, mysterious but alive.

And then, just as he was going to say yes, he had them, Josh felt a flicker of fear course through him like a current. A warning.

If he told Malachai the whole truth, would he get in his car and drive up to New Haven right then? And if he did, once he saw them, would Malachai be able to let go of them when he was so desperate for proof that reincarnation existed? When he was convinced that the stones were that substantiation? Could Josh take the chance and put Quinn at greater risk?

"Not yet. Gabriella will have them by tomorrow."

"How did this happen?"

Behind him, Josh heard Gabriella on the stairs.

"We're going to eat something now, Malachai. We'll tell you tomorrow. I'll call as soon as we know where and when we're supposed to make the exchange and pick up Quinn."

They ate in the kitchen. Josh watched her mechanically pick up the fork, bring it to her mouth, chew the food, repeat the pattern. He knew she wasn't tasting a thing, but that didn't matter. She needed the energy. When they finished, they took mugs of steaming, milk-laced coffee into the dining room and looked down at the emeralds, sapphires and ruby, watching them as if they might at any moment take flight. Except they weren't alive. They were useless chunks of rock dug from the earth, somehow transformed into treasure responsible for at least seven deaths that he knew of.

"I heard you on the phone when I came downstairs," she said. "Why did you lie to Malachai?"

"I was afraid that if he knew we had them he'd drive up here tonight to see them—and then, once he did, I'm not sure he'd ever let them go."

"You want these as much as he does, don't you?"

Josh nodded.

"But *you're* not taking them."

"Quinn's your child."

"But I remember what you told me before Quinn was taken. You said all you wanted was some way to prove that reincarnation exists. You're the one who thinks he's going crazy, who's been obsessed for so long. Whose life has fallen apart. How can *you* let them go?"

Josh stared at the stones and considered how he'd found out about them. How Rachel had remembered something she hadn't been aware she'd ever known. And how the fabric of their pasts had been woven together in a way that defied logic. Shouldn't the way he found the stones—indeed, the very fact of these stones' existence—prove it for him once and for all? There were so many incidents and revelations in the past four months that should have been proof enough for him. Why weren't they?

For the same reason that interviewing three thousand children still hadn't been enough for Malachai or Beryl.

"You know," Josh said, taking his eyes off of the glittering gems and turning to Gabriella, "tomorrow night at this time, you'll be here with Quinn."

She closed her eyes as if in silent prayer. When she opened them, she looked down at the stones, too.

"I can't imagine what it was like, what you did today, taking these. You were almost killed in Rome, and yet you put yourself back in danger today."

"We're way past that."

She turned and stared at him for a long minute. Then she

leaned in, very quickly, put her mouth on his and kissed him. It was intimate but asexual. An expression of gratitude. "I take it back," she said. "What I said before. There's no way I'll ever figure out how to say thank you."

"I don't expect you to. This has to do with so many things that I don't quite understand—karmic debts that need to be paid, plans that have to be lived out, despite our conscious wishes or wants. You and Quinn are part of it, but not the way I thought. I'm not making sense, am I?" He was embarrassed. It all sounded like sentimental lunacy when he talked about it out loud.

"Josh, do you think you and I are connected?"

"In some past-life way?"

"Yes."

"I desperately wanted to believe we were. But no. Even when I'm with you, I can still feel her presence—she's still pulling at me."

He stood up, walked the length of the room, got as far away from Gabriella as he could, but it didn't matter, he could still see her luminous golden eyes looking at him. Right then, more than he'd ever wanted to tell anyone anything, he wanted to tell her that whatever had happened in the past didn't matter. That he could live without knowing how Julius's story with Sabina ended. That he could forget the nameless, faceless woman he thought was waiting for him. That he didn't need to keep finding proof or discover a method of photographing auras. That he didn't have to turn all these theories into irrefutable, black-and-white realities.

But he knew better.

Yesterday, he might have been able to walk away from his search.

Yesterday, Rachel hadn't yet reached into her unconscious and told him a story about a painting and a frame.

Yesterday, that same painting and frame hadn't yet offered up a treasure that they had been hiding for more than a hundred years.

Yesterday, he might have been able to walk away from the idea that some destiny was waiting for him.

One day had irrevocably doomed him to remain faithful to his past.

"Oh, God..." The words ended in a cry, as if she'd been pierced and was in pain.

"What?"

"Josh, we don't really know there aren't more of these, do we? What if there are? What if we give all twelve to this monster, and they don't work because—"

"No, that's not going to happen. He's not going to make you wait while he tries them out before he turns Quinn over."

"But what if there are fourteen stones? Sixteen stones?"

"There were twelve." He heard his own voice from a great distance, as if he were standing at one end of a long tunnel and someone at the other end had just said it.

"You're sure?"

"Yes."

She stared at him. "Wait...you know...I think you might be right." She stood up and walked quickly out of the room.

Josh followed her into the library, where she was pulling books off of the shelves, dropping them to the floor when they weren't the ones she wanted.

"What are you doing?"

"I think I remember something—I'm not sure. There may

be some kind of proof." She pulled another book off the shelf and flipped through the pages. "Yes...here it is. Here, come look."

It was a drawing of a peacock, feathers splayed.

"What is that? Why is that significant?"

"This is a copy of a drawing found in a tomb in ancient Egypt. Ancient writings described it as a golden breastplate from India that would assist the wearer in reaching his next incarnation. In each of the peacock's feathers was a precious stone. Josh, there were twelve feathers in the peacock's tail. Twelve exactly. The peacock was an ancient symbol of rebirth. Reincarnation. The stones have ancient writing on them that we know is Indus. Maybe this was where the stones were originally from."

"You can give him that, give it to him along with everything else as some kind of proof."

She was already ripping the pages out in a frenzy of activity and manic energy that he found heartbreaking. And then she laid her head down on her arms and wept. Josh watched, helplessly. No matter what he said to her, he knew it wouldn't do any good. Nothing would, except getting her daughter back.

"I think you should try to get some sleep. I know it's going to be hard, but you need the rest. You won't help Quinn if you're this exhausted tomorrow."

She nodded.

"Come on." He helped her up. "I'm going to take you upstairs."

"You're not leaving, are you?" she said in a shaky voice. The tears were still coming.

"No. I'm going to stay here. Sleep on the couch. I don't want you to be alone, not tonight."

As they walked up the stairs, she leaned on him, and he could feel how cold her skin was through her shirt. In her bedroom she lay down, too tired to get undressed, so he pulled a quilt up over her. Now that she was in bed, her sobs intensified, filling the room with her grief and her fear. He sat down beside her, bent over and put his arms around her, and they stayed like that for what seemed a long time. Suddenly she lifted her face to his, leaned in and kissed him. The anger and fury in the pressure of her lips on his surprised him. He didn't understand, but that didn't matter now; there would be time later to consider how impossible their being together was.

"I just want to get out of my head for a while. Is that okay?" she whispered.

"Yes, Gabriella. It's fine."

She wasn't gentle or patient as she took more than she gave. She ripped at his shirt and pants, pulling his clothes off him, not giving him a chance to do the same to her. He was instantly hard as he watched her undress quickly. He was barely able to glimpse her long legs, full hips and breasts because she was too fast for him. One minute she was pulling off her clothes, the next she was climbing on top of him, almost as if she was possessed.

And then she stared down at him with blazing eyes that never closed, that dripped endless tears on his chest as she tried to ride out her fear and her pain. Josh felt himself disappear into her, amazed at the heat that surrounded him. He couldn't catch her rhythm; she was too frenetic, moving in an almost trance-like craze, so he stopped trying to, instead letting her set the pace. She kept changing her speed, keeping him on the edge, slowing down, barely moving, then riding him as if there was a race she needed to win, and just when he'd feel the pressure building, she would stop, idle for a minute, not moving her hips or legs or torso but only flexing her muscles, then rushing off again.

Gabriella was raw and open and rough, and Josh wasn't sure she knew who he was anymore other than a release and a reprieve from her terrors. But even knowing that, her pressure and pulsing and pushing moved him deeply. She was surviving the only way she could, and he was determined to help her through it.

Finally she threw back her head and gripped his shoulders so tightly he felt real pain. The low moan started deep where the two of them met and meshed. It rose up, increasing in intensity, becoming louder and primitive, sounding the way he felt, as if the world was exploding and imploding at the same time, and years of grief and passion and helplessness came together and escalated into a howl that filled the room and made him turn his head aside, and this time, he wept with her.

Josh woke up alone in the bed, naked, under the covers, remembering the night before. Not so much their violent coming together as what had happened afterward. How Gabriella had fallen asleep, exhausted and spent, nestled in the crook of his arm. And how he had stayed awake, watching her, wishing that the stones were already gone and Quinn was back and this was his life.

Gabriella was in the kitchen, drinking coffee, dressed, her hair still damp and curled around her face when he went downstairs. She looked up at him and tried to smile. It was an intimate glance that reached out across the room and embraced him.

"Did you hear from Rollins?" he said, asking her the one thing that mattered.

She nodded. "He's almost done, thank God."

"Any other calls?" he asked.

"No. I'm going crazy."

"They'll call, Gabriella. They will."

She nodded. "Do you want coffee?" She started to get up.

"I'll get it."

"No. Let me. It will give me something to do. I need something to do."

After pouring it, she put a mug down in front of him and then sat down opposite him. "I can't believe what I did last night."

"You'd be surprised what grief does to people."

She looked down into her mug as if she'd find an answer there. "But...it was... I was..."

"You were reaching out, you wanted relief. Don't do this. You're under more stress than you've ever experienced in your whole life. Don't be too hard on yourself."

"It's just that..." She finally looked up at him. There was sorrow and confusion in her eyes. "I didn't use you, Josh."

"There's a Buddhist koan," he said. "A series of candles are set up on a table. The one on the right is lit, those to the left aren't. As each lit candle burns out, just before it expires, a monk uses its flame to light the candle beside it. And when that candle is about to burn out, the monk uses it to light the next candle in the row. The question is, is the flame that burns on that last candle the same flame as the one that burned on the first? The second?"

"It's the same. What do you think?"

"Not the same, but not different, either. Without the first flame none of the other candles could have been lit."

Gabriella nodded.

He went on. "We shared something. It didn't mean the same thing for both of us, but we ignited for a time and shared a burning. And we're both different for it this morning. It might never be repeated, but it won't ever disappear, either."

She bowed her head just enough for it to be a movement, as if what he'd said was a benediction, and just then, the phone rang.

Chapter 68

Friday, 10:48 a.m.

"I told you to shut her up!"

As frightened as she'd been until this very moment, his screaming at her threw Bettina's heart into a rapid rhythm. It didn't seem possible that she could be so frightened for so long and not die of it. Could he hear her heart beating?

"Why *can't* we stop and buy candy?" Quinn asked for the sixth time in a whining voice.

"Because we're in a hurry, sweetheart. Let's just be quiet and be patient."

"But I want to stop," Quinn wailed.

"I swear to God, if you don't get her to shut up, I'm going to pull over and do it myself," Carl barked from the front seat.

"She's not even three years old," Bettina answered with an edgy tone, and then froze. She'd just talked back to him. What was he going to do? She no longer imagined that under his tough exterior was a soft soul that really didn't want to be bad and hurt anyone. She'd spent the past three panic-filled days with him, and she was sure that if there had once been a human core inside of him that responded to kindness or love, it had hardened and dried up.

Bettina looked out of the car window, understanding that although she could see out, no one could see in. The car was like a coffin. Tight, closed, impossible to escape. Kidnappers usually killed their victims. She knew that. It was always on TV. How many lived? What was the percentage? She could picture a hundred newspaper headlines that she'd never paid attention to.

"Why *can't* we get candy?" Quinn asked yet once more.

"I said, shut her up. Didn't you hear me? Christ, she is getting on my nerves."

"Honey, we'll get candy after we meet your mommy. We're going to see her really soon. And then you can get candy."

"Let's stop and get candy and bring it to Mommy. I want M&M's."

Carl turned his head around slightly. "I am telling you for the last time, put a sock in her mouth if you have to. I can't deal with this now. Do you understand that? Do you get that? Or am I going to have to beat it into you?"

There was no question that he could. That he would. She wiped her hands on her jeans and stole a look at the back of Carl's head, at the two inches where his hair ended and before his shirt collar started. His skin was ruddy but soft-looking. Were there veins there? Arteries? If she leaned up to him and bit him, could she hurt him badly enough to incapacitate him and—no. He was driving. If she hurt him, he might lose control of the car and kill them all. But this was as close as she'd been to him in the past three days, after all the frustration of being helpless in that motel room, listening to the droning television for seventy-two hours, after failing to come up with any kind of counterattack.

"Let's get a candy present for Mommy."

"For fuck's sake, shut her the hell up!"

Bettina's body broke out in a new sweat; she shook, and her damn teeth began chattering again. Quinn, who had been listening to the sound for the past three days, and now associated the chattering with the man getting even more angry, broke out in loud, piercing wails.

Bettina's fear escalated. What if this was too much for him? What if he turned around now and shot them both?

"Come on, Quinnie, stop crying now. We're going to see Mommy, and she's going to be so excited to see you that she's going to cover you in kisses."

But the wailing didn't stop. If anything, it intensified.

"Fuck. Fuck. Fuck!"

"Quinnie, do you want to play a game? Your bear wants to play a game with you."

The cries were now shrieks.

"For God's sake, give her this." Carl threw a pack of gum at Bettina. It hit her on the side of the face and stung for a minute. Tears welled up in her eyes.

"What's that?" Quinn asked, the tears stopping instantly as if she'd been able to tell from the shiny yellow wrapper that this was something sweet.

Of all the bizarre things Bettina could have thought of, in the middle of this holy terror, in the back of a car being driven by a cruel, frightening man who had a gun and who she was sure had used it more than once, all Bettina could think of was that Gabriella didn't want Quinn to have gum. It was one of the rules.

Unwrapping it, she showed it to Quinn. "This is gum. I'm going to give you a piece. But listen to me, it's not the same as other kinds of candy. You don't swallow it, you chew it."

"It's not candy?"

"Yes. It's candy, but a special kind. You don't swallow it, you just chew it."

"Just give her the fucking gum. Let her swallow it if she wants. Just get her to shut up. I need her to shut up."

Bettina gave Quinn the stick of gum, forcing a laugh as Quinn put the wondrous thing in her mouth and instantly grinned as the sugar exploded and teased her taste buds.

"Don't swallow it," Bettina warned.

Quinn nodded. Kept chewing. Smiled. Kept chewing.

At least she was quiet now.

Chapter 69

> This soul needs to follow another soul in whom the Spirit of life dwells, because she is saved through the Spirit. Then she will never be thrust into flesh again.
> —Secret Book of John, The Gnostic Gospels, 185 A.D.

Friday, 1:05 p.m.

Malachai pulled up in front of Gabriella's house and sat in his car waiting. Less than two minutes later, she and Josh came out. They stood on the driver's side, talking to Malachai through the open window, filling him in on the kidnapper's instructions and going over their plans. Malachai was going to follow them in his car. If he lost them, he'd call on his cell. Once Gabriella got directions for where the switch was going to be made, Josh would call and give him the information. And most important, once Malachai was sure Josh and Gabriella were with the kidnapper, he was going to alert the police so in case anything at all went wrong, they had help.

"But you're going to explain to them how careful they have to be," Gabriella said.

"I will, don't worry," Malachai said soothingly, the way he talked to the children before he hypnotized them.

And then Malachai asked Josh if he could see the stones.

"Gabriella has them," he said, giving her the option of whether or not she wanted to take them out. But she opened her bag, extracted a padded envelope, took out the tissue-wrapped package and handed it through the window.

Malachai unwrapped them, and hunched over them. Josh couldn't see the stones, or his mentor's face, but from the incline of Malachai's head and his stillness, Josh could tell he was doing what he'd done when he'd first seen them—just kept staring.

A minute went by.

"I'd like to alter the plan. When we get there," Malachai said to Gabriella without looking up at her, still staring at the stones, "I'd like to be the one to make the exchange. I'm not emotionally involved, and I'm less likely to do anything rash. The kidnapper said you could bring someone with you. He'll be expecting you to be with a man."

"No," Josh said. "I'm going in with her."

Now Malachai looked up and gave Josh a stern glance. "These should have been mine. If I can't have them, at least let me be the one to turn them over."

Josh looked at his watch. "We need to go," he said.

Malachai rewrapped the stones and, reluctantly, Josh thought, handed the package back to Gabriella. She gripped it as if the feel of it was keeping her from losing her mind. Then he took her arm, and the two of them walked over to her car.

They spoke only perfunctorily until they were on I-95, heading east, not even knowing their final destination. After thirty minutes, Gabriella's phone rang and the kidnapper gave her an address off exit 8. Gabriella's tension electrified the air. Occasionally, Josh checked the rearview mirror and saw Malachai's Jaguar, three or four cars back, but wasn't worried about losing him. They had cell phones.

At 2:25 p.m., Josh pulled into a parking lot at a Dunkin' Donuts on the Post Road in Stamford as instructed, and they sat silently and waited, watching Gabriella's phone.

The overbearing scent of fried bakery goods wafted into the car but didn't defuse the nervousness that Josh was sure he could smell. Fear and tension has its own stench. It emanated from soldiers in battle. From prisoners on trial. From mothers whose children were in mortal danger.

When the phone rang again she reached for it so quickly it didn't ring a second time. She listened, said yes, then hung up and looked out the window and pointed across the street to a large stone church sitting on top of a small hill. It had a circular driveway, tall spires and a bell tower.

"They're in there. Right in there." Her voice wavered.

Josh drove to the end of the block. The light was red. He stopped.

Gabriella clenched and unclenched her fists. She didn't take her eyes off the church when she spoke to him. "There is no way that anything has happened to my baby, is there?" Her voice was wrenched from a place so deep inside her it sounded as if it had traveled miles to get to the surface.

"Whoever did this doesn't want Quinn, remember that," Josh said. "He doesn't want any more problems. He just wants the stones. That's all he ever wanted from the beginning. He didn't want to kill the professor or the guard. They just got in the way. No one is getting in his way now. He just wants the stones and the mantra. That's all. The stones and the mantra," he repeated, talking to her the way he had heard Malachai talk to the children when he was helping them relax into hypnosis. "The stones and the mantra." As he said it, he wondered if the man he was talking about was Alex Palmer. Was he behind the original robbery and this kidnapping? Was Rachel staying away from him until this was over, as she'd promised?

The red light was lasting longer than seemed possible. Gabriella rolled down the window and leaned out, so far that Josh's instinct was to hold her back.

"The last thing Quinn needs is for you to get hurt," he said.

Was she even hearing him?

"Gabriella, let me do this for you."

She didn't say anything.

The light switched to bright, glaring green. Josh put his foot on the gas and eased out. There weren't any other cars on the street but he still went slowly. They were almost there. He didn't want anything to happen now.

Ten yards.

Twenty yards.

Thirty yards.

Josh took a left into the long driveway. Drove another twenty yards and then pulled up in front of the church. They both got out of the car. He went around to meet her.

"For Quinn's sake—" He held out his hand.

"I need to be in there."

"Stay in the back, in the shadows."

She still hadn't handed him the package that held the stones and the mantra.

"I promise Gabriella, I'll bring her back to you."

She extended her hand. It was shaking, violently.

Chapter 70

Josh, carrying the package that contained three walnut-size sapphires, two emeralds, one ruby and a dozen sheets of paper with phonetic translations of long-forgotten Indus symbols, walked up the steps leading to the church. Gabriella walked beside him.

At the bottom of the driveway, on the street, Malachai parked and got out of his car.

Josh climbed the last of the six steps. He was on the landing. He reached out for the bronze door handle and opened it to cool air perfumed with incense.

For a few seconds, all he could see was the gloom waiting inside. After the sunshine, he was suddenly blind. But he was better than most at readjusting from light to dark from all his work behind the camera and in the darkroom, and within seconds he was reading the shadows.

He walked inside, Gabriella next to him.

Josh took ten steps up the center aisle.

A woman holding the hand of a young child stood in front of the altar. A tall, heavyset man, motionless, was to the right of them. Behind them a gold cross gleamed.

"Who are you?" the man called out. "Where's Mrs. Chase?" In the dim light, he must not have been able to see all the way to the back of the church.

"I'm right here," Gabriella called out. "Josh is my friend, the man you said could drive me here. He's here to help. He has what you want."

"Mo-o-m-my…" The cry was the sound of fear and relief exchanging places, echoing on and on in the almost-empty, hollow church.

Josh felt Gabriella start beside him. He took her arm and held her back. And then he let go and stepped forward.

Meanwhile, Carl had grabbed Quinn by the shoulder, pulled her close, and held her back with one large hand, fingers digging into the little girl's flesh. Bettina's eyes were wide with confusion, not understanding what was happening. She whimpered.

The kidnapper glanced over at her, annoyed.

Hopefully by now Malachai had alerted the police. That had been the plan; once Josh and Gabriella were inside the church, he'd make the call. Josh just had to keep everyone calm until they got here.

And then he heard the sound of soft footsteps behind him.

Josh felt a surge of relief. Thank God.

He didn't turn around. He didn't want to distract the kidnapper or give him any advance warning that the police were here.

Josh kept walking to the altar. He was five feet away when he saw it: gleaming the way the cross gleamed, almost the way the stones had gleamed in Gabriella's living room the night before.

The man had a gun.

"Let Quinn go," Josh said. "Take this and let her go." He held out the package.

And that was when the kidnapper noticed something in the shadows.

"Let Quinn go!" Josh repeated.

The kidnapper ignored him; he was staring to Josh's right. In one quick, smooth move he pulled out his gun and pointed it into the shadows.

"Who the fuck are you?" he shouted.

Josh didn't understand what was happening. Was the kidnapper crazy enough to pull a gun on the police? He turned. No, it wasn't the police, it was Malachai. What the hell was Malachai doing here? There was no time to reason it out. Not now. But there was time for Josh to realize one thing: the police weren't on their way. Malachai, for some reason, hadn't called them.

"Hold your hands out and keep them out," Carl said to Malachai. "I don't know who the fuck you are, and I don't want any trouble."

Malachai held out his hands.

On the altar, Bettina's teeth started to chatter. Loudly enough for Josh to hear.

Carl turned to her. "Shut the fuck up."

Quinn's lower lip quivered.

Josh took one step closer to the altar. "Let the baby-sitter go—you don't need her anymore," he said calmly and evenly. "She's only going to get in your way. Let her come down here and wait with Mrs. Chase."

This was his last chance to get Bettina out of there so she could go and get help. The church was dark enough that the kidnapper wouldn't be able to see if Bettina stayed or left.

Bettina's teeth were still chattering. The repetitive sound shattering the deep, cavernous silence.

"The noise is driving us all crazy," Josh said to the kidnapper, sympathetically. "Let her go."

Bettina was staring at him.

Carl was staring at her.

Call the police, Josh mouthed carefully, hoping she wasn't yet in shock, hoping there was enough light on him that she could make out what he was saying.

"Wait down there," Carl ordered.

Taking off down the steps, Bettina ran toward the back of the church, toward Gabriella.

Josh didn't turn around. Hopefully she'd understood what he'd asked of her and would get help.

Carl's attention returned to Malachai. "So I asked you who the fuck you were."

"I'm not here to make any trouble," he said. "Take the package, let go of the little girl."

As Malachai talked, the kidnapper's eyes narrowed and he cocked his head as if he was making a great effort at listening. Then he smiled. As if something sweet had occurred to him. "The money was supposed to be deposited in my account, but it wasn't."

Why was he telling Malachai that? Josh wondered.

"I'm sure you'll get your money when you deliver the package. Take it. Let the little girl go," Malachai ordered.

The man shook his head. "Only if the money's there, along

with whatever else I was supposed to pick up. Is it? Is what's owed to me in there?"

"Tell me how much money it is, and I'll get it for you," Josh pleaded. "I'll get it right now."

The kidnapper laughed. He pointed his gun at Malachai. "It's him that owes me the money. He's the one who's the fucking liar."

"What are you talking about?" Malachai asked, astonished.

"I've got what they call an ear for voices," Carl said. "I know who you are."

"Oh, do you, now?" Malachai asked, sounding imperious, except for a slight nervous hesitancy on the last word.

"Yeah, I do. I know exactly who the fuck you are."

And suddenly so did Josh.

A dozen small moments slipped into place. It was Malachai, desperate for the stones, desperate to prove reincarnation, who had orchestrated all of this; from the very beginning, years ago, on a snowy day in a chapel at Yale where Gabriella had gone to feel closer to her mother and met a priest—either Malachai himself or someone he'd hired—who gave her what turned out to be the map to the treasure. Malachi arranging to have the stones stolen. Malachai making that last effort to be the one to handle the exchange, knowing full well Josh would never agree. Malachai, the master magician. Certainly he was capable of using artifice and disguise, ruse and subterfuge. But Josh wouldn't have imagined that Malachai was also capable of the horrendous acts that had been committed in the quest for this grail. Murder and kidnapping.

The past isn't always a pathway to the future. It can be a punishment, too. That was what reincarnation was about, wasn't it? The temptation to repeat the past, the courage not to.

Josh was remembering Rome and Malachai discussing his father, who'd never given him a chance because of an older son who'd died before the second son was born.

What if I am that firstborn reincarnated, Malachai had mused. *Wouldn't that ruin my father's life, to know that now? That he had me all along and lost me twice?*

Yes, this was all Malachai's composition: his symphony of revenge.

"So are you going to give me what you owe me or not?" the kidnapper grunted.

"Let go of Quinn," Josh said.

"You shut up," Carl said to Josh, and jutted his chin toward Malachai. "This is between him and me."

Malachai took a step closer to the altar, and then another. "Let go of her."

"And give up the only currency I have? I don't give a shit what else goes down, man. I want the money!" he screamed.

Josh understood the rest of it now. The kidnapper was supposed to exchange the child for the stones and then get away. Malachai would be there in the church with Josh and Gabriella. Not a suspect. One of the child's saviors.

And then later—that night or the next day—there would be another exchange, and Malachai would retrieve the Memory Stones and the translations. They would belong to him, and he could do what he'd been waiting to do for so long—he'd rape the past.

Or at least he would try.

"So do I get the money or do I take the kid?" he snarled at

Malachai. "This kid belongs to a professor—I'm sure she'll pay to get her back! You'll pay, won't you, Mrs. Chase?" He asked, calling out to the back of the church.

"Yes!" Her voice was strong and sure and tortured.

Quinn, either from the sound of her mother's voice or the pain of her captor's fingers digging into her shoulder, started to cry.

"Shut up!" Carl screamed at her.

It looked to Josh as if the man's nerves were starting to fray.

The crying grew louder, filling up the church.

Carl trained his gun on Quinn. "Do you have any idea how sick I am of listening to this kid wailing? Of getting jerked around? I want my money. Now."

Quinn's sobs escalated.

Josh stared at the kidnapper's finger on the trigger, but out of the corner of his eye he glimpsed Malachai moving slowly toward him. "Give me the stones, Josh," he whispered as he reached out. "Let me handle this."

"What do you think you're doing?" Carl screamed, brandishing the gun.

Quinn's sobs reached a level that was earsplitting.

Josh didn't know what he saw that foretold the accident, but he knew what was going to happen a split second before it happened, and he threw himself forward, shoving Quinn back and out of the way and out of the path of the kidnapper's gun.

He heard a shot and then its echo. As the echo died out he heard the sound of Quinn crying, and as she ran past him, he felt her body fan his face, a little breeze. He smelled fire. He heard Quinn shrieking out for her mother.

She was fine, he thought. Finally, she was fine.

From somewhere behind him, Josh heard Gabriella emit a soft, small moan. The pain that she expelled with that one sound must have weighed a million pounds.

Josh didn't feel anything except surprise until the burning started, and then he could smell the jasmine-and-sandalwood perfume and the exhilarating feeling of time turning on itself and washing the pain away…

Julius is running fast through the streets of Rome. He can't go fast enough. He stayed in the temple too long with his brother. Wasted—as it turned out—precious time trying to save Drago's life, only to fail. Only to lose him. He will not lose her, too, he thinks. Sabina has been underground now for twenty hours. Her air will be starting to run out. She will be waiting for him. Worried. Not understanding why he is taking so long. Will she start digging? Can she get out of the tomb by herself with just the knife? Or will she pass out from lack of air before she thinks to start digging?

He can hear the footsteps behind him.

All he can do is go faster.

Faster.

Faster.

He has to get to the tunnel. It will only take a quarter of an hour to crawl through to the back wall of the tomb, where he will finally dig through to her side, inside the tomb, and get her out, and then together they'll crawl back through the tunnel and disappear while it is still dark.

They've arranged for a safe hiding place for the night, where they will wait until Sabina's sister, Claudia, brings the baby in the morning, along with her half of the Memory Stones, and they'll spend the rest of their lives with Rome behind them.

Through the thick curtain of the centuries, Josh heard Gabriella saying, "Hurry, he's been shot. He's bleeding."

He turns the corner and sees the thugs waiting for him. They must have figured out which way he was running and come around the other side to cut him off. There are six of them. Laughing and spitting out their rough epithets. He can't turn back. The only chance he has is to do what they won't expect.

Julius gulps down a huge mouthful of air and then takes off, running faster than he thought he'd be able to, almost flying, speeding right toward them, not caring that they aren't moving. They will. Their instincts will push them to the right or to the left and he'll slip through.

He sees a knife flash, but he doesn't let it stop him.

Sabina is waiting. She can't have much air left.

He runs faster.

They are laughing.

"Your temple is gone, do you know that?"

"All of them, gone."

He runs at them, but he was wrong. One of them isn't stepping aside. He lunges forward.

The blade flashes.

Julius feels the pain. Doubles over. Gags. They all laugh, congratulate one another. One of them kicks him. Blood drips from the wound in his side, black in the night. One of them sees it, though, and points.

"He's making a sacrifice to his gods, his blood on the altar. Let the stuck pig go, let him bleed to death."

They leave. Sound leaves. Julius stands up, staggers. The pain makes him double over. It doesn't matter. It is only a minor irritation, a nuisance. He has to get to the tunnel he dug himself. He has to crawl through it and save Sabina, who is waiting for him to rescue her so they can, together, rescue their daughter, and together, the three of them, start a new life, so he stumbles on.

Gabriella was calling his name. "Josh? Josh? Can you hear me?"

He looked up at her, wanting so badly to stay in the present with her.

"Josh?" She was holding Quinn in her arms. The little girl stared down at him. There was a flame in the child's wide eyes, burning into him, and Quinn was whimpering. "Daddy, Daddy, nooooo. Daddy, noooo."

Julius can see Sabina holding their baby in the minutes before she passed her over to her sister. He had bent down over his child—a goodbye. Her eyes looked up at him. There was a flame in her fierce eyes, burning into him. How could such a tiny baby look at him like that? he'd thought.

He was back in the present, forgetting all of that, remembering, there was more than one criminal here, more than one man who must be stopped. Josh saw Malachai's face moving out of his line of sight. He saw his eyes flash the same way they had always flashed whenever he'd talked about the stones. Josh needed to push up through the pain to tell them that Malachai was getting away, that he was taking the stones with him. Josh had to break through this haze of time folding back on itself to tell them to go after him, tell them Malachai was the one who had plotted out this whole charade, that he had the stones now, and he was getting away.

He had all of the stones now and he was getting away.

He had all of the power.

He was dangerous. Not just in the present. But for the future.

But when Josh tried to speak, all that came out was another sound: a long, drawn-out, soft *shhhhh* as he tried to quiet this child who was part of another child who was part of him, but Quinn continued crying, saying the same word over and over, "Daddy, Daddy."

So it had been Quinn whom he had been fated to help. Not Rachel. Not Gabriella. It was the baby he and Sabina had not lost as much as saved. Their child. Now this child. She had been saved again.

"Daddy, Daddy."

The ringing was back. But this was a different sound. Circling closer. When he realized what it was, Josh tried to smile. The siren meant Bettina had understood what he'd silently asked her to do. Everything would be fine now. Malachai wasn't paying attention to the sound; there would be no time for him to get away. The police would stop him. It was all fine now. The kidnapper. Malachai. They'd both be trapped.

It takes whatever strength he has left, but somehow Julius manages to drag himself down into the tunnel. The pain from his wound has turned to fire and the fire is devouring him. His insides are aflame. He gasps for a breath but he can't get any air in his lungs. He can't breathe. Julius cannot breathe. Panic fuses with pain. Sabina is waiting for him just at the end of this passageway, on the other side of that dirt wall. He tries to inch forward toward it. He can't. Can't even lift his head from the grime and muck and stones. So, this will be his tomb, too. This dank, dark narrow space. Here he will turn to dust and bones, rubble and ruin only a dozen breaths from Sabina. A dozen breaths that he doesn't have.

His pain was ebbing, turning into colors that were swirling behind his eyes. His skin buzzed. Josh was made of blinding light, enough to illuminate a whole city, a light that invigorated him even as his eyes closed and he slipped into the familiar zone of another life, of a life in the past that had gone wrong, that he had finally put right.

If he died now, would someone see that strange aura above his own head?

What life would he live next?

They say when you die, your life flashes before your eyes. For Josh, it was all of them, the people he'd photographed, the people he'd known, the people he'd loved, the people he'd been, so many people. The human chorus. The music of souls.

AUTHOR'S NOTE

While *The Reincarnationist* is a work of fiction, whenever possible I relied on the facts of history and preexisting theories about the subject of reincarnation to construct the backbone of this tale.

Life in ancient Rome, paganism, early Christianity and ancient beliefs in reincarnation, as well as the Vestal Virgins, are as history recorded them. So are the descriptions of Vestals' duties, domicile and temple, as well as the rules they lived by. Their vows of chastity were sacrosanct, and they were buried alive for breaking them.

I have taken liberties when discussing their involvement with the Memory Stones—which are wholly my own invention, as are the Memory Tools.

Many of the locations in this novel exist. The Riftstone Arch is in Central Park; the Church of the Capuchins is where I describe it in Rome. Several tombs of Vestals have been discovered in various locations around Rome, but Sabina's was not found, as there is no record of a Vestal by that name.

The Phoenix Foundation does not, unfortunately, exist. And while Malachai and Dr. Talmage are entirely fictitious, I was inspired by the amazing Dr. Ian Stevenson, who has done past life regressions with over 2,500 children.

Josh, Natalie and Rachel experience past life regressions in ways that are similar to those of people I've met and read about, but their stories are entirely my invention.

My own reading and research into reincarnation theory has been an ongoing process, and what I described in these pages was culled from the tenets and writings of those who have studied and believed over thousands of years. Included at the end of this novel is a list of books for those of my readers who wish to delve further into this fascinating concept.

Please visit Reincarnationist.org for more information.

ACKNOWLEDGMENTS

This is my ninth published novel and the one I have been writing the longest, since before I even knew I wanted to be a writer, when my mother first introduced me to the idea of reincarnation. I missed her a little less while I was working on this book and I'm certain she would love it best of all.

There are so many people I'd like to thank, starting with Loretta Barrett, Nick Mullendore and Gabriel Davis of Loretta Barrett Books for all their hard work and excellent advice. Thanks to the whole team at MIRA Books—especially Donna Hayes, Dianne Moggy, Alex Osusek, Laura Morris, Craig Swinwood, Heather Foy, Loriana Sacilotto, Katherine Orr, Marleah Stout, Stacy Widdrington, Pete McMahon, Gordy Goihl, Ken Foy, Fritz Servatius and Cheryl Stewart, Rebecca Soukis and Sarah Rundle. I am indeed blessed to have all of these amazing people in my corner and behind this book. It's been a wonderful experience—thank you.

Thanks to Mayapryia Long, who gave me the right information at the right moment. For support, advice, information or just great conversation, thanks to Mara Nathan, Jenn Risko, Carol Fitzgerald, Judith Curr, Mark Dressler, Barry Eisler, Diane Vogt, Amanda's father, Suzanne Beecher, David Hewson, Shelly King, Emily Kischell, Stan Pottinger, Elizabeth's fiancé, Simon Lipskar, Katherine Neville, the Rome-Arch Listserv, Meryl Moss and all the International Thriller Writers.

My gratitude to each bookseller, librarian and every reader.

As always to my loving family: Gigi, Jay, Jordan, my father and Ellie.

And to Doug Scofield, for the calm in the storm, the eternal optimism and the music.

Suggested Reading List

Beloff, John. *Parapsychology: A Concise History.* St. Martin's Press, 1997.

Bowman, Carol. *Children's Past Lives: How Past Life Memories Affect Your Child*. Bantam, 1998.

Chitkara, M. G. *Buddhism, Reincarnation and Dalai Lamas of Tibet*. A.P.H. Publishing Corporation, 1998.

Chopra, Deepak. *Life After Death: The Burden of Proof.* Harmony, 2006.

Cott, Jonathan. *The Search for Omm Sety: A Story of Eternal Love*. Warner Books, 1989.

Darling, David J. *Zen Physics: The Science of Death, the Logic of Reincarnation.* HarperCollins, 1996

Faulkner, Raymond, translator. *The Egyptian Book of the Dead: The Book of Going Forth by Day.* Chronicle Books, 2000.

Fenwick, Peter, and Elizabeth Fenwick. *The Truth in the Light: An Investigation of Over 300 Near-Death Experiences.* Berkley Publishing Group, 1997.

Gauld, Alan. *A History of Hypnotism.* Cambridge University Press, 1995.

Head, Joseph and Sylvia Cranston. *Reincarnation: The Phoenix Fire Mystery*. Julian Press, 1977.

Jung, Carl Gustav. *Man and His Symbols.* Pan MacMillan, 1968.

Jung, Carl Gustav. *Memories, Dreams, Reflections.* Pantheon, 1989.

LaGrand, Louis E. *After Death Communication: Final Farewells.* Llewellyn Publications, 1997.

Sabom, Michael B. *Recollections of Death: A Medical Investigation.* Harper & Row, 1982.

Shroder, Tom. *Old Souls: The Scientific Evidence for Past Lives.* Simon & Schuster, 1999.

Stevenson, Ian. *Children who Remember Previous Lives.* University of Virginia Press, 1987.

Stevenson, Ian. *Reincarnation and Biology: A Contribution to the Etiology of Birthmarks and Birth Defects.* (2 vols.) Praeger Scientific Publishers, 1997.

Stevenson, Ian. *Unlearned Language: New Studies in Xenoglossy.* University of Virginia Press, 1984.

Tucker, Jim. *Life Before Life: A Scientific Investigation of Children's Memories of Previous Lives.* St. Martin's Press, 2005.

Weiss, Brian L. *Many Lives, Many Masters: The True Story of a Prominent Psychiatrist, His Young Patient, and the Past-Life Therapy That Changed Both Their Lives.* Warner Books, 1988.

Woolger, Roger J. *Other Lives, Other Selves.* Crucible, 1987.